## Praise for Brian Klein

'A rarity . . . a sequel that's just as good as the original' *Scotsman*

'A wild rollercoaster that's thrilling from the beginning to the end' *London Economic*

'Buckle up . . . a page turner that is impossible to put down till the very end' *Reader's Digest*

'Action packed, fast-paced and filled with amazing twists . . . great characters too!' *Female First*

'With this explosive sequel, author Brian Klein has cemented his position as Britain's most exciting thriller writer' *SWNS*

# BRIAN KLEIN

# THE LAST REICH

C

CONSTABLE

CONSTABLE

First published in Great Britain in 2024 by Constable

1 3 5 7 9 10 8 6 4 2

Copyright © Brian Klein, 2024

The moral right of the author has been asserted.

All rights reserved.
No part of this publication may be reproduced, stored in a retrieval system, or
transmitted, in any form, or by any means, without the prior permission in
writing of the publisher, nor be otherwise circulated in any form of binding or
cover other than that in which it is published and without a similar condition
including this condition being imposed on the subsequent purchaser.

A CIP catalogue record for this book
is available from the British Library.

ISBN: 978-1-40872-102-5

Typeset in Crimson Text by Hewer Text UK Ltd, Edinburgh
Printed and bound in Great Britain by Clays Ltd, Elcograf S.p.A.

Papers used by Constable are from well-managed
forests and other responsible sources.

Constable
An imprint of
Little, Brown Book Group
Carmelite House
50 Victoria Embankment
London EC4Y 0DZ

An Hachette UK Company

www.hachette.co.uk

www.littlebrown.co.uk

*To Neil and Faie,*
*my mum and dad,*
*to whom I owe so much*

# Prologue

El Calafate, Argentina

June 2022

John Franklin was seconds away from meeting his maker. As the discredited former presidential candidate crossed the deserted street in the centre of El Calafate, heading towards a black SUV, he'd no idea he was the moving target of a lone gunman sitting at a small table outside a run-down café less than thirty yards away.

A hidden wireless earpiece saved his skin. It broke into life, emitting a brief crackling sound, and a second later the unmistakable voice of his driver alerted him to the imminent danger.

'Sir, there's a hostile located across the street, twenty degrees west. He monitored your exit from the museum and has a weapon aimed directly at you. Shall I take him out?'

Franklin stiffened slightly and furtively shot a look to his left before speeding up the pace of his walk and then breaking into a fast jog. The momentary glance told him all he needed to know. The man with the gun had every reason to want him dead, even though he was a blood relative.

'Intercept but don't take him out . . . just disable him.'

Three seconds later, a .50 calibre round fired from a Barrett M107 semi-automatic sniper rifle ripped into the right shoulder of the would-be assassin and the sheer force of the impact propelled his body backwards. The gunman was hurled out of his rusty metal chair while the small handgun he was holding slipped from his grasp, clattering onto the sidewalk. His head slammed against the concrete paving stones, and although he didn't lose consciousness, he was too dazed to offer any resistance to what followed.

The Lincoln Aviator sped forward from its stationary position and screeched to a stop outside the café. The driver jumped out and heaved the motionless body off the ground, hauling it into the back of the SUV. Moments later, the front passenger door was yanked open and Franklin leaped inside, barking orders as he slammed it shut.

'Get moving, Hugo. Head straight for the farmhouse.'

As the Lincoln pulled away at speed, Franklin half turned over his left shoulder and stared down at the dishevelled figure whose bloodied body was splayed across the back seat. The man was barely awake but his blue penetrating eyes glared back at his half-brother exuding pure hatred. Franklin's lips parted to display a Joker-like grin.

'Don't worry, Daniel. Everything's going to be just fine.'

A moment later, a clenched fist smashed into the abducted man's temple and everything went black. As a result, he didn't feel the sharp prick of the hypodermic needle that followed shortly after.

* * *

When Daniel Anderson woke almost twenty-four hours later, his brain felt as if it were floating in a dense fog, accompanied by a soundtrack of a thousand bass drums which assaulted his senses. A series of random questions battled their way through the mist as he struggled to find clarity.

What happened outside the café? Who shot him? Where was he? Right now, he'd no answers. His eyes gradually regained their focus and he endeavoured to get his bearings. He was lying in a large bed that appeared to have no restraints, dressed in a blue cotton hospital gown. His right shoulder and arm were heavily bandaged and two IV lines were hooked up to metal stands that supported transparent plastic pouches of blood and antibiotics. He felt no pain in his right arm, which he put down to the drugs doing their job.

The room was large, bright and neatly decorated with an aquamarine floral-print wallpaper that teamed nicely with the royal-blue deep-pile carpet. The ceiling was low and the brown wooden beams that ran across it were typical of a classic farmhouse.

Daniel turned his head and stared out of the large casement window centred in the side wall and took in the view of rolling green hills dotted with moving white blobs that he assumed were sheep. For a brief second, he wondered if he was back in Australia, but his thoughts were interrupted by a sudden movement in the far corner of the room that caught his eye. He hadn't noticed the presence of the elderly nurse, who sprang to life the moment she witnessed signs of her patient waking up.

'Where the hell am I and who . . .'

He shouted in vain as the woman flew out the door with an energy that belied her age. It was as though she'd spotted a fire in the room and needed to report it. He could just about hear her muted voice, but his limited Spanish meant he'd no idea what she was saying or who she was talking to. He didn't have to wait long for an answer. Somehow, he guessed the approaching footsteps belonged to the man he'd travelled halfway around the world to kill, but right now that was the last thing on his mind. Daniel was far more interested in his own survival and possible escape. However, laid up in bed, unarmed and badly injured, the odds of achieving either of those objectives didn't look too good.

The sunrays now bursting through the open door meant John Franklin's elongated shadow entered a moment before he did. He was wearing his trademark red baseball cap that, as usual, appeared to be cemented to his head. His cornflower-blue eyes were focused, unblinking, on Daniel. Franklin's chiselled facial features were partially camouflaged by a straggly yellowish beard, pebbledashed with small grey intruders. He was casually dressed in a blue gingham shirt, neatly tucked into some suitably worn Levi's 501s. The Western look was finished off with a pair of chocolate-brown leather cowboy boots. Franklin marched across the room and came to a stop by the bedside, next to the metal medical stands.

'Daniel, that was very foolish behaviour on your part back at the museum. Hugo normally goes for a kill shot. Fortunately for you, and much to his disappointment, I instructed him to resist his primitive instincts.'

Franklin allowed the hint of a smile to widen slightly on his pursed lips. Daniel held his gaze for a few seconds before speaking for the first time.

'What do you want from me, John – a round of applause? A few weeks ago you put a five-million-dollar bounty on my head and now you expect thanks for preventing your trained ape from taking me out. You're a sick bastard, and even if it's not me, someone out there will take you down. It's just a matter of time.'

Franklin's smile disappeared but he ploughed on with his rehearsed charm offensive.

'Daniel, ordering your killing was a rare error on my part for which I apologise. In time I'll explain my actions, but be clear about one thing, once I recognised my mistake, I laid a trail I knew you wouldn't be able to resist following. You see, I wanted you to find me . . .'

Daniel cut in, his voice laden with sarcasm.

'You expect me to believe this bullshit?'

'Trust me, I've two other enemies I fear far more than you, both of whom are desperate to find me. They've huge resources but no idea where I'm based and I intend to keep it that way.'

Daniel felt himself slightly relax for the first time since he'd woken up. Remarkably, he sensed Franklin was telling the truth. A rarity in itself.

'Go on.'

'Vengeance and retribution are powerful emotions, Daniel. Mossad and the Taliban have equally compelling reasons for wanting me to suffer at their hands. I took a huge risk allowing you to find me, but I want, no, I need you on my side. Never forget, we share the same bloodline, our grandfather's – the blood of the Führer, and right now, brother, we need each other more than ever.'

Daniel listened intently and nodded as a sign for Franklin to continue.

'In the coming weeks and months, as you recuperate, we'll talk frankly about many things as we plot our revenge on our enemies . . . together.'

Daniel could feel himself being seduced by Franklin's overtures, but enjoyed the fact that, for the first time in their relationship, his half-brother was addressing him as an equal.

'John, have you thought about what the Taliban might do to you if you ever fall into their hands – they're savages.'

Franklin moved closer and leaned down over the bed, so his head was just inches above Daniel's face. His voice dropped to a whisper.

'I've had many sleepless nights thinking about just that, but don't worry, I've taken precautions.'

# Chapter One

*The Little Fox*, The Indian Ocean

September 2023, Fifteen months later

The turquoise waters of the Indian Ocean glistened under the relentless rays of the midday sun as the white super yacht cruised majestically across the water, hugging the northern coastline of Mauritius, as it made its way towards Madagascar.

Unusually, the sixty-four crew on board the two-hundred-and-forty-foot cruiser had only two VIP passengers to attend to. That didn't make their life any easier, however, because one of them was the boat's owner, and John Franklin was as uncompromising as ever, always demanding the impossible from his staff at breakneck speed.

His companion, Daniel Anderson, was far more chilled, but thrived on the incessant, almost manic, energy generated by his older half-brother, and they were as one when it came to achieving their goal. Both were driven by two powerful and destructive motives: destiny and revenge, an intoxicating cocktail that made them a credible threat to contend with, particularly as their ambitions were backed by unlimited funding courtesy of a giant Nazi nest egg, residing in a covert Swiss bank account.

The half-brothers were the only remaining grandchildren of the man universally regarded as the most reviled dictator of the twentieth century. Seventy-eight years earlier, Adolf Hitler had fled his war-torn bunker in Berlin at the tail end of the Second World War and created a new identity in Southern Patagonia, where he lived with his wife, Eva Braun, and his faithful lieutenant, Martin Bormann, under the alias Franklin. The choice of surname was a deliberate nod to one of America's most revered presidents, Franklin Delano Roosevelt, as Hitler's long-term plan was for one of his direct descendants to become the political leader of the most powerful country in the world. To this end, in 1946, he had fathered a son, Richard, who'd moved to San Francisco in his early twenties, where he ran a massive pharmaceutical corporation, backed by millions of dollars Bormann had stealthily moved out of Germany during the last few months of the war. Richard Franklin went on to father five children, four boys and a girl, all from different mothers, and now, many years on, only John and Daniel were left.

During the previous fifteen months, they'd worked relentlessly, skulking in the shadows, using their power, wealth and influence to create an unholy axis of evil, comprising a small number of leaders of extreme right-wing fascist political parties and high-profile terrorists based across five continents. These men, who proclaimed themselves saviours rather than politicians, were riding the tide of economic meltdown created by a global energy crisis, war in Europe and soaring inflation. They'd grabbed power and influence as desperate people searched for answers outside of regular democratic politics to put bread on the table.

Franklin and Daniel were relaxing on a couple of loungers, enjoying a light lunch on the pool deck: a Caesar salad washed down with a bottle of Cloudy Bay, a much sought-after New Zealand Sauvignon Blanc. Daniel looked quite different from the clean-cut young man who'd confronted his half-brother the previous year in El Calafate, due to the bushy blond beard now sprouting on his face.

The pair were in the middle of discussing the recent election of a new president in Equatorial Guinea, a high-yield oil-producing state in Africa. His political campaign had benefited from a donation to the tune of fifteen million dollars, courtesy of one of their black bank accounts. The whirring sound of helicopter rotors interrupted their conversation, and both men looked up towards the west. Franklin was the first to spot the incoming aircraft. The H225 twin-engine Super Puma was his latest toy; a twenty-eight-million-dollar purchase, making it the most expensive helicopter in the world. On board was a ragbag collection of right-wing fanatics whom Franklin had been nurturing for a while. Some of them already held political power, others were on the brink.

'Here they come, Daniel. Lambs to the slaughter. We'll take soundings from them on their state of readiness to enact Operation Atonement, and once they've left, I'll bring you up to speed on my plans for our old friends, Vargas and Hembury.'

Franklin drained his wine glass and placed it on a small coffee table next to a black leather-bound folder that he flicked open, allowing Daniel sight of two monochrome headshots of the detectives. Both had red crosshairs stamped across their faces.

Daniel took a sip from his glass and savoured the unique taste of his favourite white wine that never failed to deliver. His smile morphed into a grimace.

'John, it's time for retribution.'

\* \* \*

Daniel sat next to Franklin at one end of the highly polished black walnut table that comfortably seated their ten guests. Brushed-chrome nameplates, perfectly spaced around it, identified the eclectic group of neo-Nazi political leaders and terrorists who'd been summoned to the covert meeting. They'd travelled from five continents and Daniel couldn't help thinking their gathering resembled a meeting at the United Nations, except Franklin was no secretary-general and the main topic on his agenda was the complete antithesis of world peace.

Seven spoke English, and the three who didn't had access to a set of black Bluetooth earbuds placed next to their nameplates. They were linked to a small group of translators in a nearby room who were poised in front of their microphones, waiting for Franklin to begin the meeting. They'd been recruited by a private head-hunting agency that had lured them onto the boat with the prospect of earning the equivalent of three months' salary for this one job. Sadly, they'd never get the chance to enjoy their windfall. Carefully arranged around the inner circle of the table were ten brown leather attaché cases, each of which had the initials of the respective recipient embossed in gold lettering.

Most of the men had never met in the flesh before, although they were aware of each other and their fearsome reputations. The common denominator was Franklin, their secret paymaster, who lined their pockets with millions of dollars through illicit bank transfers. The former US presidential candidate rose from his seat and cleared his throat as a signal that the meeting was about to get underway.

'Gentlemen, welcome on board *The Little Fox*. In case you're wondering about the cases, they each contain five million dollars in cash which, knowing how busy you all are, is a small thank you from me and Daniel for your attendance at this intimate get-together. I know I normally transfer funds to your private accounts, but my father always taught me that cash is king, so spend this unexpected bonus on your wives, girlfriends or whores and enjoy this token of our esteem.'

General Okoi Okonkwo, who'd recently led a military coup in another beleaguered African state, smiled like a great white, displaying all his teeth, as he leaned forward and raised the case in front of him high into the air. An instant later he began violently banging it on the veneered tabletop. Within seconds, the other guests followed his lead in a bizarre, frenzied demonstration of gratitude. Franklin milked the moment before lifting his arms in a gesture that acknowledged the reaction but called for silence at the same time.

'Friends, September twenty-fifth is only weeks away, so we have much to prepare and discuss. Let's get to it.'

# Chapter Two

T roy Hembury was living on borrowed time and he knew it. An inoperable grade three brain tumour meant he'd never reach a ripe old age, but right now he was determined to make the most of his life, despite the death sentence. He'd cheated the grim reaper the previous year when his body had taken a severe battering in a firefight in Israel. Hembury had been part of a covert anti-terrorist task force created by the FBI and Mossad, who'd combined resources to combat an attack on Israel's water supply, masterminded by John Franklin, with the backing of the Taliban. During a shoot-out at a desalination plant in Ashkelon, he'd risked his life to save his friend and colleague, Nic Vargas, and had miraculously survived two close-range gunshots to the abdomen, thanks to the remarkable skill of a surgeon in Tel Aviv.

As a reward for his heroic efforts, the sixty-two-year-old former LAPD lieutenant was offered the post of head of internal security at the White House, a role far more challenging than he could ever have imagined when the vice president first proposed it. He was the first African American to hold the prestigious position and felt truly honoured to accept it. Hembury had over a hundred security staff working directly under him and shouldered the responsibility for guarding against potential cyber-attacks as well as physical ones.

He'd been a career policeman for almost forty years, a divorcee with very few ties, so he'd happily upped sticks from his home in Los Angeles and rented a two-bed condo in the fashionable Georgetown neighbourhood of the US capital. The apartment was carved out of a red-brick Italian-style villa located on Grace Street Northwest, less than two miles away from his world-famous workplace at 1600 Pennsylvania Avenue.

Hembury's weekday routine involved a twelve-minute commute in his dark blue Toyota RAV4, which ensured he was normally sitting behind his desk inside the West Wing of the White House by six a.m.

It was Friday morning and his thoughts were already drifting towards the following night when his beloved LA Clippers were arriving in town to play a pre-season friendly against the Washington Wizards at the Capital One Arena. As he closed the street door of his apartment block and sauntered down the concrete steps leading to the sidewalk, he automatically reached for his car key inside his jacket pocket and glanced towards the SUV in its normal spot about twenty yards away. He'd no reason to notice the man sitting in the driver's seat of a black Ford Focus, parked on the other side of the street about thirty yards away. He was facing the opposite direction, his eyes glued

7

to the wing mirror which he'd deliberately angled to observe Hembury's departure. His gloved hands were resting on his knees, a small detonator in one and a smartphone in the other.

As Hembury's leading foot hit the pavement, the bomber flicked a switch and all hell was let loose on the quiet suburban street, courtesy of a vehicle-borne improvised explosive device. The ear-piercing blast and shock wave created a booming thunderclap heard by thousands within the city, including the incumbent of the Oval Office just over a mile away. The fire-ball that ensued, spewing out white-hot metal and glass debris, rocketed skywards over two hundred feet and a thick plume of black smoke formed a treacherous cocktail with the ignited contents of the Toyota's fuel tank. The sheer power of the explosion catapulted Hembury's body high into the air like a rag doll, along with dozens of pedestrians who were close to the centre of the blast. Four of them died instantly and grotesque, blood-soaked body parts rained down onto the street alongside hundreds of fragments of twisted metal wreckage.

The bomber's passive facial expression didn't alter as he watched the horrendous carnage he'd unleashed play out behind him. Moments later, he sent a pre-written WhatsApp note to a smartphone over five thousand miles away in a suburb of Buenos Aires. The recipient of the message was standing in the doorway of a small shoe shop in a narrow side street in San Telmo, the oldest neighbourhood in the city. She glanced down to confirm the content of the message, then her eyes locked onto a narrow driveway leading to a small car park beneath an apartment block, which served the sixteen residents of the building. She knew full well that parked in Space

12 was a silver VW Golf Mk7 that she'd spent three hours working on overnight. She checked the time on her phone before retrieving a small detonator from her coat pocket. Seconds later, a massive explosion ripped through the concrete-pillared car park and putrid smoke poured out onto the street, totally obscuring the red-and-white wooden entrance barrier.

Three floors above, in Apartment 12, Chief Inspector Nicolas Vargas of the Buenos Aires Police Department was abruptly woken from a deep sleep by the seismic blast rocking the foundations of the building. Vargas was one of the city's senior detectives, having held his rank for well over a decade and was regarded as having the most astute brain on the force. He was a widower who'd lost his wife many years earlier and had slept alone ever since, never quite coming to terms with the reality of his loss. Despite being a striking-looking man in his early fifties, he'd no interest in filling that void and instead distracted himself with an unrealistic workload, which meant his mind was permanently juggling far too many complex cases, which was just how he liked it.

Vargas could feel the walls of his bedroom vibrating from the after-effects of the explosion, and as he struggled to focus his senses, his phone pinged. His deep-set caramel brown eyes flickered as they peered through the darkness at the familiar green WhatsApp icon. When he read the message, the Chief Inspector knew he'd been the target of the attack.

# Chapter Three

Washington D.C., United States

Hembury propped himself up in his hospital bed and reached across to the bedside locker for his cell. Apart from a pounding headache, courtesy of mild concussion, and some minor scrapes and bruises, he was unharmed. Any doubts he may have had concerning the motive for the bombing evaporated when he caught up with the WhatsApp message that had landed on his phone immediately after the blast. It was identical to the one received by Vargas.

> I'm sure you both realise these little incidents have simply been a warning. As you can see, I have the resources to take you out whenever I want and trust me your deaths will happen before the end of September. For now, I'm content to know you'll be constantly looking over your shoulder, wondering where the next strike will come from.

If the content of the message was threatening, the signature was chilling: no name or initials revealed the identity of the sender, just a red swastika emoji sitting on a black background. As Hembury stared at the Nazi image, his screen broke into life, registering an incoming call from Vargas in Buenos Aires.

'Nic, you beat me to it. Are you okay? That bastard Franklin is evidently back.'

'Tell me about it – but I'm fine. Thank God you're okay too. I've been trying your cell for the last two hours, so you really freaked me out. My apartment's not looking too clever, though, and as for the car . . .'

The two friends spent the following few minutes bringing each other up to speed with details of their respective blasts. Vargas was horrified to hear about the innocent civilians who'd lost their lives in the Georgetown bombing. It was currently the lead news story in the United States, with wild media speculation as to the true motive of the car bomber, which, given the sensitivity of the situation, the FBI was keeping firmly under wraps.

'Troy, car bombs normally fall into two categories – those used to kill the occupant of the vehicle in a specific assassination attempt and those used to kill as many people as possible who are in close proximity to the bomb, like the Oklahoma City car attack. It's clear both our bombs fall into the second category. That lunatic had no intention of taking us out this time – he just wanted to let us know he's gunning for revenge.'

Hembury adjusted his position in the hospital bed so he was more upright.

'I get that, but why now? We've heard nothing for well over a year, and what's the significance of the end of September?'

Vargas was sitting at a corner table in a small coffee house a few hundred yards away from his apartment block, which had been evacuated immediately after the blast. He downed the dregs of his Americano and struggled to come up with a logical reply. Before he could offer anything helpful, Hembury cut back in.

'Nic, I've got Berrettini on the line, which is hardly surprising given the circumstances. I'll call you back.'

Mike Berrettini, the deputy director of the FBI, had worked with both men the previous year on the extraordinary case involving a biological attack inside Israel that was masterminded by the same man who'd just declared his hand as the source of the bombings: former Republican presidential candidate John Franklin. The three detectives had formed a mini taskforce, working closely with the director of Mossad to thwart the plan to sabotage Israel's water supply, and since then Berrettini had led an international manhunt to track Franklin down, with little success.

Hembury's mouth gave way to a wry smile as the deputy director's familiar voice boomed down the line.

'Troy, what the hell? The blast is the lead story on every network. You definitely okay?'

'Woah, Mike, slow down. I'm fine. What do you know about the bombings?'

'I know Franklin was behind them and it's clear he's gunning for you guys.'

Hembury couldn't help but be impressed by the way Berrettini cut through any small talk and came straight to the point.

'Mike, how on earth can you know that so quickly?'

'Easy, the arrogant bastard sent me a WhatsApp.'

# Chapter Four

Washington D.C., United States

Twenty-four hours after the attacks, Vargas, Hembury and Berrettini gathered in a secure meeting room on a subterranean floor inside the J. Edgar Hoover building on Pennsylvania Avenue. Vargas had taken the red-eye from Buenos Aires and travelled straight from the airport to FBI headquarters to discuss the latest intelligence the deputy director had put together. It was the first time in over a year the three men had met in the flesh.

After a round of bear hugs, they sat down at an oblong metal table with Berrettini taking his place at the head and Vargas and Hembury sitting either side. Berrettini gestured towards a glass coffee percolator and a white ceramic tray containing a selection of croissants and Danish pastries.

'Help yourselves, guys. Make the coffee strong. I think you're going need it.'

Hembury smiled and did the honours, pouring out three steaming cups, while Vargas grabbed a pain au chocolat, which he devoured in a couple of mouthfuls. Berrettini took a large gulp of black coffee and then fired up his laptop. The Italian-born deputy director wasn't an imposing man in the physical sense: his short stubby frame carried at least two stone in excess weight, his ratty black hair, which crowned a rotund olive-skinned face, was showing early signs of receding, and his unkempt beard was heavily frosted. Despite his modest appearance, though, Berrettini was recognised as a brilliant strategist with one of the sharpest intellects in the Bureau. His ice-cool brain moved seamlessly through the gears as he began the briefing.

'In a few minutes, we're joining a Zoom with Sir Christopher Denton, the director of GCHQ in the UK, but before that I need to bring you guys up to speed, and the first question I'm sure you're both desperate to hear an answer to is – why now? Why has Franklin come back into play at this time?'

Hembury shuffled in his seat and glanced across at Vargas who acknowledged the look and then switched his gaze back to Berrettini.

'As you know, despite our best efforts, we've failed miserably to track his whereabouts. In fact, we've had no confirmed sighting since May 2022, over sixteen months ago, when we know he was in Israel. The trail went cold a long time ago and the sad truth is, he could be anywhere.'

As the deputy director drew breath, Vargas cut in.

'Mike, what if the bastard is hiding out on another boat? A leopard never changes its spots.'

'We've obviously been down that route but it's a dead end. There are over ten thousand luxury yachts out there – it's needle in a haystack territory, if indeed that's the type of hide he's gone for. The fact he's suddenly emerged from the shadows to threaten you guys is, I believe, no coincidence. It's helped confirm a hypothesis I've been working through for a while. Our analysts at the NSA have been collaborating with the Brits at GCHQ, monitoring a constant line of chatter between neo-Nazi groups and militants across the world, which indicates an imminent coordinated event sometime in the next few weeks. We're seeing traces of communications between groups that have previously never worked together, so we fear something big is in the pipeline. A key word that's appeared regularly in the chatter is "wolf", which got me thinking that—'

Hembury exploded from his chair like a human Jack-in-the-Box.

'Jesus – Wolf was the Führer's nickname. You think Franklin is involved in this?'

'Up until yesterday, it was just intuition and I couldn't join the dots, but now he's shown his hand, there's little doubt he's somehow involved. For all we know, he could actually be—'

Berrettini never completed the sentence because an alert on his laptop indicated his Zoom call was ready to go live. Vargas and Hembury gathered close as he introduced them to the director of the UK's intelligence, security and cyber agency, who was sitting behind his desk in Cheltenham. The FBI Deputy Director cut straight to the chase.

'Chris, thanks for jumping on the call. What's the latest intel at your end?'

Denton was GCHQ's eighteenth director and, at forty-two, the youngest person to hold the role since its formation in 1919. A former intelligence chief at MI5, he'd been instrumental in shaping government counterterrorism strategy following four coordinated suicide bomb attacks on London's transport system that had rocked the capital on 7 July 2005. He was a beanpole of man, standing six foot three with a body weight of just eleven stone and an angular head that resembled an axe blade. But despite his slightly gawky appearance, when he spoke, his light hazel eyes burst into life like a pair of Bunsen burners and his words were as lean as his physique.

'Gentlemen, it's clear the car bombs were connected to recent disturbing chatter our analysts have been monitoring online. One of the code words used between the two bombers and their handler was *Sühne*, a word that's come up at least three times in the last few weeks. As far as—'

Berrettini knew he was speaking for his two colleagues when he interrupted Denton mid-flow.

'Chris, our German isn't too hot. What does it mean?'

'Its literal translation is "atonement", but that could be a red herring, because often code words aren't used literally. Anyway, more specifically, what I can tell you is the perpetrator in Washington hired a black Ford Focus in Detroit using fake ID and made the five-hundred-mile journey to Georgetown, where he prepped and detonated the bomb outside your apartment, Mr Hembury. He dumped the vehicle in an underground car park in Arlington and then vanished. The only CCTV we have of him is far too wide to help with any specific identification, which tells us we're dealing with a specialist operator who we assume is no longer in the country.'

No one spoke for a moment and then Vargas broke the silence with a question.

'What about the goon that hit my apartment? Where did he detonate his bomb from?'

'They were partially hidden in a shop doorway across the street, but, Chief Inspector Vargas, the question you should be asking is, where was *she* based? Your bomber was a woman.'

# Chapter Five

*The Little Fox*, The Indian Ocean

Deshi Ivanov combined outstanding physical prowess with an exceptional IQ of 182. A Chechen national, she was born in Grozny in 1994 and was only a child when the United Nations declared her home city the most destroyed war zone on earth, after an estimated eight thousand civilians were killed in a bloody three-month siege during the Second Chechen War.

Two days after her seventh birthday, she watched in terror as her mother was raped and murdered by a group of young Russian soldiers high on drugs and alcohol, while her father, one of the leaders of the separatist movement, was crucified and hung from an electric pylon located on the outskirts of the city. Somehow, Deshi survived these horrors and at the same time looked after her twin brother, Vakha, who was traumatised by the brutal loss of his parents.

At the end of the siege, the siblings were captured by Russian forces who burned their tiny wooden house to the ground before transporting them, along with a small group of other children, to an orphanage in Novosibirsk, the largest city in Siberia. They languished there, in appalling conditions, for almost a year before a remarkable stroke of luck changed their lives forever. A childless eccentric oligarch's widow, Yelena Komarova, adopted them as a pair and overnight they swapped the squalor of a state orphanage for the luxury of a twelve-bedroom mansion on the Agalarov Estate, a private gated community for billionaires located about thirty miles outside of Moscow.

Deshi loathed everything Russian, including and especially her adoptive mother, but was smart enough to play the game and take advantage of the opportunities a privileged upbringing and education could offer. By the time they were eighteen, she and Vakha were fluent in English, French and German. Deshi was awarded the status of 'Master' in the Russian martial art Sambo, a combat sport developed by the Soviet Red Army in the 1920s that combined judo and jujitsu. In their final year at a private school, the pair were chosen as head boy and head girl and their proud mother made a substantial donation to a prominent college in Oxford that helped secure them places on an international relations degree course. But Deshi had other plans for their future that involved an entirely different type of studying.

Her physical and mental skills had not gone unnoticed by a Moscow-based senior recruiting officer for the military's elite special operations force, Spetsnaz. She and Vakha cut a striking duo; both standing almost six feet with sculpted muscular frames topped off by coal-black hair and dark brown eyes. In September 2012, the twins joined the covert elite unit, walking away from their previous lives and never speaking with their adoptive mother again. They were fuelled by a deep-rooted anger and hatred that wasn't specifically focused on the Russian nation, but on a humanity that had allowed their parents and thousands of their people to be butchered in such tragic circumstances.

The Chechen twins were fast-tracked under the watchful eye of the unit's notorious commander, Nestor Zakharov, and during an intense four-year period, they honed their skills in sabotage, counterterrorism, hand-to-hand combat, guerrilla warfare and assassination. During that time, they took out targeted enemies of the state, both within Russia and internationally, and it transpired the pair were natural born killers. Deshi grew extremely close to Zakharov, who treated her with the reverence of a father. Those inside the unit who witnessed their relationship were convinced it was sexual, but it never went that way, as the commander saw Deshi as the daughter he'd always wanted.

Then, one day, just as suddenly as they'd deserted their adoptive mother for a new life, Deshi and Vakha once again mysteriously vanished from sight, leaving no trace of their whereabouts. When they re-emerged a few months later, it was as freelance assassins, and their employer was the dark web. Their earnings skyrocketed to anything between one and five million dollars a hit, depending on the difficulty of the assignment and the profile of the target.

Daniel Anderson had first become aware of them in December 2022 when Franklin had tasked him with the job of recruiting a full-time head of security on a one-year contract who'd be prepared to do whatever was required, however challenging or distasteful. After protracted negotiations, a twenty-million-dollar deal was agreed, and the first time Franklin met Deshi and Vakha in person on board his super yacht, he left the meeting concluding the fee for the twin killers was nothing short of a bargain. He'd wanted an attack dog to help with the complex events he had planned for the coming months and, much to his delight, he'd landed two for the price of one.

Less than an hour after they boarded *The Little Fox*, Deshi and Vakha were summoned to a debrief with Franklin in the massive glass-and-metal loggia that made up most of deck five and which served as his office. The pair took their normal places on a cream leather two-seater couch in the centre of the vast space, opposite Franklin and Anderson, both of whom were ensconced in matching club chairs, cold beers in hand.

Deshi took her employers through a blow-by-blow account of recent events, detailing the success of the car bomb attacks in Buenos Aires and Washington. Anderson couldn't take his eyes off the Chechen assassin and was more than happy to sit back and listen to her detailed report, but Franklin was clearly distracted, focusing instead on his iPad Pro, digesting his latest emails and keen to move on. He brazenly cut her dead mid-sentence, reminding everyone in the room who was the boss.

'A pleasing result that rattled some cages – precisely the intention, and it created a diversion that served its purpose, but now we need to concentrate on our primary targets, which are far more challenging.'

Franklin paused for a moment, a scornful smile appearing on his face; a coded message to ensure there was no danger of complacency breaking out amongst his highly paid staff. His right hand skimmed smoothly across the top of the table to

21

retrieve a grey folder that he brandished in the air as though it were a hand grenade.

'We'll spend the next few hours running through every detail in here, confirming we're happy with the key timings and collaborations. Tomorrow morning, we leave on reconnaissance trips to Europe and America. Daniel, you and Vakha will travel to Reno and then on to New York. Deshi, you and I will head to Florence. Any questions?'

# Chapter Six

Florence, Italy

The ancient Roman city of Florence lies in a valley alongside the river Arno, surrounded by rolling hills, and is considered by most academics to be the birthplace of the Renaissance. Celebrated for its culture, art and history, its world-renowned museums, galleries and churches make it a magnet for millions of tourists every year.

The Grand Cavour, a majestic boutique hotel carved from a medieval palace, is another jewel in the centre of the city, located on the Via Del Proconsolo, directly opposite the acclaimed Bargello Museum. Its spectacular rooftop cocktail bar, the Divina Terrazza, offers breathtaking panoramic views of the sensational skyline, including the magnificent Cathedral of Santa Maria del Fiore.

John Franklin and Deshi Ivanov were in the bar, standing next to a low glass wall which encircled the small terrace, drinking in the stunning views as they looked out towards the north-east of the city. Franklin's gaze was transfixed on a large green copper dome sitting regally on a quadrangular

Moorish-style structure that to the untrained eye could easily have been mistaken for a typical Byzantine Christian church. Built in the mid-nineteenth century, the Tempio Maggiore was indeed a place of worship, but its congregation was Jewish, and the synagogue was the largest and most admired in Italy. Franklin continued to stare at it before breaking the silence.

'That monstrosity is the reason we're here. It shares a personal history with my family and carries a debt that needs to be paid.'

Deshi found herself facing the back of his head.

'What does that mean in terms of the schedule?'

'It means I've chosen it as the location where you and I will be based on the actual day of the attacks. It's my chance to seek revenge on behalf of my grandfather.'

He paused momentarily to savour the story he was about to recount.

'During the war, German soldiers occupied this city for just over a year and the army used the synagogue as a storage unit for artillery and small armoured vehicles. When events began to turn against us in August 1944, my grandfather was forced to order the evacuation of the troops. The Führer gave explicit instructions to senior Nazis to blow up key strategic bridges and buildings before leaving, and top of the list was this symbol of Jewish faith. He knew its destruction would deal a devastating blow to Jews across Europe. Our soldiers placed over a dozen explosive devices inside the building and wired them to detonators a couple of blocks away, but a meddling old janitor who'd been hiding inside the building disabled all but one, so when the explosion occurred, our troops believed their mission had been accomplished but in reality, there was hardly any serious structural damage. So, one deranged old bastard, who wasn't even a Jew, thwarted the entire operation. When my grandfather heard about the fiasco, he ordered the immediate execution of the soldiers involved.'

Deshi nodded and glanced down at her watch; a gesture Franklin registered as he turned away from the viewpoint.

'Yes, you're quite right, we shouldn't be late for our dinner appointment. That would show a lack of respect and we need to keep Signor Ricci fully onside.'

Franklin leaned across her to reach for his tumbler of bourbon resting on a high circular table a few feet away. He drained the glass, placed it back down and headed for the exit. Deshi glanced at her coupe containing a Negroni, thought better of it and followed him down the stairs.

# Chapter Seven

Florence, Italy

The four armed guards dressed in military fatigues patrolling the front gates of the Tempio Maggiore showed little interest in the group of three tourists who joined the back of the small queue waiting to enter the synagogue through a glass kiosk to the left side of the building. The two men in the party had their baseball hats pulled low over their foreheads and the young woman's long black hair was drawn back and covered by an olive-green headscarf. To complete their disguise, they each wore large-framed sunglasses, all of which ensured their facial features would be unrecognisable if picked up by security cameras.

As soon as they passed through the ticket office and entered a large garden surrounding the Jewish temple, they hung back in a huddle, pretending to read some engraved inscriptions on the front wall. A handful of visitors passed by and made their way inside the building, leaving them alone outside.

Franklin turned to study the façade of the magnificent structure, known as the Great Synagogue of Florence. The exterior was modelled on Arab Byzantine architecture, with a dominant central green dome, perfectly framed on either side by two arched towers that supported smaller onion domes in the Moorish Revival style. The front walls were entirely clad with Italian travertine, its resemblance to Jerusalem stone a clear nod to the Holy Land. Franklin glanced over his shoulder at the large set of grey wrought-iron gates at the main entrance that were permanently locked for security purposes.

'Signor Ricci, how will you and your men penetrate the building?'

Armando Ricci was the self-proclaimed leader of the Roman National Party, an anti-Semitic white supremacist group founded in Naples ten years earlier. It pursued a biological form of racism that believed the Italians were a race, connected not by language but by blood. As well as targeting Jews, their hatred also focused on migrants and LGBTQIA+ people, whom they categorised as subhuman.

Ricci was a short stub of a man who appeared to be almost as wide as he was tall. His clean-shaven head disguised a receding hairline and his deep-set circular brown eyes and flat nose combined with his plump face to create the appearance of an angry bulldog. He'd the barrel chest of a canine and the growl to go with it. As a young man, Ricci, who in those days was a fervent communist, had attended Bologna University to study political science. But his ideology soon took a sharp turn to the right after being groomed by a fascist lecturer who introduced him to *Mein Kampf*, the autobiographical manifesto written by Adolf Hitler while serving nine months in Landsberg prison in Bavaria for treason. For Ricci, a devout anti-Semitic fascist, the opportunity of working with and for the Führer's grandson was an honour beyond belief.

'Signor Franklin, we plan to use two vehicles in a coordinated strike. A Transit will pull up twenty yards from the entrance and six of my men, armed with AK-103s – thanks to your funding – will take out the guards before they have time to react. At the same moment, an unbranded articulated lorry will arrive and unload a Patria armoured vehicle, which will smash through the gates and enter this garden where it will pull up at the entrance to meet with the rest of my men. Then we—'

'How many people does the Patria carry, as we'll both need to be inside it?'

Deshi cut in as Ricci was mid-flow, and the bulldog flashed his teeth in anger; but he held back, as he knew the woman was an elite killer and a close ally of Franklin's. He also registered the fact Franklin would be joining him in person on the day of the attack, so his annoyance turned to elation.

'That will indeed be an honour for myself and my men, and as for the vehicle, it can hold up to twelve plus a three-man crew. I only plan to have six men inside, so there will be plenty of room for both of you. Together, we'll transform this place of worship into a giant burial ground.'

Franklin placed his hand on Ricci's shoulder as a gesture of approval.

'Let's go inside the synagogue, so I can get a feel for the place.'

The midday sun streaked through the six horseshoe-arched stained-glass windows, illuminating the Ten Commandments above the wooden ark on the back wall. Every surface of the interior was decorated from top to bottom with hand-painted designs featuring scrolls, floral motifs and geometric patterns. The colour palette was a heady mix of red, blue and gold and the entrance lobby, where they stood, featured a Venetian marble floor laid in arabesque design with the number 1882 inset into the tiles, marking the year the synagogue opened. The seating was provided by dozens of dark brown oak pews that ran the length of the prayer hall, broken up by three aisles.

Franklin led the way forward along the centre one, heading towards the ark. Halfway along, he came to an abrupt stop, as his lead foot pressed into a pronounced dip in the floor. Ricci was quick to offer an explanation.

'The floor is uneven here because during the war a bomb—'

'Signor Ricci, I don't require a history lesson about this dreadful place. I know exactly what happened here, which is one of the reasons I wanted to see it for myself.'

'I apologise, Signor Franklin, for any misunderstanding on my part.'

Deshi was busy taking a good look around and weighed in with another question. She pointed to a long wooden grille running along the right-hand side of the hall, behind which were two rows of wooden seats.

'Why's that area cut off?'

Ricci was relieved to have a chance to show off his knowledge without threat of rebuke.

'It's reserved for the wives of the most important men in the community – a sort of VIP area. The rest of the women are seated upstairs.'

He pointed to a gallery that formed a three-sided horseshoe on the upper level with six rows of seating.

'On the day concerned, every single seat will be filled. Almost two thousand Jews will be inside – a perfect killing field for us.'

Franklin was relishing every moment and had one final question for his fascist guide. 'What about the head of the synagogue? It's vital we take him out as a clear message to any survivors in the community.'

The bulldog bared his teeth for a second time.

'Don't worry about that, Signor Franklin. My men have studied an image of Rabbi Raphael Zolli. He's top of the list.'

# Chapter Eight

Reno, United States

The Silver Dollar Bar on Lakeside Drive in Old Southwest Reno claimed to possess the biggest selection of tequila in the state of Nevada, which suited Trump-supporting Republicans and members of extreme right-wing political groups down to the ground. The establishment was set over three floors, with small square black-and-gold booths that provided a haven for fascists and neo-Nazis to vent their bile without fear of being overheard. Daniel and Vakha were huddled together on a banquette, strategically chosen, in a corner of the top floor, waiting for their guest to arrive.

They were due to meet John Nicks, a notorious Holocaust denier and advocate of the white genocide conspiracy theory that claimed the existence of an organised Jewish plot to eradicate the dominance of white people. Nicks was the leader of the White National League, an underground group based in Nevada with tentacles spread deep across mid-America. He was a giant of a man who looked as though he'd just stepped

31

out of a WWE ring and was best known for his cartoonish thick black beard that earned him the nickname 'the Pirate' from his devoted followers. His greatest claim to fame thus far was his role, alongside five devotees, in ransacking Nancy Pelosi's office during the infamous Capitol Riots. However, in a subsequent face-to-face meet with John Franklin, the Führer's grandson had informed Nicks his Trump-supporting gesture would prove to be an irrelevance when compared to the significance of the attack on the world order he'd soon be taking part in.

Franklin had insisted Daniel and Vakha travel to Reno to meet with Nicks as a sign of respect but, more importantly, to hand him a fake passport, enabling him to travel incognito because Franklin knew he was on the FBI's watch list. The three of them would then take the red-eye to New York later that evening.

They were almost an hour early for the rendezvous and Daniel was bored and irritable as the young Chechen assassin was not known for his sparkling conversation. He reached across and grabbed a handful of pistachios from a round ceramic dish on the centre of the table and was about to pick up his cell phone to read his emails when Vakha hit him with a question from left field.

'Mr Anderson, did you really create Jack Pitt and *Secret Tombs*?'

Daniel hadn't seen that one coming and hesitated for a moment before replying. 'Yeah, I did, along with three brilliant game designers. Why do you ask?'

Vakha's eyes beamed with excitement and he leaned closer.

'Because it's my favourite PlayStation game of all time. I

smashed all the levels in the five versions and picked up every bonus treasure along the way. I can't believe you were the brains behind it – you're not much older than me.'

Daniel's mood immediately softened and he made the decision to reveal a secret part of himself to a virtual stranger; intimate information only a handful of people in the world knew about.

'Vakha, my life story is far stranger and more unbelievable than any fictional storyline I created for Jack Pitt. I was born in Los Angeles but my mother died shortly after my birth and, because my father's identity was unknown, I was passed over to an adoption agency that sent me seven thousand miles away to Australia. My adoptive parents always said I was special, and when I was five, they told me who my father was and, more importantly, who my grandfather was. They explained he was one of the greatest figures in history and that I was his direct descendant. They said the Führer's blood flowed through my veins and my destiny was mapped out for me.'

Vakha was totally absorbed by Daniel's revelations and shook his head in disbelief. 'So, you and John are half-brothers?'

'Yes, and there's more to the story. When I was twenty-one, I inherited fifty million dollars from a secret bank account belonging to my father's estate. That was obviously mind-blowing. It allowed me to fund Wolf Productions and bring in amazing talent from the gaming world. Then Jack Pitt was born and the rest is history. Suddenly, we found ourselves in the same league as the big boys. *Secret Tombs* was right up there with *Call of Duty*, *Street Fighter* and *Grand Theft Auto*. I was living the dream. Then, shortly afterwards, I discovered I had three other half-siblings spread across the world, as well as John. In the last sixteen months all of them have died, leaving just the two of us as the sole surviving descendants of Adolf Hitler, along with John's son, who he has no contact with. That's why we've no choice but to fulfil our destiny . . . it's our inheritance.'

He paused, grabbed a Heineken bottle from the table and took a huge swig. Vakha looked on in amazement, not knowing what to say next. Neither spoke for a while before Daniel broke the silence.

'What about you and Deshi? You guys have obviously made more money than you can ever hope to spend. What drives you on? Why are you here?'

Vakha was equally ready to unload his remarkable back story.

'When we were small children, the Russians slaughtered our parents and wiped out our entire village while the rest of the world watched on. Nobody said a word or raised a finger.'

Vakha's eyes watered and he could feel himself choking up. But he wasn't quite finished.

'Just like you and John, it's us against the world.'

The two men got lost in exchanging stories but Daniel kept a close eye on the time. Nicks was now late and if he didn't arrive soon, they'd have to go without him. When he finally turned up, he made a half-hearted sheepish excuse blaming a Mexican Uber driver for trying a supposed short cut to the bar that added forty-five minutes to the journey. The leader of the White National League proceeded to rattle off a tirade of abuse about him.

'The beaner was lucky I didn't cut him up. Bastards like him have taken jobs from decent hard-working people. It's a real pisser they never let Trump finish that wall.'

Nicks's signature beard was littered with bits of food and Daniel suspected the true reason for his lateness was a spur-of-the-moment detour to the McDonald's he'd spotted earlier at the corner of the block.

'This is a serious operation, Nicks, and I've no time for bullshit. You're behind schedule and we need to catch a plane. Vakha has your passport. Let's go.'

Nicks guiltily wiped the remnants of a burger from his beard. He needed to up his game fast, now he was playing in the big league.

Daniel glared at the fascist known as 'the Pirate'.

'Jesus Christ, Nicks. I hope you're up to this.'

# Chapter Nine

Rockville, United States

Berrettini had secured a safe house for his two friends in the small city of Rockville, about thirty miles northeast of Washington. He was genuinely concerned for their welfare following the bomb attacks and had installed two agents inside the house and one in the large garden that surrounded the property on three sides.

Hembury was happily beavering away in the open-plan kitchen, prepping scrambled eggs on the stove when the FBI deputy director burst through the front door armed with a laptop case and a brown paper bag stuffed full of croissants and Danish pastries. His mood was buoyant as he laid out plates on the kitchen table and grabbed a carton of fresh grapefruit juice from the fridge.

'Troy, forget the eggs. These croissants are warm, as is my news.'

A few seconds later, Vargas emerged from one of the bedrooms. As the three men sat down around the table, Berrettini set up his laptop. The desktop file he opened contained several security camera stills and videos taken at an airport passport control booth. They showed three men as a group and individually, none of whom were instantly recognisable to Vargas or Hembury, who was the first to question the footage.

'So, what are we looking at here, Mike?'

Berrettini clicked on the photo featuring a colossus of a man with a distinctive liquorice-coloured beard, dressed head to toe in stonewashed denim.

'These images came through to me from the NSA just over an hour ago. They show three men arriving at JFK, having flown in from Nevada. This guy is the one who initially raised alarm bells at the agency, because his passport details were a mismatch with his facial recognition. His name is John Nicks, a neo-Nazi who runs a white supremacist group based in Reno. We know from video footage he was involved in the Capitol Riots, and he's on our internal terrorist watch list. The first question we need to answer is – why would he enter New York State under an alias?'

Vargas leaned in towards the laptop to take a closer look at the frozen image to try and work out its relevance. Berrettini could see both his friends were bewildered, so he ploughed on.

'Okay, now we get to the really interesting part. Once we spotted Nicks, we ran images of his two companions through our facial recognition system and, bingo, we got a massive hit.'

He flicked through to another image featuring a much younger man.

'Any ideas?'

Vargas and Hembury shook their heads and remained silent.

'Okay, I'll put you out of your misery. You're looking at an image of Daniel Anderson, Franklin's only remaining sibling who, up until this morning, we believed was dead, as we've heard nothing of him since the Israeli episode fifteen months ago. He's also travelling under a false passport, using the name Matt Dempsey, who one of my colleagues tells me is a fictional character in one of his computer games. Apparently, he's an anti-hero.'

Vargas took in the striking features of the Führer's grandson, whose ash-blond hair and crystal blue eyes confirmed his Aryan credentials.

'Damn. Of course it is. The beard threw me off. What about the third man?'

'No match there – we've no idea who he is. But, as none of us believe in coincidences, Anderson's sudden appearance accompanied by a known terrorist doesn't bode well. The timing must relate to Franklin's recent activities. The question is – why has he gone to New York and what the hell is he up to?'

Hembury had quietly demolished a croissant while the other two were talking, but his eyes had remained transfixed on the screen.

'Look, we know from our meeting with the head of GCHQ there's a major terrorist operation in the pipeline and the Hitler boys are clearly in the mix. Maybe New York is the target. Do we know where Nicks and Anderson are staying?'

'Yes, they checked into the Pierre on 61st Street on the Upper East Side. Right now, we have them under surveillance. I've organised a Bureau chopper for us. We'll be in New York in a couple of hours. Pack a bag and let's get out of here.'

As they rose from the table, Hembury glanced back at Anderson's frozen image. His instinct told him something was off.

'Strange choice of hotel – why would they want to stay in that part of town?'

If Hembury had known the Pierre was located just four blocks away from the largest synagogue in New York, he'd have had his answer.

# Chapter Ten

New York, United States

Anderson's deluxe grand suite on the thirty-ninth floor of the Pierre offered unparalleled views over Central Park and the magnificent city skyline. John Nicks drank in the splendour of the ornately decorated lounge where he was sitting with Daniel and Vakha, discussing plans for the following twenty-four hours. The classical grandeur was a visual reminder of the unbridled power and wealth Franklin and his associates possessed. At last, he was operating with influential people who shared his twisted view of the world and he felt relevant.

Daniel was holding court while Vakha was busy checking over a Beretta M9 semi-automatic pistol that had been delivered to the hotel concierge a few minutes earlier concealed in standard Amazon packaging. He'd opted for the A3 version that offered an extended magazine chambering seventeen rounds as opposed to the standard ten.

Daniel smiled, watching the childlike pleasure the young assassin experienced as he carefully weighed the weapon in the palm of his hand, and then turned away from Vakha to address Nicks.

'John, I'm keen to check out the temple and hear your detailed plan for the attack. There's a possibility Vakha and I will join you on the day, although ultimately that's Franklin's call.'

Nicks roughly stroked his beard with his right hand, a tic that usually signified a surge of excitement in the brain of the white supremacist.

'As you've so much choice of where to be on the actual day, Daniel, that would be a real honour. I've scheduled a visit tomorrow morning to the Emanu-El Synagogue, but before then we have a meeting with the six members of our group who'll form the assault team. One of them works as a night janitor in a container warehouse in Brooklyn. The meeting's scheduled for eleven tonight.'

Daniel rose from his armchair to signal the session was over.

'Okay, I suggest we stay in our rooms for the rest of the day and meet downstairs around ten thirty. John, I remember you said in Reno you like seafood. I suggest you check out the lobster and crayfish club sandwich on the room service menu.'

Nicks could feel himself salivating at the prospect and began to stroke his beard again.

\* \* \*

The matt black Bell 412 chopper, with no identifiable markings, smoothly descended onto a helipad a few blocks south of the FBI New York field office on Foley Square in Lower Manhattan's Civic Center neighbourhood. Berrettini led his two colleagues inside the seventies-built, forty-one-storey tower block to the twenty-third floor, where he kept a small office and a tight group of fifteen seasoned agents who monitored local terrorist threats in the city. Waiting for them in a windowless meeting room was his New York chief, Ralph Kennedy, a long-serving agent who'd graduated from the field to a senior management position within the Bureau.

After a brief round of introductions, Kennedy opened his laptop, which was connected to a slide projector, and ran through several black-and-white videos featuring their three targets. The CCTV footage showed them signing in at the hotel reception desk, entering and exiting a lift and then walking along a corridor on the thirty-ninth floor.

'We've access to the hotel's internal security camera system that shows the three men spent just over an hour together in Anderson's suite before Nicks and the unidentified third man went to their own rooms. Since then, they've ordered food and stayed apart. We've three agents in the foyer standing by to visit their rooms whenever they leave, and additional teams parked up at the front and rear of the hotel ready to follow them whenever they go. For now, it's a waiting game.'

\* \* \*

Franklin and Deshi decided to snatch an early supper with Ricci in Florence's most celebrated square, the Piazza della Signoria, before heading for Peretola Airport and the comfort of a private jet that would return them to the sanctuary of *The Little Fox*, now moored off the Madagascar coastline by Manafiafy beach.

Ricci, who evidently loved the sound of his own voice, was droning on about the literary merits of *Mein Kampf* when Deshi, who'd tuned out long ago, cut in.

'Mr Franklin, don't react, but the two men sitting at three o'clock were on the rooftop terrace last night. They caught my attention because they were drinking Diet Coke, even though that place is known for its cocktails. This evening they sat down at their table about a minute after we arrived, so there's no doubt they're watching us. They're dressed as Westerners, but I'd guess they're of Asian or Middle Eastern origin and looking at the bulges under their jackets it would appear they're both carrying.'

Franklin felt his stomach churn as he furtively checked out the two men. He was pretty sure he knew the identity of their employer, so these two guys represented his worst nightmare. He turned to Deshi, who instantly read her boss's mind and slowly rose to her feet. She casually strolled between the circular tables laid out on the square, pausing at one positioned just to the left of her targets. She leaned down and asked the young American couple who were quietly enjoying their cappuccinos for a light, knowing full well they weren't smokers, as there was no ashtray on their table. The two men immediately lowered their gaze as Deshi approached them next. She bent down to address the man closest to her and slid her right hand inside her leather bomber jacket to retrieve a Glock 19 that she pressed firmly against his ribcage. When she spoke, she ensured her voice was just loud enough for both men to hear.

'Stand up slowly and walk inside the café. Take the stairs to the right of the food counter down to the restroom.'

Following her normal protocols, Deshi had scouted the

interior layout of the café as soon as they'd arrived, so she knew the location of the rear exit in case they had to leave in a hurry.

None of the other customers or waiting staff paid any attention as she accompanied the two men inside the café and down the narrow staircase to a small empty toilet. Deshi allowed the weighted door to close behind her and immediately the man furthest away dived forward onto the hard tiled floor and rolled to his right, desperately grabbing for his pistol. At the same moment, his partner spun around and lashed out, attempting to force the Glock from her hand, but Deshi was far too quick for them. Her left hand parried the incoming blow, while she simultaneously fired a shot into the heart of her assailant. A split second later, a perfectly aimed headshot took care of his partner.

She checked both corpses for ID but wasn't surprised to discover they had none. As she exited the restroom and made her way up the stairs, she speculated the local Carabinieri would never be able to establish the identities of the two Asian John Does.

Franklin and Ricci had already departed the café and crossed the square, where Deshi spotted them standing among a throng of tourists outside the Palazzo Vecchio. As she left the café to join them, she quickly tucked a fifty euro note under one of the side plates on their table. Franklin was jumpy and desperate to get away from Ricci and the crime scene, and a few minutes later he and Deshi leaped into the back of a chauffeured Mercedes S-Class. The limo tore away, leaving a trail of black rubber on the ancient cobblestoned road, and headed straight for the airport.

Two hours later, four thousand miles away in a former

presidential palace in Kabul, Abbas Turabi, the head of international security for the Taliban regime, relayed the news of his failed operation to the supreme leader.

'We didn't succeed on this occasion but we're getting closer. Sooner or later, the American will fall into our hands and he'll answer in person for his crimes against the Islamic Emirate of Afghanistan.'

# Chapter Eleven

New York, United States

'They're on the move, sir.'

The head of the FBI's New York branch was sitting in the front passenger seat of a silver Mercedes Sprinter van parked across the street from the entrance of the Pierre, watching Anderson, Nicks and Vakha climb into a yellow cab. Kennedy was on his cell, speaking with Berrettini.

'We'll fall in behind and I'll call you as soon as we learn their destination.'

The deputy director had taken the call on speaker, so Vargas and Hembury both heard the update. He clicked off his phone and rose from his seat.

'It's too late at night to be going out to eat, something must be going down. I'll get a driver on standby. Be ready to leave as soon as we hear.'

The yellow cab drove through the vast complex of warehouses in the six-million-square-foot space known as Industry City and pulled up on 39th Street. Its three passengers had no idea they were being followed as they exited the vehicle, with

Nicks leading the way. It took the small group some five minutes to find the entrance of the storage container warehouse they were searching for, adjacent to the harbour.

Waiting by the security door was a lanky teenager with a distinctive shaven head plastered with a disturbing array of swastika tattoos. He nodded towards his leader and swung open the grey metal door, allowing the three men to enter. In the following fifteen minutes, five more men arrived, all granted entry by swastika man, who followed the last one in.

Kennedy was about eighty yards away, partially hidden by a massive sea container, monitoring events through a thermal vision scope. Behind him, in a tight huddle, crouched four armed agents who'd travelled with him in the back of the Sprinter. He lowered the device and reached for his cell. Minutes later, Berrettini, Vargas and Hembury were on their way to join him in Brooklyn.

* * *

Inside the warehouse, nine men were tightly grouped around a long wooden trestle table with Nicks standing at one end. He was pointing animatedly at a blueprint of the internal layout of the Emanu-El Synagogue on East 65th Street.

'On the day, there'll be two and a half thousand Jews seated inside – sitting ducks, just waiting to be taken out. The only obstacle in our way is the security detail who guard the front entrance and inner lobby. Most of them are former Marines and they'll be armed with assault rifles.'

Swastika man, who was standing at the other end of the table, raised his hand, asking for permission to speak.

'We've given that problem a great deal of thought and I reckon we've come up with a way to breach their security . . .'

Outside the front of the warehouse, another attack plan was being hatched with Berrettini at the helm. Based on Kennedy's briefing, he figured they faced nine hostiles inside the building. As all of them were most likely terrorists, he was anticipating a firefight. There were now four agents on-site, as well as an armourer who was busy sorting out a pair of Glock 17s for Vargas and Hembury. Each gun housed a magazine containing seventeen rounds and he supplied them both with a spare clip, just in case things turned really ugly.

The deputy director was in his element, dishing out orders to his team.

'We've more agents on the way, who should be with us in the next few minutes. Once they're here, we'll look to make a forced entry of the building. There's a second door to the warehouse that runs along the riverside, about thirty yards up. Nic, you take that entrance along with four agents and, Troy, you join up with the other four, who'll enter through the front.'

He turned to face two of his senior men.

'Patrick, you and Dan will be team leaders. Neither of the doors are guarded from the outside but we've no idea where the targets are situated inside or what they're up to. We believe all, or at least most of them, will be armed, so I doubt they'll hand themselves over peacefully. You've seen images of Anderson and Nicks – let's make sure we end up with both in custody, alive and well. Any questions?'

No one spoke. Berrettini glanced down at his watch before issuing his final order.

'Okay, it's 23.39. Both teams look to enter at precisely 23.55

and maintain comms with each other at all times, so Kennedy and I can hear exactly what's going down.'

The armourer handed out tactical gas masks to both assault teams, along with Triple-Chaser CS tear gas grenades. These specialised weapons consisted of three canisters pressed together that separated on deployment, meaning they covered three times the area of a conventional grenade, and had a burn time of thirty seconds before clearing.

Inside the warehouse, the meeting had disintegrated into a rowdy party with most of the White National League members swigging on bottles of Pilsner and passing around several cannabis joints, creating a large plume of smoke that hung obstinately above the table. Country music was blasting from a small Bluetooth speaker resting on the concrete floor and the mood was turning poisonous.

Daniel was growing increasingly irritated by the outrageous behaviour of Nicks's men and was seriously doubting the wisdom of Franklin's choice of partner. He was itching to leave and caught Vakha's eye, who picked up on his boss's unease. The two of them casually moved away from the table and began to walk towards the side entrance, about fifty feet away. They'd only taken a few paces when mayhem broke out inside the warehouse, courtesy of the two FBI assault teams and a huge blast of tear gas. Grenades rained in from two different directions, aimed at the group of men huddled around the table in the centre of the giant storehouse.

Panic set in and the first person to reach for his gun was swastika man. His eyes were burning from the acidic solution released by the canisters but his temporary blindness didn't prevent him grabbing his M16 automatic assault rifle and indiscriminately spraying rounds in the direction he believed the attack had originated from. Three of his comrades followed suit and in the chaos that followed two FBI agents were taken down by random gunfire.

Amid the havoc, Nicks had the presence of mind to grab the synagogue plans and screw them up into a tight ball. Then, with his free hand, he grabbed his Zippo lighter from inside his jacket and set light to the papers, which he threw onto the floor underneath the trestle table.

Vakha was quick to react and grabbed Daniel around the waist to steer him away from the agents who were heading directly towards them. They joined together as one, moving at high speed to their right, desperately trying to escape the gas cloud that had appeared from nowhere.

The FBI agents returned fire far more efficiently, as their state-of-the-art masks allowed them to spot distinct outlines of figures moving through the dense smoke. The first white supremacist taken out lost half his temple as a 9 mm round penetrated the right-hand side of his skull. Four more followed in a matter of seconds and Nicks, who'd dived beneath the wooden table for cover, screamed his surrender.

As the gas began to clear, the agents spotted him kneeling on the floor with his arms raised high above his head, next to a small pile of black ash. Hembury called over his comms for an immediate ceasefire.

Thirty feet away, having cleared the gas cloud, Vakha was leading Daniel towards the side entrance. Vargas and two agents were scanning that area when they spotted the two men heading for the exit about fifteen feet away. Vargas instantly recognised Daniel and screamed out a warning.

'Anderson, stay where you are. There's no way out.'

Daniel stopped but Vakha pushed him forward with such brute force he found himself rolling head first, bouncing off the concrete floor towards the exit. The young Chechen moved at lightning speed, Beretta poised, and fired off two headshots within a second of each other, taking out both the agents who'd been standing to one side of Vargas. Vakha's trigger finger was a millisecond away from firing again when a bullet blew away a large section of his brain and his body folded and slumped to the floor.

Vargas held his gun stance for a few seconds, taking in the horror of the gruesome tableau laid out in front of him: two slain agents and a young man he assumed was Anderson's bodyguard created the stench of death that surrounded him.

Daniel witnessed Vakha's shooting a moment before he disappeared through the exit and, once outside, found himself standing on a six-foot-wide strip of concrete that lay between the warehouse and the harbour. He ran for his life along the narrow pathway, desperately trying to put some distance between himself and Vargas. As soon as he reached the corner of the warehouse, he darted towards a cluster of huge containers positioned by a giant crane alongside the water. There was a narrow gap between two of them and he slipped inside it, hoping to disappear in the shadows.

He frantically tried to catch his breath as he reached for his cell and called the only man alive he knew could possibly help him. As soon as Franklin answered, Daniel began an incoherent rant.

'John . . . It's all gone to shit. Nicks's team has been taken down . . . Vargas was there . . . he killed Vakha . . . you've got to get me out of New York . . .'

Franklin's mind was reeling as he struggled to digest the implications of the hysterical outburst from his half-brother. Before he could reply, he heard the distant sound of another voice.

'Mr Anderson, walk slowly towards me and keep your hands high in the air or I won't hesitate to shoot.'

Mike Berrettini calmly issued the warning with his gun aimed at Anderson's head. Daniel edged slowly forward and emerged from his temporary hiding place, out of the shadows. His cell was still live and although it was in his right hand and a long way from his ear, he could hear Franklin repeatedly yelling his name. He was about four feet away from Berrettini, who was calling for backup on a throat mic while continuing to train his gun on him. Daniel knew there was no way out but had one last act of defiance in his kitbag. In a flash of movement, he hurled the cell towards the oily blackness of the bay and achieved significant distance, which meant neither he nor Berrettini heard the splash. Moments later, Vargas appeared, flanked by three agents, and Daniel offered up his wrists for the cuffs he knew were coming his way.

Three thousand miles away, fifty thousand feet in the air, Franklin was in utter turmoil, storming around his private plane, trying to process the fallout from the nuclear call he'd just received. He cursed the fact the engine sound from his Gulfstream was nowhere near loud enough to drown out the hysterical screaming and sobbing emanating from the toilet at the rear of the plane where Deshi had installed herself after hearing of Vakha's killing. He stood rigid on the spot as the sound changed from weeping to a guttural howl, an excruciating noise he swore sounded more like a wolf than a human.

After a few minutes, the haunting shrieks of pain subsided and Franklin's scowl slowly morphed into a menacing half-smile. Deshi would want to avenge her brother's death. He just had to harness her pain and weaponise it against Vargas.

# Chapter Twelve

## Washington D.C., United States

The High-Value Detainee Interrogation Group, better known as the HIG, was created in 2009 by President Barak Obama. It was a unique black-ops task force of high-ranking intelligence professionals drawn from the CIA, Department of Defense and the FBI, and its purpose was to interrogate terrorists immediately after their arrest to obtain information about their accomplices and upcoming threats to the United States.

The unique group fell under the jurisdiction of the FBI and its chief was Mike Berrettini. In that role, he'd called in two of his closest associates, Brad Keane from the CIA and Scott Neville from the Department of Defense, to help with the interrogation of the two terrorist suspects his team had arrested at the waterside warehouse in New York.

Daniel Anderson and John Nicks were being held in adjoining cells in the basement of a remote building in the suburbs of Washington that didn't have a house number or a zip code and technically didn't exist. The two men had been drugged during the ninety-minute flight from New York, and when they awoke had no idea where they were or that they were being held so close to each other.

In an upstairs secure room, Berrettini was heading up a small clandestine meeting with his two counterparts from the other intelligence services, along with Vargas and Hembury.

'We'll start the first round of interrogations at the same time. Scott, you'll lead Anderson's with Nic alongside and, Brad, you take Nicks with Troy riding shotgun. I'll be watching camera feeds from both. You'll all have earpieces, and I'll keep you up to speed with what's happening next door. Brad, Nicks may prove hard to break because he's been pulled in by the Feds before, but I'm hoping Anderson will crack wide open like a warm freshly delivered egg.'

\* \* \*

Franklin and Deshi were back on board *The Little Fox*, which had left Madagascar and was heading south-west towards Port Elizabeth in the Eastern Cape Province of South Africa. They were sitting together in one of the smaller lounges on the sun deck, analysing the consequences from the disastrous fiasco that had taken place in New York. Deshi's initial grief had mutated into cold white anger, which she knew could only be quelled by a revenge killing of the man who'd murdered her twin brother. Her face was contorted with pain, the sickly pallor of her skin and her puffy red eyes signs of her evident distress. Her life force was now solely driven by the need for retribution, and it couldn't come soon enough.

Franklin's mind was consumed with a completely different scenario. He suspected Nicks would keep his mouth shut but had no way of knowing how long Daniel could hold out under intense interrogation and that left him with two options: his half-brother had to be silenced or else removed from his FBI captors, neither of which seemed a realistic scenario. However, he wondered if there might just be a way. He refreshed his glass tumbler, courtesy of a bottle of Jim Beam, before floating the idea to Deshi.

'We need to mount a counterstrike before the FBI learn anything meaningful from Daniel or Nicks. You won't be surprised to know I have a resource deep inside the Bureau who's given me some priceless intel. Daniel and Nicks are being kept in a secure location they claim is impossible to breach unless we have a small army at our disposal, so that's not a live option. But my source also passed through a little gem of information that might just give us an edge and turn this scenario on its head.'

For the first time since she'd learned of Vakha's death, Deshi managed to focus her thoughts on another topic. She nodded at Franklin, urging him to continue.

'We have the address of a safe house in a sleepy little town just north-west of Washington where Vargas and Hembury are holed up. Unlike the other site, this property is unsecured or at least not as tightly guarded, which gave me an idea. What if we lifted one of them and held them in a secret place of our own? I'm sure that Italian bastard Berrettini would be more than willing to agree to an exchange – one of his friends for two of ours.'

'I want the Argentine. It has to be Vargas.'

Franklin heard the desperation in her voice and felt the need to re-establish his authority in the hierarchy of their weird relationship.

'I'll decide which one we target, and remember, we need both alive until our operation has played out. They need to witness the scale of our attacks and understand the power of my legacy. Then they can die. I promise you can have the pleasure of taking out Vargas any way you want. I'll hand him to you on a plate, but for now he and Hembury are more useful to us alive. Now, let's get on, we've a great deal to do and little time to put together an elite team to work with you on the extraction in Rockville.'

Franklin drained his glass and switched his focus away from Deshi towards his black iPad Pro, resting on a small side table. Deshi took the cue and silently slipped away. Despite the assurances she'd heard from her boss, she'd only one thought playing on her mind.

Once Deshi had departed the lounge, Franklin logged in and opened a file entitled *Das Endspiel* – 'The Endgame' – which was buried deep in his iCloud drive. It required an encrypted passcode to get into and its contents had never been shared with his inner circle. Franklin was a cunning psychopath who trusted no one, not even his half-brother, and this key part of Operation Atonement had so far been kept secret. The hint of a poisonous smile broke out on his lips as he viewed the contents of the document. It was an incredibly ambitious and outrageous plan that would create waves across the globe, and now was the time to bring it to fruition.

# Chapter Thirteen

## Washington D.C., United States

**B**errettini was crammed into a small space hardly bigger than a broom cupboard. His bulky frame was perched on a high-backed brushed-metal stool jammed up against a wooden shelf that supported four sixteen-inch colour monitors. They displayed live feeds from two cells located on the other side of a solid concrete wall. The FBI deputy director checked his digital watch which confirmed the time was 10.00. The interrogations were about to begin.

His eyes flicked between the four screens: two security cameras from each cell. A strip of white gaffer tape stuck across the top of the monitors gave the name of each suspect. In both instances one camera offered a close-up of the detainee while the second showed a wide shot taken from behind their head, favouring the two interrogators. Berrettini felt like a tennis umpire preparing to follow the live action about to play out in front of him. As he stared at the stony faces of Anderson and Nicks, both harnessed to their chairs by heavy-duty black leather straps, he wondered who'd crack first. He wasn't a gambler but had he been, he'd have placed all his money on the young Australian.

Scott Neville, number two in the Department of Defense, was Berrettini's equivalent and an old hand when it came to this line of work. He'd drilled the truth out of dozens of hardened terrorists who'd initially appeared unbreakable. He was in his early forties, tall and lean with a gaunt face, aquiline nose and sharp features, which gave him a hawk-like appearance. Vargas, who was sitting alongside him, felt way out of his depth and slightly uncomfortable but reconciled that feeling by reminding himself of what was at stake. Neville opened with a barrage of words that sounded just as threatening as any physical assault.

'Daniel, this is very easy for us. The fact is – you don't exist. You've been missing, presumed dead, for almost sixteen months, which means you get no call to a lawyer or a loved one, if you even have one. We can do whatever we want and no one out there will ever know. How do you fancy a spell at Guantanamo? One injection, one flight and that's where you'll wake up in a nicely pressed orange boiler suit. So don't waste my time with bullshit. There's no way out for you.'

Daniel tried his best to protect himself from the verbal assault by tuning into the mindset of his computer game hero, Jack Pitt, who'd often faced adversity but always beat the odds, however heavily stacked against him. The only difference was, Pitt lived in a fantasy world – this was real life. Daniel knew he'd never survive the horrors of Guantanamo. For now, though, while he considered his options, he maintained eye contact with his enemy and remained resolutely silent. Neville was an astute interrogator who'd done his homework on

Daniel and correctly interpreted the lack of response to his opening salvo.

'This isn't one of your pathetic video games, Daniel. This is real life. Jack Pitt and his cronies can't save you from what's coming your way.'

Daniel blinked for the first time, a telltale sign the master interrogator chalked off as a minor victory.

'It could take hours, days or even weeks but, believe me, you'll tell me everything I want to know, so why bother playing the hero? After all, you're the bad guy here, and in the real world bad guys like you get their asses hung out to dry.'

By comparison, in the adjoining cell Nicks was only too happy to talk, offering up a wall of words laced with the defiance of a zealous terrorist prepared to die for his cause, although that option wasn't on offer. Brad Keane, head of special ops in the CIA, had come across plenty of Islamist fanatics who were content to die rather than talk but was a master at keeping them alive while taking them to the very edge of the precipice, where the pain was so unbearable that eventually they cracked, spilling their guts in return for the welcome escape of death. Nicks continued with his mantra, repeating his rehearsed script verbatim.

'I'm an American citizen and I know my human rights. Under the constitution, I've the right to take the Fifth and I'm entitled to legal representation. You've no mandate to detain me and, as far as I can see, nothing to charge me with.'

Nicks's heavily bearded face broke into a defiant grin displaying his nicotine-stained teeth, which resembled two rows of condemned tombstones. Keane sat back and listened with the hint of a knowing smile creasing his lips. His hairy fingers slightly adjusted his tortoiseshell glasses, which magnified his toad-like eyes. Above them, his thick, bushy eyebrows formed a black bar across his forehead. He was seriously hirsute. His entire body was covered from head to toe in wiry black hair and Hembury thought he looked Neanderthal.

'You asshole. Do you really think a pathetic piece of shit like you, who's out to kill innocent American citizens, deserves any human rights?'

'I'm an American citizen and I know my human rights. Under the constitution, I've the right to take the Fifth and—'

Keane leaped from his seat and smashed into Nicks's body with a wrestling-style body slam that sent the white supremacist sprawling across the stone floor, while still firmly strapped to his chair. He pummelled his face with a flurry of punches before easing off but remained crouched over Nicks, who lay motionless on the floor like an upturned crab. Keane stared down at the reddened face that was already beginning to bruise up.

'Nicks, as far as charges are concerned, how about travelling across the country using a fake passport for starters?'

Berrettini was settling into his chair preparing for the long haul when his cell buzzed, signalling an incoming WhatsApp. As soon as he saw the message, he recognised the swastika emoji Franklin had used before.

Halt the interrogations for twenty-four hours and I'll cut a deal. I'm ready to end this feud once and for all and come in.

Berrettini read the message twice before alerting the

interrogation teams to the new development. Two minutes later, all five men were sitting in the meeting room above the cells digesting the implications of the message. They were sceptical about Franklin's motives, especially Hembury, who was the first to challenge it.

'That sick bastard has ice running through his veins. I wouldn't believe a word he says. There's no way he's ever going to hand himself over to us, so what's his play?'

Vargas backed up his colleague's initial assessment and was equally bemused.

'Why twenty-four hours. What possible difference can that make?'

Berrettini held up his cell and began to punch in a reply.

'There's only one way to find out. Let's call his bluff.'

The reply didn't take long to write.

Okay, but if you don't appear, the interrogations resume and we'll come looking for you.

# Chapter Fourteen

Washington D.C., United States

Because of the urgency of the situation, Franklin had sent Deshi to Washington in his private jet which, remarkably, was capable of making the eight-thousand-mile flight from Port Elizabeth to Washington non-stop. The Gulfstream G650ER, which cost just over seventy million dollars, was one of three he kept on different continents; an extravagant perk that came from being one of the richest men on the planet. All of them had lavishly designed interiors that featured some of the most sought-after artwork in the world.

Franklin had initially insisted Deshi would need a small support team on the ground, but it didn't take long for her to persuade him she only required the aid of a competent driver and a safe location to keep the prospective hostage; the rest she could take care of by herself. Besides, now her brother was gone, she loathed the idea of working with people she didn't know or trust.

The Gulfstream landed just before midnight at a small private airport about forty miles west of D.C. Deshi was met outside the terminal by an operative Franklin had recruited courtesy of the dark web. It was a high-risk decision bringing in an outsider at short notice but the likely consequence of waiting longer to find a vetted terrorist, dedicated to his cause, wasn't an option.

Mo Leonard was a highly decorated former Marine who'd served in both Gulf War campaigns and now made a living as a mercenary, operating mainly on the infamous Tor Browser, where an endless supply of anonymous clients was eager to engage his unique talents.

He was casually dressed in a pair of denim cut-offs and a tight-fitting white T-shirt that showed off his impressive biceps to maximum effect. His muscular six-foot-two frame was striking for a man of his age and he kept it that way with three two-hour gym sessions a week combined with a low-fat, high-carb diet. His dark, rugged features and piercing blue eyes indicated he'd been a seriously handsome man in his younger days. Despite his youthful appearance, Deshi speculated he was probably pushing fifty, but didn't give a damn about his looks – the man just needed to be able to drive and follow orders.

Leonard's rate card varied between five and thirty thousand dollars a day depending on what he was asked to do, and he was always paid in Bitcoin. Nothing surprised him, but he found this hire intriguing as the job description was the weirdest he'd come across to date. It required a clean driving licence, a Transit van, access to a remote location close to the tiny town of Rockville where the interrogation of a hostage could take place, and the willingness to kill if necessary. The web post guaranteed a minimum of three days' work with a possible extension. When Leonard replied, insisting on an upfront payment of ninety thousand, his Bitcoin wallet alerted him within five minutes that the funds had landed. He was seriously impressed and suspected that, whatever the hire entailed, there was a good chance it would be extended, which meant this could turn out to be the biggest payday he'd ever pulled off.

He'd assumed his temporary boss would be a man and so was taken by surprise when a sole female passenger jogged down the steps of the Gulfstream onto the tarmac and headed towards the passenger terminal. Even from a distance, he detected the young woman had a certain aura about her. There was something special in the way she held herself, and when they met a couple of minutes later, he sensed he was dealing with a serious player who operated on a far higher level than him.

It was her eyes that told the story – there was a coldness behind them he surmised could only belong to a natural born killer. They appeared to embody a high voltage current that could shoot out and scorch a man without warning. He wasn't afraid of her, but instinctively knew he'd be working with a woman the like of which he'd never come across before.

She approached him in silence and not a word was spoken as they walked together across the small airport car park where his rental Transit was waiting. She threw her soft overnight bag into the narrow gap behind her seat, strapped on her belt and nodded, issuing a silent command to start the van.

As instructed, he'd already completed his first day's work, monitoring the comings and goings of a large house in a quiet street in a middle-class suburb of Rockville and was keen to report his findings, but knew better than to jump in like an eager recruit and kept quiet until he was asked the question. The wait only lasted until they hit the highway.

Deshi was reading a WhatsApp message from Franklin and Leonard heard what sounded like an angry groan. He looked out of the corner of his eye, saw her eyes were closed and took the opportunity to read her screen.

> Whichever one you take, they must stay alive so we can make the swap. Remember, Vargas has a great deal of personal suffering coming his way on the day of the attacks. Keep your head.

She opened her eyes, closed the message and slipped the phone inside her jacket pocket before speaking for the first time.

'Tell me everything you know about the house. What movements have there been?'

Leonard was slightly spooked by the directness of her question but didn't flinch and kept his eyes firmly on the road.

'As requested, I kept surveillance on the property from six this morning until two hours ago when I left to come and meet you. Just after seven two men exited the property dressed in jogging gear. They ran east along the street before turning north at the first block they reached. There was very little traffic about and I figured my Transit would be far too conspicuous if I tried to follow, so I stayed where I was, and thirty minutes later, they reappeared, retracing their steps. I guess somewhere along their route they turned and headed back rather than completing a circle.'

Deshi had retrieved her cell and was looking at the location on Google Maps, trying to work out where the joggers might have stopped before doubling back.

'What about the two men – was either of them olive-skinned or African American, like the photos we sent?'

'Impossible to tell. I was parked up a good two hundred yards away facing forwards, so all the action was in my wing mirror, which made it impossible to confirm a definitive visual on their faces. Any closer and I may well have been spotted. Besides, they were wearing dark hoodies pulled down over the front of their heads, which made a visual even tougher. What I can tell you is, one of the men was constantly looking around as he ran, almost as though he was a bodyguard for the other one. They didn't run next to each other like friends, if you know what I mean. An hour after they returned, about eight thirty, three men left together in an SUV and returned just before I left to meet you.'

Although she was frustrated by the vagueness of the reply, Deshi was also impressed by the precautions Leonard had taken during the surveillance operation. He was obviously a pro and that was good to know. It was clear either Hembury or Vargas was out running under the watchful eye of a federal agent – but which of them was it? She prayed it was the Argentine.

'Okay, tell me about our storage venue.'

'I didn't have much time to sort somewhere but I've hired a remote property in Laytonsville, a tiny town in Montgomery County, about ten miles north of Rockville. It's a small run-down farmhouse set in about twelve acres, so no nosy neighbours to worry about. I found it online and it's dirt cheap, so shouldn't arouse any suspicions. I know you said three days, but I had to hire it for the week. I hope that's okay.'

Deshi continued to warm to her new assistant who was constantly surprising her and nodded her approval.

'Let's head there now for a few hours' rest and then I want to be parked up in Rockville no later than six thirty.'

* * *

The rental property Leonard had booked showed no resemblance to the images he'd seen online. Rather than a farmhouse, the structure they entered was nothing more than a small tenant cottage that hadn't seen any love for a long time. It offered a single open-plan room downstairs with a portable stove and fridge tucked in one corner and two tiny bedrooms above with a Jack and Jill bathroom. The only furnishings were a wooden kitchen table with three chairs on the ground-floor level, and upstairs a couple of double beds squashed up against the side walls. Leonard was deeply embarrassed by the hovel and expected to be bawled out, but Deshi was surprisingly cool.

'Guess the owners couldn't believe their luck when you rented this dump, but it'll do for our purposes. No one will come looking for us here.'

Leonard responded with a sheepish grin. He realised he was beginning an extraordinary adventure and had no idea how it was going to play out.

Deshi placed her overnight bag on the table and took out a cellophane package containing balls of string, a black cloth blindfold, a set of leather restraints and a packet of plastic ties. She ripped it open and spread the contents across the tabletop, then produced a small transparent box that contained a medical syringe and a small 50 ml glass bottle of colourless liquid. Finally, she removed a Glock 19 with a double-stack, fifteen-round magazine and a silencer, which she knitted together with the assurance of an experienced assassin. Leonard watched the scene play out in front of him as if it were a Netflix drama and was intrigued to know what the spherical object was Deshi had left inside the bag but decided it was safer not to ask.

'Benefits of hitching a private plane ride, I guess. No customs or immigration arseholes to ruin your fun.'

Deshi almost broke a smile but suppressed it, choosing to ignore the comment and instead issued her next set of orders. She'd no intention of forming an attachment to Leonard, even though she found him strangely attractive, which baffled her, because he was old enough to be her father.

'We'll grab a few hours' sleep and then we leave at five forty-five. I'll take one of the bedrooms and you put together a couple of chairs down here, just in case we get any unexpected visitors.'

Deshi was exhausted and within seconds of lying down on the rock-hard surface disguised as a bed, the blackness of sleep enveloped her mind. The first image she saw was Vakha as a young boy, repeatedly kicking a football against a wall in the tiny yard outside their family home. The calmness of the dream was broken by the sudden appearance of an armed Russian soldier who appeared out of nowhere. Vakha had his back to him, so had no idea he was there. The dream mutated into a nightmare as the soldier lifted his rifle and Deshi yelled at her twin to run, but before the tormented scream left her mouth, a bullet ripped open the back of his skull. His tiny frame collapsed in a pathetic heap and Deshi stared at her brother's fallen body and then looked across at the face of the man who'd pulled the trigger. To her astonishment, it wasn't the face of an anonymous Russian soldier that stared back at her smiling. It was a face she recognised only too well. It belonged to Chief Inspector Nicolas Vargas.

# Chapter Fifteen

Rockville, United States

The Transit eased to a stop exactly halfway along Crabb Avenue, about two hundred yards away from the safe house where Vargas and Hembury were staying. The journey from the farm cottage had taken less than thirty minutes. Deshi checked her digital watch: 06.15. That meant they'd less than an hour to wait, assuming the joggers kept to the same routine Leonard had witnessed the day before. She'd had already run through the operational plan twice on the journey but now they were stationary she repeated it to him for a third time, word for word.

The following forty-five minutes seemed to last an eternity, but eventually the digital alarm on her watch confirmed it was seven. Her eyes were glued to the wing mirror of the van but there was no sign of movement outside the safe house. She cursed under her breath in her native Chechen as she acknowledged she'd no Plan B to revert to if this one failed. Then, at 07.12, two figures emerged from the front gate of the house, immediately turned left and began to jog up the street away from her.

Deshi strained her eyes as she desperately tried to identify the men, but the distance made it impossible, and within a matter of seconds they'd reached the first corner and turned left again, disappearing out of sight. For a moment, she felt a chill of despair flood through her body and then she drew down on her passionate belief in fate, the only religion she believed in. She'd an unrelenting trust in destiny that had so far guided her through adversity and brought her to where she was today. That instinct reassured her that one of the joggers was Vargas and it rarely lied to her.

And if it was the Argentine, Deshi knew she'd have no choice but to ignore Franklin's plea for patience. She'd have to fulfil her need to punish the detective with a slow and agonising death. After that she would vanish, a trick she'd successfully pulled off many times before and one that would ensure she'd never have to see the American psychopath again. Sadly, it also meant she'd have to take out Leonard, which was a great shame, but if she were to disappear, no loose ends could be left behind.

Deshi glanced across at the former Marine who nodded and gunned the van engine into life. The Transit set off on a short trip, coming to a stop on the opposite side of the avenue to the corner where the joggers had turned left a couple of minutes earlier. This gave the van occupants a clear sightline down the side street.

Nothing happened for about twenty minutes, and then Deshi exited the van, crossed the avenue and positioned herself about ten yards away from the corner, hugging a newly cut hedge that surrounded the corner property. Her cell was in her left hand and the Glock was partially concealed in her right

72

one, held in a vice-like grip. She controlled her breathing, consciously lowering her heart rate, and displayed the poise and cunning of a lioness patiently stalking her prey.

When Leonard saw the joggers turn back onto the side street, he sent a pre-arranged WhatsApp to Deshi's cell. She registered a tiny vibration tickle her palm and pocketed the phone, slid the gun into the right-hand pocket of her leather flying jacket and began to walk. As soon as she turned the corner, she spotted the two men heading straight towards her and slightly quickened her pace. They were no more than fifty yards away and the distance between them rapidly shrunk until they were almost face to face. At the crucial moment, the timing of her move was immaculate and neither man had a chance to react before she revealed the Glock and fired a single kill shot that pulverised the right cheekbone of the FBI agent. The impact of the close-range shot sent his body spinning sideways, tumbling across the sidewalk onto the street.

The other jogger stopped dead in his tracks, desperately trying to process the brutal killing he'd just witnessed. Deshi registered his skin tone and hardly drew breath before barking out an order.

'Hands high and turn around slowly so your back is facing me.'

The man knew he'd no choice but to comply. He completed the turn, his eyes locked on the twisted corpse of the agent who'd been tasked with protecting his life. For a moment he was mesmerised by the bloody husk of bone and gore that filled the space previously occupied by the agent's face, but his focus was broken by a sharp sensation in the side of his neck caused by a hypodermic needle and his mind emptied into a black void.

The van screeched to a halt alongside the two fallen bodies. Leonard leaped out of the transit and flung open the rear doors. He moved onto the sidewalk where he helped Deshi bundle the drugged man into the back of the van. He was just about to slam the doors when she waved her right arm high in the air as a gesture for him to wait. She leaned forward to take a closer look at the face of her hostage and studied it in detail for the next few seconds. As she stood, she signalled for Leonard to close the doors. He glanced across at her, a burst of energy coursing through his veins.

'That went like clockwork. You happy?'

It was impossible to tell from her poker face if the body of the unconscious man stashed in the back of the Transit belonged to the man she really wanted.

# Chapter Sixteen

Laytonsville, United States

When he opened his eyes and tried to focus, the blackness was still there, which made no sense. Then he realised he was blindfolded and his hands and legs were bound tightly to what felt like a wooden chair. He was disorientated and it took him a while to work out the back of the chair was lying flat on the floor, weighted down, which meant he was facing the ceiling. His thoughts were scrambled but slowly began to clear and he remembered the shooting – the brutal killing of his protector. Then he recalled the woman with the Glock. Who the hell was she?

The restraints were so tight he could feel them cutting into his skin, causing an excruciating burning sensation. He felt like a trussed turkey, wrapped inside a straitjacket with no room to manoeuvre or flex a muscle. Whoever had bound him knew exactly what they were doing and there was no point wasting precious energy trying to escape. All he could do was wait and see what their next move would bring.

As it turned out he didn't have to wait long. After a few

minutes, he heard a door open and the sound of approaching footsteps. Moments later he felt a hand brush against his forehead as it reached for the blindfold and removed it in one fluid movement. The room was dimly lit and it took a few seconds for his eyes to adjust from total darkness to a murky gloom. As his focus sharpened, the face of the woman who'd taken out his FBI bodyguard came into view.

Her features seemed strangely familiar but, then again, he was sure he'd never met her before. There was something about her that reminded him of someone, but he couldn't nail it. When she spoke, it was almost as though she'd read his mind.

'Yes, Mr Hembury, I look almost identical to my brother, which is not a surprise as we're twins. Vakha was killed a few days ago in a warehouse in New York and I need to learn every detail concerning his death. Fortunately for you, you're not the man who pulled the trigger or right now you'd be suffering far greater pain than a few rope burns but believe me, your life still hangs in the balance and your survival depends on what answers you give me in the next few minutes.'

Hembury's memory rewound to New York and the storage warehouse in Industry City where he and Vargas had joined forces with an FBI combat team and taken part in a firefight, leading to fatalities on both sides. They'd deployed tear gas grenades to give themselves an edge and, even though they'd been wearing tactical masks, the bulk of the shoot-out had taken place in a smoky haze, so Hembury hadn't witnessed the shooting of the young man he now knew was called Vakha. Besides, he'd been far too busy trying to keep himself alive.

It was only in the aftermath of the shoot-out that Hembury

had seen Vakha's face, when he'd been confirming the identities of corpses from both sides. It was the young man's death mask he now concentrated hard on visualising, and he was stunned by the striking resemblance between Vakha and his sister. Suddenly everything made sense. He instinctively knew if he was going to survive her death threat, he'd need to improvise an account and, what's more, it would have to be convincing.

'It was a kill or be killed situation. Your brother was trying to help Anderson escape – I guess he was his personal bodyguard?'

Hembury paused, having floated the question, but Deshi's ice-cold stare prompted him to keep talking.

'My colleague, Nicolas Vargas, had two FBI agents with him, and as they closed in on your brother and Anderson, Nic yelled at them both to drop their weapons. I heard it clearly – I was only about ten feet away.'

Lies, but Hembury felt they were his only hope of staying alive. He could feel Deshi's vengeful eyes burning into his very soul as he continued with his tale.

'Vakha was an incredible marksman. He took out the two agents with consecutive headshots – the speed between them was like nothing I've ever witnessed, and then Vargas brought him down with a kill shot of his own because he knew he'd be next. As I said, he had no choice but—'

In a moment of uncontrolled rage, Deshi lashed out with the gun barrel, whipping it across the right-hand side of Hembury's face, smashing his cheekbone into pieces, sending him into a state of semi-consciousness. The sickening sound of the crack boomed through his ears and the unexpected timing of the blow meant the initial pain from the impact was amplified because he'd not been prepared for it. Almost instantly, the soft tissue around his cheek area spurted blood at an alarming rate, drenching one side of his face, and a small, jagged fragment of bone protruded through his skin like a miniature rhino horn. Even though he was barely awake, he let out an anguished scream that came from a place so deep inside he didn't know it existed. He could hear the woman yelling at him, but her voice was just a distant echo masked by an overwhelming sensation of unbearable agony.

'Vakha was far too good to leave himself exposed like that. Tell me the truth, did Vargas execute him?'

Hembury's mind was far too muddy to offer up a coherent answer, even if he could've made out the question, but then a perfectly placed karate kick landed on the side of his skull, just above his left ear, acting as an instant anaesthetic. The pain disappeared and everything went black.

\* \* \*

Berrettini and Vargas were sitting in the kitchen of the safe house digesting the implications of the catastrophic events that had played out a few hours earlier. Both were still reeling from the fallout. The FBI deputy director had been briefed on the shooting of one of his agents and the kidnapping of Hembury and was bringing Vargas up to speed. A few minutes earlier Franklin had sent a new WhatsApp message to Berrettini containing a proposition. Vargas was holding the FBI man's cell, reading it for himself.

I told you I would cut a deal – just not the one you expected. Now it will be on my terms, not yours. I want a hostage exchange. Anderson and Nicks in return for Hembury. Before you argue that's unfair, let me point out I will execute Nicks as soon as he's in my custody, so it's really Anderson for Hembury. In two hours I'll send through a link. Don't waste your time trying to trace it – its origin is impenetrable, even with your resources. I'll be on it and you'll see Hembury is alive. I want to see you and Vargas as well as Anderson and Nicks.

Vargas passed the phone back to Berrettini who was typing an email on his laptop. He pocketed it and paused working the keyboard.

'That bastard is a control freak, and despite his bullshit, I'm putting our tech guys all over the link once it arrives. Meanwhile, I'll organise a connection to the interrogation house and move Nicks in with Anderson so they can share a camera. You and I can log in from here.'

Vargas nodded and took a giant slurp of coffee before replying.

'That son of a bitch really caught us with our pants down. How the hell did he know where we were staying – and why take Troy and not me?'

'He's got to have someone working inside our intel division on his payroll. Could be one of many and right now we're too stretched to track them down. As for Troy, I think it was pot luck. His obsession with running every morning made him vulnerable once they knew where you guys were based. Let's hope he's alive and safe because I don't trust a word that comes out of Franklin's mouth.'

# Chapter Seventeen

## Laytonsville, United States

Franklin let rip with one of his trademark rants and this time Deshi was on the receiving end. He was testing a Zoom link from his boat to the tiny cottage in Laytonsville when he caught sight of Hembury's hideous pulp of a face that had swollen to the size of a large melon.

'For Christ's sake, the man looks like he's done fifty rounds with Tyson Fury – what the hell have you done to him? I told you to keep him in one piece, you stupid bitch. Your temper may have cost us everything.'

Deshi was indifferent to her boss's outburst but for now was happy to feign contrition. All of that would change the moment she laid eyes on Vargas. She tried her best to conjure up an apologetic expression, while the psycho continued his rant.

'No more screw-ups, Deshi, or you might find yourself reunited with your brother far quicker than you imagined. Now, patch him up the best you can and put him in a dark corner for the Zoom. Frame a loose body shot and let's hope he doesn't still look like Frankenstein's monster when I next see him.'

The computer link went dead and Deshi glanced away from the screen. Leonard was standing a few feet away shaking his head in disbelief, having witnessed the tirade she'd just received.

'Your boss is a bundle of laughs. Why would you put up with that shit?'

'Because he's my only route to finding the man who killed my brother. I'll put up with a mountain of shit or whatever it takes to make that happen. After that, once I've avenged Vakha's death, all bets are off and I'll happily blow that American psycho's brains out.'

\* \* \*

The link worked perfectly and the computer screens at all locations divided neatly into four symmetrical segments. Top left, seated together, were Vargas and Berrettini and, top right, Anderson and Nicks. Bottom left was Hembury, who'd been strategically positioned a long way from the computer camera and, despite benefiting from some hastily applied make-up courtesy of Deshi, still looked like an extra from a horror movie. Bottom right was Franklin, sitting in front of a dark mahogany wood background, wearing his trademark red baseball cap. He'd planned to run the meeting, but Vargas went off like a rocket.

'What the hell have you done to Hembury! Troy, can you hear me? Can you talk?'

Deshi had released the arm restraints a few minutes before the Zoom went live and Hembury summoned up every ounce of strength he had left to raise his right arm and muster a pathetic wave. He murmured a handful of words that were impossible to hear and had Vargas yelling at the screen.

'Bring him closer to the camera!'

Franklin cursed under his breath as his worst fears played out. He frantically tried to take back control.

'Mr Hembury is fine where he is. Now, let's get down to business—'

Vargas edged forward so his face was less than an inch from the split screen.

'Get one of your goons to bring him up to the computer or this call is over!'

Berrettini hastily scrawled a note on the desk pad in front of them: *Calm down.*

Vargas either didn't see the note or ignored it.

'Last chance, Franklin. Move him now!'

Franklin nodded his acquiescence. Suddenly, the ghostlike image of Hembury disappeared when Deshi turned her iPad face-down on the tabletop so Leonard could move him closer without any danger of being seen on camera. Once Hembury was positioned a few feet from the table, Deshi framed up the camera again.

Vargas gasped when he saw the hideousness of his best friend's face.

'Troy, can you hear me – can you see me?'

Hembury's vision was non-existent in his right eye and blurred in his left, but he understood what was going on and tried hard to strengthen his voice when he eventually spoke.

'Nic . . . I'm okay . . . well, I'm . . . alive.'

Franklin's concern that Hembury's facial injuries might

hijack the meeting had proven correct and he made a mental note to punish Deshi for her reckless behaviour. His eyes switched from Hembury to the screen displaying Anderson and Nicks.

'Okay, let's not waste any more time. Before I explain how the hostage exchange will work, I need to hear from my people. Daniel, have you and Nicks been coerced in any way that I need to be aware of?'

Anderson stared straight down the lens of the tiny camera on top of the computer on a table in his cell and smiled before responding.

'No, we've just sat back and listened to their bullshit threats. They've learned nothing. John, I always knew you'd come through.'

Franklin soaked up the compliment and felt empowered to take back full control of the meeting.

'Listen up. This is how the hostage swap will play out. In five hours' time, at precisely seven this evening, you'll deposit Anderson and Nicks on the sidewalk outside the safe house in Rockville where one of my operatives will collect them in a Transit. Should there be any attempt on your part to follow by vehicle, helicopter, drone or even satellite, I'll be informed by the same person who passed the location of the property onto me. If I learn you've not followed these instructions to the letter, your friend Hembury will be blown into a thousand pieces. Once I know my people are safe, I'll tell you where he's being held.'

Berrettini had managed multiple hostage exchanges before but never one as one-sided as this. He also realised that, following Vargas's outburst, he badly needed to establish himself as the lead negotiator on their side.

'That's not the way these things happen, Franklin. The exchange needs to be simultaneous, or it won't happen.'

Franklin relished the interruption because it allowed him to play his ace card. He ploughed on, ignoring the interruption.

'At seven, when you release Anderson and Nicks, refresh this feed and you'll see a live image of Hembury. In the top corner of the screen there'll be a clock displaying a two-hour countdown. The timer is linked to a detonator that will trigger an explosive device inside the property, where your dear friend is being held. Now, I anticipate that by eight fifteen my colleagues will be safely in the air and on their way back to me. Only then will I send through the address. The good news is it's no more than a few minutes' chopper ride away, so you'll have plenty of leeway – well, about half an hour, I expect – to locate Hembury and get him out before the explosives go off.'

Berrettini couldn't believe what he was hearing and let rip.

'This is total bullshit! How can we trust you to give us Hembury's location once you know Anderson and Nicks are safe? We've learned from hard experience not to believe a word you say.'

Franklin was desperate to deliver his *coup de grâce*.

'Because, Mr Berrettini, this is my game and my rules, and if you don't agree to them and the swap doesn't take place exactly as I've outlined, the bomb will still go off at nine and your friend will suffer a brutal and undignified death. His body will be pulverised into so many tiny pieces a burial will be quite unnecessary.'

A smirk crossed Franklin's face as he prepared to log off knowing that, once again, he was holding all the levers of power.

'I expect Anderson and Nicks to be on the sidewalk at seven.'

With that, his screen turned black, indicating he'd left the Zoom call. Deshi had viewed the entire meeting from a position just outside Hembury's framed shot. She was the only person who knew Franklin was lying. He'd instructed her to set the detonator on the bomb she'd brought with her to go off at eight twenty-five, not nine. The man was a double-crossing psycho who'd set a death trap for the FBI rescue force. He'd no intention of allowing Hembury to live once Anderson and Nicks were free.

# Chapter Eighteen

Laytonsville, United States

Berrettini slammed the laptop shut, rose from his stool and stormed across the kitchen to the fridge, where he grabbed a couple of beers and passed one across to Vargas. His cheeks were glowing – a combination of anger and frustration at just how easily he'd been outmanoeuvred by Franklin.

'He's got us by the balls and knows it. Unless we can find that location in the next five hours, we're screwed.'

Vargas opened his beer but didn't take a drink.

'I just want to wipe that arrogant smile off the sick bastard's face and finish this once and for all, but our priority right now has to be Troy's safety and if that means playing the game by Franklin's rules, so be it.'

Berrettini nodded and reached for his cell.

'Yep, you're right, and the first thing I need to do is draft in a chopper and an HRT team to facilitate his rescue.'

\* \* \*

Deshi reattached the leather restraints on Hembury, even though he could barely move under his own steam, and then signalled to Leonard to meet her upstairs. She followed him into one of the bedrooms where they stood uncomfortably close to each other by the foot of the bed in the only available floor space. Franklin had given her specific instructions on how the hostage exchange should be handled, and part of that brief entailed lying to Leonard about his role – a lie that ensured a death sentence for him.

Deshi was a highly trained mercenary who'd killed many times at close quarters. She'd also been responsible for the deaths of dozens of strangers using explosive devices, so struggled to grasp why she felt so troubled about setting Leonard up – a man she'd known for less than twenty-four hours. Her emotions had been mangled since her brother's death and she hadn't yet found a way of processing the grief that was clogging up her thoughts. Her rational decision-making never allowed sentiment to cloud it but right now she was bewildered by her own feelings and had to work hard to switch to autopilot.

'Franklin wants me to pick up Anderson and Nicks in the Transit and drive them straight to the airfield where his pilot is waiting. You're to stay here with Hembury until eight-thirty to ensure he doesn't escape, and then get the hell out of Dodge just before the FBI rescue team arrives.'

Their faces were no more than twelve inches apart and Deshi tried to avoid eye contact as she issued his death warrant but found it impossible to avoid his gaze. Leonard sensed something was slightly off but couldn't tell what. The tension between them in the tiny room was almost unbearable. It was so strong it was tangible – you could almost touch it, grab it by the hand or cut it with a knife. Leonard felt awkward and couldn't wait to get away as quickly as possible.

'I can't see our friend downstairs having the strength to work his way out of the restraints or get out of his chair, let alone leave the cottage but, fair enough, I'll see it through if that's what the paymaster wants. I'd better get my ass into town and hire another set of wheels. I want to be nowhere near this place when that bomb goes off.'

Franklin's blatant lie regarding the time the bomb was set to explode was gnawing at Delhi's psyche but she remained silent as Leonard edged forward, attempting to squeeze past her. He moved slowly, expecting her to turn slightly to one side to create a bit more room so he could pass by, but she held the space, forcing him to brush up against her, and for a moment they came face to face with their bodies touching. Both felt the same surge of electricity. Deshi's arms sprung out like a pair of coiled springs, smacking Leonard hard in the abdomen, forcing him backwards onto the bed. In the same movement, she flung herself on top of him and their mouths locked, joining them as one. The sex that followed was primitive and frantic, providing an unexpected moment of release. Both were hungry for each other and yet neither seemed to really understand why it was happening. Not a word was uttered, and when it was over Deshi seamlessly reverted to her role as leader, once again issuing orders, as though the episode had never taken place.

'Sort a car out as quickly as possible while I stay with Hembury. As soon as you return, I'll leave for Rockville, park up a mile away from the safe house and wait until just before seven to collect the men.'

Leonard slid off the bed and stopped by the door before he exited the tiny room. He turned to face Deshi. His emotions were shredded but just like her he acted as though nothing had happened.

'Just checking, I leave the house at eight thirty, a few minutes before the Feds arrive, and the bomb goes off at nine, right?'

Deshi detected a slight hint of scepticism in his tone, as if he suspected she'd lied and wanted to test her. But reason told her there was no way he could possibly know about the bomb being set to go off at 8.25, while he was still inside the cottage with Hembury. For a moment she thought of her favourite insect – a female praying mantis, who eats her male in a brutal act of cannibalism immediately after mating – and casually buried the query.

'You got it. Make sure you get out exactly at eight thirty.'

The sex was forgotten and the old Deshi was back. Lying through her teeth.

* * *

Berrettini had been busy. It was 18.53, just seven minutes away from the opening salvo of the hostage exchange. Anderson and Nicks had been transported from their cells in Washington to the safe house in Rockville, where they were being kept under guard in the large basement. An FBI hostage rescue team of six specialists, led by a former Marine commander, Ted Johnson, had arrived an hour earlier in a UH-60 Black Hawk, which had landed in the large rear garden of the property. It was on standby to take off at two minutes' notice, as soon as Franklin revealed the details of Hembury's location. The chopper could hold up to twelve passengers, which meant there was plenty of room for Berrettini and Vargas to hitch a ride.

\* \* \*

Deshi checked her watch, hit the Transit ignition and headed towards the safe house. Her facial features were well disguised, courtesy of a handful of props she'd brought with her from South Africa. Her natural black hair was hidden beneath a short, spiky acrylic blonde wig and her face was concealed behind a ghost-face latex mask, leaving only her dark brown eyes visible. It was her second visit to the location, so she knew exactly where to go, and at 18.59 she parked up outside the front gate of the safe house. A security camera mounted on a black metal pole inside the grounds monitored her arrival, which Vargas and Berrettini watched on a black-and-white monitor in the hallway.

One minute later, Vargas opened the front door and led Anderson and Nicks through the garden to the gate that opened onto the street. As agreed, he held his position and allowed them to continue alone while he watched the masked driver of the Transit deliver a hand signal, gesturing for them to make their way to the back of the van, where they opened the rear doors and disappeared inside. Vargas shook his head in despair at a procedure that took less than thirty seconds and facilitated the freedom of two international terrorists who knew the minute details of Franklin's operational plan.

As Deshi watched the two men disappear inside the rear of the Transit she glanced back towards the house and was distracted by a shaded figure standing just inside the gate.

Suddenly her regard for the well-being of the hostages evaporated. The man she was staring at was her brother's killer, and for a moment a blind rage took control of her senses, urging her to pull out her Glock and gun him down on the spot. But then the rational side of her brain kicked into gear and brought her back to her senses. Vargas was a tempting target, but she knew that within seconds of pulling the trigger she'd be surrounded by FBI agents who'd take her out. Besides, the Argentine deserved a far more drawn-out and agonising death, so for now her weapon stayed where it was. Franklin had promised her there would be a new opportunity down the line – for now she just needed to be patient.

The engine was idling and as soon as the transit's doors slammed shut, she floored the gas pedal and sped down the road before heading north-west towards the private airport. Vargas made his way back inside the house and joined Berrettini, who was still standing in the large hallway next to the monitor on which he'd watched the handover take place. Close by was a small table with an open laptop on it, which was now the focus of his attention. Berrettini's face was etched with concern and when Vargas saw the image on the screen, he understood why. Hembury was centre frame, tied to a chair, and it was impossible to tell if he was conscious because there was no obvious sign of movement, although it appeared as though his left eye was open.

In the top corner of the picture was a digital countdown clock that displayed 01.59.55. The FBI deputy director and Vargas stared at the screen; their eyes glued to the timer. It was the countdown to Hembury's death and both men viewing the gruesome image knew it. What they didn't know, however, was the footage they were watching was an edited recording of their friend, which had been filmed earlier. As ever, Franklin was manipulating events and calling the shots.

'Nic, it's a waiting game. Can we trust Franklin to come through with the location before it's too late?'

Vargas didn't have an answer but couldn't take his eyes off the image of his friend, who could very soon be breathing his last.

# Chapter Nineteen

Montgomery County Airpark, United States

The traffic had been heavier than the van's navigation system had predicted and it was 19.52 when Deshi parked up on the tarmac less than thirty feet away from the Gulfstream that was fuelled and ready to go. The private airport was practically deserted, so they pretty much had the entire facility to themselves. She strolled around to the back of the transit to check on her live packages and opened the rear doors to find Anderson and Nicks sitting cross-legged towards the back of the van. She'd lost the wig and mask earlier on the journey and Anderson recognised her immediately and sprung to his feet.

'Deshi, it's great to see you. I'm so sorry about Vakha . . . He died trying to save me.'

She ignored his sentiments and with a robotic movement reached inside her flying jacket for her Glock. Both men watched in terror as she raised it and fired a single shot that entered the right ventricle of Nicks's heart before he had a chance to utter a word of protest or offer any resistance. For a moment Anderson feared he was next, but with the same clinical precision Deshi pocketed the gun and turned towards the plane.

'What the hell was that about?' Anderson yelled after her.

She didn't bother to face him when she replied. Her voice was a monotone.

'Franklin's orders. Now let's get out of here.'

Three minutes later, they were on board the jet and Deshi sent a WhatsApp message updating Franklin. He was in his state room on *The Little Fox*, relaxing on his king-sized bed, enjoying a glass of his treasured bourbon. He checked his watch, it was 19.55, Washington time. Once again, he ran though the calculations in his head. Timing was everything, and for his plan to work perfectly he needed the FBI helicopter to land just before 20.25, which would ensure Vargas and Berrettini would witness the explosion live, with the possible bonus of a few FBI agents being taken down if they were close enough to the cottage when the device went off.

* * *

Berrettini finally received the WhatsApp message from Franklin revealing Hembury's location at 20.16 and two minutes later the Hawk was airborne. The FBI deputy director was strapped in at the rear of the chopper alongside Vargas and seated in front of them was the six-man hostage rescue team. Shortly after taking off, the pilot came through their headsets.

'Arrival time currently 20.23 and on the ground shortly after.'

Vargas gave a thumbs up to Berrettini. For both men, the next few minutes couldn't pass quickly enough.

\* \* \*

The Gulfstream knifed into the sky and settled into its cruise at fifty thousand feet. Deshi was jumpy, checking her cell every two minutes. It was 20.18. Seven minutes to go before the bomb would go off. She visualised Leonard sitting inside the cottage, keeping watch over Hembury, waiting until eight thirty before leaving. Except he never would.

She was anguishing over whether to warn him, but knew if she crossed Franklin, she might lose her only route to Vargas, and she couldn't jeopardise that. She forced herself to look away from her cell and turned towards the window, staring out at the pure white landscape of fluffy clouds that created a stunning vista.

Deshi tried every mental trick she knew to switch her mind away from Leonard but at 20.20 she cracked. She punched his contact on her cell, and he answered after two rings.

'Get out. Get out right now. You've got five minutes. The device is set for 20.25.'

She ended the call and closed her eyes, praying she'd given him enough time. Hopefully Franklin would never discover she'd crossed him. He'd simply assume Leonard had died in the explosion alongside Hembury, just as he'd planned. And if ever he found out the truth, she'd handle it when the situation arose.

\* \* \*

The Black Hawk pilot keyed his radio to give an update.

'Two minutes from the co-ordinates, so we're heading down. Keep your eyes peeled, we should have a visual any moment of the location.'

Vargas checked his watch – 20.23. They still had thirty-seven minutes before the bomb was due to go off. Enough time to get Hembury out. Ninety seconds later the Hawk circled fifty feet above the cottage, its LED beam clearly illuminating the site. Berrettini came on the radio.

'Great work, guys. That must be where they're keeping him. How close can we land?'

'Very close, sir. Probably twenty yards away, directly south of the—'

Suddenly the Hawk was rocked sideways by a massive blast of scorching hot air shooting upwards from an enormous explosion below. For a moment, everyone on board believed they were going down, but the pilot rode the wave of turbulence and pulled the chopper upwards with an incredible manoeuvre that virtually forced the nose of the Hawk in a vertical line. In a matter of seconds, he'd stabilised the helicopter at a safe hover height of two hundred and fifty feet above the raging inferno below.

Vargas stared out his window at the carnage below – bewildered and shocked. He knew no one inside the cottage could have survived the blast. In fact, the billowing black smoke and flames simply masked the reality – the tenant cottage no longer existed. It had vanished. Without warning he felt an excruciating pain in the pit of his stomach – the same pain he'd experienced fourteen years earlier when his wife Sophia had died.

# Chapter Twenty

Laytonsville, United States

L eonard lay prostrate, concealed by a thick copse of pine trees about fifty yards to the east of the cottage, listening as the Hawk circled above. It was the only natural camouflage on offer within a square mile of open fields, random trees and small bushes, and he figured he'd no choice but to wait for the chopper to land before he could make a safe escape to the hire car. It was parked up on a random piece of tarmac a couple of hundred yards away that gave direct access to a track that ran behind the cottage.

Five minutes earlier he'd received Deshi's warning and was out of the cottage in less than two. He'd been bemused by the call but had no time to process it. He just needed to stay alive and that meant getting out fast. As soon as Leonard had opened the front door, he'd heard the distinctive sound of the Black Hawk's rotors approaching from the north and knew it was too risky to head directly for the car. The lack of cover from above meant he'd be a sitting duck. He'd made it to the sanctuary of the trees about ninety seconds before the chopper descended at speed through the low cloud cover, where it hovered directly above the cottage.

Moments later, he watched the UH-60 perform an awkward dance in the sky as it was struck by a hot funnel of air generated by the furnace below. The pilot had somehow wrenched the Black Hawk upwards and now, from a higher starting position, the chopper was beginning a fresh descent, looking for a secure landing spot just outside the perimeter of the fireball. Leonard knew he'd no choice but to remain in his hiding place.

Inside the Hawk, Commander Ted Johnson was barking instructions as the chopper engaged in an emergency landing procedure. Johnson was a man who looked as though he'd been built from a pack of Lego bricks. His enormous chest was square, as was his head and jaw, and his hair looked as though it had been pressed by an iron.

'I've called in firefighters, but they won't make it for another thirty minutes. Once we're down, let's see how close we can get to the site, just in case Hembury made it out. As soon as we land, fan out in standard one-eighty formation facing the building, just in case any hostiles are out there waiting to give us a surprise welcome.'

Berrettini and Vargas were still stunned by the explosion and the realisation that Franklin had outsmarted them yet again, this time with horrific consequences for their friend. But Johnson's voice booming down their headsets brought them back into the moment and they clung to the vague hope that somehow Hembury had survived the blast.

Had the Hawk broken cloud cover just ninety seconds earlier, they'd have witnessed a bizarre sight. When Leonard left the cottage, he wasn't alone. He was cradling a man's limp body in his arms, as if it were a baby. The former Marine regularly benched one hundred and twenty kilos in the gym, so carrying Hembury's ninety-five kilo frame was a cakewalk.

He'd moved at a remarkable pace given the weight and awkward shape of his payload, and once he'd reached the refuge of the trees, he'd carefully placed Hembury on the grass, resting him on his back. The former police lieutenant was in a semi-conscious state, a consequence of the beatings he'd received and an overload of painkillers Deshi had administered, but he still understood what was happening around him. He was physically too weak to move his body but managed a croaky whisper. Leonard kept one eye on the descending Hawk, which was landing about two hundred yards away, and moved his face next to Hembury's to try and hear him.

'Why . . . why would you . . . save me?'

Leonard arched an eyebrow, struggling for a truthful answer. His last-minute decision to save his hostage had been instinctive.

'Maybe because somebody saved me. Call it karma.'

'The girl? Who . . . is she?'

Leonard frowned this time before replying.

'Just enjoy the rest of your life and treat every day as a bonus.'

Leonard's eyes switched back to the Hawk. He could tell by the change in the tone of the rotors it would only be a matter of seconds before the engine was cut and the FBI agents would be on their way. He rolled onto his side and moved his mouth close to Hembury's right ear.

'Can I trust you to help me now? I've got to make a two-hundred-yard belly crawl to reach my car. Will you keep quiet for the next ten minutes and give me the time I need? After that you can let the Feds know where you are.'

Hembury struggled to respond. Leonard wasn't sure if he was laughing or choking.

'You'll have . . . all the time you want . . . I can't stand up . . . wave . . . shout.'

Leonard's gaze was fixed on the chopper and when he saw the doors push open, he knew he was out of time. He looked at Hembury's pathetic, beaten-up face and made another call based on instinct. He reached for the Beretta firmly stuffed down the waistband at the back of his jeans and placed it in Hembury's right hand.

'Okay, I'm going to trust you. Give me those ten minutes and then shoot your heart out to get their attention.'

Hembury felt the cold steel of the gun in the palm of his hand and slowly wrapped his index finger around the trigger. Before he had time to reply, Leonard had set off, writhing across the grass like a hungry viper hunting down a rat.

In the opposite direction, the FBI agents had formed a semi-circle and were methodically making headway towards the remains of the cottage where the fireball had dramatically reduced in size and most of the wooden structure had already burned to the ground.

Hembury had every intention of keeping his side of the deal with the man who'd saved his life and was painfully attempting to count to six hundred. Twice he almost blacked out and forgot where he was, and on each occasion erred on the side of caution when he restarted the count. By the time he reached the magic number, almost twelve minutes had passed. He began to apply pressure to the trigger, but his finger felt as though it had a lead weight tied to it, so even that simple task felt beyond him. The man had told him to shoot his heart out, but he wondered if he could manage even a single round.

Hembury knew he was close to passing out and dredged up every ounce of physical and mental strength he could muster in a final attempt. The gunshot rang out across the open terrain almost at the same moment his mind drifted off into a black chasm. Across the field, less than one hundred yards away, Johnson yelled a warning to his men, who'd instinctively dived to the ground for cover.

'Hostile fire coming in from the trees directly north-east. Fan out, keep low and let's nail them.'

Vargas and Berrettini had been instructed by Johnson to stay inside the Hawk while he and his team secured the area. They watched as the special agents slowly made their way towards the copse where the shot had originated from. Even though there had been no more shots fired, the agents were still being cautious in their movements when Johnson spotted Hembury's prone figure. His body was partially concealed by the trunk of a pine tree, but his head and torso were clearly visible, as was the Beretta that had slipped from the grasp of his right hand.

As Johnson approached to within six feet, he keyed his radio.

'Possible ID on our hostage. Not sure of his status. No sign of body movement. I'm by the second tree to the right of the copse. No evidence of hostiles. Moving in to check vitals.'

Vargas and Berrettini stared at each other and then forgot all protocol as they leaped out of the open door of the Hawk and sprinted across the field towards the trees. Neither knew if their friend was alive, but at least for the next few seconds there was a glimmer of hope that hadn't existed moments earlier. Vargas felt tears streaming down his face as he ran flat out across the field as though his own life depended on it. He didn't know if they were tears of pain or joy.

Johnson had been joined by three of his men, one of whom was a paramedic. He was kneeling over Hembury, holding his wrist, frantically searching for signs of life. Within seconds he confirmed a weak but stable pulse.

Johnson's voice blasted down Vargas and Berrettini's earpieces.

'The hostage is alive. Confirm – hostage is alive.'

His voice was so loud it drowned out the distant sound of a car engine firing up a few hundred yards away. Leonard floored the gas and headed in the opposite direction; forever grateful his hostage had kept his side of the bargain.

# Chapter Twenty-One

*The Little Fox*, The Indian Ocean

The mood on board the super yacht was euphoric. After a celebratory reunion in the loggia, Franklin invited Deshi and Daniel to join him in his inner sanctum, an area on the fourth deck he normally kept off limits. The three were sitting together in a small screening room that adjoined Franklin's master bedroom suite. Daniel had lived on *The Little Fox* for over a year without knowing of the cinema's existence and wondered why they were there and what new revelations were about to be unveiled by his older brother.

The decor was a rich mix of red velvet and gold panelling that covered three walls. A white projection screen, framed by a set of matching red curtains, was fixed to the fourth. There were only six seats, split neatly into two rows of three. They were classic cinema seats that had once belonged to a renowned movie theatre in Times Square that had closed decades earlier. Each chair was covered in dark red velvet cloth that matched the walls and had popcorn and drinks holders attached to the arms. By contrast, there was nothing classic about the ceiling-mounted state-of-the-art 5K projector unit which produced high-quality images to rival any contemporary cinema in a high street mall.

Franklin held court, sitting in the middle seat of the second row. Deshi and Daniel were in the wing chairs of the front row, half-turned away from the screen, facing him. He'd a black plastic remote in his right hand which he was waving around like a baton but as yet nothing had appeared on the screen.

When they first sat down he insisted on a full report and Deshi completed her debrief before Daniel brought him up to speed regarding his time at the hands of Berrettini's interrogators. Deshi had gilded her report with a thin veneer of lies. She knew exactly what the psycho wanted to hear and that didn't include him discovering she'd tipped Leonard off about the early explosion. She truly despised Franklin and imagined he viewed himself as a modern-day Bond villain, an Ernst Blofeld-type megalomaniac, convinced he could take on the world. She listened to him spew his venom and concluded he only needed a white Persian cat perched on his lap to complete the cliché. But her impassive expression revealed none of these thoughts. Instead, she maintained eye contact and pretended to be absorbed by his every word.

'So, Hembury and our mercenary were incinerated together, plus Nicks is dead. Boom – no loose ends. Deshi, you did a magnificent job which has earned you a healthy bonus.'

He waited for her display of appreciation before continuing. The actress in Deshi faked a smile of gratitude. She played her role to perfection, even though she knew she'd betrayed her boss and definitely hadn't earned a bonus. In Franklin's eyes, she'd redeemed herself from the mistake she'd made when she'd mashed up Hembury's face ahead of the Zoom call. In the end, as he saw it, everything had worked out perfectly and he purred with satisfaction that his plan had played out so well.

'We can only hope Vargas and Berrettini saw their buddy blown to pieces. Trust me, the Argentine will have suffered great pain witnessing his best friend's death, and, as I promised, we have another personal lever to assault him with before I allow you to kill him.'

Franklin was droning on about his own hatred for Vargas when Deshi felt a buzz from her cell, tucked inside her front jean pocket. Her phone was on silent but she knew she'd just received a text or WhatsApp and was curious because she didn't share her number readily. She'd no interest in what Franklin was saying and interrupted him mid-flow to ask for directions to the nearest bathroom. He was perplexed by her timing but told her where to go and continued his rant to the other half of his audience.

As soon as she reached the corridor, Deshi retrieved her phone and clicked on the new WhatsApp message.

Thanks for the tip-off. I got out just in time and also saved the hostage. Don't know why but it felt right. Can you call me? M

Deshi cursed under her breath, stunned by the message. She'd intended to delete and block Leonard's number but hadn't got round to it yet. How stupid had she been, allowing her feelings to jeopardise such a vital operation? She deleted the message and his contact as fast as she could, as if the speed of her response would somehow wash away the consequences of her actions.

By the time she returned to the cinema, Franklin had changed topics and was heaping praise on Daniel for, as far as she could tell, basically keeping his mouth shut. As soon as she retook her seat, he flicked the remote towards a sensor that killed the lights and brought the projector to life.

'This is it – Operation Atonement, the culmination of a life's work, which you two are extremely fortunate to be part of.'

A 2D map of the world appeared and on it were fifteen red lights identifying cities spread across five continents. A strapline centred in the top third read: *Operation Atonement, 25 September 2023*. The map was interactive, and when Franklin clicked on one of the city icons, the image cut to a specific synagogue identified by its name. The locations were spread across the globe from Africa to Australia and included capital cities in Nigeria, New Zealand, Hungary, India and Canada.

Franklin was enjoying himself, highlighting his favourites. He resembled a magician waving his magic wand around, landing on different synagogues and then clicking on a second embedded link that detailed the local time of the attack, the specific group allocated to carry it out and the name of its leader. Deshi and Daniel had the identical thought at the same moment: what would happen if the file fell into the wrong hands? The information it contained would expose the entire operation.

Franklin paused on an image displaying the striking façade of the Dohány Street Synagogue in Budapest, an eclectic mix of Byzantine, Moorish and Gothic elements.

'This monstrosity happens to be the largest synagogue in Europe. It holds three thousand people and on Yom Kippur will be full to the brim, like all the targets on the map. Jews are a hypocritical people who, across the world, roll out for their annual visit to their local place of worship to repent for sins they've committed throughout the year. Most synagogues will even have overflow services taking place in reception halls within the structure, so our fifteen targets will account for well over thirty thousand Jews.'

Although Daniel was impressed by the visuals, he was slightly puzzled by the content of the presentation as it contained information he already knew, although he appreciated some of it would be new to Deshi. Equally he didn't want to burst his half-brother's bubble.

'John, it's very cool seeing everything laid out like this but I'm not sure what I'm learning other than confirming 9/25 is destined to be the new 9/11. Are you sure this level of detail needs to be written down, though? I wouldn't want this file to go rogue and fall into the wrong hands. It pretty much tells the whole story and—'

Franklin didn't allow him to finish the sentence.

'That's precisely what we want to happen.'

Daniel and Deshi glanced across at each other, unsure what kind of rabbit Franklin was about to produce from his fantasy hat. Once he saw he had their full attention, he cut to the chase.

'This entire operation is nothing more than a smokescreen for the main event. We want, in fact, we need, this file to be seen by Berrettini, so he alerts counterterrorism forces around the world, who'll focus their resources on protecting the named locations and remain blind to the real threat. I'd go as far as to say it's essential—'

Daniel was swiftly losing patience at being kept in the dark.

'John, for once in your life, stop grandstanding. What the hell is the real threat?'

Franklin remained silent, enjoying the moment, then clicked on his remote and a fresh image appeared on the screen. Only this time it wasn't a building, instead it was the face of one of the most famous men in the world.

# Chapter Twenty-Two

Washington D.C., United States

The private wing of the Walter Reed Medical Centre, the US Army's flagship hospital in Washington, was normally reserved for three-star officers and above. The new occupant of Room 8, on the third floor, was a former police lieutenant without any decorations, but the secrecy surrounding his admission and the security outside his room suggested to medical staff he had to be a five-star general.

Two armed soldiers kept guard either side of the door and a third was positioned at the far end of the corridor. Inside the room, Hembury had regained consciousness and Berrettini and Vargas were standing next to his bed, captivated by his tale. All of them were baffled by his last-minute reprieve, courtesy of one of his kidnappers. He was surprisingly lucid considering the physical battering he'd taken, mixed with the cocktail of drugs his captors had pumped into his body to keep him sedated. They were slowly wearing off and had been replaced with an intravenous line feeding fentanyl into a vein in his left hand.

The right side of his face was concealed by fresh bandages following three hours of surgery where fibrin glue, a sealant favoured by plastic surgeons, had been applied to close the cuts caused by his smashed cheekbone that had been reset at the same time. His voice was badly slurred and gravelly but surprisingly strong.

'The woman was clearly in charge. I suspect she was receiving her orders directly from Franklin. She took down the agent with a single headshot and was responsible for the redesign of my face. The thing—'

Vargas couldn't resist cutting in.

'Let's be honest, Troy, it can only be an improvement. People pay thousands for facial remodelling and yours has been taken care of by the military free of charge.'

Vargas couldn't tell if Hembury smiled because it was impossible to see what was going on under the bandages, but he spotted a glint in his friend's left eye. Berrettini wasn't so amused.

'Troy, ignore that moron. What were you saying about the woman?'

'She spoke good English but had a strong Eastern European accent – could well have been Russian. The thing is, I got the distinct feeling it wasn't really me she was after.'

Hembury paused as he thought carefully about the best way to explain her obsession with his friend. Vargas noted the hesitancy.

'Go on . . .'

'Nic, the young man you killed in the warehouse – the guy who was trying to help Anderson escape, was her brother . . . her twin. I told her it was self-defence – that you'd no option, but she wasn't buying it. She repeatedly called it an execution and vowed revenge. That's why she was so pissed she got me and not you.'

Berrettini noted the pained expression on Vargas's face. He was clearly shaken by the revelation.

'Okay, we'll revisit that. Now tell us about the guy who saved your life.'

'He was a pro, no doubt about it, but I'm guessing he was a hired hand. I don't think they had any history and he was clearly subordinate to her.'

Berrettini nodded.

'Not that subordinate. Saving your life looks to have been a spur of the moment decision – a major breach of protocol. We have to assume neither the woman nor Franklin have any idea he did it.'

Vargas had regained his composure and leaned forward, his face only inches away from Hembury's.

'Troy, for once we might just have an edge on Franklin. As far as he's concerned, you were obliterated by the explosion. For now, let's keep it that way.'

\* \* \*

The frozen image on the projector screen was a headshot of a distinguished middle-aged man who appeared far older than his fifty-eight years. Grizzled hair framed a prominent fore-head etched with permanent worry lines that resembled a set of badly ironed creases. His perceptive brown eyes were partially concealed by hooded lids and beneath them hung two pouches of saggy skin. An owl-like nose, heavy jowls and

111

square jawline completed the features of a face known to millions of people around the world. A face that belonged to Shimon Stern, the longest-serving prime minister in Israel's history.

'If you want to kill a snake, you have to cut off its head.'

Franklin sneered as he took a moment to savour what was coming next.

'What better message could we send to Jews around the world to show them they are no longer safe, than by killing the Israeli prime minister and the US ambassador to Israel, another Jew, in one wonderful coup on their Day of Atonement?'

The image changed to an exterior shot of the Great Synagogue in Jerusalem.

'This is where both men will be begging God for forgiveness on September twenty-fifth and I've a plan to take them out.'

Anderson was stunned by this new information. He knew the risks in attempting to strike at the very heart of Israel.

'John, we've never discussed this – it's madness. The security will be off the chart. You can't suddenly throw this into the mix without months of planning.'

Franklin's nostrils flared at the blatant challenge to his authority.

'Daniel, please don't patronise me. This plan has been long in the making. Our grandfather, the Führer, initiated it over fifty years ago. Plus, for good measure we'll still take out one significant synagogue in five different continents by doctor-ing the file Berrettini receives. It will only reveal ten of the fifteen targets, which means we'll still have a little icing on our cake.'

'But why would he believe the file is genuine?'

'Because I plan to set up our friend – that gullible fool, Armando Ricci. Closer to the time, the Italian police will receive a tip-off that the Roman National Party is planning an attack inside Italy. When they search his residence, they'll find a hidden folder on his laptop containing the file detailing the attacks on ten synagogues around the world. Under interrogation, he'll fold like a cheap deckchair and tell them I'm personally joining his assault team, which is planning to hit the Tempio Maggiore in Florence. That intelligence will draw Berrettini and Vargas to Italy like moths to a flame when, in reality, the three of us will be over two thousand miles away in Jerusalem.'

Deshi hadn't spoken throughout the presentation, until now.

'What about the Argentine? You promised he'd suffer as a direct result of the attacks.'

Franklin responded with a click on the remote and a fresh image appeared of an elderly couple. The picture was clearly taken on a long-lens surveillance camera.

'My dear, I haven't forgotten. These are Vargas's beloved in-laws, practically his only remaining family and the last link to his dead wife. They're members of the Templo Libertad in central Buenos Aires, and every year they make an appearance on Yom Kippur. It's one of five synagogues that won't be on the file Berrettini receives. I even know their seat numbers, which ensures they'll be prime targets when the attack takes place. Can you imagine the pain Vargas will suffer when he learns of their deaths – especially now he's just lost his closest friend? He'll be devastated, and that's when you can step in and finish him off.'

Despite the contempt she felt for Franklin, Deshi was dazzled by the arrogant display of deviousness and ingenuity being flaunted by the man she referred to as the psycho.

# Chapter Twenty-Three

Al-Karameh, Jordan

17 February 1969

On 4 February 1969, Yasser Arafat became chairman of the Palestinian Liberation Organisation, known more commonly throughout the world as the PLO. It had one single policy: the destruction of the State of Israel, which it had opposed since its foundation twenty years earlier on 14 May 1948.

Just ten days after he was elected, his assistant presented him with an intriguing invitation that had arrived at his base in Al-Karameh in Jordan via a courier. The letter was from a self-confessed sympathiser in South America who wished to make a substantial donation to his cause in return for a face-to-face meeting. Arafat read the typed document with little or no interest and was about to screw it up and dispose of it when he saw the signature. He was no historian but knew the significance of the name Martin Bormann. He'd been Adolf Hitler's personal secretary, no less, and loyal henchman throughout the Second World War. Swift research revealed that Bormann supposedly died in Berlin in April 1945, trying to escape the Russians, who'd encircled Hitler's bunker where he was holed up, but his body had never been found. That fact alone made the invitation intriguing and irresistible.

Three days later, Arafat travelled eight and a half thousand miles on a challenging thirty-five-hour journey that involved five flights taking him from Amman in Jordan to the tiny town of El Calafate in South Patagonia. Although the invitation had insisted he travel alone, the PLO leader was a suspicious operator who'd survived many attempts on his life by his shrewd use of bodyguards, so when he arrived at the obscure farmhouse named El Blondi, he was accompanied by three devoted soldiers, all armed to the teeth.

They were greeted at the entrance to the house by a young man in his early twenties accompanied by an attractive female translator. The man was a perfect specimen of the Aryan race: blonde-haired and blue-eyed, and his opening gambit, even in translation, was a killer.

'Mr Arafat, welcome to El Blondi. My name is Richard. Martin and my father are very much looking forward to meeting you. Sadly, my father is in poor health and is reaching the end of his days, but his mind is still as sharp as ever. My apologies, your men will not be allowed to sit in the meeting but are welcome to enjoy the hospitality of the house. One last thing. When you speak to my father directly, always address him as "Führer".'

Arafat was stunned. Like the rest of the world, he believed Adolf Hitler had been dead for over twenty years. He began to wonder if he'd wasted his time; if he'd been conned by a group of fascist fantasists hidden away in the ass end of Argentina who still supported the Nazi dream of world domination. All that changed five minutes later when he entered the pine-panelled study with Richard and the translator. He saw a man who he assumed must be Bormann standing like a faithful lapdog to the side of a large mahogany desk, behind which sat the shrivelled shell of a man – who was, undoubtedly, Adolf Hitler. The hair was wispy and grey, and the moustache had gone, but the piercing blue eyes, as cold as a glacier, were staring straight at him.

For the first and only time in his life he felt starstruck, and sensing he was in the presence of greatness nervously adjusted his distinctive black-and-white chequered keffiyeh before bowing in reverence.

'Führer, it is the greatest honour of my life to meet you.'

Hitler was seventy-nine and reaching the end of his life. His body was riddled with cancer, and a few minutes before Arafat had entered the study, Bormann had injected him with diluted cocaine that dulled the pain and kick-started his brain. The stimulant normally lasted for about an hour before wearing off, but the immediate effect of the drug was remarkable. The Führer was like an old toy springing into life after receiving fresh batteries.

'Welcome to my home, Chairman Arafat. I am a huge admirer of your organisation's ambitions. We have much in common and a lot to talk about.'

During the following thirty minutes, the four men discussed their shared objective – the destruction of Israel.

As Hitler's stamina began to wane, Bormann took control of the meeting.

'We will, of course, finance your cause, allowing you to source arms and fund black ops attacks against the Israelis. It is essential we form an unbreakable bond that will eventually allow us to achieve our goal. It's—'

Hitler emitted a quiet groan and slowly slumped forward onto the desk. The energy burst supplied by the cocaine had run out. Bormann was used to witnessing this behaviour and hardly missed a beat.

'Moving forward, Richard will be your sole contact. He'll run the bank account and ensure you have everything you need. In the short term, I wondered about the possibility of a hit on the Israeli prime minister, Eshkol – decapitate the snake?'

The diminutive Arab smiled for the first time.

'What's the famous saying, "Great minds think alike"?'

When Arafat returned to Jordan after an exhausting seventy-hour round trip, he concluded the marathon journey had been well worth his time. Not only because of the new alliance he'd formed and the unlimited funding it would bring, but because for a few minutes he'd breathed the same air as the only man on the planet who hated Jews more than he did.

# Chapter Twenty-Four

Washington D.C., United States

After the exposure of the safe house in Rockville, Vargas moved into a spare room in Berrettini's house on 14th Street in the fashionable Capitol Hill neighbourhood, just a short drive from FBI headquarters. As befitted the deputy director, the townhouse was considered a safe property, but security had been beefed up by the presence of four agents – two worked the perimeter and two were based inside the house.

It was early evening and Berrettini and Vargas had just returned home after visiting Hembury at the military hospital where he was making great strides and was in good spirits. Berrettini had thrown together a spaghetti carbonara, one of only three Italian recipes in his cooking repertoire. The two men were sitting at the end of a small dining table working their way through large plates of steaming-hot pasta, washed down by the contents of an ice-cold bottle of Pinot Grigio. Vargas was devouring his meal and was impressed by the Italian's culinary skills.

'Wow, Mike, you've kept this talent secret – totally delicious.'

'It's all thanks to my mum, she's the original Italian mamma. When I left home for college, she was terrified I'd starve, so she taught me three recipes and I've lived off them ever since. So, tomorrow night it's ragù, and Wednesday my pièce de résistance, homemade lasagne.'

Vargas laughed and wrapped more pasta around his fork.

'Talking of family, I have to disappear for a couple of days.'

Berrettini arched an eyebrow.

'I know it's not great timing but I've no choice. The day after tomorrow is the fourteenth anniversary of Sophia's death. Every year, I meet up with her parents and her sister to visit the grave. It's a date I can never miss.'

Vargas's voice began to break. Even after such a long time, he still found it painful to talk about the sudden loss of his wife. The truth was, he'd never recovered from the trauma of her premature demise due to a brain tumour and, in a romantic sense, he'd never been able to move on. He'd lost the love of his life. He started to tear up and Berrettini stood from the table and walked across to give his friend a deep bear hug. Neither man spoke, and shortly after they broke off the embrace Vargas disappeared into his room to begin packing.

\* \* \*

The Pertutti café in the south-western corner of Plaza de Mayo claimed to serve the best chocolate churros in the whole of Buenos Aires. It had been established more than a hundred years earlier and an urban myth claimed Eva Perón would often stop off for a cappuccino and a churro on her way to the pink presidential palace, less than two hundred yards away at the opposite end of the square.

It was also a regular breakfast meeting place for Vargas and his long-term assistant, Juan Torres. Both men had a sweet tooth and their breakfast order never wavered. They'd worked together as a team for over thirteen years and Torres wanted it to stay that way. He'd refused so many promotions, the chief of police had given up offering.

Vargas had returned from Washington to Buenos Aires on the red-eye and arranged the meet to bring his colleague up to speed because they hadn't spoken since the car bomb explosion in the basement car park of his apartment block.

Unusually, Vargas was dressed in a smart black linen suit with a white shirt and thin black silk tie, while Torres was far more casual in a pair of cream chinos paired with an open-necked blue cotton shirt. Vargas was due to see his in-laws at midday, which allowed him plenty of time to explain why he'd disappeared to Washington immediately after the blast. He hadn't quite finished his debrief when Torres interrupted.

'Boss, last week while you were away, chief inspectors in the city were called to a high-level meeting with the commander and I was sent in your place. The mayor was there, along with a guy called Hector Correa – the current head of intelligence and security for Latin America. As of now, the city's threat level has moved from general risk to severe because of an intelligence warning of an imminent terrorist attack on prominent locations in the city. The mayor isn't going public with it right now, but all districts have been put on high alert and a list of possible targets has been prepared. Surely, it's got to be connected with the chatter GCHQ warned you about and Franklin's attacks on you—'

'Christ, how big is this conspiracy? What's that bastard up to? Juan, can I see the list?'

Torres leaned down and lifted an iPad from his brown leather satchel, put on a pair of John Lennon pebble glasses and checked through his emails until he found the appropriate one. He shared the screen with Vargas, who leaned across the table.

'Usual high-level targets, boss. The National Congress, presidential palace, police headquarters, the opera house, and so on.'

Vargas checked through it and nodded.

'Yes, nothing jumps out. I'll need to update Berrettini, though. As you say, this can't be a coincidence.'

'Boss, how long are you here for?'

'Just today for Sofia's annual memorial and then I'm heading back to Washington tomorrow.'

Vargas glanced down at his digital watch.

'It's a good one-hour drive to Tablada, so I'd better get going. Keep in touch, Juan, and let me know if you hear anything more specific.'

The two men embraced and Vargas departed, his thoughts turning to a far more personal crisis, one that had lasted fourteen years and showed no sign of abating.

* * *

La Tablada cemetery housed over one hundred and fifty thousand Jewish graves and one of them belonged to Vargas's late wife, Sophia.

At five minutes to twelve he trudged through the imposing double-domed entrance and made his way past the permanent Holocaust memorial. He weaved through hundreds of headstones until he reached the first open stretch of land, without any graves, which he knew so well. From there it was a ninety degree turn and a further five-minute walk until he reached the spot. He felt as though he could have made the journey blindfolded, and in an emotional sense he did.

Waiting for him by Sophia's grave were three familiar figures: his in-laws, Gabriel and Rebeca, along with their remaining daughter, Nadia, who'd flown from her home in Israel for the annual pilgrimage. All were dressed in black, and Gabriel held a Hebrew prayer book in his right hand. As soon as they saw Vargas approach, they turned to face him, and a series of tearful hugs ensued. It never got easier for any of them. Sophia had been taken far too early and the pain still had a tinge of rawness that time simply couldn't heal.

They stood in a tight family group as Gabriel recited the traditional mourner's prayer. Although the book was open, he never glanced down; the words were so deeply engraved on his heart.

After some moments of silence, they took turns to step forward and lay a small pebble on the end of the grey marble stone that covered Sophia's grave. Vargas was the last to complete the ritual and spent a while with his eyes firmly shut, trying to recall some of their favourite times together and the happiness they'd shared.

After leaving the cemetery, Vargas and Sophia's family returned to central Buenos Aires where they visited Templo Libertad, the synagogue where he and Sophia had married, fourteen years ago. The rabbi had been in place for over twenty years and had officiated at their wedding ceremony. Vargas knew he'd be waiting to greet them, as always, ready with words of comfort before he and Gabriel would recite the same memorial prayer spoken at the cemetery. Vargas didn't speak a word of Hebrew, but he'd heard the prayer, the Mourner's Kaddish, so many times, he quietly joined in with a phonetic rendition of his own, which seemed to provide a crumb of comfort.

It was early afternoon and the vast interior of the synagogue, which held some seven hundred people, was pretty much deserted, except for about forty tourists and a dozen local orthodox worshippers, liberally spread out across the low wooden seating areas. Gabriel took his regular position about halfway down on the right-hand side, while Rebeca and Nadia sat almost directly above him, as women were seated in the upstairs gallery, a traditional segregation that had remained a constant in synagogues across the world for centuries.

Vargas had left the prayer hall to wash his hands in the bathroom, just off the large entrance hallway, and was walking back down the aisle when he spotted something a bit off, something that didn't feel quite right. A dumpy, middle-aged man dressed in a pair of dark blue slacks with a matching polo shirt was standing on the other side of the prayer hall taking photos with his Samsung phone. His facial features were partially hidden by a wide, flat-brimmed gaucho hat that dwarfed his head but at least added a bit of height. At first, Vargas assumed he was just

124

another tourist taking holiday snaps of the most famous syna-gogue in Argentina, but then, on closer inspection, he realised the photographer was more interested in his father-in-law than the beautiful stained-glass windows twenty feet above him. Vargas couldn't be sure he was right – and the idea seemed preposterous, but then the man switched his viewpoint upwards to Rebeca and Nadia and continued clicking.

# Chapter Twenty-Five

Buenos Aires, Argentina

Mauro Cabrera didn't normally believe in luck, but on this occasion, he couldn't believe the gift that had magically fallen into his lap. Was it a fluke or coincidence? He simply didn't care. He just planned to take full advantage of the situation.

The Victory Nationalist Party, of which he was a prominent member, was a small neo-Nazi group which had been banned in April 2017 through a ruling by the Argentine Court of Justice but continued to operate underground. The party's leader, Bruno Guzmán, claimed that towards the end of the Second World War Hitler had identified Argentina as the future of Nazism. He constantly referred to an unsubstantiated comment the Führer had supposedly made in his infamous bunker, days before the Russians arrived: 'Argentina will provide the next leader of the Nazi Party.'

As ludicrous as this sounded, Guzmán still managed to attract thousands of dedicated followers who passionately supported his vile doctrine that spoke of the annihilation of the

Jewish race. The party's online publication, *The Iron Fist*, broke new ground in Argentina by establishing a regular platform for neo-Nazism and anti-Semitism.

Cabrera was one of five senior party members who formed a small council working directly for Guzmán, and was also part of the strategy team planning the Yom Kippur attack on the Templo Libertad. He was on his third scouting mission when he spotted Gabriel arrive and take his usual seat. Cabrera had studied photos of Vargas's father-in-law supplied to him by Guzmán. Gabriel was top of the killing list – a priority hit, so when Cabrera saw the man himself enter the synagogue, he couldn't believe it. He decided to take some pictures of Gabriel and his family in situ to further ingratiate himself with Guzmán and the mysterious American his boss talked about who was financing the entire operation.

His dreams of a tasty bonus instantly evaporated, however, when he spotted Vargas striding towards him through the wooden pews. He knew precisely who the chief inspector was and his relationship to the targets. Panic set in. He slid his phone into his trouser pocket and started walking rapidly down the centre aisle in the opposite direction. Vargas responded by quickening his pace and was less than fifteen yards away when Cabrera lost his nerve and hit the gas pedal. For an obese man, he was surprisingly light on his feet, and his swift dart towards the exit morphed into a fast jog and then, within seconds, a full-on sprint. He dashed through the front entrance and took a hard left onto the busy side-walk, dodging groups of pedestrians, with Vargas in hot pursuit.

As he reached the end of the block, he didn't bother

looking over his shoulder; he could sense Vargas closing in. He ran across the road, heading for the entrance of the iconic Teatro Colón, hoping it would offer an escape route through its warren of exits leading onto four different streets.

The busy one-way avenue comprised four lanes of traffic, and as Cabrera cleared the third his luck ran out. His eyeline was firmly fixed on the two enormous glass entrance doors belonging to the theatre and he never saw the eight-wheel articulated truck approaching at speed from his right. The astonished driver slammed on the brakes – Cabrera had appeared out of nowhere, and there wasn't a chance in hell of the juggernaut stopping in time. The impact was brutal and Cabrera's body was thrown high into the air with such ferocious velocity it appeared to horrified onlookers as if it were weightless. He was dead long before he crashed onto the sidewalk, colliding with a streetlight for good measure, before coming to rest in a hideous crumpled heap.

Car horns and frantic screams bellowed out around Vargas who'd witnessed the shocking collision from less than ten yards away. As he approached the body, he sidestepped the gaucho hat, now gently rolling on the kerb as though it had a life of its own. He'd desperately wanted the suspect alive – he had so many questions to ask – but at least there were the images on the phone that would confirm his suspicions.

He was the only person moving towards the twisted corpse; everyone else seemed to be running away. Vargas leaned down over Cabrera's body to search for the cell when his eyes fixed on a small pile of twisted metal and plastic

– the guts of the Samsung that had been pulverised during the impact.

He cursed under his breath; yet another dead end. The entire case was a jigsaw. He knew once he put all the pieces together it would present a true picture, but right now he just didn't have enough of them.

\* \* \*

The third-floor hotel room at the Holiday Inn airport hotel in Buenos Aires was bleak and sterile and aptly fitted Vargas's mood as he silently slid out of his black linen suit and threw the pants, tie and jacket into his open carry-on bag which rested on the crumpled wafer-thin sheet on top of the single bed. He glared at the items in utter despair, knowing he would see them in exactly twelve months' time when he'd don the same clothes once again for the annual ritual.

He stripped naked and trudged into the tiny shower where he welcomed the sensation of boiling hot jets of water battering his skin, although they failed to wash away the permanent ache that absorbed every fibre of his being. He bathed in self-pity as he questioned his entire existence – a fifty-two-year-old man with no meaningful personal life whatsoever, who survived on the rare moments of gratification his work provided as a means of staying relevant and having something to live for.

He desperately wanted the release crying offered but just heaved instead because he'd no tears left. Gradually his thoughts drifted away from his private heartache to the menacing spectre that cast a dark shadow over his life and possibly that of

Sophia's family. Franklin the tormentor was out there weaving a new web of evil. Vargas sensed the endgame was approaching and vowed to his late wife he would finally bring his enemy down and save her family, even if it turned out to be the last thing he ever did.

# Chapter Twenty-Six

Minnesota, United States

January 2011

John Franklin was riding a wave of political euphoria, transporting him on a one-way ticket to the Oval Office. His polling was extraordinary, not just in relation to the other contenders for the Republican presidential nomination, but also against the Democratic incumbent, a president who'd lost his way and was suffering the lowest approval ratings in history. In head-to-head polls, Franklin appeared a shoo-in to take the keys to the White House in the upcoming November elections and pretty much unstoppable.

Under the Machiavellian guidance of his father, Franklin was travelling the country on a whirlwind tour of thirteen swing states, attending an endless number of rallies, fund-raisers and TV appearances, reinforced by the biggest marketing campaign in US political history, which positioned him as the 'great unifier'. His father's pockets were remarkably deep, filled as they were with unlimited funds supplied by Franklin Pharmaceuticals, the third largest drug company in the world.

John had just taken part in a packed Friday night rally in Rochester, Minnesota, where he'd whipped three thousand adoring supporters into a frenzy as they'd joined in with his 'Let's unify America together!' chants and cheered him to the rafters of the giant airport hangar.

He'd managed to escape the devoted crowd in one piece and boarded Richard's Cessna for the flight to a remote ranch in Whitefish, Montana for a long-planned strategy weekend to hammer out the schedule for the next stage of the campaign.

He leaned back in his seat to celebrate his latest triumph with an ice-cold glass of Bollinger, while his father nursed a tumbler containing his go-to bourbon.

'John, I suggest you hit the pillow – we've a long flight ahead of us.'

John waved his flute around, gesturing towards the interior of the jet.

'Dad, I'm cool. This baby will kill it in a couple of hours.'

Richard Franklin took a large gulp of whiskey before shaking his son, the presidential candidate, to his very core.

'John, we're not going to the ranch. We're heading to the Gaza Strip.'

\* \* \*

The flight time was just over twelve hours and the Cessna gobbled up the miles as it carved a route transporting them across the Atlantic to the Asian continent. Both men grabbed some shut-eye until halfway into the flight, when Richard took the opportunity to give his son a fast-track history lesson on Middle Eastern politics.

'John, back in 1969, Bormann brokered a meeting between Yasser Arafat and the Führer, which I was present at. It was the start of a thirty-five-year relationship I fostered with the Arab. Other than Iran, we became the biggest independent donor to the PLO and were directly involved in two of their highest-profile terrorist attacks: the Dawson Field episode in September 1970, when Arafat masterminded the hijacking of five international planes, and the Munich Massacre, that took out eleven of the Israeli Olympic team. It was accredited to Black September, a splinter group of the PLO, but, trust me, Arafat had his fingerprints all over it, as did I. But as the years passed, he became fat, corrupt and rich and lost his spark. It became clear to me the new boys on the block, who had the burning hunger and hatred to take on the Israeli government, were the Palestinian Justice Brigade: a small paramilitary organisation who, unlike their big brother, Hamas, have no political aspirations to rule Gaza and also rejected the Oslo Accords which called for a two-state solution in the Middle East. Their sole mantra is the destruction of the State of Israel, which makes them ideal soulmates. Our ambitions are perfectly aligned. They seek the establishment of a sovereign Islamic state within the borders of pre-1948 Mandatory Palestine. So, in 2004, shortly after Arafat's mysterious death, I switched camps and formed an allegiance with them – specifically their military wing, led by Khaled Shomani, a committed fanatic to the cause.'

He paused to pour himself a large tumbler of bourbon before continuing.

'John, you guys are of a similar age, so now it's your turn to take on that relationship.'

'Dad, are you sure it's safe? Our government has designated them a terrorist organisation. If word gets out I've met with the PJB, my shot at the White House is over.'

'Don't worry, I've covered our tracks. The ranch the media believe we're heading to is set in over eighty acres, so no one can get near it. But just to play it safe, I've arranged for my chopper to fly in and out over the weekend. Officially, as far as the outside world is concerned, we'll have spent the weekend there, planning strategy. The reason you must meet Shomani now is because once you're in the White House, the Secret Service will monitor your diary down to the smallest detail. They'll even know what time of day you go for a crap. Plus, right now your face isn't that well known outside the US but all that will change the moment you become the most photographed man in the world. Trust me, it's now or never.'

John nodded and eased back in the massive leather armchair which barely resembled a regular plane seat.

'What the hell are we going to talk about?'

Richard's mind flashed back over forty years to his first meeting with Arafat and a hint of a smile broke out on his face.

'Many things, John, including cutting off the head of the snake.'

\* \* \*

Together with the West Bank, the Gaza Strip forms the State of Palestine. It's the smaller of the two Palestinian territories and is situated on the eastern coast of the Mediterranean Sea, but politically its significance is huge. It shares its borders with Israel to the north and east and Egypt to the south-west. The strip is only twenty-five miles long and seven miles wide and in 2012 it was home to over one and a half million Palestinians, making it one of the most densely populated areas in the world.

The Cessna came in low to avoid Israeli radar and touched down safely on a makeshift runway that had been constructed in the previous forty-eight hours at a defunct airport on the outskirts of Rafah, a small city in the south of the strip. From there, Richard and John were driven in the back of a Land Rover, forming part of a three-car convoy that headed directly for Gaza City. The two cars that sandwiched the jeep were jammed full of militia.

The three vehicles pulled to a halt outside the entrance of the Al-Jalaa Tower in the West district of Gaza City. The eleven-storey building was the official base for the controversial media outlet Al Jazeera and the exterior was plastered with its signage. The international broadcaster ran its news studios and general operations from there but the building, less publicly, provided a legitimate cover for a far more sinister operation.

The Palestinian Justice Brigade had the entire fifth floor to itself and its leader, Khaled Shomani, kept an office there. It was a twelve-by-twelve box, housing nothing more than a small metal desk, a few steel chairs and a large map of the Middle East that dominated one wall.

Richard and John were escorted through the reception area over to a small bank of lifts and minutes later deposited inside the sparse room. The soldiers departed immediately and it wasn't long before the leader of the PJB appeared. John was astonished he was alone – not a bodyguard in sight, but that wasn't the only surprise.

Shomani was dressed in a traditional white ankle-length thobe with a matching keffiyeh held in place by a black cord. He was blunt faced with dark brown eyes as hard as flint and had an aura about him that demanded instant respect. The man was an enigma; the son of a Saudi tribal chief who'd been educated at Oxford and spoke impeccable English was also a cold-blooded killer, personally responsible for the deaths of dozens of Israeli civilians and soldiers. He cheek-kissed Richard twice before being introduced to John, who received a similar greeting. As soon as he spoke, John realised he wasn't a man to be underestimated.

'Richard, it's good to see you in the flesh again. Skype is no way to develop a personal bond.'

His penetrating stare switched from father to son.

'John, by coming here in person you've taken a huge risk and shown me, and our holy cause, great respect. We'll work together and achieve meaningful things in the future.'

John felt slightly in awe of the man who had a huge bounty on his head and who was nothing like he'd envisaged.

'Khaled, the risk is well worth the reward. Of course, I need to be careful, especially once I'm in the White House, but, as you know, my family believes in the long game, and we share the same single passion – the destruction of Israel.'

The Arab laughed heartily as though reacting to a joke.

'John, imagine if the global media knew the future leader of the Western world was sitting in this tiny hovel of an office, the base for the head of the military wing of the PJB. There are plenty of journalists even in this very building who'd die for a story like that.'

John laughed nervously, not sure whether Shomani had just issued a veiled threat or made an ironic observation. Either way, he moved the conversation on.

'Khaled, we'll continue with funding through existing back channels to support your rocket attacks because they seem to be having an impact. But, looking forward, what more can we do?'

The intense expression that appeared on the Arab's face indicated he knew exactly what he wanted.

'John, the rockets are fine, but they only scratch the surface. What I hope to build with you is a long-term plan for a life-changing event that'll not just change the status quo here but rock the world too. I need us to create an outrage that'll force the American people to question the wisdom of backing the Jewish state. John, I crave my own 9/11.'

John understood exactly what his new partner was seeking to achieve. Shomani wanted his name to become as synonymous with evil as that of another infamous Saudi-born terrorist: Osama bin Laden.

# Chapter Twenty-Seven

*The Little Fox*, The Indian Ocean

I t was early morning, just after sunrise, and Daniel and Deshi were sitting together on the sun deck at the rear of the super yacht from where they had a clear view of the helipad. The crew onboard the Super Puma were evidently preparing for take-off, so they wondered if there was a trip in the offing.

They didn't have to wait long for an answer. A few minutes later, Franklin emerged from a glass elevator which had brought him up to the top level of the boat. He strolled over to join them, clutching only a black computer case in his right hand. His overnight bag had already been loaded onto the chopper.

'I've some business to attend to and will be gone for two days. When I return, be ready. We'll be flying straight to Gaza to meet up with the head of the PJB's military wing to run through the planned attack in fine detail before we move on to Jerusalem. Once you leave here, you won't be returning until after the operation is complete, so bring everything you need.'

As usual, Franklin only imparted minimal information. As he turned and headed for the chopper, Daniel rose to accompany him on the short walk.

'John, where are you off to? You sure you don't want me to come with?'

'No, it's a private matter, Daniel, that only I can handle.'

Having shut his younger brother down, he climbed aboard the chopper and slammed the door shut.

\* \* \*

Incredibly, Franklin had decided to spend forty-six of the following fifty hours in the air. As soon as he transferred from the Puma to his Gulfstream, he prepared himself for a long-haul marathon, heading for the only American state set geographically in the tropics.

Hawaii comprises eight major islands that form part of an archipelago in the Pacific Ocean, some two thousand miles off the US mainland. Maui is the second largest of the group, and one of the smaller towns on the island is Makawao, on the rural north-west slope of Haleakalā on East Maui, which boasts a population of just over seven thousand. The local infrastructure offers a handful of schools, some shops and a church, meaning the town that time forgot is not on the tourist trail, not even in the roughest of rough guides. Only a few weeks earlier the tiny island had been ravaged by a series of wildfires, lethally spread by Hurricane Dora, that had decimated many of its communities, killing over a hundred locals in the process.

None of this was of any interest to Franklin, however, who'd come to visit the battered island because he knew two of the residents personally, even though he hadn't seen or spoken with either of them for the previous eleven years. One was his wife and the other his son.

In the immediate aftermath of his exposure as Adolf Hitler's grandson in February 2012, his wife, Caroline, and son, Bill, had their lives changed overnight. They became prisoners inside their San Francisco mansion, trapped by a gang of hardened journalists and paparazzi desperate to gain a word with, or even just sight of, the wife of the man dubbed 'the Counterfeit Candidate'. An exclusive image of her was worth north of half a million dollars to a freelance photographer in world syndication rights.

Caroline was billed in the media as the partner of the world's most loathed politician and was under siege from a ruthless, hungry pack. It was abundantly clear the media and the public at large didn't believe a word of her official statement, where she claimed to be ignorant of her husband's history, so all she could do was wait it out. With support from her sister and a couple of loyal friends, that's exactly what she did. She didn't leave the sanctuary of their home for almost six months. Food was delivered and Bill received tutoring from three teachers brave enough to be seen entering the house. After the November presidential election, which Franklin would no doubt have won had things gone differently, the world moved on and so did Caroline.

She reverted to her maiden name and quietly set about rebuilding her life. She knew she could never hope to find complete anonymity and sought a future in semi-obscurity, where no one would care about her past. In the end, after months of research, she opted to buy a modest three-bedroom house in a small town on the Hawaiian island of Maui. Less than a year earlier, she'd had visions of renovating the private quarters of the White House, but that was before fate stepped in and turned her life on its head.

Bill was only twelve at the time, and in the months immediately after the scandal broke, he spiralled into a deep depression. He'd lost his father, his friends and his identity. He was no longer the son of the presidential candidate whom everybody wanted to rub shoulders with. He was now the sole great-grandson of the most hated dictator in world history. Bill had counselling, as did his mother, but they were both in a very dark, unreachable place.

At first the relocation was a disaster. The tiny community in Makawao shunned them both, not due to who they were, but purely because they were outsiders from the US mainland who'd no right to be there. Gradually, things began to improve. Caroline donated five thousand dollars to a local charity that ran a small mission housing orphans from all eight of the main islands. That earned her a place on the committee that ran the institution. Within nine months she was in the chair, running the whole thing, and before long, she was on the board of five island charities and a leading light in the community. Her experience of setting up huge fundraisers for her former husband held her in good stead when it came to arranging much smaller functions on the island. It's always much easier to scale down than up.

As the years passed, mother and son successfully built new lives for themselves. Caroline was dubbed the island's charity queen and Bill excelled at high school and then college, where his exceptional mathematical brain helped him achieve a first-class honours MBA in business and finance. He had an incredible gift for numbers, aided by a photographic memory that allowed him to store an entire page of numerical information after a just a few seconds of scanning. He opted to pursue a career in investment banking and after graduating took his pick from six different banks on the island. In the end, Bill opted to join First Hawaiian Bank, which had a branch in Kahului, just twelve miles away from his home and which offered international opportunities down the line.

John Franklin was finally declared dead ten years after he disappeared, supposedly having committed suicide off the Carmel coastline, even though no body had been found. However, unbeknown to Caroline and Bill, their lives were watched almost from the moment they'd set foot on the island. Once Franklin had discovered their new whereabouts, he'd hired a private detective agency to discreetly monitor them, and for the past eleven years had received quarterly reports detailing every element of their existence in the tiny town of Makawao.

\* \* \*

The Gulfstream touched down at Kahului Airport just before five in the afternoon local time, and a silver Mercedes S-Class was waiting less than fifty feet away to whisk Franklin into town. The driver who'd been booked by the detective agency was under twenty-five, as stipulated, because Franklin figured there'd be no chance someone that young could possibly know who he was. Even though he'd undergone extensive plastic surgery, he was still paranoid about being recognised.

It was a short drive into town where the Merc parked up on West Kaahumanu Avenue, directly opposite the main entrance of the First Hawaiian Bank. Franklin was sitting in the back of the car, absorbed by reports of Bill's incredible success story. He'd read the same documents many times before but felt the need to immerse himself in them once more. The photograph that lay on the empty black leather seat next to him was like a silent passenger. It was a picture of Bill taken less than two weeks earlier. He was suited and booted, exiting the glass entrance of the bank opposite.

Franklin studied the photo and then glanced at his watch. He didn't really need the picture as a reference – his son was a carbon copy of himself at that age: tall and muscular, with strawberry-blond hair and sky-blue eyes. It was as though they'd both been created from the perfect Aryan template.

The numbers on his digital watch changed to 17.45 and Franklin knew Bill would be leaving the building any time in the next thirty minutes. For a man who'd never allowed self-doubt to cloud his decision-making, he still hadn't worked out what his opening line was going to be to the only person in the world he cared anything about.

# Chapter Twenty-Eight

Kahului, Hawaii

William Bush turned left out of the front entrance of the single-storey building and began his regular five-hundred-yard walk up the hill to the town's main car park where the bank had a concession of spaces.

He paid no attention to the silver Mercedes that tracked his progress for the first few seconds before accelerating past him on the opposite side of the road, allowing Franklin to be dropped off by the car park entrance, where he made his way to Space F24 on the upper level. It was occupied by Bill's red Ford Bronco, an eighteenth birthday present from his mum a few days after he passed his test. It was parked between a silver Chrysler and a black Bentley Franklin knew belonged to the bank's chairman. There were another ten cars on that level but, fortunately, there was nobody else around when he heard Bill's footsteps on the concrete stairway leading up from the ground floor.

Franklin was a monster, a psychopath who sanctioned killing for fun, so he found the feeling of vulnerability alien and difficult to process. He was an alpha male with a huge ego who for the first time in his life feared rejection. He quickly tapped the inside pocket of his dark blue cashmere jacket to confirm the gift he'd brought with him was safely in place and took a huge breath as Bill emerged at the top of the stairs, less than ten yards away. Franklin moved forward from behind the Bentley and came face to face with his son, who'd just reached the driver's door of his SUV. Bill was on autopilot and hadn't made eye contact with the stranger. He was about to click on the key remote when Franklin spoke.

'Bill, it's good to see you.'

It was the unmistakable tone of voice that Bill recognised a split second ahead of the eyes – the piercing blue eyes. Unbridled shock flooded his brain as the painful reality that his father was still alive hit home. The man he hated more than anyone else on the planet was standing right in front of him like a ghost.

'What the fuck? . . . This can't be . . . shit . . . shit . . . shit.'

* * *

There was a prolonged, painful silence inside the Bronco where father and son sat alongside each other for the first time in eleven years. Bill stared out of the windscreen, focusing on an illuminated green exit sign fifty yards away, shaking his head in disbelief, his thoughts scrambled. Then his bewilderment morphed into anger.

'Why the hell couldn't you just stay dead? You're a fraud – a Nazi criminal who destroyed our lives with your lies . . . and now you turn up . . . I loathe you.'

Franklin allowed Bill to let rip. It was pretty much the initial reaction he'd expected, but the pain etched in his son's voice told him that somewhere, buried deep, was a love he believed could be resurrected. That's when he went to work with the script he'd honed over a period of months.

'Your mother has poisoned your mind against me but give me a chance. Let me say my piece and once I've finished, if you want me to walk away, I promise I'll disappear. Only this time, you'll never hear from me again.'

Bill stayed silent, which Franklin, in his twisted mind, took as a positive.

'Let me start with a question. There were sixty-five million people living in Germany in the nineteen thirties who adored your great-grandfather, do you think they were all evil fascists?'

Franklin didn't draw breath to allow an answer.

'No, they were just regular people who'd been downtrodden by the rest of Europe, and he offered them hope and salvation.'

He ploughed on relentlessly with another question.

'What about my father, your grandfather? He built one of the world's greatest pharmaceutical companies that developed drugs that have saved the lives of millions of poor and desperate people across the globe. Was he an evil maniac as well or a man who pledged to fight famine and disease?'

Franklin, as ever, was selective with his information, conveniently leaving out the key fact that the global pharmaceutical empire had been built on the back of Nazi money stolen from European Jews who'd been sent to death camps. He was on a roll and continued with his well-rehearsed tale.

'Then there's the Jews. Look at the Middle East, Bill. The

Palestinian people have had their homeland ripped from their grasp and the Jewish lobby in New York has created a fantastical biblical story that's total crap, and yet most of the Western world supports an illegal Jewish state. My family – our family, has been on the right side of history and yet we've been painted as monsters. I'd no choice but to keep my birthright a secret because of the way historians have twisted the truth. Bill, it's a conspiracy – a web of lies that millions of people have bought into.'

Franklin's strategy was to place a tiny seed of doubt inside Bill's mind. He just needed a chink in the armour big enough to give him an opening to exploit.

'Bill, I want you to spend some time with me to see the flip side of the coin. I have original historical documents you need to read for yourself. They paint a very different picture to what you might have been taught at school. In a few days' time, I'm completing a huge operation that's been years in the making – it's going to be a world-changing event. Once that's over, I want to devote the rest of my life to you, son. I'll send a plane to take you away from this dump. We need time together – time that's been stolen from us. It's not too late.'

Bill had heard enough and couldn't take any more.

'You bullshitted Mum for all those years and now you're trying to do the same with me. Get out of the car – go. I don't want you anywhere near me.'

Franklin held his position. He'd played his ace cards and they hadn't worked. He needed a few more minutes but that wasn't an option when his son leaned sideways and exited the driver's door. Franklin mirrored him and rounded the bonnet to join him by the side of the Bronco, where Bill fired off a broadside.

'Just go. I need to breathe some clean air.'

'Bill, every word I've told you is true. I just need time alone with you to prove it.'

Bill searched his father's eyes, desperately looking to see if he could find any truth in them. He thought he saw a glimmer of something but wasn't sure what. He knew his father was a superb actor.

'Just say, one day in the future I did want to contact you . . . how would I go about it?'

Franklin knew, at that precise moment, he'd won. The ultimate control freak was back running the show and nothing could stop him. He reached inside his jacket pocket and retrieved a phone that he passed across to his son, who hesitated slightly before taking it.

'Bill, this is no ordinary cell. It's loaded with just one number and programmed so no calls can be made from it. When you want me, just message and I'll arrange the rest.'

* * *

Franklin was sitting in the back of the Mercedes, poring over his laptop on the short drive back to the airport, when he had a sudden change of mind. He snapped a fresh command to the young driver.

'Take me to the house in Makawao. You have the address.'

'Yes, sir. It'll be about a twenty-minute drive.'

Franklin nodded but his eyes were already focused on an email he'd just received from an old friend in Gaza, the next location on his hectic schedule. Before that, though, he had one more piece of business to attend to that was much closer.

The modest house in Jacaranda Way looked even less imposing in the flesh than it had done in the photos Franklin had seen. He sat in the back of the S-Class, peering through the tinted window at the dull exterior, wondering why his wife had chosen to live in what he considered to be pure squalor. As he exited the car, he instructed the driver to park a few hundred yards away and wait for his text.

Her black Toyota Aygo was parked on the driveway, so Franklin knew she must be somewhere inside the house, no doubt in her small office working through some mundane charity work. He'd never intended to visit her, and so wasn't quite sure what he was doing there, because his only feelings towards his wife were a mixture of hatred and contempt.

All he knew was she'd spent the last decade poisoning Bill's mind against him and needed to be punished. His long-term plan was to contract a hitman to quietly make her disappear, once Bill was fully part of his life and she was on her own. But that day was still a while off, so Franklin figured the shock of seeing him might be enough to trigger some kind of emotional turmoil that would hopefully screw up the pathetic life she'd built for herself.

He stood on the front porch for a good three minutes before ringing the doorbell. It amused him to wonder how long it would take her to recognise him, bearing in mind the thousands of dollars he'd spent remodelling his face.

Inside, Caroline was expecting a visit from two female colleagues, so when she heard the bell, she wasn't surprised. As she reached the door, she made out the faint outline of a tall man through the heavily tinted glass panels and wondered who her mystery caller was. Instinctively she ran her hand through her hair and took a glimpse in the hallway mirror to check her make-up was at least half-decent. On opening the door, she recognised him immediately and her warm curiosity transformed into ice-cold horror. Staring back at her across the porch was her worst nightmare, the physical incarnation of the torture she thought she'd buried long ago.

Then again, Caroline had never fully bought into the suicide story, but as the years went by, she'd grown to accept it even though her gut always told her to be cautious when writing off her husband. Tears welled in her eyes as her emotions veered off on a rollercoaster ride, conjuring up feelings of humiliation and raw anger towards the man who'd betrayed her and trashed her life. One feeling that was totally absent was love and she wondered at that precise moment how she could ever have loved the monster standing before her.

Franklin's stony expression offered no sign of remorse, and without speaking he barged past her into the hallway and made his way through to the small kitchen at the rear of the house. She paused for a moment before following him inside, and by the time she joined him, tears were flowing down her face, which had turned from marble white to fiery red. Her voice cracked as she screamed at the ghoul in front her.

'How dare you just appear like this? You hateful bastard, get out of my house. Crawl back to whatever stone you've been hiding under. Go now or I'll call the police.'

Franklin remained calm as the tirade washed over him.

'Don't you want know why I'm here?'

'No, just get out! Get the hell out of here . . . now!'

# CHAPTER TWENTY-EIGHT

She was hysterical and Franklin got a weird kick out of seeing her pain.

'I've come for Bill and there's nothing you can you do about it, you stupid bitch.'

Caroline's eyes fizzed as the tears were replaced by naked rage.

'Don't you ever go near my son or—'

'Or what, Caroline? The truth is, I've just spent the last hour with him and I've no doubt he'll soon be leaving this shithole to be with me. I need to cleanse him from the poison you've—'

Franklin never finished his sentence. Caroline lost control and her survival instinct took over. She grabbed a bread knife from the granite worktop with her right hand and lunged towards him like an Exocet missile. He partially parried the incoming blow with his left arm but couldn't avoid the serrated edge of the knife slicing deep into the back of his forearm. He howled with pain. At the same moment, his right hand punched her face with such force her forward momentum was stopped in its tracks and both her feet left the ground as she flew through the air to her right. On her way down, her temple smacked against the edge of a free-standing wooden display unit. The awful thud that echoed around the kitchen was testament to the size of the impact. Her body slumped to the floor and twitched a couple of times before coming to rest.

Franklin's open cut was leaking blood everywhere, but he wasn't too concerned. It was nothing more than a nasty flesh wound a dozen stitches would take care of. He leaned down over Caroline's prone body, pressing his fingertips to her wrist, and was surprised to discover a faint pulse. He was convinced he'd killed her. He dropped her hand and moved across the room to the sink where he ran cold tap water over the cut before snatching a blue cotton dishcloth that he wrapped around his arm to try and stem the bleeding.

He questioned the wisdom of grabbing a mop and clearing up the blood trail but that thought evaporated when he heard the front doorbell. He wasted no more time in the kitchen and scuttled out the back door into the garden, where he quickly surveyed his options. There was a stone-built carport to the side of the property, which he entered and walked through until he reached the front, where he stopped and furtively glanced around the side of a brick pillar to see who was waiting at the door.

Standing on the porch were two middle-aged women who appeared agitated as they repeatedly rang the bell to no avail. One of them was on her cell, no doubt calling Caroline, while the other had her face pressed close to the front door, peering through the glass panels. They were both preoccupied and Franklin seized the opportunity to casually move away from the house, walking in the opposite direction without being spotted. He messaged the driver and thirty seconds later the Mercedes came to a silky stop about a hundred yards down the road where it collected him. The driver spotted the blood-soaked cloth around Franklin's forearm the second he climbed into the car.

'Sir, I've a first-aid kit in the boot, would you like me to pull over?'

Franklin's retort was a shotgun blast.

'For Christ's sake, boy, keep your mouth shut, your eyes on the road and get me to the airport fast.'

The young man, suitably chastened, put his foot to the floor.

Franklin sat back and contemplated the likely fallout from his botched visit. He'd screwed up and left his calling card in blood for the world to see. He normally plotted every move and never wandered off-script, so cursed this rare bout of impulse he feared could jeopardise everything he'd meticulously planned.

# Chapter Twenty-Nine

*The Little Fox*, The Indian Ocean

B efore the Gulfstream departed, Franklin's driver sourced an island doctor who was more than happy to treat him on the jet and not ask any questions, if his five-hundred-dollar fee was paid in cash.

For the first few hours of the marathon return flight, Franklin's mood was sullen. He brooded over the potential fall-out from the bloody confrontation with his wife, but his socio-pathic tendencies gradually overwhelmed any self-doubt and normality was swiftly restored.

By the time he was back on *The Little Fox*, the painkillers had well and truly kicked in and his mood had brightened. He rationalised that none of the events that had taken place on the tiny Hawaiian island could conspire to scupper his ingenious plot, so for now he could park that misadventure and focus on what was coming next.

He messaged Daniel and Deshi, inviting them to his quarters for dinner, a rare offer which, of course, they both accepted. The chef had laid on a sumptuous seafood buffet at Franklin's request and the three of them were working their way through a starter of blinis smothered with beluga caviar. No one dared mention Franklin's mysterious trip – it was as though it had never happened.

Franklin contentedly reached across the table for a massive lobster claw, broke it open with a cracker, which he swapped for a stainless-steel pick, and set about scooping out the juicy meat.

'This is going to be our last night on the boat for a while, so enjoy the feast. We leave at sunrise tomorrow and the food provided by our hosts in Gaza will not be Michelin-star level, believe me.'

Franklin laughed at his own joke before taking a large swig of chilled Montrachet from his wine glass. Deshi had no intention of ever returning to *The Little Fox*; her plan was to help with the attack and then take out Vargas, after which she would disappear, but for now she needed to keep Franklin happy and so tried to keep the mood light with small talk.

'Mr Franklin, no doubt we'll be sleeping in canvas bags rather than on Egyptian cotton sheets?'

'Yes, my dear, I suspect you're correct.'

Deshi scrambled for something else to keep the conversation going. Her eyes lighted on the yacht's name etched on the dinner plate.

'Why did you call the boat *The Little Fox*?'

Daniel expected Franklin to ignore her but, surprisingly, he engaged and sprung to life.

'It's a tribute to my grandfather, the Führer. In 1915, during the First World War, he was serving in the Bavarian Army as a sergeant in Belgium when a stray dog befriended him in the trenches. They became inseparable and my grandfather affectionately called him Fuchsl, his little fox. He taught him many tricks, so much so he described him as a circus dog. He was heartbroken when Fuchsl died. It was the start of the Führer's lifelong passion for dogs, which many of his contemporaries believed he loved far more than humans. His farmhouse in El Calafate was named El Blondi after his beloved Alsatian.'

Daniel had stopped eating and hung on every word his half-brother uttered. He'd never heard the story before and kicked himself for not having asked the question. Franklin drained his glass and rose from the table, indicating dinner was over.

'Sleep well, as I need you both fully focused. In a few days we'll be creating our own 9/11.'

\* \* \*

The flight time to Gaza was just over seven hours. For Daniel and Deshi, it was their first visit to the State of Palestine. Franklin had returned every year since 2011 and always stayed as a house guest of Khaled Shomani, the enigmatic leader of the PJB's military wing. The two men were allies in every sense of the word and had been plotting the upcoming operation together for the previous three years.

Shomani's house was a converted old cinema that had been closed down by Hamas shortly after they gained political power back in June 2007. He shared it with his two brothers and their families. It was hidden away in the heart of the Old City, close to the Great Mosque, the largest and oldest in Gaza, and was surrounded by bumpy roads and dusty buildings, many damaged from recent Israeli bomb attacks.

The convoy from the airstrip transported Franklin and his acolytes along the main drag, Omar Al Mukhtar, past the Square of Unknown Soldiers to the edge of Al Zawya street market, where the car journey finished. From there, an armed escort of four militia led them down a narrow side road where they entered the building via a black steel door, partially hidden by a wooden market stall.

Shomani was standing in the centre of a huge ornately designed living room, formerly the stalls area of the cinema. He was accompanied by his two brothers, standing next to him, as well as three other men, all dressed in matching black thobes, who sat on low wooden chairs to his right. A large grey marble dining table, laden with food, dominated the main area and was set for nine. Shomani had laid on a traditional Palestinian buffet for his guests, comprising roast chicken, minced beef and spiced rice with toasted almonds, along with a selection of salads, flatbreads and dips.

He greeted Franklin like a brother and was equally courteous towards Daniel and Deshi, whom he was meeting for the first time. After introducing them to his two brothers, he led them across the room to the dining table where he took his customary place at the head and seated Franklin to his left and Daniel to his right, as guests of honour. Deshi took her place next to Daniel and Shomani's two brothers sat opposite them, while at the far end of the table the other three men, who'd not been introduced, took their places.

Just before they started the meal, Shomani rose from his seat and raised a glass goblet containing mint lemonade, a favourite

157

Palestinian soft drink. To the surprise of Daniel and Deshi, his English was impeccable, and his message was passionate and articulate.

'Welcome to my home and the home of my brothers, Malik and Yusuf. John, I trust and respect you as if you were a third brother and extend that trust to our two new guests sitting at my table. First, we eat, and then I'll take you through the operational plan in detail, step by step as, God willing, our day of destiny is approaching. We are about to create our own history, which will change geopolitics in this region forever.'

He paused and gestured towards the three men sitting at the far end of the table. 'These soldiers don't understand English but deserve our gratitude and praise as they're the martyrs who will carry out the key attack on behalf of our cause. Until then, like you, they are guests in my house and will enjoy all the comforts I can offer. They are committed suicide bombers – warriors who have pledged their lives to Allah. I will explain their specific roles later but for now they deserve a toast. The word is pronounced *In Shaa Allah*, which means, If God Wills.'

They stood and raised their goblets, reciting the toast as best they could. The recipients acknowledged the gesture and then turned their attention to the food. The feast went down well and conversation flowed. Shomani's brothers also spoke pretty good English, if not to his level, but Franklin was edgy, restless, itching to get the meal out the way so they could get down to business.

Two female servants were clearing away some of the empty platters and replacing them with baskets of pastries and cakes when Franklin leaned across to Shomani and dropped his voice to a whisper.

'Khaled, can we speak privately before you begin the briefing?'

Shomani nodded and led them into a small dimly lit corridor that ran off the main open-plan living area. Franklin, as ever, cut straight to the point.

'Can we hold the briefing without your brothers present? We're just days away now and the fewer people who know the specific details the better. For their own sakes, it might be preferable if—'

Shomani's eyes flashed with anger. At that moment, it was apparent why he was one of the most feared men in Gaza. The tone of his voice was a warning shot.

'John, you insult my brothers' integrity, therefore you insult me. I thought you respected me more than this. Maybe you and your friends should leave right now and I'll carry out the attack without you. There is no bigger offence you could give than to imply my family can't be trusted.'

Franklin realised he'd made a bad call and tried to reel Shomani back in.

'Khaled, forgive me. My ignorant remark simply reflects the enormity of what lies ahead of us and my fear of something going wrong. I apologise sincerely and welcome your brothers as my family.'

He offered his hand in friendship; the Saudi accepted the gesture and the two men embraced. Franklin immediately regretted his impromptu comment and realised he'd let his natural suspicions get the better of him yet again. Ironically, as things turned out, he should have stood firm and trusted his instincts.

# Chapter Thirty

Gaza Strip, Gaza City

Yusuf Mohamed Shomani was the eldest of the three Saudi brothers who shared a home in Gaza City. They had all grown up with the trappings of wealth, power and privilege. The brothers were educated in England and then politically radicalised in South Lebanon, where they fell under the influence of a fanatical imam who recruited them to a military training camp based in the mountains in the north of the country. Yusuf soon discovered he was not cut out to be a soldier, neither was his brother Malik, but their younger sibling, Khaled, embraced military life from the very first moment he picked up a weapon. He was uncannily talented with a gun and proved himself to be a fearless killer, who scythed a path through the ranks like a knife through butter.

In contrast, Yusuf and Malik both focused their attention on the political wing of the Palestinian Justice Brigade, where they soon progressed up the ladder, becoming leading fundraisers for the terrorist group, raising millions of dollars from Iran and Syria.

In 2010, the same year Khaled became leader of the military wing of the PJB, Yusuf became the president of the ruling council, with Malik as his deputy. Without question, the Shomani brothers were rapidly becoming the most powerful and influential family inside the organisation and were respected and feared by friends and enemies alike.

Yusuf was a bitter man, though, who resented his baby brother's meteoric rise to power, along with the glamour and acclaim that came with being the PJB's military leader. As the organisation's president, Yusuf enjoyed the status and privilege it provided, but the Palestinian people didn't give a damn about their politicians; they idolised their military heroes, who led the ongoing fight against Israel. In addition, Khaled had fathered three sons, while Yusuf's wife had only produced two girls, another cause of bitter resentment and envy.

In the end, the motive for betraying his brother wasn't money – he'd more than he'd ever need – nor indeed blackmail – he had no skeletons in his cupboard. It was the oldest reason in the world: jealousy – an emotion that had eaten him up for the last decade and had become insatiable.

By chance, a few months earlier, he and the justice minister for the Palestinian Authority that governed the West Bank had travelled to Kabul for a covert meeting with their Taliban counterparts. Over dinner, he'd heard an incredible story featuring the disgraced US presidential candidate, John Franklin, who'd betrayed the Taliban leadership. Consequently, the supreme leader had offered a bounty on the American's head of five million dollars. Yusuf wasn't interested in the money but could suddenly see an opportunity to embarrass his brother and scupper his plans. The reality was, the outrageous plot against Israel his brother was planning with Franklin could potentially make Khaled as famous and as popular as Bin Laden and, to Yusuf, that would be unbearable.

At dinner with the Taliban leaders, he'd casually let slip he might be able to supply information about Franklin's whereabouts, and as a result was given a hotline to Abbas Turabi, head of international security for the Taliban regime. A few weeks earlier, Yusuf had heard his brother on a Zoom with Franklin discussing an upcoming trip to Florence and he'd tipped Turabi off. The Taliban's kidnap attempt had failed in Italy, but this time around he'd been able to give them far more notice because Khaled had informed him about the timings of Franklin's visit to Gaza a while ago.

Yusuf's bitter resentment of his brother had reached fever pitch, and in a moment of rage, he raised the stakes with the Taliban regime: he agreed to give them the exact location where Franklin could be picked up in Gaza City if, as part of the kidnap, his brother was taken out as well. There was no love lost between the supreme leader of the Taliban and the head of the military wing of the PJB, so a deal was struck. In one brief phone call, Yusuf sold Franklin and his younger brother down the river to the devil in Afghanistan.

He also took out a perverted insurance policy in the event things didn't go as planned. He deleted Turabi's contact on his cell, and in an opportunistic moment, added it to the contacts on his brother Malik's phone under the innocuous ID of 'Amir'. He knew full well that if the number were to be checked, it would be traced to Kabul, which would be evidence enough to condemn his brother as the informer.

He knew Khaled planned to take Franklin and his guests to their cousin's restaurant in Palestine Square for lunch the next day and that was where the strike would take place. He'd be present but would arrange for Malik to be detained and miss the lunch, which would immediately place him under a spotlight of suspicion.

\* \* \*

Yusuf sat at the dining table, pretending to hang on every word his brother spoke as he outlined the plan for Operation Atonement. He'd heard it all before. If all went well the following day, it would remain just a clever plan that would never come to fruition. And if it all went to shit, his other brother Malik would have to be sacrificed to protect his own position.

Khaled's charisma was undeniable, as was the brilliance of his strategic military brain, which held Daniel and Deshi mesmerised when he enlightened them on the workings of the planned attack. He began the briefing with a question.

'What do you know about the Great Synagogue in Jerusalem?'

Before anyone could reply he answered his own question.

'It's the largest Jewish prayer house in Israel and once a year, on Yom Kippur, the prime minister pays a brief visit and it transforms into a fortress. Mossad take over the security and place a ring of steel around it with heavily armed soldiers guarding the entrance and patrolling the perimeter. Inside, plain-clothes agents mingle with members of the congregation. We don't know exactly how many, but we estimate at least thirty. Mobile anti-ballistic missiles are positioned in the grounds and, above, helicopter gunships control the airspace. Basically, on that one day of the year, the synagogue becomes impregnable . . . But is it?'

Daniel was intrigued and couldn't keep quiet.

'From that description, I'd say so, yeah. But looking at the smug smile on John's face, I guess we're about to learn it's not.'

Khaled looked towards Franklin.

'John, would you like to educate your brother?'

'No, you're doing just fine, Khaled. It's your ball game.'

Shomani nodded and continued.

'There's huge demand for parking spaces in Jerusalem – they're like gold dust. So, three years ago, thanks to John's funding, we moved into the car park business. Under the umbrella of a respected Muslim company, we bought a small underground facility in Akhad ha'Am Street, as well as a large run-down supermarket that adjoined it. The buildings are located just six hundred yards south of 56 King George Street, the location of the synagogue. The car park has two storeys above ground and two beneath, with eighty spaces on each level. As part of a development scheme, the underground floors are being extended in size, creating sixty new spaces on each level, using the footprint underneath the supermarket, which is also being knocked down to expand the upper levels. But that's not all we've been building.'

Shomani paused and reached for his laptop on the table beside him. He flipped it open and found the appropriate file, before turning it around to face his audience. The first page was split into six images showing various angles of what looked like a state-of-the-art tunnel.

'We based the design on the remarkable tunnel the Mexican drug cartel built to break out the drug lord El Chapo from prison in 2015 – although that was almost a mile long, three times the length of ours. But in engineering terms, it's quite similar. It runs off a sewer tunnel that already exists beneath the street and heads directly west towards King George Street. Of course, we're constructing the car park as well, which gives our work the perfect cover. Every day, we ship in labourers from the West Bank who are split into two teams, one builds the car park, the other the tunnel.'

Shomani clicked on a new file that showed a video of a square steel bucket running on rails, travelling through the tunnel with a man kneeling inside. From the footage it appeared incredibly straight and well illuminated by ceiling lights positioned every six feet.

'Four months ago, we completed the build and broke through into a disused cellar underneath the rear of the syna-gogue. It was partially flooded and contained old prayer books and some random artworks. The lighting was out, and the water level was about three feet. Stone steps lead up to a wooden trapdoor that appears as though it hasn't been opened for years, possibly decades. Every Sunday evening, the building is closed to the public, and that's the only time we've dared enter the cellar. I went myself about five weeks ago with our three martyrs so they could get a sense of the underground journey that awaits them.'

Daniel shook his head in disbelief.

'Khaled, it's incredible. It's beyond belief the Israelis haven't got wind of it. For a start, so many workers must know of its existence.'

'True – but, firstly, they're loyal PJB supporters and would rather die than betray us and, secondly, they've no idea where the tunnel leads or why we're building it. They're just happy to get paid well and to be helping our cause. As far as the Israelis are concerned, Jerusalem is one huge building site

– excavations, renovations and new builds are happening all across the city and the last thing on their mind is the creation of a tunnel.'

Deshi was fascinated by the detail of the works but wanted to know more about the role the three fighters sitting at the end of the table would play.

'How will the attack work?'

'We've obtained a copy of the architectural plans from 1982 when the synagogue was completed. They show that the steps from the cellar lead to the basement where there's a staircase up to a corridor on the ground floor. The rabbi's private quarters are off this and a door on the other side of his office takes you into a hallway leading to an entrance into the far east corner at the rear of the main prayer hall. All three soldiers will have twenty pounds of explosives strapped to their bodies and the detonators will be in their right hands. Each bomb will be packed with nails, ball bearings and other metal fragments to maximise casualties. We know they'll be taken down by Mossad agents, but as each soldier dies, their hand will automatically release the trigger, so their deaths as martyrs will detonate the bombs. We hope at least one of them can get close enough to the prime minister's seat to ensure he dies in the explosion. And so, finally, we will have achieved our lifelong ambition – we will have cut off the head of the snake.'

Franklin rose from his seat and began an applause that was taken up by Daniel, Deshi and Khaled's two brothers. Yusuf's face beamed with a huge smile but for far different reasons to everybody else at the table.

# Chapter Thirty-One

Gaza City, Gaza Strip

The floor-to-ceiling windows of the Skycap restaurant eleven storeys above Gaza City offered its diners incredible views of the city that were further enhanced by the stunning backdrop of the Mediterranean Sea. Down below, most citizens relied on basic food banks provided by the United Nations for survival – the World Bank having ranked Gaza as having the highest unemployment rate in the world. But for a handful of privileged people, the fifty-dollar-a-head set lunch was a luxury to be savoured. As well as serving specialities such as chicken legs dressed with thinly sliced hot green peppers, lemon and garlic, Skycap was the only restaurant in the city to also offer international cuisine such as chicken Caesar salad and club sandwiches.

Regular diners included senior directors of NGOs, government ministers, police chiefs and the head of the PJB's military wing, Khaled Shomani, whose first cousin, Gabri, owned the place.

Shomani was seated at his customary table, which ran alongside the panoramic centre window, along with Franklin,

Daniel, Deshi and Yusuf. Waiters were buzzing around taking drinks orders and Daniel was in deep conversation with his brother and Khaled.

'Last night, I thought a great deal more about the tunnel – it's a genius one-way ticket into the most guarded building in Jerusalem, but, John, I couldn't help thinking about the irony of building a tunnel. Your entire life would be so different had it not been for three small-time crooks who had the same idea back in 2012.'

Franklin's expression gave way to a rueful smile.

'Daniel, of course that thought has struck me many times, but had I become president, I could never have been this hands-on with such a hugely important operation. The fact that most of the world thinks I'm dead allows me a priceless freedom to move around. So, in many ways, I owe those scoundrels a debt of gratitude.'

Further down the table, Yusuf was on the phone to Malik, who'd been held up by an unexpected meeting with a senior minister, which Yusuf had engineered, but was now on his way to the restaurant and less than fifteen minutes away. Yusuf ended the call and checked his watch – it was three minutes before midday. It would all be over well before his brother arrived.

The main lift opened directly onto the restaurant floor and at twelve o'clock precisely, the doors slid open to reveal four Taliban fighters armed with M4 fully automatic rifles capable of unloading seven hundred 5.56mm rounds per minute.

The leader of the group raced forward, urgently searching for Shomani who was partially blocked from view by Daniel seated opposite him. Their plan was to execute the PJB leader, kidnap Franklin and be in and out within sixty seconds. Below, a getaway van was running hot outside the front of the building. Gunfire rang out inside the restaurant and petrified diners let out horrified screams as they desperately scrambled for cover behind upturned tables.

But the opening shots didn't come from the armed intruders. Gabri, Shomani's cousin, was behind the bar when he saw them exit the lift and he began spraying rounds at the uninvited intruders to his eatery from an AK-47, a gift from one of his regular patrons he kept mounted on the wall just for show. Gabri was a restaurateur, not a soldier, and most of the rounds he fired went astray, destroying thousands of pounds of lavish decor, except for one that hit its target, blowing away the kneecap of a fighter who yelled an Afghan curse before sliding to the floor, clutching his leg in agony.

The other three Taliban fighters immediately opened fire, even though they were under strict orders to capture Franklin unharmed and only kill Shomani, but the element of surprise was no longer with them – now it was about survival.

Shots were aimed at Shomani's window table and innocent diners in the line of fire were shown no mercy. Shomani dived to the ground and rolled across the wooden floor in a tight ball while reaching for his Glock 19 semi-automatic pistol, its magazine loaded with thirty-three rounds. He figured he'd only need four.

The actual firefight lasted less than thirty seconds as three headshots took care of the Taliban leader and two of his sidekicks. Gabri finished off the fourth attacker, who was a sitting target writhing on the floor, peppering his body with more than twenty rounds.

The screams continued until people realised the shooting had finished, and then started up again as the full horror of the carnage could be seen for real. Over a dozen bodies of innocent customers were strewn across the floor, some providing human cushions for the black-turbaned slain gunmen.

Shomani rose to his feet to survey the wreckage, adrenaline pumping through his veins. He wondered what the hell four Taliban fighters were doing in his favourite restaurant, but before he could begin to answer the question, he heard a haunting cry coming from behind the long table he'd been sitting at, which was now turned on its side.

He moved across and his body stiffened at the sight of Franklin kneeling over Daniel's body, which seemed at first sight to be untouched, except the crown of his head was missing. Deshi was on the floor next to them, propping them both up, her white T-shirt drenched by the blood fountain that was spurting from the cavity at the top of Daniel's skull.

Yusuf was huddled on the floor a few feet away, shaking with terror but unharmed from the shoot-out, wondering how long it would be before Khaled worked out he'd been betrayed. The answer was six hours. When the Kabul phone number was found in Malik's contacts, Khaled slit his older brother's throat while Yusuf watched him protest his innocence until his dying breath.

# Chapter Thirty-Two

Washington D.C., United States

It was Hembury's first day back at work since being discharged from hospital. He and Vargas were sitting together in a temporary office provided by Berrettini inside the Bureau's main headquarters on Pennsylvania Avenue. His face looked a lot worse than it felt. It was still puffy and bruised from the surgical procedures he'd undergone in the care of the military medical centre. He was fine about it, but Vargas wouldn't leave it alone.

'How's the Elephant Man feeling today? There must be some advantages to the cool beaten-up look, but right now I can't see any.'

'Thanks, Nic. Just the kind of support I would expect from my best—'

They were interrupted by Berrettini, who burst into the room, laptop in hand, as though it were surgically attached. He was clearly energised and had the look of a man who'd just lost a dime and found a fifty-dollar bill. In one swift movement he opened the MacBook, powered it up and gestured to them to sit down either side of him so they could see the screen.

'This is a breaking news item that aired on CNN about an hour ago. We heard about it late last night, so I can update you on the story, but first I want you to see the pictures. Take a look.'

He clicked on a link that displayed a three-minute film, recorded off-air. A young female reporter was standing outside the Memorial Medical Center in Maui, Hawaii. The story involved a near fatal attack on Caroline Bush, the former wife of John Franklin, the disgraced presidential candidate. She was in a coma, in a grave condition, with little hope of recovery following an assault from an intruder who'd broken into her house. The item concluded with a shot of her son, Bill, parking up in a red Bronco and walking through the small car park to the hospital entrance surrounded by a gang of reporters and photographers. Hembury was first to react.

'Christ, I'd forgotten all about her and the boy. He could only have been about twelve when Franklin disappeared. He looks like a younger, identical version of his father. What do we know about the attack?'

Berrettini was pumped and ready to go.

'After the scandal, Caroline became a recluse, which is hardly surprising. A few months after it died down, she moved, lock stock and barrel, to a small town named Makawao on the Hawaiian island of Maui. For the last eleven years, she's raised her son Bill, pretty much living in obscurity, until now. Two days ago, she was attacked in her home where friends found her unconscious, just minutes after the assailant left. She had wounded her attacker with a bread knife during the assault

– there was a huge amount of blood splatter at the crime scene, none of which belonged to her. And here's the juicy bit, a few hours ago one of our agents arrived on the island and is working closely with the police department. He's just emailed me the result of a DNA test on the blood at the crime scene. It belongs to John Franklin.'

Vargas sat back in his chair and shook his head.

'What the hell was he doing there? We know he's got something major in the works, so why pick this moment to reappear in his wife's life and try to kill her?'

Hembury broke in.

'Mike, none of it makes sense – it's not how he operates. And what about the blood ID? Does this mean the Hawaiian police are about to inform the world that John Franklin never really killed himself and is alive and well, bar a bread-knife wound? That would be a disaster for us.'

'No, we've got that under wraps for now. However, in the long run, who knows? But there's more. A silver Mercedes S-Class was spotted near the house around the time of the attack, and as there are only two on the island it wasn't hard to trace. It turns out it was hired by a private detective agency on behalf of a visiting client. Anyway, when the police interviewed the owner of the company, he pulled the client confidentiality crap, but that all changed when he realised the Feds were involved.'

Vargas had left his chair and was pacing around the office.

'I still don't get it – why risk exposing his existence to the world – for what?'

'Hopefully we're about to find out. We've two Zooms coming up. The first is a two-hander with the owner of the detective agency and the man who drove Franklin around the island, and—'

Hembury interrupted.

'And the second?'

'The second is with Adolf Hitler's sole surviving great-grandson.'

\* \* \*

Lee Chong had the look of a worried man. He'd run his small private detective agency for twenty-two years on the island of Maui without any serious run-ins with the authorities, and now here he was sitting in a tiny interview room in a local police station about to be interviewed by the deputy director of the FBI, two and a half thousand miles away in his Washington office. Somehow, he'd got mixed up in a possible murder attempt and he knew the Bureau had the power to shut him down if they weren't happy with his level of cooperation. He had the feeling a shit day was just about to get a great deal worse.

Chong was a Goliath, large-framed and seriously overweight – the result of far too many business lunches with prospective clients. His soccer-ball-shaped, olive-skinned face had almost caved in on itself and was framed by a mop of greasy black hair. His three chins meant he had no obvious neck, so his huge head just seemed to wobble on top of his shoulders. When he spoke, he had a surprisingly high-pitched voice for such a big man. He told everyone he was in his mid-fifties but was actually sixty-two, and at that precise moment, he felt every one of those years. He'd donned his best suit and tie for the meeting and his shirt buttons were straining at the challenge of staying in place around his enormous girth.

When he first saw the Zoom image on the computer screen, he felt his bowels loosen. He hadn't realised he'd be facing three interrogators, not just one. He tried to smile but wasn't sure his mouth muscles were cooperating and ended up pulling a dumb expression. Sitting next to him was Tom Cooper, a much younger man, who'd been Franklin's driver for his short but eventful visit to the island. Cooper was far more relaxed and genuinely excited at being the focus of such a huge story. He was casually dressed in a pair of denim cut-offs matched with a blue-patterned Hawaiian shirt that reflected his laid-back approach to the whole episode, which he was determined to enjoy. For a few hours at least, he'd become a local celebrity, which would definitely be worth a night of free drinks in his local bar.

Berrettini swiftly introduced Vargas and Hembury and began the questions.

'Mr Chong, tell us about your client who visited the island a couple of days ago.'

Chong stuttered a reply.

'W-what do you w-want to know?'

'Everything, so please don't waste our time. This incident could have a direct bearing on an imminent terrorist threat to the United States, so tell us everything you can and if it gets boring, I'll let you know.'

'His name is Brad Wolf. He's an American businessman who first retained our services eleven years ago. He wanted—'

Vargas interrupted straightaway.

'How did he contact you – was it in person?

'No, it was all done by phone and email. I've never actually met the man, not even on Zoom. He commissioned us to begin a long-term surveillance on Mrs Bush and her son, Bill, and report every month on their comings and goings. I must admit, I thought it was odd, but he said he'd pay triple our normal rate, as long as we remained discreet.'

Hembury whispered to his two colleagues.

'Par for the course. Classic Franklin, throwing money around like confetti.'

Chong couldn't hear the comment but paused, curious if he'd given them what they wanted. Berrettini glared at the screen.

'Continue, Mr Chong. Were you aware of Mrs Bush's background?'

'Yes, of course, but it was a good job and, besides, all Wolf wanted was surveillance – no contact with the subjects, so I didn't really have a problem with it. I expected it to fizzle out, to be honest, when the reports got thin and boring. Not a lot happens on the island.'

He stopped for a moment to reflect.

'Well, not normally . . . not until two days ago.'

'Go on.'

'He emailed a week ago to say he was coming to the island for a four-hour visit. He was prescriptive about the timings. I offered to meet him but he insisted we supply a driver aged twenty-five or younger, and that no one from the agency should be involved. He also specified an S-Class to take him around the island.'

Berrettini cut in.

'Mr Cooper, you were the driver. Tell us what happened.'

Unlike his one-time employer he didn't need to be asked twice. He loved the spotlight, and it soon became apparent he'd been captivated by the powerful man he'd chauffeured around the island for a few hours. Cooper delivered a blow-by-blow account of Franklin's visit, concluding by relating how quickly he'd reacted, contacting a local doctor in Kahului who'd come to the airfield and applied stitches to an open wound on his client's arm. He seemed far too pleased with himself and was clearly enamoured of Franklin. Berrettini was apoplectic with rage and let rip with a barrage of questions.

'Jesus, man, did it not occur to you a crime had just taken place – a possible murder? Are you a total moron? Why the hell didn't you inform the police?'

Even though he was two and a half thousand miles away, Cooper reeled back in his chair and all three of Chong's chins wobbled from the impact of the verbal blast. Cooper continued to shoot himself in the foot as he struggled to defend his actions.

'He seemed a good man to me. He told me he'd cut himself by accident inside the house and I believed him. And then there was the tip . . . I'd never seen a hundred-dollar bill before, and he gave me ten of them.'

# Chapter Thirty-Three

Washington D.C., United States

'What's the bastard up to?'

Vargas voiced the single thought they all shared.

Berrettini glanced down at his watch.

'Look, we've got thirty minutes before we talk to Franklin's son. Hopefully, that might throw up a few answers. Before that, there's something on my mind I want to float with you guys. You may not like it – especially you, Troy.'

Hembury looked bemused but nodded as a gesture for the FBI deputy director to continue.

'We all know how Franklin works. He's an arch manipulator, a control freak who plans every move way ahead, always hiding in the shadows. But whatever happened in Hawaii tells us one important fact – he sometimes acts on impulse, because there's no way he would have planned such a clumsy murder attempt on his wife. His MO tells us he'd have paid for a hitman to take her out and ensure he was nowhere near the scene. So we need to tap into that impulsive, reckless side of his brain. We need a way to flush him out into the open.'

Hembury smiled.

'I'm liking it so far, Mike – what's the idea?'

'Okay, here goes. We use you as a human hand grenade. Right now, Franklin thinks you're dead – blown to a million pieces by the explosion in the cottage in Rockville. So, it's time to rattle his cage, inject some self-doubt into that sick brain of his. Troy, I'm proposing we go public with you front and centre of the story. We issue a press release to the media, announcing that the head of the White House internal security team was kidnapped by an unknown terrorist group and reveal how the FBI facilitated your rescue due to the help of an insider working for the kidnappers.'

Vargas got it straightaway and turned towards Hembury.

'Troy, I like this. It offers two ways to get under Franklin's skin. He'll be furious to hear you're alive and totally pissed he's been lied to by his own people, and then he'll set the dogs on our mysterious friend who saved your ass. Whoever that guy is, we need to track him down first and be waiting.'

Berrettini cut back in.

'Nic's right, Troy. The only question is, how do you feel about putting yourself out there as a public figure?'

Hembury smiled ruefully.

'I get it, and I'm happy to be a sacrificial lamb if it helps smoke the bastard out. The sooner the better.'

* * *

Bill Bush was sitting next to his mother's hospital bed on the third floor of the Memorial Medical Center in Wailuku. She was heavily wired to a bank of machines, including an ECMO, which was keeping her alive, constantly throwing out green neon numbers, some of which occasionally dropped into the red zone.

Caroline was in a deep coma, having suffered a traumatic head wound and a stroke, meaning her survival chances were rated one out of a possible ten by the consultant who was treating her. A critical care nurse was adjusting plastic pouches of propofol and glucose that were being fed into veins in her right hand.

Bill was in turmoil, struggling to process the life-changing events of the previous forty-eight hours. It appeared as though he was about to lose a mother and gain a father he'd believed was dead. Right now, the grief and distress were more than he could handle. The door of the ICU room opened and an FBI agent appeared in the doorway.

'Mr Bush, the deputy director is ready to talk with you on the link. Please follow me, we've a private room set up downstairs.'

Berrettini had decided to handle the delicate interview on his own but, unknown to Bill, Vargas and Hembury were present, positioned just out of shot of the laptop camera. Bill's blue eyes were stained red and his greasy hair and beard growth combined to tell the story of a distraught man who hadn't washed or shaved for a couple of days. He was still in the suit he'd been wearing when his father had surprised him, although the tie had long gone, and his white cotton shirt was unbuttoned at the neck. Berrettini kicked off the interview with a gentle inquiry.

'Mr Bush, I appreciate this is an awful time for you. How is your mother doing? What's the latest?'

'She's being kept alive by machines – so not great.'

'I'm very sorry to hear that, but where's there's life there's hope.'

Bill shrugged and nervously adjusted his shirt collar.

'Mr Bush, have you any idea why your father came to the island and attacked her?'

Bill remained silent for a few seconds, although his eyes darted around the room like a couple of pinballs.

'How do you know it was my father?'

Berrettini played the game, even though he knew Bill had seen Franklin in person two days earlier.

'He left his calling card all over the house. The blood splatter matched his DNA, so there's no doubt he was there.'

'Mr Berrettini, you don't seem surprised by that. How long have you known my father was alive? And please don't lie to me.'

The FBI deputy director accepted the rebuke and continued.

'About eighteen months, give or take. Now, why do you think he attacked your mother? Why did he come to the island? Was it the first time you'd seen him since 2012 or had he visited before?'

Bill remained defensive.

'I never said I saw him. As far as I was concerned, he was dead. What do you want from me?'

Berrettini was clearly irritated by Bill's surly attitude and moved up a gear.

'Mr Bush, I really haven't got the time to waste playing games with you. I've just interviewed the man who drove your father around the island, so I know you spent twenty minutes together in the car park close to your office. What did you discuss?'

A much longer period of silence ensued before Bill opened up.

'I'd just finished work and had walked to my car when he appeared out of thin air. Up to that moment, I'd thought the bastard was dead. When I got over the shock, I told him to leave me alone, but I'd absolutely no idea he planned to visit my mother. Had I known, I'd have done everything in my power to stop him.'

'What did he want, Bill? Why did he come, and do you know where he's hiding out?'

'He wanted me to agree to spend some time with him soon. He kept saying how he wanted to prove he'd been unfairly persecuted because of his birthright. Basically, he spouted a ton load of bullshit.'

Berrettini saw an opening.

'When you say he wanted you to spend time with him – why didn't he ask you to go straightaway?'

'He said he wanted me to wait, that something big was going down soon – something world-changing.'

Berrettini's gaze switched from the computer screen to Vargas and Hembury, who acknowledged the look with a nod.

'What did he say about it?'

'Nothing. I told you exactly what he said – he didn't tell me what it was. Now, can I go back and spend some time with my mother, while I still have her?'

'One last question, for now. Did he give you some way of contacting him in the future – an email or a cell number?'

For a split second Bill thought about the burner phone his father had left with him. 'No, he just said he'd be in touch.'

For the briefest of moments, he'd glanced away from the screen and then resumed eye contact. A classic tell he was lying that all three men at the other end of the Zoom picked up on.

# Chapter Thirty-Four

Kahului, Hawaii

The fourth-floor flat on Vevau Street was in an apartment block owned by First Hawaiian Bank, located no more than a three-minute walk from its main office. The small studios were a perk offered to staff who might have occasion to work late at night.

Bill opened the door to number twenty-four, the faithful bolthole he sometimes used for one-night stands, but mainly as a sanctuary to hide away, when he couldn't face going home to his mother and just needed to be alone.

Once inside, he flopped onto the solitary sofa bed and tried to gather his thoughts. It had been an intense forty-eight hours and Bill wasn't quite sure what to make of it all. He felt inside his suit jacket and pulled out the cell his father had given him, throwing it down onto the carpeted floor. He wondered why he'd lied to the FBI and wasn't sure of the answer. It was simply that a rogue voice inside his head had warned him against betraying his father, even though he felt no loyalty to him whatsoever.

He rose and grabbed a beer from the blue Smeg in the tiny

open-plan kitchen and walked across to a wooden tea-chest in the far corner of the room, beneath the solo window inside the flat. He opened the lid and peered inside at dozens of scrap-books that had sat untouched for many years, gathering dust. Leaning down, he picked up the top one and moved across the room to a small plastic-topped table and sat down on one of the two chairs either side of it. He flicked open the cover and stared at a front page of *The New York Times* carrying a colour headshot of his father alongside a black-and-white photo of Adolf Hitler. The banner headline proclaimed, 'the Counterfeit Candidate Exposed'. Bill's instinct was to close the book, but he fought against it and began scanning the copy below the photos.

He spent several hours reading through the content of the scrapbooks and then moved on to a hardback biography buried in the bottom of the chest, *Hitler: A Study in Tyranny*, by Alan Bullock. He consumed the pages at a ferocious rate, and just after four in the morning, gave in to an overwhelming tired-ness and drifted into an exhausted sleep.

A few minutes later, a nagging voice in his brain forced him awake and Bill returned to the chest, pulled out a specific scrapbook and flicked through it until he found the article he was looking for. It was a feature in the *San Francisco Chronicle* and his eyes zeroed in on the text he'd read a few hours earlier, 'Nature or nurture? John Franklin's twelve-year old son Bill has Adolf Hitler's blood running through his veins. As his only great-grandson – which way will he go?'

\* \* \*

'Troy, are you okay to get going with this?'

Elizabeth Oakley, senior press officer for the White House, patted Hembury on the shoulder as she stood alongside him in a main corridor outside the media briefing room. She cut a striking figure with her shoulder-length platinum-blond hair, sparkling hazel eyes and oval face, combined with a catwalk body. She'd held down the prestigious post for two years and knew Hembury well because of his significant role inside the building as head of internal security.

'Let's get on with it, Liz. There's someone out there who'll be watching this broadcast whose skin I well and truly need to get under.'

The press conference was well attended by a mix of print journalists and TV reporters who'd had no idea why it had been called, and there was a buzz of excitement and expectation inside the room as Oakley and Hembury entered.

The pair told a carefully edited version of Hembury's kidnapping by an unnamed terrorist group and his subsequent dramatic rescue by an FBI task force. Very little detail was offered up, and for the journalists present it was an extremely bizarre briefing because, usually, security threats of that nature were never revealed to them, let alone the public.

Hembury took questions and remained deliberately vague with his answers, except on one specific point. As he made eye contact with the lens of a CBS News camera, he visualised that somewhere in the world Franklin would be watching a television screen, and in his mind, his words were being delivered to him and him alone.

'The terrorists behind my kidnapping realised the US government would never accede to their demands and decided to cut their losses and take my life. My last-minute rescue by the FBI was due to the remarkable bravery of an insider who was prepared to betray their cause and put their own life on the line to save mine.'

Hembury stood as a signal to the reporters in the room that the interview was over. He turned to walk away, but one of the newshounds shouted out a final follow-up question.

'Mr Hembury – was it a man or a woman?'

He searched for a TV camera lens before answering.

'I need to protect their identity, so that's a question I won't answer.'

Hembury hoped the ambiguity in his reply would create a tsunami of doubt in the twisted mind of the greatest control freak he'd ever come across. He'd intentionally put both his kidnappers in the firing line and hoped the uncertainty created would result in Franklin making another impulsive mistake.

# Chapter Thirty-Five

Gaza City, Gaza Strip

Shomani's house had been transformed into a mini fortress, with PJB soldiers patrolling the perimeter of the former cinema as well as the interior. Inside, Daniel was laid out on a massage table in one of the bedrooms, where two male servants were diligently washing his naked body. In the corner of the main living area, Franklin and Shomani were alone, sitting opposite each other on simple wooden chairs. Franklin's mood was dark. Daniel's death meant he was now on his own – the last surviving grandchild of the Führer and his only blood descendant, other than Bill, and he'd no idea where his son's head was at.

Shomani was running on a short fuse and had a number of burning questions for his American guest, but first needed to show respect to his friend for the loss of his younger brother.

'John, Sharia law dictates the burial of a body as soon as possible, preceded by a simple ritual involving bathing and shrouding the body in a white cloth.'

Franklin snarled, 'Daniel was no Muslim, Khaled. Like me, he was an atheist.'

'But he died in a Muslim country, in my care, and I hold the responsibility for his burial. The material for his shroud will be the finest available – the highest mark of respect I can offer him.'

Franklin nodded, his thoughts elsewhere, wondering why Shomani's brother had betrayed him and helped the Taliban track him down for a second time in a matter of weeks. It just didn't smell right, but he couldn't quite figure out what was behind the play that had cost his younger brother's life.

Shomani continued to lay out the details of Daniel's imminent funeral.

'The burial will take place in the morning at Sheikh Shaban cemetery, one of the few remaining in the city, as open land is a scarcity here due to the massive population problem. Daniel will have a ceremony fit for a martyr, despite his religious beliefs.'

Franklin was still distracted but managed a mumbled acknowledgement. Shomani then changed tack completely.

'John, we need to discuss the attack. Why did four Taliban fighters come to Gaza looking for you and try to take me down too?'

'What makes you think they were looking for me?'

'Don't demean our friendship, John. I'm not a fool.'

Shomani turned away and shouted a command to two men who were positioned at the far end of the vast room. They disappeared through a set of double doors and less than a minute later returned dragging the seemingly lifeless body of a young Arab across the mosaic-tiled floor. The prisoner was barely conscious. His face, testimony to a savage beating, was little more than a ruby red pulp, heavily bruised with deep gorges across the forehead and cheeks, while his eyes were badly swollen and closed. His torso was exposed and covered with open cuts; no doubt caused by multiple knife wounds. Shomani kept his eyes on the prisoner but spoke to Franklin.

'This man was waiting outside the front of the building where the attack took place, parked up in van. As they say in American movies, he was the getaway driver, except he didn't make it very far. Once the shooting started, two of my men patrolling the ground floor reception area saw him acting suspiciously. Any sane man would have driven away at the sound of gunfire, but he stayed put, presumably waiting for his friends to return from the restaurant. Less than an hour ago he confessed to my interrogators, but I want you to hear it for yourself. He's close to death, but I've kept him alive so you can hear what he has to say.'

The soldiers deposited the prisoner's body at Shomani's feet, and the terrorist leader knelt low to the ground until his face was only inches away from the mouth of the young Arab fighter. He addressed him respectfully in Arabic.

'Ghadi, if you want your body to be prepared for an honourable Muslim burial, you'll answer my questions truthfully. If you refuse, it'll be cut into tiny pieces and thrown into the Med for the sharks. I only have two questions and then I'll end the pain and keep my word.'

At first there was no reaction but then Franklin detected a slight nod of the head.

'Who sent you?'

The man's voice was a hollow whisper and Shomani had to

move even closer, so his right ear was almost touching the prisoner's mouth. His breathing was slow and heavy and his words only just audible.

'The supreme . . . leader.'

'What was your mission?'

'To . . . kill you . . . and bring . . . the American . . . to Kabul.'

Shomani translated the words and then withdrew a curved single-edged dagger from a red leather sheath around his waist and sliced the prisoner's throat with a skilful flourish. He stood and turned to look at Franklin, whose stony facial expression confirmed he wasn't surprised by the revelation.

'Come, John, it's late. In the morning we bury Daniel and after that you and I have much to discuss.'

* * *

The cemetery in downtown Gaza City was grim. Inside Sheikh Shaban, headstones had been randomly ripped out and large sections of the burial-ground had been built over with temporary corrugated housing erected by homeless squatters desperate for any piece of land they could lay their hands on. In the east quarter, an area reserved exclusively for deceased Palestinian fighters, it was a different story. This section, surrounded by a low wooden perimeter fence, showed no signs of vandalism whatsoever. Locals knew any appropriation of those graves would be seen as disrespectful to the PJB leadership and would inevitably lead to them joining the thousands of bodies buried under the earth.

Franklin stood in a tight group alongside Shomani, Yusuf and Deshi as the chief imam of the city read the short burial prayer. As was the case with all Muslim burials, the grave was laid perpendicular to Mecca and the body was placed on its right side to face the Islamic holy city. Strips of cypress wood provided a cushion between Daniel and the ground to prevent his body touching the dirt. Shomani knelt by the graveside and systematically poured three handfuls of soil on top of the corpse that was covered by a thin white shroud. He spoke the traditional funeral prayer in Arabic and then translated it for Franklin and Deshi, who followed suit.

'We created you from it, and return you into it, and from it we will raise you a second time.'

Franklin grimaced as he poured handfuls of earth onto Daniel's body and heard the splatter below. He was a man who believed emotional attachments were dangerous and should be avoided at all costs, but at that precise moment, he realised how close he'd become to his younger brother during the previous eighteen months, when they'd travelled the world together on his boat. Because of his birthright, Daniel had been the only man alive to truly understand the weight of destiny and expectation Franklin carried on his shoulders, and now he felt truly on his own.

But there was no time for reflection or regrets. He had to focus on the importance of the days that lay ahead. As the last pieces of dirt trickled through his fingers, he vowed to fulfil the Führer's pledge, made back in 1948 when the rogue Israeli state had been formed. As Hitler's last surviving grandson, he'd be the man to finally cut the head off the snake.

\* \* \*

Back at the house, Shomani led Franklin into a small basement room he hadn't previously visited. It was surprisingly Western in its decor, decked out with black Chesterfield sofas and armchairs, completely out of keeping with the rest of the former cinema's interior design. On one wall was a bank of mounted television screens, all muted and tuned to different world news services, and opposite them was a large black walnut desk that supported two computer terminals and a laptop. He gestured towards the armchairs and the two men sat opposite each other in front of the screens. Shomani poured them both a glass of mint tea and got straight down to business.

'John, I need to know the reason why the supreme leader of the Taliban wants to get his hands on you so badly. You told me about the campaign you conducted together in Israel, which came so close to succeeding, but why does he blame you for the Israeli reprisals?'

Franklin shifted in his chair and swigged a mouthful of hot tea before replying. 'Look, the supreme leader screwed up the operation. He insisted on sending along Akhtar Khairkhwa – the notorious Taliban fighter with a five-million-dollar price tag on his head, courtesy of the US military. The Israelis picked him up with their facial recognition system when we crossed the border from Jordan into Eilat. That simple mistake cost us the whole operation. Without that, we could have moved around Israel undetected.'

'What happened during the shoot-out at the desalination plant in Ashkelon, where it all went wrong?'

Franklin had ensured he was nowhere near the water processing plant when the shit had gone down. He was hiding out a hundred miles away in a quiet luxury hotel near Lake

Galilee when Mossad agents confronted the Taliban fighters. He'd never admitted that fact to anyone and had no choice but to defend his own lie.

'It was pretty bad, but like Khairkhwa I managed to escape just before the Israelis circled the plant. He made it back to Kabul and then, a few weeks later, the Israelis blew him and half the Taliban leadership into oblivion with a drone strike. I risked my life on that mission, alongside the Taliban, so I've no idea why that madman in Kabul blames me.'

Franklin smoothly delivered another lie without the hint of a tell. He knew the supreme leader blamed him for leaving his fighters exposed to Mossad at the Ashkelon desalination plant while he was nowhere to be seen. But he wasn't sure if Shomani believed him and instinctively tried to change the subject.

'Khaled, why did your brother betray me? First by revealing my location in Florence, and then right here in Gaza?'

Shomani glared back at Franklin at the mention of his older brother.

'Malik took that secret with him to the grave. I confess, his betrayal was a deep shock to me, and for once in my life I've no answer to a question that will haunt me forever.'

Shomani flipped open the lid of a small ornate ivory box resting on a side table by his chair. He lifted a Marlboro Red, lit up and inhaled deeply, maintaining eye contact all the while.

'John, the informer is dead and you're safe with me, but keep one thought in mind – I'm not the Taliban. Never lie to me, because there's plenty of room in our section of Sheikh Shaban for another plot.'

# Chapter Thirty-Six

Kabul, Afghanistan

Abbas Turabi, the head of international security for the Taliban, let rip at his assistant, Moosa Zafar, who'd run the disastrous kidnap operation in Gaza City. The two men were facing each other across a desk in what used to be the governor's office in Kabul, a former palace that now served as headquarters for the high command of the Taliban regime 2.0.

'It would appear as though the American infidel has a guardian angel. Our fighters have failed twice now to capture him, even though we had him in plain sight and, this time, we've created a dangerous enemy in the shape of Khaled Shomani. The entire operation was a catastrophe and your reckless decision to agree to Yusuf's demand to take his brother out will not end well for us. The supreme leader is incandescent with rage. The failed attack is a personal humiliation for him and now I'm tasked with picking up the pieces. I'll call Shomani myself and try to persuade him one of our fighters went rogue – that the sanctioned mission was only about capturing Franklin alive. I have permission to offer the supreme leader's word on this, as well as ten million dollars by way of an apology.'

Turabi stood to his feet, retrieved a Smith and Wesson revolver from under his thobe and aimed it directly at Zafar's forehead.

'Make no mistake, this fiasco should have cost you your life but you've one final chance to make good. Speak to Yusuf and threaten to expose his identity to Shomani unless he delivers us Franklin on a plate. Scare the shit out of him. I'm sure the potential wrath of his brother will frighten him far more than anything we have to offer.'

* * *

Franklin was back in his room, relaxing on his bed, when things turned nuclear. He'd spent the last few minutes watching CBS News, and although he was drifting off and his eyes were shut, he wasn't fully asleep when the bombshell landed.

Hembury's voice amplified through his brain like a massive thunderclap. Within moments, he was wide awake and watched in disbelief as the ghost of a dead man taunted him down the camera lens. He was mesmerised by the broadcast, and as soon as it finished, he used the digital remote to rewind, so he could hear every word again, right from the very beginning.

His initial shock simmered for a moment and then he exploded with a red-hot rage, yelling at Hembury's image on the screen, almost as if he believed the head of internal security at the White House could hear him. After a third viewing, he began to process what he'd just seen.

He was humiliated by the thought of being betrayed by Leonard or Deshi – or possibly both, working together. He needed to discover the truth and plot his revenge and that would necessitate retribution on an industrial scale. As he calmed down, the psychopathic side of his personality began to relish the prospect of what would come next. He summoned Deshi to his room for what she assumed was a debrief of the kidnap attempt, but when he spoke, he caught her completely off guard.

'My dear, do you believe in ghosts?'

They were standing facing each other; he'd hardly let her in the door, so keen was he to speak with her. Despite the calmness of his voice, Deshi knew him well enough to sense a burning anger bubbling behind his piercing eyes. She felt shivers down her spine and braced herself for what was to follow.

'You see, it appears my old friend Troy Hembury has come back from the dead to haunt me and that can only mean one thing.'

Franklin launched forward like a guided missile and delivered a vicious punch that landed on her temple, just above her right eye, taking her completely by surprise. Deshi staggered backwards but somehow managed to retain her balance, because of the wall behind her. She raised herself upright, facing him again, to see Franklin was pointing a Beretta at her head. She could see the safety was off and it was good to go.

'You stupid lying bitch. Did you really think you could betray me and get away with it? Tell me exactly how you and Leonard pulled it off or I'll blow your fucking brains out.'

Deshi had survived for twenty-nine years on her quick wits and physical prowess. She was a consummate liar. She felt the warm trickle of fresh blood on her forehead caused, no doubt, by the gold ring on Franklin's index finger, but ignored the sensation and looked her attacker in the eye.

'Mr Franklin, I know nothing, I swear. Hembury was blown to pieces in the explosion. Why do you think he's alive?'

'Don't play games with me, Deshi. He's the lead story on every news bulletin.'

He paused for a moment and picked up the TV remote with his right hand and replayed the press conference. Deshi didn't need to act her reaction. Even though she knew he'd survived, she was genuinely amazed to see Hembury relaying the intimate details of his escape.

'I set the bomb in place but was in the air when it went off. I took out Nicks as ordered and brought Daniel safely home. This has to be Leonard operating as a lone wolf, and there's only one conceivable reason he'd have done it.'

Franklin lowered the gun slightly.

'Go on – but this better be good.'

Deshi's thoughts flashed back to the warning call she'd made to Leonard, tipping him off about the exact time of the bomb detonation and then the WhatsApp she'd received a few minutes later revealing he'd taken Hembury with him.

'Look, Leonard's a mercenary – a gun for hire you found on the dark web. Hembury probably offered him millions of government dollars to set him free, and then it must have been pure luck they both got out ahead of the explosion. Leonard is the traitor here, not me. I'd never betray you.'

Franklin looked deep into her dark brown eyes, searching for the truth, but he couldn't find the reassurance he was looking for. She was either a brilliant actress or maybe she wasn't lying, but he couldn't be sure either way so, for now, he decided to play along.

'Okay, my dear, a lot of what you say makes sense. But I can't abide loose ends and I certainly won't allow anyone to make a fool of me. Leonard has to be punished for his betrayal, and your redemption lies in you taking take care of it personally.'

Deshi hadn't anticipated Franklin demanding an immediate response. She'd assumed that after they'd completed the attack in Israel and the killing of Vargas, she'd disappear, as would the problem with Leonard.

'Mr Franklin, we're only days away from Operation Atonement. Surely this can wait until after that, rather than become a distraction?'

Franklin snarled and raised the gun.

'You really don't understand me at all, do you, my dear? I can't fully focus with this betrayal hanging over me – it eats away at my brain. You were in overall charge of the kidnapping, so it's your mess to sort – so sort it. I want that bastard Leonard dead.'

Deshi knew there was no way around the madness and decided to engage, even if it meant she had to kill the man she hadn't been able to erase from her memory since they'd slept together in the cottage.

'Okay, there may be a way. He was clearly infatuated with me, and I think I could lure him over here if he thinks it's a personal request and nothing to do with the previous job.'

'Did you screw him?'

'No, but I know he wanted me, and I can use that.'

Another lie flowed effortlessly off her lips. Franklin nodded, still unsure whether he could believe a word she said.

'Do it. And do it fast.'

'I burned his number, do you have it?'

'I'll text you. Now get out of my sight.'

\* \* \*

Seven thousand miles away in Seattle, Leonard was working his way through a microwave meal that claimed to be chilli con carne but bore no more than a passing resemblance to the real thing. He was glued to his laptop, binge-watching the third series of *Narcos*. His screen time was usually focused on crime dramas he found on the streaming channels, so he'd not seen the Hembury press conference that was the lead story running on most rolling news channels.

When his cell rang, he saw the caller's name and grabbed for the phone as if his life depended on it. It was a number he'd convinced himself he'd never see again, and he felt a wave of excitement surge through his body when he heard her voice.

'I've tried to put you out of my mind, but I need to see you . . . Mo, I need you.'

There was a pleading desperation in her voice he found irresistible.

'Where are you?'

'The last place in the world you could ever imagine and probably the last place you'd want to come to.'

'Don't worry. I'll be there.'

# Chapter Thirty-Seven

Gaza City, Gaza Strip

Deshi sat on her bed for a while, methodically working through her options before reporting back to Franklin. He'd moved into the main living room and was deep in conversation with Shomani when she found him. He glanced across and signalled for her to join them.

'My dear, I trust you've some good news for me?'

'He's coming. He'll be here sometime tomorrow evening.'

Franklin purred like the well-serviced engine of a Rolls-Royce.

'Excellent, tell me more.'

He nodded towards Shomani.

'I've told Khaled about our friend, Mr Leonard.'

Deshi was surprised Franklin had mentioned his failed attempt to kill Hembury but figured Shomani must have seen the CBS News piece by now, so it made sense.

'Leonard's flying into El Arish Airport in northern Egypt, which is only thirty miles south of the Gaza border crossing at Rafah. It's a soft border, unlike the Israeli one in Kerem Shalom, so he'll have no problem getting through it. I'll meet him on our side in a hire car and drive to the Al-Mathaf Hotel in the city, about twenty minutes from here. I've booked a room for us, which he'll never leave – except in a body bag.'

Franklin's eyes flicked to Shomani for the briefest of moments and then settled back on Deshi. It was lightning fast, but she caught it, as well as the Arab's subtle acknowledgement. When Franklin spoke, his voice was tinged with sarcasm.

'Excellent, my dear, but don't worry about hiring a car. I'm sure Khaled will be more than happy to supply you with one from his fleet, along with a discreet follow car, just to ensure you both make it safely to the hotel. The coastal road that runs from Rafah to Gaza City is treacherous and somewhat confusing and we wouldn't want you to get lost.'

It was clear Franklin no longer trusted her, and Deshi was pretty sure she knew what he and Shomani had in mind for her and Leonard. As usual, the psycho was holding all the cards. But she'd managed to hang on to one, and she planned to play it for all it was worth. Franklin was a narcissist who prided himself on knowing everything, but what he didn't know was what Leonard looked like. That was her ace in the hole.

There were less than twenty hours to go before the former Marine arrived, and that left her with a hell of a lot to do if she were to survive another day. She'd have to move quickly, but first she had to make one more call to Leonard before he boarded his flight.

\* \* \*

The head of international security for the Taliban had two crucial phone calls to make. He glanced down at the numbers on his notepad, knowing one call was going to be easy while the other would be tricky. Turabi wasn't sure what order to place them in, but after further deliberation he decided to get the difficult one out of the way first, knowing he could then relax and enjoy the second.

He was a senior government minister in the recently formed Taliban regime that had retaken control of Afghanistan and it was highly irregular for him to speak directly with the head of the PJB's military wing. Despite their shared hatred of Israel, in many ways they were competitors, but he was acting under strict orders from the supreme leader and so had no option but to comply.

Turabi may have been a skilled politician, but he was no fighter, which is why he dreaded making the call to Shomani. He knew the Saudi-born Arab was one of the most ruthless and dangerous killers in the Middle East, and yet here he was about to try and con him.

Shomani took the call and for the first few minutes listened carefully as Turabi apologised for the attack in the restaurant, swearing on the lives of his five children that the sole intention had been to capture Franklin and nothing else. The Taliban minister then offered his ten-million-dollar sweetener as part of the apology to help demonstrate his sincerity. Shomani knew he was being lied to, but it served his purpose to play along. However, he had every intention of seeking revenge down the line. Eventually, Turabi came to the crux of the call.

'The supreme leader requests that, as a fellow Muslim, you hand the American over to us immediately. He has dishonoured Islam with his behaviour and severe retribution needs to be enacted and honour restored.'

Shomani was about to reject the offer out of hand but paused as he conjured up an idea.

'Minister, please thank the supreme leader for his generosity and tell him I'll seriously consider his request. We're on the move right now, so this is not a good time. Call me again in a week and I'll give you my answer. I might even decide to execute him on your behalf.'

Shomani knew that if all went well, the world would soon be a very different place and he could worry about Franklin then. However, in the meantime, he needed to be vigilant. The American had lied to him – he'd betrayed the Taliban leadership and would need very close monitoring. Turabi came straight back at him.

'My friend, a week is fine but please don't touch him. The supreme leader has his own special plans for handling Franklin, and I'd hate for anything to spoil them.'

The call had gone far better than Turabi had dared hope and now he relished the prospect of making the next one. It was a call he'd originally asked his assistant to make, but in the end, he'd decided there was too much at stake and he needed to make it himself.

Yusuf Shomani saw the name that flashed up on his cell and reacted as though the phone had morphed into a grenade. He hurled it across the room where it landed on his bed and continued to ring. He slipped slowly down onto a handmade Persian rug and curled himself up into a tight ball while the instrument of terror continued to vibrate on the red silk bedcover as though it had a life of its own.

Turabi persisted and called back every three minutes until, on his eighth attempt, Yusuf picked up, having had time to rehearse what he wanted to say. Despite his terror, he knew he needed to appear strong.

'Leave me alone, you bloodsucker. I kept my side of the deal, but your fighters screwed up twice, and that's your problem, not mine. I've already sacrificed my brother for your cause and that's it. Enough is enough.'

Turabi's response was a chilling laugh that rocked Yusuf to his very soul.

'You imbecile, that's not how the rules of this game work. We own you and you'll continue to help us until the American is in our hands.'

His next line might as well have been a physical punch to the solar plexus.

'I've just had a very nice chat with your brother, Khaled, who has accepted ten million dollars as an apology from our supreme leader. I wonder how he'll react when I tell him the true identity of our informer, especially when he realises he's executed the wrong brother. I really wouldn't want to be in your shoes at that point. I can only imagine the kind of slow and brutal punishment he would dish out.'

Yusuf's bowels opened and he soiled himself. His voice dropped to nothing more than a whimper.

'I understand . . . I'll help you . . . but it might be difficult for a while.'

'My friend, I'll need the details of a new location for Franklin within the next few days because I understand he's on the move. If I don't hear from you by then, you know what to expect.'

# Chapter Thirty-Eight

Gaza City, Gaza Strip

It was late afternoon and Deshi was exhausted, having spent most of the previous night in the downtown area of the city putting together the intricate pieces of a plan she hoped might just save her life.

She was shut away in her bedroom, running through a mental checklist in case she'd forgotten anything crucial, when Franklin entered without knocking. He stood in the doorway, his top lip curled up at one end forming a contemptuous sneer.

'Ready for your reunion with Leonard? Are you sure he's going to show?'

She cleared her mind and played along.

'Pretty sure. He's due to land at El Arish at five and then grab a cab to the Rafah crossing. I've arranged to meet him this side of the border at six thirty.'

Franklin nodded his approval and produced a set of car keys from the front pocket of his jeans.

'You're going to need these. Khaled's provided a Shogun for your trip. It's parked in the garage at the rear of the building.'

He tossed the keys to her and disappeared back into the corridor. Deshi collected them from their landing place on her bed and checked the time on her cell. She'd need to leave in about thirty minutes and her immediate priority was to check out the car. If her suspicions were correct, it would probably have an added extra courtesy of one of Shomani's technicians.

The three-car garage had been sculpted from the basement area of the old cinema and housed two black Land Rover Defenders, as well as a gunmetal grey Mitsubishi Shogun. It was a 2006 3.2 Warrior diesel with over two hundred thousand miles on the clock. The old warhorse had clearly seen better days. Deshi pulled the bonnet lever and checked out the engine bay, which housed a reconditioned engine from a younger model. It was clean and tidy, and to her amazement didn't contain anything that shouldn't be there. A quick inspection of the trunk offered up nothing either. She then lay on the white-painted concrete floor and rolled underneath to examine the undercarriage. The muffler, front and back axles, brake lines and exhaust were all as expected and there were no surprises. She began to doubt the instincts that had rarely failed her in the past and wondered if she'd misread Franklin's furtive glance at Shomani the previous day.

She wasn't quite done, however, and began a thorough search of the interior. But, again, the cupboard was bare. Deshi took one final patrol around the car exterior looking for anything unusual and was about to give up when she spotted something slightly awry: one of the wheel nuts on the aluminium hub fitted to the rear passenger tyre had a small black mark on it that, under closer inspection, appeared to be grease. The top half of the metal rim wasn't quite flush to the tyre, revealing a tiny gap, just wide enough to slide the side of a coin in between. She reopened the trunk, grabbed a wrench, and set about removing the rim.

The nuts turned easily, which made her suspect they'd only recently been tightened, and in less than a minute, she'd freed the rim and placed it on the ground. That was when she spotted the black metal package, no larger than a cigarette pack, gaffer-taped to the back of the aluminium wheel hub. Deshi was no stranger to IEDs, although this was one of the smallest she'd ever come across. Attached to one side was a wafer-thin magnetic GPS tracker chip, which was no doubt there for the benefit of the follow car Franklin had alluded to.

She carefully released the bomb from the tape to take a closer look and it didn't take long for her to work out how it functioned. It had no timer, so she knew it must connect by either Bluetooth or Wi-Fi to a remote detonator, and because of its size she knew it could only produce a small charge – nowhere near powerful enough to take a human life. But its strategic positioning made it a deadly weapon. Its blast would result in a full tyre blowout that would send the car careering out of control.

She was about to take the Shogun on a notoriously dangerous clifftop road, so it wasn't hard to work out the logic behind its placement. Deshi weighed the small bomb in the palm of her hand for a few seconds and then carefully strapped it back into position with the gaffer tape. She picked up the wrench and screwed the rim back into place before sliding into the driver's seat and gunning the engine into life. As she waited for the electric garage door to open, she glanced at the two Defenders and wondered which one would be used as the follow car.

The coastal road which stretched from Gaza City to the border crossing at Rafah was just over twenty miles long, and for the second time in twenty-four hours Deshi drove the historic route that ran along the Palestinian Mediterranean coast. Even though she'd made the first trip at night, it had been easy to identify the most dangerous section – a steep, narrow switchback with a sheer three-hundred-foot drop over a rocky edge and no safety barrier in sight. Seeing it in daylight confirmed she was right. Deshi was a highly trained assassin who'd set plenty of booby traps of her own. This was the perfect spot to blow a tyre and send a car hurtling out of control before allowing gravity to do the rest. For her own freshly formed plan to work, the timing would have to be perfect.

She continued her drive to Rafah, where she pulled over onto a section of hardstanding about fifty yards from the border crossing with Egypt. It was just after six, which meant she faced a thirty-minute wait before he was due to arrive. The road was strangely quiet, with just occasional traffic, so when she heard the distant sound of an approaching car, a glance in her rear-view mirror showed a black Land Rover Defender coming into view. It parked up tight to the side of the mountain, allowing the front passenger a perfect sightline of Deshi's Shogun. The distance between the two vehicles meant it was just too far for her to recognise the two men in the front seats, but Deshi was pretty confident she could guess the identity of one of them.

Shomani had provided Franklin with an English-speaking driver along with a bomb technician, who was sitting in one of the rear seats nursing a detonator with a Bluetooth connection to the IED hidden in the Shogun's wheel rim. Franklin was monitoring the Mitsubishi through the optical viewfinder of a Canon DSLR camera fitted with a 500 mm zoom lens. He could easily make out the back of Deshi's head inside the Shogun and was in prime position to cover her reunion with Leonard before they both met their maker.

Every couple of minutes, the red-and-white border barrier raised to allow a vehicle pass through, but none of them was of any interest to either Deshi or Franklin. At six forty, however, a white Chevrolet Aveo with a yellow neon light above the windscreen came to a halt at the border crossing and Deshi watched as two guards spoke with the solo male passenger sitting in the back. He stepped out of the taxi and passed them some paperwork that the senior guard worked through. Franklin took the opportunity to begin clicking with his zoom lens as he had his first glimpse of the man who'd betrayed him. His dark hair was mainly hidden by a black baseball cap and his tall muscular frame was clad in a tight white T-shirt and a pair of stonewashed Levis.

The exchange with the guards lasted for an anxious couple of minutes before they gave him the go-ahead to return to the back of the cab. Moments later, the barrier lifted, and the Chevrolet drove through the border crossing, parking up next to the Shogun, which Deshi had already exited. He spotted Deshi straightaway and leaped out of the taxi, ran towards her, and they locked in an embrace. Franklin lowered his camera, having seen enough. He turned to his driver.

'Let the whore and her ride go past and keep them in range all the way until we reach the switchback.'

# Chapter Thirty-Nine

Rafah, Gaza Strip

The black Defender tracked the Shogun as it made the testing journey back towards Gaza City with Deshi at the wheel. She could now clearly see Franklin riding shotgun in the Land Rover behind and pictured him holding the detonator on his lap.

There'd been an awkward silence inside the Shogun since they'd met up and Deshi felt the need to break the ice.

'Are you okay?'

He glanced across at her for the first time since they'd begun the journey.

'Yes, all good. Are we going straight to the hotel?'

She paused for a moment to negotiate a tricky bend and then calmly lied.

'Yes, we should be there in about forty-five minutes.'

Behind them, Franklin was getting agitated. They were less than two minutes away from the switchback and he was giving a running commentary to the bomber sitting behind him.

'Stand by . . . Wait for my cue . . . Don't go too early.'

Deshi knew they were fast approaching the lethal bend, and if her hunch was right, the attack would happen sometime in the next sixty seconds. Her hands clenched the wheel as she clinically focused on the key moves she'd mentally rehearsed dozens of times in the past few hours. The one thing she couldn't afford to do was worry about the man sitting next to her – his fate was sealed, but she needed to stay alive to avenge her brother's death. After that, she didn't care, and all bets were off.

She glanced in the rear-view mirror and wasn't surprised to see the Defender rapidly closing the gap between them. She steadied herself as she aimed the nose of the Shogun towards the approaching corner. Blood pumped furiously in her ears as she braced herself for the imminent explosion. She knew her reactions had to be perfect. Weirdly, time seemed to slow as she waited.

When it came, it sounded more like a pop than a bomb blast, but the effect was just as lethal. The rear tyre was instantly blown away and the Shogun veered violently out of control, zigzagging across the road, heading straight towards the cliff edge. Deshi's reaction time was astonishing, even though she'd been prepared. Her right foot slammed on the brake and she let go of the steering wheel, simultaneously releasing the seat belt. Her right hand grabbed the door handle, and in one flowing movement, she flung her weight against it at the precise moment the Shogun hurtled into the air, having run out of tarmac.

As the SUV soared over the cliff, Deshi launched herself out of the driver's seat with all the force she could muster. Less than a second later, her body crashed onto a rocky overhang protruding about twenty feet beneath the edge of the road. On impact, she bounced and rolled downwards like a rag doll, but she was prepared for the blow and managed to gain control of her own momentum, coming to a stop about three yards from the edge of the precipice.

Beneath her, the Mitsubishi bounced off the side of the cliff face, plunging downwards, bursting into flames moments before smashing onto the rocks below. Deshi heard the fireball explosion along with the sound of shrieking brakes as the Defender slid to a halt above her. Her body was covered with cuts and bruises, but she ignored the pain, leaping to her feet and making a dash across the rocky edge to a large section of wild plantation she'd scouted the night before which she knew would provide her with cover. She threw herself into the thorny bushes just as she heard the doors slamming. Franklin leaped out of the Land Rover and rushed to the side of the road, desperate to peer over the edge.

The first thing he saw was the flaming chassis of the Shogun bouncing against the rocks below before it slipped under the waves of a rough sea which was crashing into the side of the cliff face. Within seconds, the flames had been doused and the car was completely submerged.

Twenty feet below him, Deshi held her breath, slowed her heart rate and kept her body perfectly still. In her calmed state, she thought she could hear the psycho's frantic heavy breathing above.

As soon as the Shogun disappeared, Franklin punched the air in triumph. As a man who hated loose ends, he'd eliminated two in one exhilarating moment. He turned and walked back towards the Defender; an arrogant smile burned into his face.

Deshi heard the Land Rover roar into life, followed by the sound of the SUV pulling away, but remained static in her hiding place for a further ten minutes, just in case he doubled back. As the adrenaline receded, she felt an excruciating, thrusting pain in her left arm and realised it was most likely broken, a casualty of the fall. She emerged from the bushes and walked gingerly across the rocks for about a hundred yards before she found what she was searching for. Propped up against the cliff overhang was a small low-powered moped camouflaged with greenery she'd hidden the night before. Deshi reached for the starter key, which was already in place, and the motorbike sprung into life.

She could only manage to grab the right handlebar because her left arm hung limply by her side. The ride back into town was slow and perilous as she struggled to maintain her balance, navigating her way through dozens of twisty turns. The normal half-hour journey took more than ninety minutes but eventually Deshi arrived at the Grand Palace Hotel, a beachfront property about three miles away from the Al-Mathaf, where Franklin believed she'd booked. She retrieved the room card from her jeans pocket, entered the small lobby and headed straight for the cover of the emergency staircase. She didn't want to arouse suspicion using one of the lifts; her rough appearance would make her far too memorable. She barely made it up to the third floor without passing out from the pain and had just about enough strength to tap the card on the metal pad underneath the door handle. As she flopped onto the bed, a voice called out from the ensuite bathroom.

'What kept you?'

A moment later, a tall male figure appeared in the bathroom

doorway, his right hand nonchalantly resting against the top of the wooden frame. As soon as he saw Deshi's battered body, the huge grin on Mo Leonard's face disappeared.

* * *

*Twenty Hours Earlier*

Deshi waited till just before midnight before slipping out of Shomani's house through her bedroom window. The city was still buzzing, and it was easy to grab a cab and a driver who was willing to stay with her all night in return for the princely sum of two hundred dollars. She'd a huge amount to accomplish and only a few hours of night-time cover to pull it off, but failure wasn't an option.

Her first destination was the Grand Palace Hotel, a four-star located on the seafront, where she booked a room for three nights under an alias with a fake credit card. That was the easy part. After that, nothing else was.

Earlier in the evening, she'd called Leonard back and changed his travel arrangements without explaining why. Instead of meeting her just across the border, she'd instructed him to take a cab from the airport in Egypt directly to the Grand Palace in Gaza City, where he was to check in and wait to hear from her.

For the next two hours Deshi scoured dozens of seedy bars in the downtown area, searching for a particular type of man who'd be key to the success of her plan. Because of the alcohol ban in Gaza, they were all disguised on the exterior as cafés or restaurants with the bar always hidden away in a dingy basement or cellar. The driver knew all the likely spots and drove her around, totally bemused by her behaviour, as often she'd spend less than sixty seconds inside a joint before running out and moving on to the next. It was almost two in the morning when she found him. The Silver Mill restaurant was home to one of the grimmest bars she'd ever seen but the rugged Italian serving behind the bar was the payoff she'd been looking for.

He was tall, dark and muscular and Deshi figured probably in his early thirties. She casually pulled up a stool at the far end of the bar and waited patiently until he noticed her. Deshi knew she had a mesmerising effect on men but rarely bothered to employ her God-given gifts, as she'd little interest in pursuing romantic relationships. Sure enough, as soon as he saw her, he made his way over, greeting her with the smile of a pedigree Italian stallion. His English chat-up lines were as smooth as his smile.

'Welcome to paradise, otherwise known as the Silver Mill. I haven't seen you in this dive before – I'm sure I'd have remembered. What can I get you?'

Deshi responded with the best fake laugh she could summon, and at the same time leaned forward to grab his right hand with hers.

'You'll do for starters, but let's open with a double Jack Daniels on the rocks.'

For the next hour he hardly moved away from her, other than to serve the odd customer who demanded his attention. He was infatuated and by the time the bar closed at three he was putty in her hands. They slid inside the back of her cab and she kissed him hard on the lips. After a long embrace, she broke away and hit him with the most bizarre request he'd ever heard.

'Gio, do you trust me?'

'Why?'

# CHAPTER THIRTY-NINE

'I want you to help me with something important this evening.'

He was intrigued, captivated and nodded for her to continue.

'About five, you need to arrive at Rafah, cross the border and walk for a few hundred yards into the Egyptian side and wait. Then at six thirty I want you to catch a cab and ask the driver to take you back across the border to meet me on the other side. I'll be waiting there with a car. You need to wear a baseball cap, jeans and a T-shirt, and when we meet you need to hug me.'

Giovanni gave a cheeky smile.

'Well, that won't be hard. What happens then?'

'Then I'll drive you into town, where I've booked a suite at the Al-Mashtal for us to spend the night.'

'What the hell is this all about?'

Deshi looked deep into his puppy-dog eyes.

'Trust me, Gio.'

The besotted Italian shook his head, bewildered. He couldn't resist the adventure that lay ahead.

'Okay, I do.'

Deshi leaned in for another kiss.

'One other thing. I need to source a motorbike. Any ideas?'

'Well, my flatmate owns a moped, maybe you could borrow it.'

Deshi reached into her jeans and produced a small wad of one-hundred-dollar bills and placed it in his hand before tightly squeezing it shut.

'Give him this as a rental. I only need it for twenty-four hours.'

'Christ, that's more than the piece of shit is worth. He'll bite your arm off.'

Giovanni's flat was only a five-minute ride away from the bar, and fifteen minutes later she kissed the bemused Italian goodbye and set off in the taxi with the moped jammed in the half-open trunk. As the cab pulled away, Gio shouted after her at the top of his voice.

'See you at the border, mystery lady.'

For a moment, Deshi felt a twinge of guilt; she'd just handed the young Italian a death sentence. But then her mind clicked back into gear and she instructed the driver to take her to the border crossing at Rafah. It was on their journey back into town that she spotted the switchback. She'd earmarked it on the way out as a possibility but approaching it from the border confirmed its status as the most dangerous corner on the road. They pulled over and she asked the driver to help her carry the moped down a treacherous rocky path that led onto a precipice jutting out below the side of the road.

She wondered what was going through his mind but the promise of another two hundred dollars for keeping his mouth shut seemed to douse any curiosity he might have had. After securing the moped in position, she walked along the rocky edge, aided by torchlight, and spotted an overgrown patch of bushes she hoped might just save her life. By the time her driver dropped her back at Shomani's house, it was almost sunrise. She paid him off and carefully pulled herself up through the bedroom window, before collapsing onto her bed and falling into a catatonic sleep.

# Chapter Forty

Gaza City, Gaza Strip

Deshi stood underneath the shower, wincing, as fine jets of hot water cleansed her cuts while bitterly stinging at the same time. She glanced down at the metal plug hole and watched the blood-red water spin in a clockwise vortex before disappearing. It reminded her of the classic shower scene from one of her favourite movies. For a moment she shut her eyes to try and visualise Hitchcock's masterpiece, *Psycho*, that for some reason brought a smile to her face.

Her left arm was pretty useless, which made it tricky to balance and wash herself but, somehow, she managed it and a few minutes later, she emerged from the bathroom dressed in a white towelling robe Leonard had found in one of the wardrobes.

He was standing at the window, staring out at the Med. His thoughts pulsed with unanswered questions, but as soon as she appeared he put them to one side and helped her walk across the room to the king-size bed. Once she was comfortable, he lay down next to her, so close her wet hair flicked against his face and he could feel the warmth emanating from her damp body. He turned onto his side and gently brushed her cheek with his right hand.

'Deshi, are you up for telling me what the hell's going on or do you just need to crash?'

She managed a half-smile and spent the next few minutes taking him through the previous twenty-four hours until he was fully up to speed.

'Jesus, I thought I led a complicated life but you're on a different level. Poor old Gio.'

Deshi didn't appreciate the hint of a reprimand.

'He was a casualty of war.'

'Sure, I get it, especially as he saved my life.'

He sensed her mood and switched topic.

'Franklin sounds like a psycho. How dangerous is he?'

'Very . . . and that happens to be my personal nickname for him.'

They burst into laughter, finally breaking the thin veil of tension that had hung in the air since the moment she'd arrived in the hotel room. Deshi inadvertently brushed her left arm against his body and shrieked with pain. Leonard instinctively pulled away and reached across for a small leather bum bag on the bedside table.

'You need some painkillers and then in the morning I'll find a doctor to take a look at your arm.'

Deshi shook her head and beckoned him towards her using her good arm. She surprised herself with her next line.

'Mo, I've a better idea for taking my mind off the pain – but it involves you doing some work.'

\* \* \*

Franklin was enthusiastically making his way through a bottle of Jim Beam, celebrating the successful completion of the removal of Deshi and Leonard, which meant he was now free to fully focus on the complex upcoming events. There were only days to go before Operation Atonement went live and he'd a huge amount to set in place before then. He was sitting at the large dining table in the main living area of the house when Shomani, flanked by two of his fighters, entered the space. The terrorist chief walked across to join him and briefly placed his hand on his shoulder, before pulling up a chair.

'John, I've been briefed by my men and it appears our plan worked extremely well, even if it did cost me a Shogun.'

Franklin polished off the remnants of his glass and poured himself a fresh one.

'I'll happily replace it with a new model. Watching those traitors plunge to their deaths inside that shit piece of metal you laughably called a car was incredible. I can only hope they were choking on flames before they smashed into the rocks at the bottom of the cliff. Or maybe they drowned – who knows?

'Only their maker will know the pain they suffered. Now, what's next on the agenda?'

'A little more celebration – maybe another bottle, and then it begins. In the morning I've two Zoom calls I'd like you to sit in on – one of which will be a game-changer.'

\* \* \*

'Troy, we've had a breakthrough with the photofit. Nathan, can you bring us up to speed.'

221

Berrettini had summoned a meeting at short notice in one of the secure rooms on the eighth floor of the agency with Hembury, Vargas and Nathan Burns, the man who headed up the Bureau's technology and data division. Burns was a middle-aged string bean of a man; six foot five, without an ounce of excess weight on his bony frame. He had horse-like facial features, with large teeth, a gaping mouth and deep-set brown eyes, matching the colour of his thinning hair. For all his physical drawbacks and lack of people skills, he was a geek with an extraordinary IQ and was one of Berrettini's prized assets.

They were grouped around an oval, grey-topped table and Burns was the only one standing. He was operating a slide machine that projected onto a drop-down white screen.

'Mr Hembury, we took the photofit you created of your kidnapper with one of our artists and ran it through a facial recognition software using a new program we developed with GCHQ in the UK. It employs remarkable technology and—'

Berrettini butted in.

'Nathan, let's get to the interesting stuff.'

Burns accepted the rebuke from his boss as par for the course and cut to the chase.

'The tech allowed us to match the hand-drawn image to the face of an international terrorist – a mercenary we believe has carried out numerous high-profile assassinations around the world. He's an ex-Marine who operates mainly out of the dark web, where, no doubt, he sources most of his clients. His name is Mo Leonard but we're pretty sure he employs a number of aliases.'

The FBI deputy director was rapidly running out of patience with his technocrat.

'For heaven's sake, Nathan, move on.'

'Yes, sir. Just under twenty-four hours ago, an airport facial recognition camera confirmed a ninety-nine per cent match with this man. He was travelling under the name Jim Darlen and passed through El Arish Airport in northern Egypt where, fortunately for us, the Israelis have a feed of all the security cameras inside the international terminal, and that's how we got our hands on the intel.'

Hembury was staring at the image of Leonard on the screen, which was positioned side by side with the photofit. There was no doubt he was looking at the man who'd betrayed Franklin and saved his life.

'Nathan, that's incredible work. Leonard was definitely my saviour. You said he passed through the airport – do we know where is now?'

'Yes . . . and no.'

Berrettini raised a quizzical eyebrow, a signal for Burns to continue.

'He left Egypt less than two hours after arriving and crossed the nearby border into Gaza but then the trail went cold.'

Vargas spoke for the first time, echoing the thoughts of everyone in the room.

'Christ, is he still working with Franklin, and if so, what the hell are they doing in that part of the world?'

* * *

Deshi was perched on the side of the bed, balancing an over-loaded tray on her lap, heaped high with every single item from the hotel's extensive room service menu. She was devouring a plate of eggs Benedict, having already demolished a portion of American-style pancakes topped with blueberries and whipped cream. Leonard stood a few feet away, leaning against a chest of drawers, watching in awe as he made do with a croissant and a steaming hot mug of black coffee.

'Someone's got a healthy appetite this morning.'

Deshi ignored him and reached for a glass of fresh orange juice, so he moved on to a far more substantial topic.

'I've been thinking – now Franklin believes we're dead, maybe we should just cut and run. Disappear for a few months until the nut job hopefully gets tracked down by the FBI.'

'Not a chance, we know the psycho is heading for Jerusalem to launch an attack on the Israeli prime minister, and I'm hoping, somewhere down the line, Vargas and Hembury will show up. Once I avenge Vakha's death, we can disappear to anywhere you like.'

Leonard knew he was facing a brick wall and changed tack.

'Deshi, we've no idea where Franklin's going to base himself in Jerusalem and it's far too dangerous for you to follow him.'

'Exactly, that why it's your job.'

She hit him with a deadly smile he couldn't resist.

'How do you work that one out?'

'Two reasons. Firstly, he doesn't know what you look like and, secondly, he thinks you're dead.'

Having delivered that bombshell, she grabbed a smoked salmon and cream cheese bagel that demanded her full attention.

# Chapter Forty-One

Gaza City, Gaza Strip

With just an hour to go until the first Zoom, Franklin had joined Shomani in his state-of-the-art basement office and was bringing him up to speed with the complexities of his plan. He was still buzzing from his recent success in despatching two of his enemies, and once again believed he was the master of the universe.

'The next twenty-four hours are all about disorienting the FBI and those clowns Vargas and Hembury.'

Shomani raised a sceptical eyebrow. Franklin imitated an orchestra conductor, waving an invisible baton as he spoke.

'Khaled, it's about sleight of hand. I'm going to provide them with a big bone to chew on in the guise of a digital file that'll magically fall into their hands. It'll outline a series of coordinated attacks planned on ten major synagogues, spread across five continents, to take place on Yom Kippur. The intel will be genuine, and the FBI will alert counterterrorist agencies across the world, who'll put forces in place to prevent the attacks from taking place.'

Franklin paused and licked his lips in anticipation of what was coming next.

'They'll also believe I'll be present at one of them, which will draw Berrettini, Vargas and Hembury to Florence, to the Tempio Maggiore – two and a half thousand miles away from Jerusalem, where you and I will actually be. Very simply, I'm offering up a sacrificial lamb to create a massive distraction from the real target, the Israeli prime minister. In addition to the attack in Jerusalem, we'll hit five major synagogues across the world, none of which will be listed on the file they receive.'

Shomani wasn't quite sure at that precise moment if the American was brilliant or crazy, but he was far too committed to pull out. Besides, he'd invested years in their relationship and any opportunity of striking a blow against the Israeli State was too good an opportunity to turn down.

'And how will this file mysteriously come to their attention?'

'All in good time, my friend. One of the contributors on the first Zoom is Armando Ricci, an Italian neo-Nazi and leader of the Roman National Party. I'm going to orchestrate his arrest for planning the attack in Florence and an encrypted file will be discovered on his laptop. It'll take some time to break it open, but once they do, the FBI boys will believe they've found the Holy Grail. Ricci will panic and buckle under interrogation. I'm pretty sure he'll tell them about my scouting trip to Florence and my intention to be present for the attack at the Tempio Maggiore. Here's the beauty of it – because he believes it to be true, so will they. There's a senior detective working at Interpol, based in France, who's on my payroll. He's a sleeper I've never used, until now. That's why he's there, waiting for the moment I need him. He'll alert the Italian intelligence agencies about intel regarding Ricci's potential involvement in a terrorist attack in Florence, which'll lead to his arrest and the search of his apartment.'

He glanced down at his watch.

'Time to get ready for the Zoom. We've got ten lambs to send to the slaughter.'

The screen featured eleven contributors, including Franklin, who played the role of ringmaster. Shomani stayed out of shot but had a clear view of the large wall monitor displaying the leaders of notorious fascist groups, located across the globe. He couldn't help but be impressed at seeing representatives from countries as disparate as Australia, Italy, Canada, Nigeria and Kazakhstan.

Franklin began the Zoom call by explaining how each of them formed a vital part of a master plan that would change the world order forever. That after 9/25, Jews would no longer feel safe, wherever they lived. Spontaneous bursts of applause and cheers broke out as, one by one, the right-wing insurgents revealed the confidential details of their planned raids on synagogues in their respective cities.

Shomani enjoyed the irony of the situation, knowing they were all dead men. Thanks to Franklin's imminent betrayal, they'd be walking into a well-laid trap. The call concluded with Franklin proclaiming a call to arms.

'Gentlemen, we're on the verge of creating history – a global event that'll be talked about long after we've departed this earth. A mortal blow to Jews everywhere. My grandfather would be very proud of all of you.'

Then, bizarrely, he spontaneously performed the infamous Nazi salute and everyone followed suit. Shomani, even though he shared the American's hatred of Jews, winced with embarrassment at the outlandish sight he was witnessing. Before Franklin wound up the Zoom, he turned his attentions towards Ricci.

'Armando, can you stay on the line? I need to go through a few things with you. Everyone else, you know what's at stake. Go out there on the twenty-fifth and create your own place in history.'

Within seconds, nine of the feeds cut to black as the contributors signed out of the call, leaving Ricci and Franklin on their own. The Italian was intrigued and excited to be singled out from the group for a one-to-one conversation with the Führer's grandson and resembled an exuberant lapdog, awaiting its next command from its owner.

'How can I be of assistance, Mr Franklin?'

'Armando, I'll be frank with you. I'm concerned about the robustness of some of our friends' plans. They seem riddled with inconsistencies and are poorly thought through – unlike yours, which is why I require your help.'

Shomani watched in awe as Franklin played Ricci like a violin.

'During the next twenty-four hours, I'll review them all, but I'm especially worried about the ones in Lagos, Sydney and Boston. Armando, I'd like you to do the same and send through your recommendations for any changes you feel are required to enhance their chances of success. I'll email you an encrypted file containing detailed breakdowns on all the operations. You'll need to source a burner cell so I can send through the passcodes. Once you're into the file, destroy the phone, as without the codes, it will be impenetrable.'

Franklin was building lie upon lie. He knew full well the FBI would be able to break into the file, but the more Ricci bought into his tale the better.

'Thank you for showing such trust in me, Mr Franklin. Are you still planning to come to Florence?'

'Armando, wild horses couldn't stop me. I'll be flying out in the next couple of days.'

'What about the girl – will she be coming with you?'

Franklin glanced across at Shomani before replying.

'Deshi? No, she'll be elsewhere.'

# Chapter Forty-Two

Gaza City, Gaza Strip

T he second Zoom had a very different dynamic because Franklin knew the five participants had every chance of succeeding with their attacks. The targeted venues were some of the most iconic synagogues in the world and all held huge significance for the Jewish community in their respective cities.

They were sited in five different continents. In the heart of Le Marais, the Jewish neighbourhood in Paris, the Synagogue des Tournelles was one of the most spectacular in Europe, adorned as it was with stunning metal framework designed by Gustave Eiffel, the man who created the most famous tower in the world. In America, the enormous Temple Israel in Michigan boasted the largest reform congregation in the country, while the Great Synagogue on Wolmarans Street in Johannesburg was known as 'the crown jewel of Orthodox Judaism in South Africa'. In the Sydney suburb of Bondi Junction, the Central Synagogue was the largest in the southern hemisphere and, finally, the Templo Libertad in Buenos Aires was one of the most esteemed synagogues in South America and, more relevant for Franklin, included Vargas's in-laws amongst its congregation; the true reason he'd chosen it.

The man tasked by Franklin to lead the assault in the Argentine capital was Bruno Guzmán, the leader of the Victory Nationalist Party. He was a Hitler fanatic and edited the online publication *The Iron Fist*, which had a red swastika as its logo. Guzmán's plans had suffered a recent setback when one of his senior lieutenants was killed in car accident a few hundred yards away from the synagogue. A disastrous incident he'd no intention of mentioning to Franklin when it was his turn to reveal his attack plan.

'Señor Franklin, the Templo Libertad is surprisingly poorly protected and we're confident our soldiers can enter through the main entrance without too much resistance. I'll personally lead the attack with three of my best men armed with M4 carbines, purchased with funds you kindly provided. The nearest police station is a seven-minute drive away and we believe we can carry out the carnage required and be long gone before they arrive on the scene.'

Shomani could tell Franklin was far more interested in the details of the Buenos Aires attack than the other four and the reason soon became apparent.

'Bruno, that's good to hear, but let's focus on Vargas's family. They have to be taken down ahead of anybody else.'

Guzmán was primed for the question.

'It is my personal priority. We have the seat number for Gabriel Kapel, as well as those of his wife and daughter. If you'll allow me to share my screen, I'll show you the floorplan.'

Franklin gave him access and a split screen appeared displaying two images detailing the interior seating plan of the temple. Three red crosses marked the precise locations of the Kapel family's seats.

'Excellent, Bruno. I have one more essential task I need you to carry out, before you and your men leave the scene.'

Guzmán instinctively moved closer to his computer screen to ensure he didn't miss a word.

'Of course, Señor. What might that be?'

'I want clear photographic evidence of the Kapels's corpses, all three of them. Really shoot them up – they need to be as grotesque as possible. I can't wait to forward them to their beloved son-in-law.'

\* \* \*

Franco Mancini was the head of L'Agenzia Informazioni e Sicurezza Interna, the security agency inside Italy, more commonly known as AISI. It was formed in 2007 and worked closely with counterparts across the world such as MI5 and the FBI, and its famous motto, *Scientia rerum rei publicae salus* meant 'Knowledge of issues is the salvation of the republic'.

Mancini was a former Italian Marine who'd risen through the intelligence ranks at breakneck speed, and the seniority of his position, at the relatively young age of forty-two, meant he reported directly to the prime minister. He was viewed by most politicians and civil servants as the second most important man in Italy, but he personally disputed that claim as he considered his role in protecting Italian nationals far more important than running the day-to-day affairs of the country.

He was a handsome man, tall and slim, with a shock of black hair and probing dark brown eyes that sat above a perfectly sculpted set of cheekbones. He was renowned for his Canali suit collection, which fitted his elegant frame perfectly, along with suitable matching accessories. Mancini prided himself on being the best dressed intelligence chief in Europe. One of his closest friends was Mike Berrettini, and the physical contrast between Mancini and the FBI deputy chief was comically stark because, despite his Italian heritage, Berrettini was short and rotund and rapidly losing what was left of his hair.

Mancini was sitting in the front of an unmarked police car in a quiet cul-de-sac in downtown Naples, having just helicoptered down from Rome on a journey that took just over fifty minutes. Alongside him was his assistant, Aldo Casella, and parked up behind them was a black Sprinter van concealing four special agents, armed to the teeth and waiting for the green light.

Mancini checked his watch, it was almost ten at night, which meant it was four in the afternoon in Washington. Before sanctioning the break-in, he decided to place a call that Berrettini answered after just one ring.

'*Ciao*, Mike. How goes it?'

The FBI deputy director was always happy to hear from his opposite number in Italy and a huge smile broke out on his face.

'Tough times at the moment, my friend. Deep in a case I just can't break open. Hey, it must be nearly ten over there – what's happening?'

'Mike, I'm just about to search the apartment of the leader of an infamous neo-Nazi group here. We've had a tip-off from Interpol that he's planning an attack on a synagogue in Florence, specifically on Yom Kippur. I know there's a lot of chatter on the intel radar about something major coming up and wondered if this event might be part of a bigger picture. It's probably just an internal issue but I'll keep you informed in case something else emerges.'

Berrettini knew his friend had great instincts and something in his gut told him this might be the break he was waiting for.

'Franco, I'll wait to hear. Good luck with the raid, my friend. *Ciao.*'

Inside his seedy first-floor apartment, Armando Ricci was enjoying the company of two underage whores, a once-a-month treat he granted himself off the back of funds received from supporters who purchased his racist online magazine. A thick haze of cannabis hung in the air, which complemented the music blaring out from a radio tuned to a sixties greatest hits station. Ricci was pumped full of drugs and blissfully snorting a line of cocaine from the ridiculously flat stomach of one of the anorexic girls, when the crunching sound of his front door being demolished by a battering ram instantly cleared his senses.

Four armed agents poured into his flat and swept through the living room, before bursting into the bedroom where they found the two girls semi-comatose on the bed and Ricci, just about on his feet, stumbling around a small free-standing unit, frantically reaching for a weapon he knew was in the top drawer. Within seconds, the barrel of a Beretta AR70 assault rifle was jammed hard against his right temple. He immediately gave up any resistance and melted to the ground in a messy heap.

Mancini appeared in the open doorway and surveyed the scene before barking out his orders.

'Take the scumbag to the airport and pull this flat apart. We need his phone, laptop and any other communication devices.'

# Chapter Forty-Three

Naples, Italy

Hangar five at Capodichino International Airport in Naples normally accommodated up to six small private jets, but the sole aircraft parked up inside was the fifteen-seater Leonardo AW139 helicopter Mancini had flown down in from Rome. A few yards away, Ricci sat in a metal chair restrained by black leather arm ties, facing the intelligence chief and his assistant. He appeared to have shaken off his drug-fuelled stupor and was brazenly ignoring their questions, repeatedly demanding his right to contact a lawyer. It was a stalemate that showed little chance of being broken.

As well as four of his agents, Mancini had brought Lorenzo Conti, his senior tech guy, on the flight from Rome. He was busy working away in a small prefab office in one of the corners of the hangar. Ricci's iPhone had thrown up very little and Conti was now working through a MacBook Pro that contained a number of unseemly racist hate emails, but nothing incriminating linking the Italian fascist to a possible attack on the Tempio Maggiore in Florence.

Conti was focusing his attention on a stubborn desktop file that was heavily encrypted and password protected. He had immediately briefed his boss about the rogue file, which was mysteriously titled 'OA' and Mancini had wasted no time placing a second call to Berrettini, requesting his help.

'Mike, our Nazi boy is staying schtum, and so far, there's nothing that backs up the tip-off we received from Interpol, but my tech guy has found an encrypted file. It could be Ricci's porn collection, for all I know, but I think it's worth sending over to you in case your team can bust it open. The truth is, I've nothing concrete to justify holding him much longer.'

'Franco, I get it. I'll put our best guys on it, and I'll forward it to my contact at GCHQ as well. The British have unique software that might find a way in.'

Mancini returned to the hangar and sat down opposite Ricci, who was slowly gaining in confidence the longer time passed without any sign of his being charged. He greeted the intelligence chief with an arrogant smirk, which instantly vanished when he heard Mancini's opening gambit.

'Armando, I'm looking forward to viewing the contents of the file named OA on your MacBook. You probably thought it was impenetrable, but right now there are software technicians in Washington and London cracking it open.'

The naked horror on Ricci's face spoke volumes and told Mancini everything he needed to know. He'd tried a bluff – he'd no idea if the file's contents could be accessed, but the thought of whatever information it contained being revealed was clearly a terrifying prospect for Ricci. Mancini chanced his arm again.

'Anything to say?'

Ricci avoided eye contact but remained silent. Mancini shook his head, stood up and walked away, knowing it was now a waiting game. It was almost three hours later when the breakthrough occurred. Berrettini knew as soon as he read the WhatsApp from Sir Christopher Denton, GCHQ's director, that something huge was about to break.

> Mike, take a look at the decoded file I've sent through on our safe email link and then call me straightaway.

For the next fifteen minutes, Berrettini sat at his desk viewing the file, mesmerised by the content he was reading. The deeper he dug into it, the worse it got. He realised he was looking at plans for a coordinated set of attacks due to take place in ten countries, across five continents, in a few days' time. The sheer scale and precise detail embedded in the file was incredible – almost unbelievable – but he feared it was all true and suspected one man's fingerprints were all over it. That the file had been uncovered on the laptop of a lowlife Italian terrorist was remarkable, but sometimes in the counterterrorist business you needed a stroke of luck and it appeared, for once, that that was the case here.

As he searched through the file, he felt as though he were holding a stick of dynamite with a short fuse. He knew he needed to take the contents directly to the president and the head of homeland security, who'd want to share the information it contained with other heads of state across the world whose cities were in the line of fire, but before he did anything there was a call he had to make first. Mancini recognised the number and picked up straightaway.

# CHAPTER FORTY-THREE

'Mike, any luck with the file?'

'Franco, the guys at GCHQ busted it wide open and the content is mega. I'm reporting directly to the president, who'll no doubt be contacting your PM in the next few hours along with other world leaders. I can't say too much except you need to know the attack in Florence is live and your fascist boy is up to his neck in it. But there's much more at stake.'

Mancini was stunned by the revelations but recalled the look on Ricci's face when he thought the contents of the file might be exposed.

'Mike, what can I do to help?'

Berrettini bit his lip hard before requesting a huge favour from his friend.

'Franco, I'm gonna need you to break a few rules – big ones, but I think it's the only way.'

Mancini hardly paused before replying in his native tongue.

'*Regole, quali regole?* Rules, what rules?'

'Great, here's what I need you to do.'

# Chapter Forty-Four

Naples, Italy

I n the following hour, Mancini did indeed break every rule in the book when it came to human rights and recognised international law. Ricci was injected with a massive dose of propofol, which knocked him out within seconds, before being bundled into the back of a van and driven to a private US airstrip two miles away, where he was transferred to a Lockheed C-5 Galaxy US military plane that immediately took off on a four-and-a-half-thousand-mile trip to Washington.

Naples boasted a huge US naval base and was home to the United States Sixth Fleet, which was strategically situated there as a bulwark against potential Russian aggression in the Mediterranean. There were over ten thousand American troops stationed at the base, which is why they required their own airstrip and terminal.

Apart from the aircrew, the only passengers on board besides Ricci were Mancini and two of his agents. The flight time was just five minutes short of eight hours, including a mid-air refuel somewhere over the Atlantic.

It was four in the morning local time when the Lockheed touched down at Fairchild Air Force Base in East Washington. It came to a halt at the far end of the fourteen-thousand-foot runway, where three men were standing by the side of the tarmac waiting to board.

About twenty minutes before the military plane landed, a large dose of the stimulant modafinil was injected into Ricci's right arm, which brought him to his senses. He'd no idea where he was but the sparseness of the interior and the five-part harness securing him in his seat informed him he was on a military aircraft. There was a large open space ahead of him, stretching for about twelve feet to where Mancini and his two agents were sitting facing him. His mind was a blur, but he knew enough to realise things weren't looking good, and when three strangers boarded the plane, he figured they were about to get a lot worse.

Berrettini was flanked by Vargas and Hembury. After a swift greeting with Mancini, they came and stood as an intimidating group a few feet in front of Ricci, who remained seated. The FBI deputy director went straight for the jugular.

'Armando, you're in very deep shit. So deep, pretty soon you're going to drown in it.'

Ricci's eyes widened and pinged around his face like a couple of spinning plates, as he desperately tried to rationalise the situation.

'Where am I? Who are you?'

'You're on American soil and in the hands of the FBI, but none of that matters because, the truth is, you don't exist anymore. The Italian authorities were only too happy to hand you over and now you belong to us. Armando, we own your ass, and if you fail to cooperate fully, this Lockheed will take you on a one-way trip to Guantanamo where you can look forward to being castrated without an anaesthetic, daily water-boarding sessions and abuse of the worst kind from many of the depraved inmates who are already there.'

Berrettini paused to allow his threat to well and truly sink in, and then subtly nodded to Vargas who was prepped to play the role of good cop.

'Or you can tell us everything you know, cooperate and walk away from this whole episode and crawl back under the rock you came out from.'

Ricci was still reeling from Berrettini's verbal assault but instantly grabbed the lifeline Vargas had thrown him.

'What do I need to do?'

Just as Franklin had predicted, the Italian fascist collapsed like a bad soufflé. Berrettini took over the reins.

'We've seen the file, Armando, so we know about the Tempio Maggiore and the other targets. We believe the American, John Franklin is the hidden force behind these coordinated attacks and the first thing I want you to do is confirm it.'

Ricci hesitated for a moment and then bowed his head in an admission of defeat.

'Have you ever seen him personally or were all your dealings remote?'

'I met him a few weeks ago in Florence. He came on a scouting trip with a woman to visit the synagogue.'

Hembury jumped in.

'Describe her to me.'

Ricci painted a picture of Deshi and Hembury nodded to

Berrettini, confirming the Italian was telling the truth. He'd just heard a perfect description of the woman who'd kidnapped him in Rockville. The Italian kept his head bowed as he continued his betrayal.

'I took him through my plan, which he approved, and then he explained to me in great detail the significance of the Tempio Maggiore to his family. His grandfather was Adolf Hitler. He'd tried to destroy the synagogue during the occupation in 1944 but was badly let down by his troops on the ground. Now, Franklin sees it as an opportunity, eighty years on, to fulfil one of the Führer's visions, as the synagogue is by far the most revered in Italy. He believes staging a massacre there would scar its Jewish heritage forever. It's so important to him, he chose it as the location he'll personally attend on the twenty-fifth.'

Ricci stopped, realising he'd probably gone too far by the startled reaction from the three men standing in front of him, but there was no going back.

'He plans to be right there, fighting alongside me and my men. He's flying over in a few days' time.'

'Ricci, you may just have earned yourself a ticket back to Naples. We've far more to discuss before I sanction that, but right now you're still in the game. Never forget, though – we own you.'

Berrettini gestured to Vargas and Hembury and the three of them turned and walked down the aisle of the aircraft until they were out of earshot. Vargas spoke first.

'Mike, this is incredible. We need to send Ricci back to Naples and keep him in place until Franklin arrives. Then, when they enter Florence, we take them down.'

Hembury had the final word.

'Guys, I feel the finale is approaching and at last we're going to catch that son of a bitch with his sticky fingers firmly in the cookie jar.'

# Chapter Forty-Five

Gaza City, Gaza Strip

S homani was in his basement office watching Fox News
when the story broke. Although it wasn't the lead on the
bulletin, he instantly realised the huge significance it
held for him and Franklin and went in search of his American
partner.

Franklin was upstairs in the main living area, talking on his
cell, when he saw the PJB chief approaching. He gestured to
him, indicating he was almost done on the phone. Unusually,
he was doing a great deal of listening and very little speaking.
When he saw the look of concern carved into Shomani's face,
he quickly wrapped the call.

'Khaled, why such a long face?'

But before Shomani could reply, Franklin ploughed straight
on.

'Whatever it is can wait a moment – I've some big news.
That was my Interpol contact on the phone. Since he placed
the tip-off with Italian intelligence, things have moved apace.
He doesn't have all the details yet, but the bottom line is they

grabbed Ricci and broke into the file. Since then, counterter-rorist agencies across the world have been notified of the upcoming attacks. They've clearly bought into the intel and have begun checking its viability and will no doubt conclude everything is legit. There's no way of knowing if Ricci informed them of my plans to meet in Florence, but if I were a betting man, I'd put my shirt on the wimp cracking once they confronted him with the contents of the file. I expect them to cut a deal so they can leave him in place to await my arrival.'

Shomani nodded his approval but was eager to give his own update.

'That's all good, John, but I too have news – only I fear it might compromise our entire operation in Jerusalem. Take a look for yourself – this story broke about ten minutes ago.'

Shomani handed his iPhone to Franklin. It was open on the Fox News App home page.

'It's the third story.'

Franklin only needed a few seconds to scan the news item before a malicious grin formed on his face. He handed the cell back and delivered his next line as a proclamation.

'This development gives us a real chance of blowing 9/11 out of the water.'

The item that triggered his reaction was the US president announcing a surprise last-minute two-day trip to Jerusalem to visit the Israeli prime minister and help celebrate Yom Kippur. It wasn't a big story, but for Franklin its significance was enormous, because it meant the US president would be inside the Great Synagogue, no doubt standing next to the Israeli prime minister when the suicide bombers launched their attack.

'John, I don't see it quite that way. You realise this means the Secret Service will be all over the site – checking everything. They may well discover the tunnel on one of their sweeps and then we're done. All that work and all those years of planning for nothing.'

'No, I'm sure that won't be the case here. Reading between the lines of that press release, the old fool of a president is claiming he wants to demonstrate the strength of the American–Israeli relationship, but the truth is he's bombing in the polls and needs to solidify the Jewish vote ahead of next year's election. Once again, the Jewish lobby is pulling the strings behind the scenes. This is obviously a last-minute decision, which allows no time for the Secret Service to do their usual diligent checks of the locations he'll visit. They won't even have time to ship the Beast over.'

'What the hell's that?'

'It's the president's ride when he's on a foreign trip and the Secret Service are worried about his welfare. It's fourteen feet long, ten tons in weight. An armour-plated Cadillac with five-inch-thick windows that can stop a .44 magnum bullet. It's a bomb-proof monster on wheels. With this short notice, they'll rely on Mossad to do the dirty work for them – probably the only intelligence service in the world they trust, and we know that to date, they haven't discovered the tunnel and it's been there for a good few months now.'

Shomani began to relax but shared another concern.

'You realise if we take down the president, we're basically declaring war on the United States.'

'Khaled, imagine how bin Laden must have felt a few days before 9/11. He'd have had the same fears and reservations you're experiencing right now. You wanted to create your own slice of history, and this is your chance to gain immortality. If this works out, no one will ever mention him again, but your name will become legend.'

\* \* \*

Hembury was sitting in a small side office inside the FBI headquarters on a Zoom call with his colleague Elizabeth Oakley, the senior press officer for the White House. He was pushing her for information regarding the president's sudden decision to visit Israel.

'Liz, to be frank, this is the worst possible time for POTUS to be on a foreign trip. Mike Berrettini at the FBI has just become aware of multiple potential international terrorist attacks scheduled to take place on the twenty-fifth – the day he'll now be in Jerusalem. I think, under the circumstances, he should reconsider the trip and stay on home soil.'

Oakley was extremely fond of Hembury but he was overstepping the mark.

'Troy, anything security-related inside the White House is your call – but once POTUS steps outside the front door, forget it.'

Hembury grimaced but knew by the tone of her voice he'd nowhere to go. Oakley saw his reaction and softened her voice.

'Look, Troy, this is a political call the old man feels forced to make because he's definitely going again in 2024. He needs to keep relevant, and the Middle East is one of his most reliable cards and a banker with the New York lobby.'

Hembury's next port of call was Berrettini, who'd been having similar thoughts since he'd heard the news regarding the president's upcoming trip.

'Great minds, Troy. I've set up a call with Bekher for later today to discuss that very subject. I'll let you know how it goes.'

Doron Bekher was the Mossad chief. He knew all about John Franklin's heritage and obsession with destroying Israel, following a biological attack he'd launched eighteen months earlier on the country's water supply, along with a small group of Taliban fighters. He viewed Hitler's grandson as a live and serious threat, and when Berrettini brought him up to date on the latest intelligence, he took it extremely seriously.

'Mike, I get your concerns, but it doesn't sound as if the lunatic's targeting Israel this time round. Firstly, you just told me we aren't on the list you found on the encrypted file, and, crucially, POTUS only made the decision to visit Israel twenty-four hours ago. There's absolutely no way Franklin could have anticipated that – even I didn't know he was coming. Any potential attack on one of our synagogues would have to have been months in the making – even years, so that can't be on his agenda.'

'I get the logic, Doron, but, still, the timing couldn't be worse.'

'Mike, if you want to know the truth, I'm pissed by the whole thing. Both leaders need a lift in the polls, which is why this has come from nowhere. I haven't even seen a schedule and yet I'm supposed to be responsible for POTUS's safety while he's over here. There's no time for his own team to prep anything, so it's all down to us – it's a total clusterfuck.'

Thirty minutes after the Zoom call with Bekher, the FBI deputy director briefed Vargas and Hembury and began planning their next move.

'Ricci arrived back in Naples a couple of hours ago and Mancini has an agent inside his apartment to keep a close eye on him in case he goes rogue. We have ears on his cell too, so if Franklin calls, we'll hear every word. Ricci believes he'll arrive the day before the attack, so I suggest we get there twenty-four hours earlier. We'll work closely with Mancini and his team on the ground and decide the best strategy once we learn more about the specific details of the operation.'

Vargas had another concern gnawing away at him.

'Mike, what about Leonard and his trip to Gaza? That's a hell of a long way from Florence.'

'I know, Nic, but follow the logic. After Troy's press conference Franklin must have worked out that Leonard betrayed him – although we still don't know why and given that madman's track record, he'll have issued a death order as a reprisal. We have to assume the trip to the Middle East has nothing to do with Franklin. In fact, if I were Leonard, I'd want to put as many miles as possible between me and him.'

Vargas nodded in agreement.

'Makes sense, Mike. I guess I was following my gut rather than my head. Let's talk about Florence.'

# Chapter Forty-Six

Gaza City, Gaza Strip

Yusuf Shomani was living on his nerves. He'd sold both his brothers down the river, and thanks to his deceit, one was dead at the hand of the other. And the Taliban wasn't done with him yet – he was still on the hook, even though he stubbornly refused to answer his cell, which displayed six missed calls from the same number – a number that belonged to his controller, Abbas Turabi.

Yusuf needed to escape the incessant calling, although he knew the best he could hope for was a short-term reprieve to clear his head. He picked up the phone and sent a short group text to his two bodyguards, informing them he was leaving the house in fifteen minutes. All senior government ministers had at least one guard, but as the brother of the head of the military wing of the Palestinian Justice Brigade, he was seen as a potential target for the Israelis, which is why he had two.

After sending the text, he switched the phone off and threw it on the bed before heading out to the seediest part of town with the sole ambition of getting totally wasted.

Outside the side entrance of the former cinema, his two bodyguards were in place, waiting by a black Land Rover. He leaped into the back and set off downtown, oblivious to the two motorbike riders parked up about fifty yards along the street, who pulled away and fell into the SUV's slipstream.

\* \* \*

Four international borders to the east, two thousand miles away, Shahzad Al-Faruq, the supreme leader of Afghanistan, was wrapping up his bi-weekly meeting with Abbas Turabi, his head of international security. Al-Faruq, who was also known by his religious title Amir al Mu'minim, Commander of the Faithful, enjoyed unlimited power within the Taliban regime. The office he held had been created almost twenty years earlier by Mullah Mohammed Omar, who'd founded the Taliban in September 1994 in Kandahar.

Al-Faruq wasn't a man used to repeatedly issuing the same order and his ice-cold demeanour reflected his displeasure with his government minister.

'Abbas, where are we with the American? We've had two failures already and I won't accept a third. You need to deliver him so retribution can be handed out. If you can't fulfil that simple task, I'll appoint someone who can.'

Turabi knew he was fighting for his life as well as his job.

'I've two elite fighters in Gaza, ready to act on my word, and expect to hear from my informer in the next twenty-four hours with information concerning the American's movements. He's a house guest of Shomani's but I'm told he'll be on the move very soon.'

The supreme leader's eyes narrowed and he moved closer to Turabi until their faces were barely inches apart.

'One more thing, take out the PJB chief. I've no intention of parting with ten million dollars. And bring the American back here . . . alive.'

'What about the informer, Shomani's brother?'

Al-Faruq didn't reply but his silence told Turabi everything he needed to know.

* * *

Yusuf made straight for his favourite bar, a dive hidden away in the downtown area, pathetically disguised on the exterior as a spice shop. The Hamas government had banned the sale of alcohol inside Gaza back in 2009 and, after the legalisation was passed, bars like the Dragonfly simply went underground. There were dozens of them dotted around the area, if you knew where to look, frequented by the Palestinian elite, who were more than happy to blatantly flaunt the rules. While his brother, Khaled, observed the strict Muslim code on alcohol, Yusuf regarded its consumption as a necessity rather than a vice.

Inside the basement bar, he hooked up with a small group of cronies and began downing vodka shots as an aperitif before grabbing a two-hundred-dollar bottle of Jack Daniels and retreating to a small corner table on his own. Outside the front entrance, his bodyguards remained vigilant, having parked the Defender in a nearby cul-de-sac.

The alcohol worked well as an anaesthetic and Yusuf began to unwind for the first time in days. He spent the following two hours steadily working his way through a bottle and a half of the imported American whiskey before staggering back up the stairs and onto the street.

His bodyguards had witnessed similar behaviour many times before, but this time, Yusuf seemed way more inebriated than usual as he staggered between them, struggling to keep his balance. The guards were far too distracted keeping him on his feet to notice the two Taliban tribesman stealthily approach from behind, seeming to come from nowhere.

Both fighters were armed with a pulwar, a traditional Afghan sword with a curved blade made from Damascus watered steel and inlaid with an Islamic inscription. The speed of the assault was breathtaking, and as they attacked Yusuf's bodyguards, the terrifying sight of the lethal blades spinning through the air acted as an instant sobering agent. Yusuf ran forward, leaving his men to fend for themselves in a battle they had little chance of winning.

He made it around the corner where he saw the Defender parked up. Remarkably, he was reasonably steady on his feet, and he dashed towards it only to find the central locking was in place and that's when he realised one of his bodyguards must have the keys. The cul-de-sac was bathed in darkness and the only light was provided by the full moon overhead. He desperately looked for a way out. He daren't turn back, so he made a run for a couple of giant steel wheelie bins parked up against a high brick wall that blocked the end of the street. Within a couple of strides, he lost his footing and slammed forwards onto the unforgiving concrete surface, taking most of the impact on his face and chest.

He heard the sound of footsteps approaching the street corner and scrambled onto all fours, rolling into a hiding place behind one of the bins. He knew his face was badly cut and felt as though he'd broken his nose in the fall, but his facial pain was the least of his worries. Yusuf felt like a wounded animal, easy prey for a predator, and suspected there were at least two of them less than fifty yards away.

Nothing happened for a few minutes, and he began to think he might be safe when he heard a strange noise in the alley. It was a soft bouncing sound, hard to identify, a bit like a recurring thud. Yusuf peered through the crack between the bins and saw two red footballs rolling towards his hiding place. It was hard to be sure of anything in the gloom until one of the balls gently rolled to a halt about six feet away from the front of the bins. The first thing that hit him was the stench, and then he focused in on the distorted bloody head of Abdul, one of his guards. His bulbous blood-shot eyes were wide open, blankly staring upwards towards the black sky.

Yusuf felt a wave of sickness and slumped forward, retching violently. His stomach was bloated with alcohol, and he puked a mix of bile and gastric acid down the front of his white thobe. For a few seconds, he lay motionless on the ground, his face coated in his own vomit, and then suddenly he felt a powerful hand grab his hair by the roots and violently jerk his head upwards until he came face to face with one of the Taliban men. Standing alongside him was his partner, who held a blood-coated sword in one hand and a cell phone in the other, which he rammed against Yusuf's left ear. Turabi's voice pierced the eerie silence.

'My friend, it seems as though you've been trying to avoid me, and as you can see, that's impossible. I'll always find you, wherever you try to hide. Now, if you want to avoid the same fate as your bodyguards, you'll tell me where and when I can lay my hands on Franklin and your brother.'

The mixture of alcohol and terror acted as a weird stimulant and Yusuf's survival instincts kicked in. He knew he just needed to pass on the information and stay alive long enough to disappear. He had the funds to start a new life anywhere in the world.

'On the twenty-fourth and twenty-fifth, they'll be in Jerusalem. I don't know the actual address but you'll find them in an apartment on the ground floor of a small car park on Akhad ha'Am Street.'

There was silence on the line as Turabi digested the information and decided he believed it. Then he shouted a command down the phone and the last thing Yusuf saw was the glint of a curved blade bearing down at speed towards his neck.

# Chapter Forty-Seven

Jerusalem, Israel

August 2021

T he three men dressed in Western garb stood in a tight huddle outside the main entrance of the Great Synagogue on King George Street in Jerusalem, appearing to be admiring the magnificent façade.

The name and design of the Jewish house of worship was inspired by the Second Temple, which had been destroyed by the Roman emperor Titus in 70 BC, and the lavish marble-floored interior was a nod to King Herod, arguably the most ambitious builder in the ancient world. The structure was dripping with the history of Judaism, and an inscribed dedication outside the front entrance read: 'For the six million Jews who lost their lives in the Holocaust . . . A house of prayer for Jews of the world, so that we the Jewish people may live'.

Franklin turned to face the Shomani brothers, Khaled and Yusuf, with a look of utter disdain etched on his face.

'The inscription disgusts me but I'm proud to see my grand-father's legacy is so prominent on the outside of this monstros-ity. If all goes well with our plans, this place will no longer be considered a safe haven for Jews across the world to come and visit. It will become a shrine to the dead, including the Israeli prime minister, like the 9/11 memorial in the centre of New York.'

To the untrained eye, the three visitors dressed in jeans and T-shirts looked like regular tourists, but for the two Arabs, wearing typical Western clothes was an alien experience, and this was the only occasion in their lives they'd ditched their traditional thobes and keffiyehs.

They moved inside and entered the huge prayer hall that seated a two-thousand-strong congregation. The interior style was designed to unify the Jewish faith, so while the walls were decorated in classic Ashkenazim style, the seating layout was based on a traditional Sephardim synagogue.

Enormous stained-glass windows, featuring stunning imagery, broke up the side elevations and five separate giant panes above the ark symbolised the Books of Moses. They were designed to face south so that during daylight hours they were almost impossible to gaze at; a reminder to worshippers pray-ing inside of how Moses had been forced to cover his eyes at the sight of the burning bush. The stunning windows were comple-mented by imposing crystal chandeliers that hung above the women's section. Everything inside the Great Synagogue had been designed by world-renowned architects, which made it one of the most beautiful prayer halls in the world.

They sat down in a quiet area towards the rear, at least twenty yards away from the nearest person, but still kept their voices at a conspiratorial level. Yusuf was leading the conversation as he'd done most of the prep work prior to the visit. He pointed across to a row of seats in the centre of the magnificent building.

'That's where the prime minister and the American ambassador usually sit, along with a number of other high-ranking dignitaries. According to the floor plans of the building we acquired at some cost from a civil servant in the local planning department, that door at the far end, to the right of the ark, leads into a small hallway where the rabbi keeps an office. Past that is a stairway that leads to the basement, where at the far end is a disused cellar that runs deep underground. That has to be our way in if we've any chance of keeping the location of the tunnel under wraps.'

Franklin nodded his approval.

'Yusuf, this is very impressive. The only obvious problem is the vast distance between the entrance door to the prayer hall and the location of the prime minister. It's odds-on the Mossad agents inside will take out our suicide bombers before they can get close enough.'

'Not necessarily. Of course, we need a bit of luck on our side, but I believe that in the chaos created by the attack, one of our martyrs might just make it across the space and detonate close enough to take him out.'

Khaled Shomani spoke for the first time since the group had moved inside.

'Yusuf has done an amazing job. Bearing in mind the tunnel won't be ready for a couple of years, I hope the quality and range of the suicide vests will have improved tremendously by then. Now, let's take a walk outside so we can show you our latest purchase as, thanks to your funds, we are now property owners and developers in the heart of Jerusalem.'

The six-hundred-yard walk to Akhad ha'Am Street took just under five minutes with Yusuf leading the way. They came to a stop outside an unimposing two-storey car park that was joined on one side by a single-storey supermarket. Yusuf placed the small backpack he'd been carrying onto the pavement and reached inside for a brown A4 envelope.

'This contains all the relevant paperwork. As well as acquiring the freehold to these two properties, we've full planning permission, which came as part of the sale, to create a brand-new parking facility with two and a half times the footprint of the current set-up. Parking is at a premium in this city, so our new car park will be a welcome addition. The beauty of the project is it provides a perfect cover for daily removals of earth and rubble, some of which will come from the creation of our tunnel. We've a brilliant Palestinian engineer on board who'll be running the project, and surveyors' reports indicate the earth surrounding these buildings is suitable for such an ambitious project.'

Yusuf paused and pointed back along the route they'd walked.

'The engineer believes we can literally go in a straight line from here to the synagogue.'

Franklin cut in.

'How long will it take to construct?'

'Probably twelve to eighteen months, depending on what problems arise once the excavation work gets underway.'

Franklin glanced back towards the Great Synagogue before turning to face Khaled. 'Finally, a realistic chance of cutting the head off the snake.'

# Chapter Forty-Eight

## Gaza City, Gaza Strip

Shomani was grief-stricken and incandescent with rage, bursting to exact revenge, after his brother's brutal slaying. He paced his office, screaming orders in Arabic at two of his men, while Franklin stood in the corner watching the drama unfold. The American didn't need an interpreter to understand the gist of what was going down. Once the PJB fighters departed, Shomani turned his fire towards him.

'This was nothing less than an assassination. Yusuf was weak but the guards were two of my best men, and all of them were slaughtered on the street – decapitated. I've lost both my brothers in a matter of days and, John, I think you're the cause of this bloodshed.'

Franklin could sense a fiery blast of anger heading his way and fought back.

'Khaled, I know the attack in your cousin's restaurant was aimed at me, but if the Taliban are behind this killing, then it can't be about me because they targeted Yusuf this time.'

He paused for a moment, seemingly overcome, conjuring up an Oscar-winning grimace.

'Yusuf, your beloved brother, was a good man who was instrumental in planning the attack in Jerusalem. Now we need to carry it out to honour his death. This is not the moment to get distracted or lose our nerve.'

Shomani thought for a moment, digesting Franklin's words, before replying.

'Maybe you're right – perhaps this is a warning shot aimed at me – punishment from the supreme leader for harbouring you in my home. But right now, I need to find the men who carried out this crime against my family. There was so much blood and gore left behind on the street, it's possible at least one of them was wounded during the attack, so we're checking hospitals and independent doctors in case anyone needed treatment overnight. Every hotel, every guesthouse, every hostel will be contacted. Trust me, we've informers everywhere in the city who are loyal to our cause. If the killers are still here, my men will hunt them down.'

\* \* \*

Armando Ricci was in his apartment in Naples but wasn't alone. He was being monitored twenty-four hours a day by Mancini's team of agents, one of who was standing next to him in the tiny kitchen when an incoming WhatsApp message landed on his cell from Franklin.

Arriving late afternoon on the 24th. I've booked three rooms at the Cavour. One of them in your name. I assume everything is in place. F

Ricci immediately showed it to the agent, who took a screen-shot and sent it through to his chief. As soon as he saw it, Mancini called Berrettini.

'Mike, we're in business. Franklin just confirmed with Ricci he's arriving in Florence on the twenty-fourth, the night before the planned attack. The hotel he's booked is just a few minutes' drive from the synagogue.'

Berrettini felt the hairs on the back of his neck stand on end. He almost had his nemesis in his clutches.

'Franco, that's great news. I've a company jet on standby and we plan to fly out to be with you by midday on the twenty-fourth. Let me know if you hear anything else.'

The FBI deputy director ended the call, left his office and raced down the corridor, eager to impart the news to Vargas and Hembury in person.

\* \* \*

No one in downtown Gaza City knew if Doctor Usman Malouf held a licence to practise medicine – there were rumours he'd been struck off many years ago for carrying out illegal abortions, but somehow he scratched a living dishing out medical treatment to those who didn't really care about his credentials but required confidentiality.

When he heard on the grapevine the PJB's military wing was offering a five-thousand-dollar reward for information regarding any recent covert medical care, he quickly made his way across town to pay a visit to Shomani's residence. The two guards positioned by the side entrance checked his fake medical credentials and then brought him inside to meet the terrorist leader, who was in his office with Franklin.

Malouf stank of booze and looked a dishevelled wreck. He was a difficult man to age; his unkempt grey beard could easily have belonged to a man anywhere between his mid-fifties and seventy. He was a bag of nerves and his eyes darted in his head with a mix of excitement and fear as he sensed he was in touching distance of an enormous payday. When he recited his tale, both men were shocked. It wasn't the story they were expecting to hear. Malouf had no idea who the American was and so played everything towards one of the most feared men in Gaza.

'Master, a few nights ago an American sought me out in my home and offered fifty dollars to accompany him to his hotel to attend to his companion – I assume his wife or girlfriend. She was covered in—'

Shomani was disgruntled and dismissed the phoney doctor mid-flow.

'This isn't the information I was looking for. You can go.'

But Franklin raised his arm towards Malouf as a gesture for him to remain. He was intrigued by what he thought he was hearing and asked Shomani for a proper translation. Once he heard it for himself, he was curious to learn more.

'Khaled, let's hear what's he got to say.'

Shomani wasn't interested but nodded to Malouf to continue. The doctor was confused but picked up where he'd left off.

'The woman was covered with cuts and grazes and her left arm was badly broken. She explained she'd fallen off a moped but I knew she was full of lies, otherwise she'd have gone to the

Al-Shifa Hospital in the city for treatment, rather than pay me cash to visit her in a hotel room.'

Shomani continued to interpret and Franklin could hardly contain himself.

'What did she look like? Describe her to me.'

By the time Malouf had finished his account, Franklin didn't bother to ask Shomani to translate. He knew for sure the doctor was talking about Deshi and guessed her male companion had to be Leonard. The startling revelation was a sledgehammer blow to his senses. How on earth had they managed to fool him, yet again? He'd seen them plunge over the cliff with his own eyes. But that was a question he planned to ask Deshi in person, when he had a gun pressed firmly to her head.

He reached inside his front jeans pocket and retrieved a handful of hundred-dollar bills that he flung across the room towards Malouf, who lost any pretence of dignity as he scrambled across the tiled floor mopping up the notes. Franklin fired off a final demand at the sham medic.

'What's the hotel name and room number?'

Malouf didn't need to wait for Shomani's translation, although he still hesitated, hoping the American might flash a bit more cash for the information. However, Franklin was in no mood to negotiate and replaced the question with a command.

'Tell me, you creep.'

'I remember now. It was the Grand Palace Hotel, Room 315.'

# Chapter Forty-Nine

Gaza City, Gaza Strip

Shomani's immediate priority was arranging his brother's funeral before they left for Jerusalem, so he'd no appetite to join Franklin, who was obsessed with paying a surprise visit to Deshi and Leonard.

'John, the girl has already made a fool of you at least once. Why not let it go? As you said earlier, we've no time for distractions.'

'Khaled, you know me better than that. I just need a weapon, two of your best men and a vehicle with a driver – then I'll take care of it myself.'

Shomani rose from his seat.

'Okay, give me an hour and I'll arrange for a Defender to be out front with a three-man team. You'll find a Beretta in the right-hand drawer of the desk in my office. It's loaded with a fifteen-round clip – help yourself.'

Franklin rubbed his hands together as if he were trying to start a fire without any sticks.

'Perfect.'

It was only forty-five minutes later when he emerged from the former cinema and jumped into the front of the Land Rover, next to the driver. He nodded in the rear-view mirror to the two fighters sitting in the back, as the Defender pulled away and set off on the fifteen-minute journey to the hotel.

The driver of a hired red Chevrolet Spark, parked twenty yards up the road, let them pass by before gunning his engine. At the same time as he hit the gas, Mo Leonard clicked Deshi's contact on his cell. She picked up immediately.

'Definite ID on Franklin leaving the house with three goons. No sign of luggage or Shomani, so I think this is just a local trip, not the big repo to Jerusalem. I'll stay well back and let the tracker do the work – the psycho's probably doing some shopping.'

Deshi laughed her approval.

'Cool. I'm going to jump in the shower but update me by WhatsApp and stay safe.'

Twenty-four hours earlier, Leonard had hidden cheap trackers on both the Defenders when they'd been left briefly unattended on the side street outside the former cinema. Their Wi-Fi signal was synced with an app on his iPhone, which had a range of just under a mile. He was also in possession of a twenty-year-old Glock 18 he'd bought from a small-time arms dealer in the flea market that opened every day in the main square of the old town. The purchase of the semi-automatic pistol only came with six rounds, but for an elite assassin it was enough to take down half-a-dozen hostiles.

The tracker did its job and Leonard maintained a steady quarter-of-a-mile distance between the Chevrolet and the Defender. He wasn't familiar with the city's layout and so had no idea where Franklin was heading until the Defender turned left onto Al Rashid. His heart missed a beat and a giant knot tightened in his gut – it was the only street in the city he knew, because it was the location of the Grand Palace Hotel. He instinctively slammed his foot on the gas and grabbed his cell with his left hand and hit the last call icon. Deshi answered after just two rings and Leonard screamed down the phone.

'The psycho knows where you are and he's almost outside. Get out! Get out now!'

Deshi kept speaking and Leonard cursed when he realised it was her voicemail he was shouting at. He hit redial and once again Deshi's pre-recorded voice came on the line. Then he remembered their last conversation – she was in the shower.

'Shit . . . shit . . . shit.'

He continued to hit redial as he pushed the underpowered Chevrolet to its limits. The Defender parked directly outside the front entrance of the hotel. Franklin leaped out of the SUV and marched into the foyer accompanied by the two armed fighters. They moved swiftly past the reception desk, headed for a small bank of lifts and took the first available one to the third floor. As they exited, the signage on the wall sent them left along the corridor, where they passed several doors on either side until they reached Room 315 at the very end of the passage, which was positioned face on.

Leonard crashed two sets of lights and blasted his way through the rush-hour traffic. He was less than two hundred yards away from the hotel when Franklin gave the green light to one of Shomani's men to shoot the lock and smash the door down. Inside, Deshi had just stepped out of the shower and was still in the bathroom. Her left arm was in a sling, and with some difficulty she'd wrapped a bath towel around her torso and was trying to fold a smaller one around her hair with her free hand when she heard the gunshot. She'd left her pistol on the bedside table closest to the bathroom, and as her survival instincts kicked into gear, she threw herself through the open doorway and rolled across the carpeted floor at breakneck speed towards it, ignoring the excruciating pain from her left arm. But a second shot cracked above her head, and combined with Franklin's booming voice, stopped her dead in her tracks when she was still four feet away.

'Hold it right there or I'll blow your head off.'

She turned to face her former boss – the ruthless psychopath. He was flanked by two Arabs, and at that precise moment three guns were trained directly at her. Franklin's face was wearing the twisted smile she'd witnessed many times before, and for the first time in her life, she sensed her own death was inevitable. There seemed no way out.

Her body towel had fallen away during her desperate attempt to reach her gun and Franklin leered at her exposed breasts before speaking again. This time he lowered his voice. It dripped with derision.

'Deshi, you really are a remarkable lady. Such a waste of a promising young life.'

The Chevrolet screeched to a halt in the middle of the narrow street outside the hotel entrance, blocking the traffic behind. Leonard didn't even pause to turn off the engine as he leaped out the car, the Glock firmly gripped in his right hand, and sprinted across the sidewalk, carving a path through bemused pedestrians, causing panic and chaos as he headed towards the hotel foyer. His route took him straight past the front of the parked Defender and the alert driver immediately texted one of his comrades inside the hotel. The recipient felt the buzz of an incoming text and pulled it out to read the message before turning towards Franklin.

'A gunman is on his way up.'

Deshi seized the momentary distraction and made another frantic dive for her gun, but Franklin predicted her movement and fired a second shot aimed at her head. But she was a moving target and the round struck the bottom left-hand side of her neck, piercing her throat. The wound opened up like a geyser, spurting a huge blood spray high into the air.

Franklin was already on the half-turn, yelling out orders to the two fighters.

'Kill the gunman and finish off the girl.'

He bolted towards the fire exit door like a scalded cat, while the soldiers crouched down with their knees bent and bodies arched forward, taking up a classic firing pose, aiming their weapons at the empty corridor outside the bank of lifts. They had a clean line of sight, which meant it would be almost impossible for them to miss the gunman as he exited.

Down below, Leonard bounded through the reception area at warp speed, entered an open lift and punched the third-floor button.

Around the same time as Leonard made his way up, Franklin exited the hotel, sprinted across the sidewalk and leaped into the back of the Defender, screaming at the driver to pull away. The Land Rover was partially blocked by the front wing of the Chevrolet and it took three attempts before the driver was finally able to ram it out of his path and drive off at speed, disappearing down the street.

The two fighters heard the ping of an approaching lift signalling its arrival and braced themselves, but Leonard was far too seasoned a campaigner to take such an obvious risk. He'd been in a similar situation once before in a shoot-out in a Mexican hotel corridor and that near-death experience was burned into his memory. He prepared to execute an armed combat military exercise he'd learned in the Marines when breaking into an exposed hostile area. As the doors slid open, he dropped to the floor at the back of the lift, lay down flat on his side and began a sideways barrel-rolling motion that built up momentum as he crossed the threshold of the lift and entered the corridor.

Bullets whistled through the air three feet above him, filling the empty space exactly where he'd have been standing had he made the expected vertical exit from the lift. The bemused fighters needed a split-second to readjust their guns to a lower trajectory but that was all the time Leonard needed. He fired off two headshots, the first pulverised the left eye socket of one of the gunmen and the second created a small crater, dead centre, on the forehead of his compatriot. Leonard remained perfectly still for a moment, eyes fixed on the broken door to his hotel room, calculating the odds of Franklin hiding inside or having already fled the scene.

Screams rang out from hotel residents who'd heard the gunfire, and he figured he had five minutes tops before the hotel was flooded with reinforcements. He sprang to his feet and moved swiftly but cautiously along the corridor until he reached the doorway of his room. He paused and listened. At first, all he could hear from inside was the constant hum of the air-con, but he shut his eyes and concentrated and detected something else. As soon as he heard it, he knew exactly what it was. It was the sound of heavy, uneven breathing – a sound he'd heard countless times before on the battlefield, a sound he associated with death.

Leonard's mind was tormented with foreboding as he moved stealthily through the doorway, his body slightly bent forward, both hands clutching the Glock as he scanned the bedroom for any sign of Franklin but, within moments, he sensed the psycho had long gone.

Deshi's naked body was spread across the bed, her right hand clutched to her throat, desperately trying to stem the relentless flow of blood exiting the wound. Leonard's heart sank to his boots, but his military instincts kicked in and he ran towards the bed where he gently raised her head from the duvet and cradled it against his chest. He grabbed the small towel that was still wrapped around her damp hair and created a double layer cushion that he rammed tightly against the open wound. She was gurgling droplets of blood through her slightly parted lips, which dripped down her chin onto her chest, and she was clearly struggling to breathe. He held her softly in his arms and continually whispered her name. At first there was no response, and then, miraculously, he spotted a hint of recognition in her bloodshot eyes. She struggled to say something, but no sound came out, and Leonard dipped his face down, so he was almost touching hers. Then he heard her speak, although her faint voice was almost unrecognisable.

'Mo . . . I'm sorry . . . I got you into this . . . Get away . . . Get far aw—'

Her voice stopped abruptly and the life force behind her eyes vanished. Leonard continued to caress her face gently and then lost control and began sobbing hysterically. He'd only cried once before when, as a twelve-year-old boy, he'd said goodbye to his mother, his only parent, and now he was mourning another woman he loved who'd been taken away from him too soon.

Then the mental discipline he'd learned in the Marines that taught him how to operate in survival mode took over, as it was designed to do. He gently lowered Deshi's lifeless body onto the bed and moved away. He registered he'd almost run out of time if he was going to have any chance of making it out alive and kick-started his brain to run on automatic. He moved into the bathroom and ripped off his blood-soaked T-shirt, flinging it to the floor. Next, he scrubbed his face, hands and arms under the hot tap in the sink and, for a moment, his emotions overwhelmed him, as he felt flushed with guilt as he cleansed his body of Deshi's fresh blood.

Still dripping wet, he ran back into the bedroom and almost tore the wardrobe door off its hinges to rummage through some clothes to find a fresh top. Then he punched in the four-digit code to open the wall safe, grabbed his passport and wallet, and without a passing glance at the bed, darted out of the room and headed down the same set of stairs Franklin had used only minutes earlier.

Leonard exited the building into a side alleyway. As he entered the main street, he saw a group of angry drivers, working as a team, pushing the banged-up Chevrolet with half its front wing hanging off to the side of the road. He spun around the other way and began walking at pace. He'd only covered fifty yards when a black Defender flew past, heading for the front entrance of the Grand Palace Hotel. He didn't break stride but casually crossed the street, allowing him to innocently glance over his shoulder and witness five of Shomani's fighters pile out of the SUV and rush into the hotel entrance.

It didn't take long for Leonard to hail a cab and he headed straight for the border crossing and the sanctuary of El Arish International Airport on the Egyptian side. He needed to get thousands of miles away from the madness as quickly as possible. His mind was in utter turmoil – as a freelance assassin he'd pushed the boundaries many times before but, on this occasion, he knew he was out of his league. Franklin and his associates played by different rules and operated on a far higher level. He sank back into the black leather seat in the rear of the taxi, closed his eyes and allowed the darkness to envelope his mind as he thought about the future he'd just lost.

# Chapter Fifty

Gaza City, Gaza Strip

Back inside the converted cinema where Shomani was based, the mood was sombre. One of his chief lieutenants had just reported on the bloodbath he'd discovered on the third floor of the Grand Palace Hotel. He was furious he'd lost two more of his elite fighters – one of whom was a second cousin – and that yet again, Franklin was at the epicentre of the chaos. As well as sanctioning a clean-up at the hotel, Shomani insisted on a complete news embargo on the incident, which was accomplished by one quick phone call. The last thing he needed was press interest when he was about to mount a perilous attack on Israel. His friends at Hamas controlled the media inside Gaza with an iron fist and a call to the head of internal security ensured details of the firefight would never see the light of day.

Franklin was perched on the edge of his bed, his mind still buzzing from his confrontation with Deshi, when Shomani entered the room, determined to confront him about the disastrous episode.

'John, your recklessness has cost the lives of two more of my men – all to satisfy your ego. Despite our history together, you're rapidly becoming a liability rather than an asset.'

Franklin had no idea how events had played out after he'd left the scene and only had one thought on his mind.

'Is the girl dead?'

'Yes, she bled out, but that's not my concern. Her friend blew the heads off two of my men and then escaped from the scene. Who the hell is he?'

'Leonard's an assassin. He has no further beef with us – we won't hear from him again, but at some point in the future, when things calm down, I promise you I'll track him down and hand him over.'

Shomani seemed to accept the answer but wasn't done.

'Okay, but the attack on the girl was totally unnecessary and cost lives – another bad call, John.'

Franklin felt cornered and instinctively moved into full manipulative mode without showing the slightest trace of self-doubt.

'Khaled, Deshi was a disrupter, set on sabotaging our operation in Jerusalem, which I'm sure she planned to expose. Remember, after she faked her own death a few days ago, it would have been simple for her and her boyfriend to leave the strip – no one was looking for them – but she refused that option and chose to stay and spy on us. What does that tell you?'

Franklin knew the true reason Deshi had remained in Gaza: her obsession with killing Vargas meant she'd no choice but to follow him to Jerusalem in the hope the Argentine would show up, but Shomani didn't need to hear the truth – just a plausible lie. Franklin didn't leave space for the PJB leader to react.

'Let's talk about Jerusalem – when do we leave and how do you plan to cross the border?'

Shomani was no fool and made a mental note to revisit the conversation, but for now he had bigger fish to fry.

'Since the Israelis built the wall, there's only been two possible routes into the country – the Erez Crossing in the north and Kerem Shalom in the east. Erez is as tight as a drum and too risky, but the eastern crossing is far more porous. It's not a people border – it's only used for large trucks carrying goods in and out of Israel. When it first opened in 2010, about twenty passed through each day. At that time, every vehicle was thoroughly checked by the border guards, but now over four hundred use it on a daily basis and only one in twenty gets properly looked over.'

'So that's our way across?'

'Yes. We own a Volvo FMX with a forty-foot container that regularly makes the crossing, always carrying a selection of white goods – refurbished fridge-freezers and washing machines. There's a large hollowed-out section in the bottom of the container we use to move men and weapons across the border. Even if we get randomly selected to be checked, the prospect of moving over fifty heavy appliances is far too much hassle for the border guards. We've not been properly searched in over fifty crossings.'

Franklin was suitably impressed.

'What time do we go?'

'Tomorrow morning at eight. It's the busiest time for traffic, so we'll be part of a giant queue of over a hundred trucks. John,

I've done it many times before and it's not the most comfortable of rides, but once we're clear of the border, the driver will pull over and let us out.'

Shomani stood to leave and then had a final thought.

'Maybe don't eat too much tonight – it's going to be a tight squeeze in the trailer; you, me and our three martyrs.'

* * *

Berrettini had briefed Vargas and Hembury on his call with Mancini and the three of them were preparing for their upcoming night-time flight to Florence.

'Everything's in place for Franklin's arrival. We've no idea how he's entering Italy but once he meets up with Ricci at the hotel, his ass is ours. A soon as we have him in custody, Mancini's agreed we can fly him straight out of the country; no paperwork or going public. Only then can we give clearance to the government agencies in the threatened cities to make pre-emptive strikes on the terrorist groups planning the synagogue attacks.'

Hembury chipped in.

'Mike, I'm surprised some of them haven't already made a move.'

'To be honest, it's not been easy to get them all to hold the line, but I stressed the point to my counterparts that if we spook Franklin ahead of the attacks, he'll disappear only to return sometime in the future with a fresh operation. They seem to have bought into that argument for now, and if things play out the way we hope, we can give them the green light to move at least twelve hours before the attacks are due to take place.'

Hembury checked his watch.

'Guys, I've a lunchtime meeting downtown. What time is wheels up?'

'It's a late one – we fly at eleven, so let's meet back here at ten and we'll share a car to the airfield.'

Vargas was the first to rise from the table. He also had a meeting scheduled that was playing on his mind. He left Berrettini's office and made his way back to the makeshift one he shared with Hembury, knowing it would be empty as his friend was already on his way out of the building. Once he was back at his desk, he fired up his laptop and placed a Zoom to Buenos Aires, where his assistant, Juan Torres, was ready and waiting. After a couple of minutes catching up, Vargas brought up the reason for the call.

'Juan, we have confirmed intel that on the twenty-fifth there are ten synchronised attacks planned on synagogues across five continents. We know exactly what terrorist group will be involved in every case and pretty much how they plan to mount the attacks and—'

Torres interrupted his boss with the obvious question.

'Are we on the list?'

*'No, we're not, but I'm still concerned about the welfare of my in-laws, who'll be attending the Templo Libertad. To make matters worse, my sister-in-law Nadia, who flew over for Sophia's annual memorial, has decided to stay for Yom Kippur, which means there are three of them to worry about.'*

'But if it's not on the list, surely there's no threat?'

'Juan, I know this sounds odd but, ever since my encounter with that goon at the synagogue a couple of weeks ago, I've felt uneasy. Can you take four of our best officers with you on the day to reinforce their in-house security?'

Torres hesitated briefly before replying.

'Boss, while you're on leave I'm taking my orders directly from that hard-ass Delgado, and there's no way he'll sanction a move like that based on a hunch.'

He paused for a moment to reflect and then came up with a plan.

'But I'm owed a few days off, so I'll book it out and spend the day fasting alongside your father-in-law, even though I'm a good Catholic boy. How does that sound?'

Vargas managed a half-laugh but couldn't shake off the terrible sense of foreboding he knew didn't really make much sense.

'Thanks, Juan, I really appreciate it. I know it's crazy but I've a feeling in my gut I just can't shake off.'

Torres had the final word.

'That's good enough for me, boss.'

# Chapter Fifty-One

Washington D.C., United States

The Roy Edwards Cancer Center, which operated out of the Johnson Memorial Hospital in south-west Washington, was considered the leading facility in the state for brain tumour treatment.

Troy Hembury had been an outpatient there for almost two years, under the care of their chief physician Professor Andrea Rosenberg. Back in January 2022, Hembury, then based in Los Angeles, had been diagnosed with a grade three brain tumour that was inoperable and most likely fatal. A combination of chemo and radiation therapy, plus an inexplicable amount of good fortune, had minimised the growth of the tumour since the initial diagnosis. When it was first detected, it was just over an inch in size and had remained that way, defying initial medical expectations that it would grow twice as large in a matter of months. Hembury had often been referred to as a miracle patient, but in recent weeks he'd been suffering severe headaches that were almost unbearable and failed to respond to the strongest of painkillers. A week earlier he'd visited the centre for an MRI scan, and at the same time Rosenberg had dispensed a course of fentanyl tablets, a synthetic opioid analgesic similar to morphine but fifty times more potent. The fact they'd hardly touched the sides in dulling the pain made Hembury fear the worst when she booked him in to discuss the findings of the recent scan. As he sat across the desk from the professor in her state-of-the-art office, he wondered just how grim the diagnosis was going to be.

Rosenberg was in her mid-forties, with an elegant, petite frame, elfin-like facial features and an intuitive set of dark brown eyes. She was at the top of her game and regarded as one of the leading practitioners in her field by her peers. In her right hand was a white folder containing the latest scans, which she'd been checking through just before he arrived, although it wasn't the first time she'd analysed them.

Hembury kicked things off with a slightly sarcastic blunt opener.

'Doc, I'm not feeling much like a miracle man right now. Has my luck run out?'

She glanced down at the file yet again before fixing Hembury with her steady gaze. He was a man she'd grown fond of and who'd become a friend, which she knew was always a mistake in her profession.

'There's no way of sugar-coating it, Troy – it's not looking good. The tumour has almost doubled in size in the last three months. We don't know what the trigger was, but the cancer is spreading at an alarming rate and that's the reason for the severe head pains. Has the fentanyl helped?'

Hembury had expected bad news, but this was the worst possible. It meant he had little time left.

'The medication just makes me feel drowsy but doesn't really dull the pain.'

There was a brief silence and then Hembury faced up to the elephant in the room. 'How long?'

'Troy, if we don't make some sort of intervention, we're looking at two, maybe three months at best. The pain is going to become more regular and intense, and you won't be able to function on your own. We'll need to admit you at that point to try and make the last few days bearable.'

Hembury could tell how hard it was for her to tell him this news and tried to manage a comforting smile.

'It's okay, Andrea. The last two years have been a bonus, so I've nothing to complain about, but what do you mean by an intervention?'

'Troy, can I talk to you as a friend and not your physician?'

Hembury's lips formed a quizzical smile as he nodded.

'I remember when we first met, you told me you were a bit of a gambler. It could be that now's the time to put all your chips on one last roll of the dice.'

'Go on.'

'My colleague, Professor Edward McKinley, and his research team have been running clinical trials on a promising new drug called bezomide. It penetrates the DNA inside cancer cells and prevents them from multiplying, which massively improves the survival chances for people with astrocytoma – your aggressive type of adult brain tumour. The trials are in their infancy and we don't know much about the potential side effects and are only offering it to patients who—'

'Who have no hope, Andrea. I get it. Where do I sign?'

'Troy, if you're absolutely sure, we'll start you on a course immediately, but I have to warn you, it may still be too late.'

'Give me some odds to cling on to.'

The professor grimaced and took a few seconds before replying.

'I'd say maybe two, three per cent, but then miracles do happen. They're rare, but I've seen them first hand. Can I ask, is there someone close you want to discuss it with first?'

Hembury slowly rose from his seat considering her question. He was a divorcee with no children or siblings – in fact no family to speak of at all.

'Yes, there is someone – although the timing couldn't be worse.'

\* \* \*

Vargas was sitting in a corner booth in Martin's Tavern, a family-run Georgetown institution that dated back to 1933. The fêted bar boasted of visits from every president from Harry S. Truman to Joe Biden, and its fabled history included a rumour that John F. Kennedy had proposed to Jackie in one of the booths back in 1953.

Vargas knew it was one of Hembury's favourite drinking hangouts, although he'd never been there himself until now, and wondered why his friend had suggested meeting there for a liquid lunch. He was nursing a glass of cold beer when Hembury appeared carrying a pint glass of his own, although the content inside it was jet black with a pearly white head.

'Nic, before you ask, the reason I love this place so much is that it pulls the best draft Guinness in Georgetown – and that includes the three Irish bars.'

He took a long swig before sitting down alongside Vargas in the curved red leather booth.

'What's up, Troy? We've a shitload to prepare before we fly out tonight. This better be good.'

Hembury took another large swallow of the Irish liquid gold.

'Nic, I've just come from the cancer centre. I had a consultation with the professor reviewing a set of scans I had last week.'

Vargas felt a physical pain surge in his heart. He dreaded what was coming next.

'Troy, you've not said anything for months, so I stupidly thought all was well.'

'So did I until a few weeks ago, when I started suffering far more severe headaches – a new level of pain to anything I'd experienced before. Opioids were a waste of time and all I could do was crawl under the duvet in the darkness and pray for them to ease up. At the beginning they lasted for about fifteen minutes, but recently they've often gone on for twice as long. Sometimes they can be anything up to an hour.'

Hembury choked up and Vargas, who was already teary-eyed, leaned across to grab his oldest and closest friend. The two men hugged tightly as tears flowed down their faces. Despite their ten-year age gap, they were closer than any blood brothers could ever hope to be and, for Vargas, the thought of losing his friend was unbearable. It brought back the pain of Hembury's kidnapping and the gut-wrenching feeling when the cottage in Laytonsville exploded. He feared he couldn't go through that again. Eventually they broke out of the embrace and Hembury was the first to speak.

'Look at the state of us. Imagine if Berrettini walked in right now.'

Vargas laughed through the tears, which he was busy wiping away from his cheeks with a paper napkin.

'Don't fool yourself, Troy. He'd be just as bad. He thinks he's the third musketeer.'

It was Hembury's turn to laugh as the two men began to regain their composure.

'Before you ask, I've probably only got a few months left – maybe three at best. They're going try one last treatment – a brand-new drug that's still in development, but I'm not holding my breath. The only reason I'm sharing this with you is because the professor warned me I could have a seizure at any time. Potentially, it could happen in the next forty-eight hours when we're in Florence and that's why I had to tell you.'

Vargas was distraught but sensed Hembury was reaching out for his strength and support and the last thing he needed to see was an emotional wreck.

'What about Mike, do you plan to fill him in?'

'Absolutely not. There's no way he'd let me fly out with you guys and I have to see this through. I want to be right by your side when we finally nail Franklin. Nic, promise me you won't say a word.'

There was a note of sheer desperation in Hembury's voice and Vargas was in no frame of mind to deny his friend's plea.

'Don't worry about Mike, I promise to stay schtum.'

Hembury managed a smile that emanated pure warmth and even a tinge of happiness. Vargas understood his friend needed a purpose to stay alive so he could continue to fight the evil enemy burrowing deep inside his brain. The prospect of finally bringing Franklin down was probably the only medicine on earth that could keep him going for a few more weeks.

'I get it, I really do. But tonight, we're going be in the air for over eleven hours. What if you have one of those headaches when we're mid-flight? Troy, are you really sure you can do this?'

Hembury drained the last of his Guinness.

'Nic, I've never been more certain of anything in my entire life.'

# Chapter Fifty-Two

Wailuku, Hawaii

Sheila Adams, an agency ICU nurse, had just entered Caroline Bush's room on the third floor of the Memorial Medical Center to carry out a routine check, when three alarms triggered at the same time. A quick glance at the line of red lights manically flashing on the bank of machines by the side of the bed indicated her patient's blood pressure, pulse and respiration rates were dropping like a stone. Adams hit the red alert button and the emergency recovery medics arrived within ninety seconds, but despite their best efforts, they were unable to save their patient.

The previous week, Bill Bush had spent twelve hours a day at his mother's bedside and returned each evening to his small studio flat, less than ten minutes away, for some respite. It was just after sunrise, and he was driving to the hospital for his daily vigil when his cell rang. As soon as he saw the number, his heart sank. He knew it was over.

A few minutes later, when he entered the tiny room he'd come to know so well, there was a serenity he'd never sensed before. The first thing that struck him was the change in ambience: the machines were off and his mother was no longer connected to them by a spaghetti of IV tubes.

He warily approached the bed and leaned down to gently kiss her face. Her cheek still had a slight glow of warmth, which surprised him and was strangely comforting. Bill spent the following half hour sitting on his own with the woman who'd single-handedly brought him up since the age of twelve – the only parent he loved. He held her hand softly in his, and gradually the germ of an idea began to form in his mind.

Fifteen minutes later he found himself on a different floor of the hospital, sitting in an office facing the senior consultant who'd treated his mother since her admittance following the assault. The clinician expressed his condolences before explaining the reason behind her rapid deterioration earlier that morning.

'Mr Bush, you knew your mother's chance of recovery was always extremely low. The truth is, her body never recovered from the initial trauma of the attack, which was extremely severe.'

As the doctor continued to speak, his words disintegrated into a vacuum – a background wall of noise, as the phrase 'her body never recovered from the initial trauma of the attack' echoed in Bill's mind. As his thoughts began to crystallise, he knew exactly what he needed to do next.

He drove directly back to his studio apartment. Once inside, he made straight for the old tea-chest containing a bunch of scrapbooks and newspaper cuttings. He wasn't interested in any of them but was searching for something else he'd recently stashed away at the bottom of the storage box. It didn't take long to locate what he was looking for. He grabbed the burner cell his father had left with him and moved across to the small kitchen table in the corner of the room where he drew up a chair.

He powered up the phone and as soon as the screen illuminated, clicked on the contacts icon. He wasn't surprised to see a single entry, simply identified by the initials JF. Bill stared at it for a while and then rose and walked across to the fridge where he grabbed a bottle of Heineken that he downed in a matter of seconds. He'd heard of 'Dutch courage', and in this case the ice-cold lager did the trick. He messaged as instructed and Franklin called back in less than a minute. Bill thought he knew exactly what he wanted to say, but when he heard his father's voice on the end of the line all that changed.

It was early morning in Hawaii and the thirteen-hour time difference meant it was evening in Gaza. Franklin was lying on his bed, wide awake and restless, contemplating his trip to Jerusalem the following morning.

'Bill, how are you? It's so great to hear your voice.'

'Aren't you even going to ask how Mum is?'

From the get-go Bill had strayed off-script and he cursed himself for such an amateur mistake. He needed to focus and keep his father on side – at least for now. Franklin couldn't have seemed less interested as he replied.

'Yes, of course. How is she?'

Bill took a deep breath and then returned to the storyline he'd planned.

'She's still in a coma – there's been no change. The doctors think it could continue for weeks, if not months. But since I've been on my own, I've had a chance to think, and I know what I want to do – what I need to do right now.'

Franklin listened intently, fascinated to hear where his son was heading.

'Go on, Bill.'

'Dad, I want to come and spend time with you. Learn more about you. Try to understand you. When I was a kid, you meant everything to me. You were my hero . . . my dad. And then one day you disappeared, and everyone around me told me you were a bad guy – an evil man I should try and forget. Well, I did that for over eleven years, but now, knowing you're alive and seeing you . . . it's made me think. You told me you were involved in something major, and I want to experience it with you, whatever it is. Dad, I need to see you, and it has to be now.'

Franklin was normally devoid of emotion, but when he heard Bill refer to him as 'Dad', he was genuinely moved and wasn't quite sure how to frame his response.

'Son, just give me a few days and then I'll fly you out to meet me. It's just not the right time—'

Bill knew if he was to have any chance of changing his father's mind, this was the moment to play his ace card. He went for the jugular and the lies flowed smoothly.

'Dad, I've spent the last week reading everything I could lay my hands on about you and your grandfather. A lot of what you told me is starting to make sense. For over a decade you lied to me – letting me believe you were dead; you betrayed me. Now's your chance to make up for all those years. I must get out of this place right now, before I go mad. I can't just sit in a hospital room and stare at her. Dad . . . I beg you, please show some faith and trust in me and let me share in what you're doing. Let me be the son you've always wanted. If not now, when?'

Bill was drained, having delivered an Emmy-worthy perfor-mance, but now came the wait to see if he was going to collect the statuette. There was a long pause on the line as Franklin's brain filtered through his options. For once in his life, he was slightly overwhelmed and couldn't think straight.

'Okay, I'll arrange for a plane to collect you later today. I'll text you on the burner with the details.'

Bill smiled inwardly as he took a deep breath.

'Dad, where am I going?'

Another long pause followed.

'The Middle East.'

As soon as Franklin cleared the line, Bill switched phones and placed a new call.

* * *

Vargas and Hembury had returned to Berrettini's house to pack their overnight bags in preparation for their red-eye flight to Florence. Nothing more had been said about Hembury's illness as both men knew they needed to focus their thoughts on the following forty-eight hours. Hembury's mood was surprisingly good, probably because he felt a huge weight had been lifted following the lunchtime session with his closest friend.

The FBI deputy director was also there getting ready for the trip to Italy and couldn't resist teasing Vargas.

'How's your Italian, Nic?'

'*Parlo un po—*'

Before he could finish his reply, Berrettini's cell burst into life and his curiosity was piqued – he didn't recognise the international number. When he answered, he wasn't disappointed by the identity of the caller.

'Mr Berrettini, this is Bill Bush.'

'Bill, it's good to hear from you. How are you and, more importantly, how's your mum doing?'

It wasn't lost on Bill that a relative stranger had asked about his mother's welfare when his father hadn't.

'She's gone . . . she passed a couple of hours ago. The truth is she never stood a chance of recovering from the beating she got from my father. But that's not the reason I'm calling.'

Berrettini wasn't sure where the conversation was going but sensed something significant was about to unfold.

'I'm sorry to hear your sad news, Bill, but please go on.'

'You told me to call you if I heard from my father.'

'Yes, I did, and have you?'

Berrettini tensed up in anticipation and flicked the call on to speaker to allow Vargas and Hembury to hear.

'You see, I lied about the meeting with my father. As you no doubt guessed, he did leave me a way of getting in touch. He gave me a burner cell with instructions to message any time. We've just spoken and he's sending a plane to collect me in a few hours to take me to him.'

'That's incredible, Bill. I'm not going to ask why you're doing this but thank you. We know where your father's heading and we're also just about to fly to Italy so—'

'Italy? No, my father's in the Middle East.'

# Chapter Fifty-Three

Washington D.C., United States

The three men's expressions were identical, each of their faces engraved with a look of disbelief. Berrettini was deeply sceptical about this latest information. It just didn't make any sense.

'What the hell? Are we being played by another Franklin – is Bill lying to us? This could be a total red herring to draw us away from Italy.'

Vargas shook his head.

'Mike, I think the boy sounded straight-up. His mother's just died following a brutal attack from Franklin. He killed her. I get the impression he loathes his father and wants to bring him down. Do you think he's kosher, Troy?'

Hembury nodded in agreement.

'Look, we know Leonard was spotted in Gaza just two days ago, so now that intel makes sense if Franklin's out there too.'

The FBI deputy director wasn't buying it.

'But what about the file? We know the planned attacks are genuine and, besides, there's absolutely no way that punk Ricci was lying when he told us Franklin was meeting him in Florence. Don't forget the maniac was recently there in person, along with his female accomplice, scouting the actual synagogue and the back story about Hitler failing to destroy it back in 1944 checked out.'

He paused for a moment to gather his thoughts.

'Nic, I'm not taking this on face value. Let's set up a Zoom with Franklin's son. I want to see the whites of his eyes. Unless he convinces me otherwise, we're sticking with Italy as planned.'

\* \* \*

Bill was still in his studio apartment when the Zoom call began. It had been less than an hour since his initial conversation with Berrettini. Long enough for him to consider the implications of what he was about to do. He'd just lost his mother and now he was poised to betray his father. He wondered if he was doing the right thing, even though he loathed the man whose bloodline he shared and was desperate to cleanse his soul from the vile stench of Nazism, a horrific inheritance he despised.

Berrettini chaired the call from his end, with Vargas and Hembury sitting alongside.

'Bill, I appreciate this must be a difficult time for you. From our point of view, it's critical we know exactly what your father told you and when.'

Bill settled into his chair and took a deep breath before replying.

'To be honest, there's not much to add to what you already know, except that fifteen minutes ago I had a short message exchange with him on the burner cell about the plane he's sending to collect me.'

'Tell me precisely what he said.'

Bill picked up his cell and scanned the messages.

'Okay. He sent me a text saying, *Plane will land at Kahului Airport at 1430.* I replied pretty much straightaway, *Great I'll be there. I'm excited. Where exactly am I flying to?* He came back with *Middle East.* Clearly, he doesn't want to say exactly where, and I didn't want to push it.'

Berrettini was impressed with the young man's response.

'Good thinking – you don't want to spook him. Bill, I've a couple of questions I require totally frank and honest answers to before I decide how we act on this information. Our problem is we have pretty firm intel your father is on his way to Italy.'

'Go ahead, sir – I'm ready.'

'Firstly, what makes you sure your father isn't lying about the destination? Maybe he suspects you're in contact with us and is using you to funnel misinformation?'

Bill shook his head.

'I don't think so. Initially when I contacted him, there was no way he was prepared to entertain me joining him, and he wouldn't say where he was, but I squeezed him to the limit. I made it clear, if he wants a relationship with me, it must start right now. Plus, I spouted some bullshit about beginning to understand my heritage, which he lapped up.'

'Why are you so willing to sell your father out?'

Bill flew out the traps with a response that was nothing short of ballistic.

'Because I hate his guts. I loathe him and everything he stands for. Eleven years ago, he destroyed my life and my mother's, and then just as we were rebuilding them, he crawls out of the woodwork and brutally murders Mum. I need to purge myself of his Nazi bloodline. To me he's a rabid dog and I want – no I need you to put him down.'

Even an experienced campaigner like Berrettini was startled by the vitriolic outburst he'd just witnessed.

'Bill, give us five minutes and we'll pick this call up again.'

Berrettini cut the Zoom and turned to his colleagues.

'Well, what do we think?'

Vargas was first out of the blocks.

'Not a doubt in my mind, Mike – unless the boy's a top Hollywood actor. That outburst came straight from the heart. If Franklin is in Gaza, possibly with Leonard – the question is why? There's nothing there for him, so it can't be a destination in itself. It has to be a landing zone from where he's plotting some kind of operation. Are we talking Israel once again?'

Hembury was quick to back Vargas up.

'Mike, my gut tells me Bill is telling the truth, in which case Franklin set Ricci up as a fall guy and the Florence angle is fake. I think we change our flight plan and head to Gaza and warn Bekher about a possible attack.'

Berrettini heaved a mighty breath, reopened the laptop and a minute later Franklin's son was back on the screen.

'Bill, we're going to support you on this but we need your total cooperation. I still have an agent on the island. He'll meet you somewhere outside the airport where he can put a micro tracker in your cell. That way we'll have a fighting chance of knowing where you land and where you're taken. I'm also going to give you my number. You can call or text me any time. We suspect you're going to Gaza City, probably via

Egypt. We'll also fly there, but we'll enter through the Israeli border.'

'Gaza? What the hell is he doing there?'

'We're not sure yet, but whatever it is, it won't be pretty. I'll pass your number on to my agent and he'll arrange to meet you shortly. Good luck, Bill, and travel safe.'

\* \* \*

Three hours later Bill arrived in a taxi at the airport, having had a successful rendezvous with the FBI agent who'd fitted the tiny tracker, no bigger than a drawing-pin head, inside his cell, next to the battery. He walked through the small terminal entrance moments before Franklin's private jet landed on the runway and watched as the Gulfstream taxied towards the terminal and came to a halt no more than fifty yards away.

Having gone through the formalities of checking in, which simply involved flashing his passport to a bored uniformed woman, Bill walked briskly through the glass double-door exit onto the runway and made his way towards the jet. He was pulling a small roller case behind him and carrying a black leather computer bag in his free hand. The automatic stairs had already dropped down into position, and waiting for him at the bottom was a smartly dressed young man, who was clearly Eastern European.

'Mr Bush, my name is Wojciech. It is a great pleasure to meet you. I've worked for your father for almost five years and it's my job to ensure you have a pleasant and safe flight.'

Bill mustered the best false smile he could manage.

'Well, Wojciech, the first thing you can do is tell me exactly where we're flying to?'

'I'm afraid I'm only at liberty to tell you we're travelling to the Middle East via a quick fuel stop in Vietnam.'

Bill grimaced but didn't push the point as he moved towards the steps. As he did so, Wojciech sidestepped smoothly and blocked his path.

'Oh, one last thing, Mr Bush. I need you to hand over your cell phone and laptop before you enter the plane.'

# Chapter Fifty-Four

Gaza City, Gaza Strip

At first glance, the forty-foot container attached to the Volvo FMX truck appeared no different to the other ten parked up alongside in the large industrial warehouse on the outskirts of the city.

The back doors were wide open and four men were busy loading it up with a hotchpotch of reconditioned fridges, freezers and washing machines, carefully avoiding a three-foot-square area of floor space about halfway down, beneath which was a steel trapdoor just wide enough for a human to drop down through. It had been cut from the fake metal floor, which had been raised by two feet and ran the entire length of the container.

It was a claustrophobic space, big enough for up to eight people to hide inside so long as they lay flat. The floor was cushioned by six wafer-thin mattresses sewn together that reeked of stale urine and faeces. There was no natural light, so the stowaways relied on torches, once they were hidden inside. Tiny air holes had been randomly drilled into the floor, which was basically a roof to the huge rectangular coffin, designed to smuggle suicide bombers across the border.

Franklin and Shomani were standing a few feet away from the rear of the unbranded container, watching the loading take place.

'John, I've made this trip at least five times in the last eighteen months and I need to warn you, this will not be a pleasant experience for a man who's used to travelling the world in a private jet. There is some good news, though – we won't be inside it for long. We're fifty miles from Jerusalem, but we'll be released by the drivers once we're safely across the border. The biggest delay will come while we're queuing to go through the crossing – that'll probably take an hour, so in total, we'll be inside the compartment for about ninety minutes.'

Franklin was only half listening, because he was staring across at the three PJB fighters standing in a tight group about ten feet away. They were holding neatly folded green fabric suicide vests prepped with several 'pipe' cylinders, filled with explosives that weren't yet attached to detonators. He turned away from them to face Shomani.

'Tell me about the bombers – what's their background? Are you convinced they'll see it through? Without them, we've nothing.'

The PJB leader reared up, clearly indignant at the query.

'John, do not question my competence in such an important matter. These men have been groomed by a leading imam in our community and trained in one of the mountain camps specifically for this moment. They're ready to become martyrs in the name of Allah.'

Franklin brushed off the reprimand and peered into the back of the lorry.

'What happens next?'

Shomani glanced down at this watch.

'All five of us squeeze past the machines and drop down through the opening into the space underneath the false floor. Then three fridges will be pushed into position on top of the trapdoor. After that, we're effectively sealed in. The two drivers upfront will keep me informed of our progress via a walkie-talkie. They're elite fighters from my personal guard who'll stay with us in Jerusalem throughout the operation and, hopefully, accompany us on the return journey. You ready to go?'

Franklin nodded and moved towards the rear of the container. Ten minutes later, he was lowered into the black hole by one of the drivers and immediately his senses were invaded by the appalling stench inside the compartment. Shomani was already inside, lying on his back. He called across to him.

'John, are you okay?'

Franklin's stomach heaved and he was forced to swallow his own vomit. It took him a moment to fully clear his throat, and before he could reply, an ear-piercing screech of metal scraping against metal reverberated throughout the compartment. The trapdoor slammed shut and a cloak of darkness enveloped the space.

\* \* \*

The FBI jet maintained a forty-thousand feet cruise and was halfway through its six-thousand-mile journey. Berrettini had agreed to switch the flight plan from Florence to Tel Aviv, which was an hour's drive from the Erez border crossing into Gaza. The FBI deputy director had his cell glued to his right ear, and by the grim look on his face, the news he was hearing was far from welcome. When he came off the call, Vargas and Hembury waited anxiously for a debrief.

'Yet again, that bastard Franklin is one step ahead of us. Our agent in Hawaii, Dan Mellow, met up with Bill, successfully loaded the tracker into his cell and it's working perfectly.'

Vargas jumped in.

'So, what's the problem?'

Berrettini shook his head.

'Mellow watched Franklin's plane take off hours ago and yet the tracker shows Bill's still on the ground at Kahului Airport. Franklin's people obviously took his cell off him, so now we've no way of knowing where's he's going, and he's got no way of telling us.'

'Christ, every time we think we have an inside track, we get hit with a curve ball. What's our next move?'

'I'm going to place a call to Bekher and warn him we believe Franklin's hiding out somewhere in Gaza, planning a fresh attack on Israel.'

Berrettini needed to wait over an hour before Bekher was free, and when he came on the line, it was clear the Mossad chief was not in the mood for small talk.

'Mike, POTUS lands in less than two hours and he's travelling straight to the US Embassy in Jerusalem where he'll meet the prime minister. Then the two of them will travel to the Knesset for a special sitting and make a joint address, after which they go to Beit Aghion, the PM's state residence, for a banquet with the great and the good. Bearing in mind we've had just over forty-eight hours to plan this, the security implications are a total nightmare, so, to be honest, I've got very little headspace left for whatever you're going to hit me with.'

'I get it, Doron, so I'll cut straight to it. I'm with Nic and Troy and we're on our way to Tel Aviv – we should be there in about five hours. We've sketchy intel that indicates Franklin is currently in Gaza, planning an imminent attack somewhere in Israel, possibly on a synagogue. I get how busy you are right now, but can you do one thing? Can you close the border crossing for the next forty-eight hours, until the twenty-sixth?'

Bekher let out a maniacal laugh.

'Mike, that's impossible. I'd need much firmer intel to pull a move as big as that, especially with so much else going on.'

'Doron, I'm telling you, that bastard is planning something for the twenty-fifth—'

'Okay, I get it. Look, the best I can do is send an emergency order through to the border police to enhance random checks on vehicles crossing the border and ensure every single one is properly inspected for the next twenty-four hours. It's going to cause chaos and huge delays, but I'll do it. Send me the last image you have of Franklin so I can forward it with the order. Mike, I've got to go, but if you need anything while you're here, just ask.'

\* \* \*

Franklin didn't normally suffer from claustrophobia but found the brutal confinement of his hiding place almost unbearable. Even though he was in total darkness, his coping mechanism was to keep his eyes tightly closed, attempting to shut his surroundings out, particularly the foul stench that hung in the air.

The scene inside the secret compartment was surreal. The three bombers were murmuring the noon salat prayer while Shomani kept in regular contact with the driver via a walkie-talkie.

The border crossing was only twenty-five miles from Gaza City and the Volvo truck covered the distance in just over forty minutes. As it approached the checkpoint, the queue of similar trucks and large vans snaked back around the twisty road for about two hundred yards from the crossing. Shomani had a brief radio exchange with the driver and then spoke to Franklin for the first time since they'd departed the warehouse.

'We're at the border. The driver says the queue is shorter than normal for this time of day – there's about fifty vehicles in front of us, so as long as we're not pulled over for extra checks, we should be through in less than an hour.'

Franklin mumbled an acknowledgement but kept his mouth firmly closed as he was in imminent danger of retching. The queue moved quickly, and once the truck reached the crossing, the exchange between the drivers and guards was cursory: paperwork was handed over to one guard, while a second took a brief look inside the back at the cargo. As soon as he saw the tower of white goods packed tightly inside the container, he indicated to the co-driver to close the doors and they were sent on their way.

Ten minutes later, when they were almost two miles inside Israeli territory, the truck pulled over into a lay-by and the driver and his comrade leaped out of the cab and opened the rear doors. They immediately began moving the machines around until they'd cleared a space above the secret trapdoor, which they slid open. The sudden burst of daylight that flashed into the compartment was blinding, but nevertheless welcome, and Franklin was the first to be heaved out of the hellhole. Fresh air had never tasted so sweet, and a few moments later, he was standing on the roadside together with Shomani, who was talking on his cell. The three suicide bombers had also exited their hiding place and were huddled together a few yards away. The PJB chief finished his call, turned to Franklin and pointed towards a black Jeep Wrangler that had just pulled into the lay-by and was parking up next to the truck.

'John, we're going to complete the journey in a bit more comfort. My men will take a short break here and then continue the drive inside the truck.'

As precisely the same moment Franklin and Shomani settled in the back seat of the jeep, the senior guard at the Kerem Shalom border received an urgent confidential email from Mossad's Tel Aviv office instructing him to begin thorough individual checks of every vehicle passing through the crossing for the following twenty-four hours. He cursed with frustration as he anticipated the chaos the order would create for him and his colleagues. He clicked on an attachment that displayed a fuzzy colour headshot of Franklin wearing his trademark red baseball cap. The guard glared at the image and shrugged before turning to a colleague in the guardhouse.

'Print this photo and hand out copies to the guards. Whoever this bastard is, he's just ruined my day.'

* * *

Bill was the sole passenger on his father's private jet. Apart from Wojciech, everyone else on board was crew. The decor dripped pure opulence, the result of a grotesque interior design budget that matched the seventy-million-dollar cost of the jet itself. He was seated in one of six cream, full-grain leather armchairs, designed and built in Italy, each comfortably big enough to accommodate two adults. The scarcity of seats freed up a huge amount of floor space inside the jet, which was home to a massive bedroom, cinema and sauna. The floor was covered with a selection of seventeenth-century silk Isfahan rugs from Persia and the walls were lined with hand-painted, embroidered de Gournay wallpaper, broken up by priceless artworks which Bill speculated had been stolen from German Jews eight decades earlier.

The sheer absurdity of the luxurious surroundings was not lost on Bill, who detested his father's blatant display of obscene wealth. It demonstrated a total lack of class, but right now, it was nothing more than a distraction because he was far more concerned by the loss of his laptop and his two cell phones: his personal one, which contained the tracker, and the burner he'd received from his father. He felt exposed and alone but knew he still had one trick up his sleeve; a unique God-given talent he possessed that might prove to be a game-changer down the line: his photographic memory. Aged eight, he'd been diagnosed with an eidetic memory, which meant he could retain visual images – objects, words and numbers – in his short-term memory far longer than the average person. In theory, he could memorise an entire Shakespeare play after one read, although not surprisingly, he'd never put that to the test. Far more relevant right now was the benefit of having Berrettini's cell number imprinted on his brain. The question was, once he met up with his father, would he be able to lay his hands on a device to be able to use it.

# Chapter Fifty-Five

Jerusalem, Israel

T he black jeep nimbly negotiated its way through the one-way streets in Jerusalem, before turning into the entrance of a car park development on Akhad Ha'am Street. The building work was ongoing, but the newly extended multi-storey parking complex was seriously taking shape, and when Franklin emerged from the rear of the Wrangler, he was blown away by the transformation that had taken place in the two years since he and Shomani had purchased the site. The PJB chief had made four visits to the development in the previous nine months to monitor the construction of the tunnel, and so was far more familiar with its progress.

Franklin made his way up the central ramp designed to take vehicles from the newly extended ground floor to the upper levels and Shomani accompanied him.

'Khaled, your brother did a great job with this development. It's a shame it'll never see the light of day. After tomorrow, the Israelis will tear this place down and no doubt blow up the tunnel that I'm desperate to visit.'

'John, be patient for a few more minutes. I've planned a run-through with our three martyrs as soon as the truck gets here, and we'll accompany them on the scout. Right now, let's go to the apartment, shed these clothes and grab a shower to rid ourselves of this stench.'

* * *

The jet with Berrettini, Vargas and Hembury on board touched down in the military section of Ben Gurion Airport in Tel Aviv, a perk laid on by Bekher. Waiting for them on the tarmac was a blacked-out Range Rover, accompanied by a local Mossad agent. As they walked down the steps of the jet, Berrettini's cell pinged to signal an incoming WhatsApp message from the Mossad chief.

> Mike, sorry I can't be there to meet you but it's frantic here. Sent one of my very best men to look after you. Forget the hotel – you're my guests, so you'll be staying at one of our safe houses in Tel Aviv.

The FBI deputy director was flanked by his colleagues as he led them towards the world's most luxurious SUV.

'Bekher came through at the last minute, which means he's taking the threat seriously, although he clearly has his hands full looking after POTUS.'

The thirty-minute journey from the airport to the port area where the safe house was located allowed time for the Mossad agent who was driving to introduce himself. Yossi Ezra was the grandson of a former Israeli prime minister and one of Bekher's most valued and trusted assets. Like most Israeli men, his features were dark and brooding, with brown penetrating eyes and a mop of carbon black hair. Ezra was surprisingly short for an elite agent, but his five-foot eight-inch frame was carved from solid muscle, and he held a prestigious black belt in the Israeli martial art known as Krav Maga; a lethal combination of aikido, karate and boxing techniques that focused on executing offensive manoeuvres in one-to-one combat. He glanced in the rear-view mirror to take a better look at his three VIP passengers.

'Gentlemen, welcome to Israel. My job is to assist you any way I can. The chief gave me a quick briefing over the phone. He feels it would be reckless and frankly pointless to enter Gaza at present, unless we've some idea where the target is based. The border checks have been significantly tightened, as you requested, so hopefully, your man won't make it across. Rest assured, if you do receive strong information on a precise location in Gaza City, we'll alert our assets over there and look to take him out.'

Hembury, who was sitting directly behind the Mossad agent, didn't take in a word Yossi said. His head was lowered and his eyes squeezed shut, as he massaged his forehead with both hands. Berrettini was sitting on the passenger side with Vargas wedged in the middle, but the FBI deputy director still noticed his colleague's obvious discomfort.

'Troy, are you okay?'

Hembury didn't reply immediately, and before Berrettini could probe any further, Vargas cut in.

'Mike, I think all of us desperately need a bit of shut-eye before we're fit to function. Yossi, how far to the safe house?'

The Mossad agent glanced down at the sat nav.

'About another twenty minutes.'

Vargas leaned slightly forward.

'Okay, put the hammer down.'

* * *

The one-bed apartment tucked away at the rear of the ground floor of the car park formed part of a lateral conversion, using the space previously occupied by a run-down supermarket. The interior was clean and sparsely furnished, with white-washed walls, grey lino flooring and Ikea furnishings.

Franklin and Shomani took turns in the black-tiled shower room, where the piping hot water managed to cleanse their bodies of the foul smell that seemed to have permeated their skin. By the time they'd dried off and changed, the truck had arrived and dropped off the three suicide bombers who were now assembled in the open-plan living room.

Franklin was getting edgy, desperate to see the tunnel, and Shomani was now ready to oblige. He beckoned the American to follow him into the bedroom, where he walked across to a run of white wardrobes and opened the door of the last one. It was empty inside, except for a few wire hangers that he brushed to one side. He bent forward and removed the back MDF panel to reveal a door-sized opening, carved out of the back wall. Franklin's eyes nearly popped out of his head as he leaned over Shomani's shoulder to peer into the hidden void, where a series of ceiling lights burst into life, activated by motion sensors.

Franklin and the three suicide bombers followed Shomani along a narrow concrete ramp that sloped downwards for about fifty feet. At the bottom, the ground evened out and the cement-walled corridor widened into a rectangular opening that revealed the entrance to the state-of-the-art tunnel. When Franklin caught a glimpse of it, he gasped as he took in the spectacular sight laid out in front of him. The fully illuminated eighteen-hundred-foot structure stretched straight ahead in a perfect line as far as the eye could see. He shouted across at Shomani, his voice bursting with excitement.

'A straight line directly into the heart of the Jewish state.'

A narrow-gauge iron rail track, usually found inside a coal mine, had been laid the entire length, and resting on top of the wooden sleepers, were three battery-powered steel mine carts, each big enough to hold a large man.

Shomani gestured towards them and Franklin hauled his body into the middle one, directly behind the PJB chief. Inside the bucket-shaped carts were two large buttons: one green, one red. Shomani hit the power and his cart set off, closely followed by Franklin's. The steel buckets soon reached their ten-mile-per-hour limit, and it took just under two minutes to reach the far end, where they disembarked by a concrete stairway which led to a trapdoor, carved out of the cellar floor of the synagogue. Shomani pointed up towards it as they stood side by side at the foot of the staircase.

'This is as far as we go. We need to walk back and manually push the carts as they only run in one direction.'

Franklin looked slightly bemused, until Shomani explained the logic.

'There's no need for them to run both ways – our martyrs aren't coming back.'

# Chapter Fifty-Six

Amman, Jordan

As Franklin's private jet came in to land, Bill peered out of the window and was surprised to see the signage that greeted him on the front of the huge terminal below. The Queen Alia International Airport in Amman was the largest in Jordan and only a seventy-five-mile drive from Jerusalem, which is why Franklin had chosen it as an entry point to Israel. As the plane taxied down the runway, Wojciech appeared in the cabin and joined him.

'Welcome to Jordan, Mr Bush. We've a two-hour car journey to our destination, where you father is waiting to greet you.'

'No more games – where is he?'

'Patience, Mr Bush. You'll know soon enough. Let's go.'

The black Mercedes S-Class exited the airport car park and headed north-west towards the King Hussein Bridge, which marked the border crossing into Israel. It was early evening and heavy traffic slowed them down, but once they crossed the bridge and entered Israeli territory, they hit the highway and headed straight for Jerusalem. Bill had never been to the Middle East before, so kept a constant vigil on the road signs, and as they reached the outskirts of the city, it became apparent they were heading for the Israeli capital.

He'd had plenty of time on the long-haul flight to figure out a way of alerting Berrettini and it was time to put his plan into action. Realistically, he knew it had about a fifty-per-cent chance of succeeding but it was the only idea he'd managed to come up with and decided if he was going to give it a go, it was now or never. He glanced down at his watch and spoke to Wojciech, who was sitting up front alongside the driver, for the first time on the journey.

'How much longer?'

'Depends on the traffic but thirty minutes max.'

Bill raised his voice and mixed in a huge dose of desperation.

'No, I can't wait that long – I'm busting for a crap. We need to stop, or I'll shit myself.'

Franklin's employee stuck to his script.

'I'm afraid I've strict orders from your father to bring you directly to him.'

Bill upped the ante and turned the screw.

'For Christ's sake, Wojciech. Have you seen my dad when he truly loses it? If I mess my pants, due to your stupidity, I guarantee you'll be out on your skinny Eastern European ass.'

He allowed the threat to hang in the air for a few seconds before following it up with, 'Now get that idiot beside you to pull over at the next services or get my father on the line. It's your choice.'

Bill had timed his outburst perfectly because he'd just spotted a three-mile sign for an upcoming petrol station. Wojciech didn't reply but leaned across to the driver and relayed a brief message. Five minutes later, the Mercedes left the highway and pulled into the Sonol car park. He braced himself – it was game on.

Wojciech followed him into the large shop that formed part of the service station, where Bill headed straight for the men's lavatory situated at the rear of the store. He reached the door and waited for his escort to catch him up before continuing the abuse.

'Are you planning to come in and wipe my ass?'

Wojciech was already reeling from the verbal assault he'd suffered in the car and was in no mood to take another dose, so held his position just outside and allowed Bill to enter on his own. Inside, there was a block of six cubicles on the left, facing a run of urinals and sinks on the right. At first sight, there was no one else present and Bill cursed under his breath, but then he heard the sound of a toilet flush, and a few moments later, a scruffy Israeli teenager emerged from the end cubicle.

Bill guessed he was probably a student as he was wearing the classic uniform: a Save the Planet T-shirt with an image of Greta Thunberg, along with ripped denims and a pair of black Converse trainers. His greasy shoulder-length hair clearly hadn't seen shampoo in a while and the strong smell of cannabis that followed him out the cubicle indicated he'd just finished a toke. He took a furtive glance at Bill as he moved across to a sink, where he began washing his hands. It was a cursory gesture and a few seconds later, he walked towards the door, where Bill had maintained his position.

'Do you want to earn the easiest hundred dollars of your life?'

The teenager was clearly taken aback and stopped in his tracks, a quizzical expression plastered across his face. Like most Israelis, he was proficient in English and his reply was not what Bill expected to hear.

'Are you a pervert or something?'

'No – no. I've lost my phone and I just need to borrow yours to send a text – simple as that. But I need to do it right now. What's your name?'

'Nathan.'

'Look, Nathan, I'm not kidding.'

Bill reached inside his jacket and pulled out a wad of twenty-dollar bills, peeling off five and gesturing for the young man to take them.

'Who do you wanna text?'

'Just a friend . . . but it's really important I tell them where I am. I just need your phone for thirty seconds.'

Nathan pulled his cell from his back pocket.

'If it's worth a hundred, then it's probably worth double that.'

Bill knew he'd no time left to negotiate and was terrified Wojciech would appear at any moment. He added five more notes to the stash.

'Okay, two hundred's fine. Now, pass me the phone.'

Nathan grabbed the money from Bill's outstretched hand and stuffed it in his front pocket.

'No way, I'm not letting go of this. Give me the number and the message.'

Bill clenched his fists, bubbling with rage. Every second he wasted threatened his plan. He slowly called out the digits and as soon as he saw Nathan had set up the text, he dictated the message.

Jerusalem. Not my cell but will try and send location
address when I can.

Nathan punched in the words and hit send.

'Are you some kind of spy?'

As he glanced up from his cell, he just caught the back of Bill
leaving the washroom. Outside in the shop, Wojciech was still
on guard, standing in the same position. As soon as he saw Bill
emerge from the toilet, his face contorted with contempt.

'That was a long crap. Promise me you won't tell your father
we stopped off.'

Bill flashed a beaming smile.

'I won't, if you won't.'

# Chapter Fifty-Seven

Jaffa, Israel

The safe house was located in the old port of Jaffa, a few miles south of Tel Aviv. Its three new guests were just settling in when Berrettini received Bill's text. He was in the kitchen, rustling up some food for himself and Vargas, while Hembury was in his room taking a nap.

'Nic, you need to see this.'

He passed his cell over and Vargas read the message.

'Damn, another game-changer. Bill did well to lay his hands on a phone. He's a smart kid.'

'Yes, well, look who his father is.'

Vargas leaned across the breakfast bar and reached for a mug of steaming hot coffee, freshly made by Berrettini. He took a sip and reflected for a moment.

'Exactly, so can we really trust him?'

'That's the million-dollar question, which we'll learn the answer to in the next twenty-four hours. Nic, you go and wake up Troy and I'll call Yossi – we're heading to Jerusalem tonight.'

Yossi Ezra was still at the wheel of the Range Rover, five minutes away from his apartment in downtown Tel Aviv and the prospect of a well-earned night's sleep. This was his tenth consecutive day at work and he couldn't wait for his head to hit the pillow, but all that changed when he saw Berrettini's number flash up on the dashboard screen.

'Yes, sir. What's going on?'

'Yossi, I need you to return to the safe house. We need to get to Jerusalem asap. I'm sure you guys must have somewhere there we can stay. Can you call the chief and give him a message from me?'

Yossi had already slowed the car and was in the process of making a U-turn.

'I'm all ears, sir. Go ahead.'

'Tell him he can call off the border checks in Gaza. The bastard's already in the country and hiding out somewhere in the capital.'

\* \* \*

The Mercedes entered the Old City of Jerusalem through the Damascus Gate entrance, heading for the car park site, a couple of miles away. Bill's gaze was permanently focused through the passenger window, memorising street names along the route. His computer brain had no problem storing them in an imaginary Filofax he could recall at any time: left onto King David Street, straight across Plumer Square onto Ze'ev Jabotinsky Street, and then right onto Akhad Ha'am Street.

The Mercedes slowed as it turned left into what appeared to Bill to be a building site, where it came to a halt. The driver emerged from the front seat and opened the back door, gesturing for him to exit. He'd arrived in the heart of Jerusalem, and although it was his first visit, thanks to his eidetic memory, he knew precisely where he was.

Wojciech drove off in the Mercedes without saying goodbye, leaving Bill in the care of a tribesman who led him towards the apartment. He was puzzled by the location, which was clearly a car park development, but figured all would become clear soon enough. What wasn't apparent was how he would lay his hands on another cell phone, now he was inside his father's lair. It was a short walk and Bill followed his escort into the apartment, where he was immediately struck by the hive of activity taking place inside the open-plan living area, but, strangely, there was no sign of his father.

Three Arab men dressed in traditional white thobes and matching keffiyehs were huddled in the far corner, taking turns filming themselves on a cell phone that was attached to the top of a black metal tripod. It was a confusing tableau, and even though Bill didn't speak a word of Arabic, he could tell emotions were running high.

'They're thanking Allah for the opportunity to become a martyr and saying goodbye to their loved ones and friends.'

Bill instantly recognised the unmistakable voice of his father and spun around to discover him standing in the hallway alongside another Arab who had an impressive air of authority about him. Franklin did his best to muster a welcoming smile and extended his right hand, which suited Bill because he'd no appetite for a fake hug. Franklin had mixed emotions on the arrival of his son. It represented another potential victory for the control freak but was also a distraction he could do without, less than twenty-four hours before the attack was due to take place.

'Bill, let me introduce you to a very old family friend, Khaled Shomani. Khaled is the military chief of the Palestinian Justice Brigade and has partnered me on this operation.'

Shomani could tell by the stunned expression on Franklin's son's face, that he'd no idea what he'd walked into.

'Bill, I'll leave it to your father to explain the precise details of the huge blow we're about to deliver against the Israeli oppressors.'

He paused to gesture towards the suicide bombers, who were sitting on the floor, checking their newly filmed video messages on their cells, and sticking Post-it notes on the back of the phones with the entry PIN codes.

'These men will become legends in Islamic history – martyrs whose names will be immortalised in the story of our conflict with the Jews. Ahmed and Farouk are brothers and Hamza is their first cousin. They've spent years preparing themselves for this moment. After the attacks take place, I'll send their videos to a contact we have at Al Jazeera and the world will see the faces of the three men who died to cut the head off the snake.'

Bill felt as though his brain was about to go into meltdown as he tried to digest and make sense of what he'd just heard from Shomani. He knew his father was a monster but had no idea he was also on the verge of becoming an international terrorist. It was as though he were stuck in a nightmare, then reality kicked back in as his father gestured towards the bedroom.

'Bill, come with me. I want to show you the tunnel.'

* * *

The drive from Tel Aviv to Jerusalem took less than an hour and it was early evening when Yossi delivered his three VIPs to the King David Hotel, deep in the heart of the city centre. As the Range Rover pulled up in front of the magnificent pink limestone façade, he glanced in the rear-view mirror.

'Gentlemen, because of the presidential visit in the city tomorrow, all our safe houses are crammed with Secret Service agents, so the chief booked rooms for us all here. I'm staying with you for the duration of your visit. He's authorised me to provide you with weapons, so I need to go and collect them from an armoury close by and I'll drop them into your rooms shortly. Mr Berrettini, you're booked into a junior suite with a lounge the chief thought could work as a meeting room for you guys.'

The FBI deputy director leaned forward and patted the Mossad agent on the shoulder.

'Thanks, Yossi. He's right, we've got a lot to talk about. No doubt you'll find us all in my room when you get back.'

Check-in was quick because they were the only guests in reception, and a few minutes later, they assembled in Berrettini's suite, desperately second-guessing what Franklin was up to. They grabbed beers from the fridge before moving across to the spectacular floor-to-ceiling windows in the lounge area that offered a stunning view over the Old City of Jerusalem. Vargas guzzled down the contents of his green Peroni bottle and let out a huge sigh.

'Right now, Franklin is somewhere down there, within touching distance, planning some kind of offensive on the very day the President of the United States rides into town. Surely, from what we already know, it has to be a synagogue?'

Berrettini maintained his gaze over the Old City but shook his head.

'Remember what Bekher told us. Firstly, the Great Synagogue in Jerusalem has a Mossad ring of steel around it, as well as dozens of agents inside. It's protected from both land and air attacks and is pretty much impenetrable. Secondly, POTUS only announced his visit a few days ago, so there's no way he can be the target.'

Hembury, who was still recovering from the brutal sledge-hammer attack on his brain that had laid him low during the car journey from the airport, moved closer to one of the giant windows until his nose was almost touching it.

'Bill is also somewhere down there, probably reunited with his father by now. We really need that kid to come through.'

Berrettini glanced down at his watch.

'As soon as Yossi returns with the weapons, I suggest we try and grab a few hours' shut-eye. I suspect tomorrow will be a bastard of a day.'

\* \* \*

Less than a mile away from the hotel, Franklin was also preparing to turn in for the night, although he'd far too many endorphins pumping through his brain to contemplate sleep. He was finally within touching distance of fulfilling the legacy he'd inherited from his grandfather.

The tiny living area inside the apartment had been converted into a temporary barracks, with Shomani, his two fighters and the three suicide bombers utilising three double mattresses that were randomly spread across the wooden floor of the living room.

Franklin and Bill had no choice but to share the bed in the tiny bedroom that concealed the entrance to the tunnel. A situation that pleased neither of them, especially Bill, who was desperate to find an excuse to leave the apartment and try to locate a phone. He lay on top of the sheets, fully clothed, with his eyes clamped shut, pretending to be asleep, but like his father, his brain was wired.

Franklin had shown him the tunnel and taken him through the plan, so he could see the inevitable consequences and massive disruption in world order should the US president and the Israeli prime minister be taken out in a terrorist attack in the Middle East.

As he fought against jet lag, he came to the mind-numbing conclusion he was probably the only person alive who could prevent this horror show from happening.

# Chapter Fifty-Eight

Jerusalem, Israel

25 September 2023, Yom Kippur
Day of Atonement

B ill wasn't sure what time he finally drifted off, but when he was woken up at six a.m. by the sound of prayer chanting, he felt as though he'd only managed to grab a couple of hours' sleep. It took him a few seconds to gather his thoughts and then everything came sharply back into focus, and he knew exactly what he needed to do.

There was no sign of his father, just a deep imprint on the sheets next to him that was still warm to the touch. The only bathroom in the apartment was in the hallway but Bill spotted a small sink in the corner of the bedroom, leaned over it and splashed ice-cold water on his face, jolting his senses into gear. He was about to check out the chanting when he noticed the far wardrobe door was partially open, which explained why his father was no longer in the bed. He figured the maniac was somewhere down below, inspecting his beloved tunnel.

Bill opened the bedroom door, coming face to face with the source of the chanting. It was an intriguing sight. The mattresses had been pushed to one side and had been replaced by rows of prayer mats for Shomani and his five men. They were on their knees, facing east towards Mecca, chanting the dawn Fajr prayer, the first of five they recited daily. He felt like an intruder and instinctively retreated to the bedroom, just as his father emerged from behind the wardrobe.

'It's good you're up, Bill. I need to talk to you. Let's go outside and get away from that horrendous din.'

They walked out of the apartment at the back of the car park and kept going until they reached the entrance. Bill used the opportunity to look across the street, searching for a nearby shop, hoping he could find a believable excuse to nip out and visit it in the next hour.

Franklin leaned on a freshly plastered section of the wall and turned towards his son.

'Bill, I want to fill you in on my plans for the aftermath because we'll need to disappear from the scene as soon as the attack happens. The Israelis will look to shut down the city, so we'll have to move fast to beat the roadblocks. They'll also close the border you came through last night as it's so close to Jerusalem. The timings are critical, and you need to be across them. The prime minister and president will arrive at the syna-gogue at nine and the attack will take place an hour later. As soon as it happens, Wojciech will be waiting for us here with the Merc and we'll head south to Eilat, where there's a soft border into Jordan. Once we reach Aqaba, a short helicopter ride will take us up to Amman, where my jet will be ready to go.'

Bill slipped back into acting mode and feigned excitement.

'Incredible. You seem to have thought of everything. What happens then?'

'We return to my boat and spend the next few months cruising the world, getting to know each other. I'll finally have the time to educate you on the truth about your family history – as opposed to the fiction you've learned at school or heard in the media.'

Bill wasn't really paying attention because he'd spotted a small supermarket only fifty yards away that might prove to be his salvation. Someone inside was bound to have a cell. He pointed towards it.

'That sounds great, Dad. Is it okay if I pick up some gum from the store over there? Can I get you anything?'

Franklin's tone changed as he turned up the heat on his son.

'Bill, we're about to create history with the biggest world event since 9/11. We're in lockdown. Nobody leaves this site. For the next few hours, I want you right by my side.'

* * *

The platter resting on the coffee table, laden with breakfast croissants and pastries, remained untouched, as did the bowl of fresh fruit next to it. Berrettini was pacing the lounge in his suite while Vargas and Hembury stood next to each other by the window, looking down on the Old City. None of them was in the mood to eat and they were surviving on a cocktail of strong black coffee and stress as they waited for something to break their way.

Berrettini checked his watch for the third time in ten minutes – it was just before eight.

'Guys, I've a call with Bekher coming up. He can only give us two minutes because he's under the cosh, but it's better than nothing.'

Vargas turned away from his window vigil.

'Mike, I hate being this passive. It feels like we should be tearing the city down, brick by brick, looking for Franklin, rather than waiting for a possible tip-off from his son.'

The FBI deputy director nodded in agreement and checked his cell again.

'Okay, here we go. I'll put the phone on speaker. Guys, jump in any time, he knows you're with me.'

Moments later, Bekher's familiar voice boomed through the room. The echo confirmed he was travelling in a car.

'Mike, I'm on my way to the synagogue – the PM and the president are arriving at nine and I'm chaperoning them for the three hours they're inside. Then at midday POTUS leaves for the airport, boards Air Force One and we can all breathe again. Just to reassure you, every Mossad agent in the country is currently in the capital, so my resources are stretched to hell, which is why I can only spare you Yossi. Mind you, he's worth two regular agents all day long. Any update on Franklin and his whereabouts?'

'Not yet, we're waiting for his son to come through with a location. How do I contact you if he does?'

'After nine, my cell will be set to do not disturb, because I'll be inside the synagogue, standing next to the PM. Mike, I'll put your number on favourites so if you call, I'll know.'

Berrettini could sense the Mossad chief was desperate to wind up the call.

'Okay, Doron. I wish you well over the fast, and if it's any consolation, none of us is eating a thing – we've lost our appetites.'

Bekher laughed in response and Berrettini glanced at his colleagues in case either of them had anything to add before the call ended. Hembury took the cue and chipped in. He glanced at the three Beretta handguns resting on the coffee table.

'Doron, it's Troy – thanks for the hardware.'

'No problem. Let's hope you guys don't need to use it.'

As Bekher signed off, there was an unspoken consensus in the room: none of them shared the Mossad chief's optimism.

# Chapter Fifty-Nine

Jerusalem, Israel

25 September 2023, Yom Kippur
Day of Atonement

With just over an hour to go, the suicide bombers were sitting cross-legged on the floor of the apartment, making last-minute adjustments to their vests. There was an uneasy tension hanging in the air as the clock ran down and every passing minute seemed to last an eternity. Bill was seated next to his father at the small round dining table in the centre of the room, watching the final preparations take place, in total silence. Shomani was standing alongside his martyrs, looking on intently as a physical pillar of support.

The green fabric vests were worn like regular waistcoats and had been tailored to fit as tightly as possible. The men took turns helping each other put them on, tightening the four straps stitched on the back. Resting in the middle of the table were three hand detonators – palm-sized plastic units with long, thin fuse wires, designed to run along the inside of the arm and connect to one of the explosive tubes sewn into the vest, which was then joined to seven more. The detonators had live manual triggers, which would be firmly held down in a tight hand-grip and activated on release. The prospective martyrs knew the moment they were killed, their hands would go limp, releasing the tension and instantly setting off their explosive-filled vests.

Franklin was fascinated by the detonators, but Bill's gaze was focused on three other objects which lay on the table and held far more interest for him. The cell phones belonging to the suicide bombers were invitingly laid out in a neat line, yellow post-it notes stuck to the back of each one, with their respective PIN codes. Bill desperately needed to get his hands on one of them for a few seconds but failed to see how he could he pull it off without being noticed. Shomani said a few words in Arabic to the three fighters and then walked across the room to join Bill and his father.

'I'll be taking the men down in about fifteen minutes and plan to travel with them along the tunnel to see them safely through the trapdoor of the cellar before returning. I assume you'll both want to join me?'

For the first time in years, Franklin felt truly alive. Every sinew in his body was energised now the moment he'd feared would never happen, was less than an hour away.

'Khaled, we'll be with you all the way and—'

Bill interrupted his father mid-flow and went for an all-or-nothing play.

'Dad, I suffer from claustrophobia. It's so bad I can't even use a lift. Last night, you'll remember, I didn't spend more than two minutes in the tunnel with you. I simply couldn't cope.'

Franklin's face turned puce with naked anger as he released a torrent of abuse.

'Any son of mine needs to show backbone. This is a historic moment in our family's war against the Jews and if . . .'

Shomani had heard enough.

'John, we've no time for this distraction. Bill can stay here with my two drivers, who'll keep him safe. As soon as we return, I'm leaving with them in the same truck we arrived in, and I believe you've sorted your own transport.'

Franklin glared daggers at his son who'd embarrassed him in front of the leader of the PJB. For Bill, though, the humiliation was worth it. Shomani continued as though the fiery interlude had never happened but played his eyeline exclusively towards Franklin.

'Timing-wise, my men will enter the cellar at nine-fifty, which means you and I will have time to walk back to the entry point of the tunnel before the explosions are triggered at ten. We'll hear and, no doubt, feel them go off but be far enough away to be safe.'

* * *

The cars carrying the prime minister and the president were choreographed to arrive outside the front of the Great Synagogue at the same time, so the two leaders could enter together. The president had spent the night at the American ambassador's residence, while the Israeli prime minister was travelling in from his home on Smolenskin Street in the upscale neighbourhood of Rehavia.

Bekher was waiting in position by the main entrance of the

synagogue to meet the two world leaders and accompany them inside. The prime minister emerged first from his car, along with his wife and, a few seconds later, the president exited his vehicle, accompanied by his ambassador and two Secret Service agents who followed in their wake.

As the Mossad chief escorted them inside the imposing building, the small group walked past lines of plainclothes agents and overtly armed military personnel who were guarding the exterior. Ironically, they were all in the wrong place because the threat to the politicians' lives was coming from underneath the structure, not outside it.

Once inside, the VIP party swiftly took their places in the centre of the spectacular prayer hall, which was full to the brim, with every seat taken. The morning service was well under way and as soon as they reached their seats, they draped black-and-cream woollen prayer shawls across their shoulders, to blend in with the rest of the congregation. The two leaders were positioned next to each other, with Bekher flanking his prime minister, while the president sat alongside his ambassador and the Secret Service agents.

Bekher's eyes flicked around the huge space, identifying over thirty elite Mossad agents strategically located in all four corners of the synagogue, close to every potential entry point. As soon as he confirmed they were in position, he took a deep breath and, for the first time in twenty-four hours, allowed himself a moment to relax, believing that for now, the two men in his care were in a safe place.

\* \* \*

Berrettini watched the arrival of the leaders on the large flatscreen in the lounge of his suite, along with Vargas and Hembury. As soon as he saw them disappear inside with Bekher, he turned away from the TV and walked across to the windows overlooking the city. The mood in the room was sombre and he was the first to address it.

'Guys, this is unbearable. We can't just sit around doing nothing. Nic, can you call Yossi and ask him to meet us out front in five. Let's go to the area near the synagogue and get a proper sense of what's going down.'

Vargas nodded and glanced at the Berettas on the table.

'Are we arming up?'

Berrettini nodded in the affirmative. A few minutes later, the Range Rover departed the grand entrance of the King David Hotel and headed west with Yossi at the wheel.

'Where are we heading, sir?'

Berrettini was staring at his cell, watching live coverage of the president's visit unfold on CNN World News.

'Let's start with the synagogue and go from there.'

# Chapter Sixty

Jerusalem, Israel

25 September 2023, Yom Kippur
Day of Atonement

I
t was just after nine forty-five and Shomani and Franklin had already walked the full length of the tunnel and were standing together in the open space beneath the floor of the cellar, the entry point to the synagogue. At the other end, the suicide bombers were climbing into the solid steel mine carts, about to begin a short one-way trip. The hand detonators were still not connected to their vests – that final step wouldn't happen until they were in the corridor inside the synagogue, seconds away from entering the prayer hall.

Franklin watched as the mini train made its way steadily towards them. The only sound inside the tunnel was a low hum as the carts effortlessly glided along the rails, but all he could hear was the pumping of his heart filling his ears. His brain was overloaded with anticipation and excitement. His distorted view of the world, polarised by his unerring faith in the virtues of Nazism, confirmed his belief that the slaying of two of the most prominent leaders of the Western world was totally justified. As far as he was concerned, the hideous attack was long overdue and the culmination of his life's work.

\* \* \*

Inside the apartment, Bill was running out of time, and he knew it. Shomani's drivers, who didn't speak a word of English, showed little interest in him but were hanging around in the main room, leaning against a wall just a few feet away from the table where the phones were sitting. They were tantalisingly close, yet still out of reach.

One of the men was glued to his cell, working his way through the levels of a mobile version of *Call of Duty*. His partner, meanwhile, was constantly switching his attention between Bill and the wall-mounted TV that was tuned to CNN.

Bill was desperate to create a brief distraction but was bankrupt of ideas. In the end, he went for a simple play, a last-ditch plan he figured was probably destined to fail, but he'd run out of options.

He walked into the small open-plan kitchen and poured himself a black coffee from a glass percolator resting on the granite worktop and filled two extra mugs at the same time. He casually moved across the room with a mug in each hand, heading for his two babysitters. As he anticipated, *Call of Duty* man shook his head and grunted, not bothering to look up from his screen, but his colleague nodded and extended an arm to grab a mug. Bill passed it across, and at the critical moment, deliberately reached forward a touch too quickly, so the side of it collided against the man's outstretched fingers, spilling boiling coffee over his right hand. He let out a cry, followed by an Arabic curse, as the ceramic mug smashed into pieces on the wooden floor, its contents instantly forming a black sticky pool.

Amazingly, the other fighter only glanced up from his game for a moment when his colleague brushed past him, frantically heading for the kitchen, where he continued to curse as he held his hand under a cold water tap at the sink.

The brief hiatus was all the time Bill needed to palm the phone closest to the edge of the table and slide it into the front pocket of his jeans. For a second, he remained rooted to the spot, holding his breath in case his sleight of hand had been noticed, but both men were preoccupied for entirely different reasons.

Bill made his way into the bathroom, locked the door, and rested his weight against it as he retrieved the cell. His hands were shaking, as was his entire body, and for an agonising moment, he struggled to press the power button. After a heart-stopping few seconds, the screen burst into life. The first thing he noticed was the digital clock displaying the time – 09.56. He punched in the PIN code from the Post-it note and clicked on the text icon. Then, the unimaginable happened – his infallible photographic memory failed him for the first time in his life. His brain froze, and as hard as he tried, he couldn't visualise Berrettini's cell number. A wave of terror engulfed his brain as he realised his superpower had deserted him just when he needed it most. He was so frantic, he'd no idea he was talking out loud.

338

'Come on . . . come on . . . focus, you moron . . . think . . . think.'

He desperately racked his brains, but his concentration was blown apart by a harsh banging on the door. One of Shomani's men was standing outside, shouting in Arabic, ordering him to open up. Suddenly, an image crystallised in his mind: a ten-digit number, black on white. He punched the numbers into the cell. The banging became more ferocious, and Bill feared the door was about to burst open, along with his heart, which was pumping a staggering one hundred and fifty beats a minute.

'Hold on . . . I'm having a piss. Wait.'

Bill typed in a short message, hit send and moved away from the door towards the toilet, where he prised open the top of the cistern, flung the cell inside and closed the lid. He pulled the flush handle and moments later opened the door where *Call of Duty* man greeted him with a threatening glare. Bill faked a smile, shrugged his shoulders and walked straight past him. As he moved into the hallway he glanced down at his watch – 09.58.

\* \* \*

The three bombers had travelled from the cellar up a twisty staircase, through the basement, and were now standing inside the rabbi's empty office, less than ten yards away from a corridor and door that opened directly into the rear of the prayer hall. Each man carefully attached the end of the fuse wire to a fixing on their vest, enabling a live circuit with the detonator. Ahmed, the youngest of the three, struggled with the straightforward task because his hands were trembling, and he wasn't convinced he'd made a secure connection. Farouk, the nominal leader of the group, checked his watch – 09.59. His voice dropped to a whisper as he turned to his fellow martyrs.

'Let's go. Praise be to Allah.'

Ahmed stopped fiddling with his wire, praying to his god he'd done enough.

Inside the synagogue, Shimon Stern, the Israeli prime minister, had been called up from his seat by the rabbi to help carry the handwritten scrolls from the enormous wooden ark at the back of the prayer hall. He was proudly standing next to the rabbi, clutching the giant scrolls to his chest, while the congregation sang a familiar prayer. The president was intrigued by the ritual and leaned across the empty seat vacated by Stern to whisper in Bekher's ear.

'Doron, this must be a real honour for your prime minister.'

'Yes, Mr President. It's called an aliyah, a privilege normally only granted to the most senior and esteemed members of the community.'

He pointed to a wooden platform with a reading podium in the centre of the hall, close to where they were seated.

'In a few moments the prime minister will carry the scrolls to the bimah, where the rabbi will read from them. It really is a huge honour.'

\* \* \*

Everyone inside the Range Rover heard Berrettini's cell ping. Vargas and Hembury held their breath as the FBI deputy director scanned the message.

Three suicide bombers tunnelling into Great Synagogue. Entering from rear. 10 a.m. Franklin and PJB leader in ground-floor apartment. Car park – Akhad Ha'am street.

Berrettini exploded.
'Jesus Christ! Yossi, how far is Akhad Ha'am Street?'
'Three, four minutes.'
'Make it two – Go . . . go . . . go!'
The agent's right foot almost went through the floor as it bore down on the throttle and the huge SUV surged forward like a rocket. Berrettini hit Bekher's contact on his cell, praying his friend would pick up.

Inside the synagogue the Mossad chief's cell rang and dozens of angry heads turned in his direction, wondering what idiot was rude or stupid enough to forget to switch their phone onto silent. Bekher's instinct was to kill it but then he remembered the identity of the only contact he hadn't blocked on the do-not-disturb setting. He clicked the green icon and Berrettini's voice roared down the speaker.

'Doron – three suicide bombers have tunnelled in. Coming in through the rear of the prayer hall—'

Bekher keyed his radio, which was on an open setting to all agents inside the synagogue.

'Three hostiles wired up. Shoot to kill. They're coming from—'

Before he'd time to complete the order, the door to the right-hand side of the ark flew open.

# Chapter Sixty-One

Jerusalem, Israel

25 September 2023, Yom Kippur
Day of Atonement

Farouk led the charge, and within seconds of bursting through the door, set eyes on the most famous face in the Middle East. He'd expected his target to be sitting more than thirty feet away in the centre of the giant prayer hall, but Shimon Stern, the man he'd been indoctrinated to hate more than any human on the planet, was standing directly in front of him, less than ten feet away.

For the briefest of moments, he locked eyes with the Israeli leader before launching himself like a cannonball in a desperate attempt to get as close as possible. A cascade of bullets rained in from multiple directions, ripping his torso apart, and a split second before his hand went limp and his body exploded mid-air, the last sight he witnessed was a look of sheer terror on the face of the Israeli prime minister.

The explosion rocked the building to its very core and the

sound of the blast that echoed around the prayer hall was deaf-
ening, shattering the huge stained-glass windows positioned
above the ark. The two other bombers, who were only a handful of steps behind their leader, vanished in the smoke cloud,
and in the following few seconds, their bodies were riddled
with bullets from a relentless onslaught of rounds cutting
through the grey haze, tearing them to shreds. Only one of
their suicide vests detonated, so Ahmed's vision of entering
paradise through jihad, with its promise of seventy-two
virgins, was cruelly denied him, due to a pair of shaky hands
and a faulty connection.

Terrifying screams drowned out the sound of gunfire, as
lethal shrapnel from the bombs flew through the air indiscriminately, along with thousands of deadly shards of coloured glass
that rained down on the petrified congregation like multi-
edged knives. Unbridled panic was unleashed as hundreds of
horror-struck people streamed down the aisles, searching for
an escape from the chaos and carnage.

The two Secret Service agents hurled themselves at the
president, bundling him to the ground, taking on the role of
human shields. Bekher performed an identical manoeuvre
on the American ambassador, but despite his heroic action,
his thoughts were focused on the fate of the man he'd the
responsibility of protecting at all costs, the leader of the
Israeli people, who he feared had been wiped out in the
initial explosion.

Eighteen hundred feet away, at the entrance to the tunnel,
Franklin and Shomani heard the blasts and felt the aftershock
that rocked the huge underground structure. Franklin experienced a massive surge of excitement, although his initial

exhilaration was slightly tempered by the perfectionist side of his brain that wondered why he'd only heard two explosions.

\* \* \*

Yossi manoeuvred the bulky Range Rover through the narrow streets with the dexterity of a Formula One driver. The SUV screeched to a halt outside the car park development on Akhad Ha'am Street, less than two minutes after the first explosion shook the interior of the Great Synagogue. Everyone inside the vehicle heard the blasts, even though they were hundreds of yards away. They knew their worst fears had been realised and could only pray for the lives of the people trapped inside. There was nothing they could do to help them, so for now, they needed to focus on catching the twisted mastermind behind the attack, who they believed was somewhere inside the building site they'd just arrived at.

Franklin and Shomani raced back into the apartment, grabbed a few personal items and were ready to leave when they caught sight of the CNN news report on the wall-mounted TV, which was transmitting live pictures across the world from outside the front of the synagogue. An aerial drone shot captured the enormity of the attack as huge plumes of black smoke billowed skywards through the gaping hole on the back elevation of the synagogue where the giant stained-glass windows had previously been in situ. Down below, hundreds of terrified people were flooding out of the entrance like a frantic colony of ants, desperate to find a haven. The news anchor had a sombre tone to his voice as he provided commentary on the distressing footage. Franklin and Shomani were glued to the screen, listening with bated breath to the latest update.

'It's believed two suicide bombers broke into the giant prayer hall just after ten this morning, and despite being gunned down by Mossad agents, managed to detonate their explosives. It's feared dozens of people have been killed in the attack, with many others being seriously injured. I can confirm the President of the United States has already been evacuated from the building by the Secret Service, along with the US ambassador, and although they were both hurt, it's believed neither has suffered life-threatening injuries. However, unconfirmed reports claim Shimon Stern, the Israeli prime minister, may have been killed in the atrocious attack, but I stress, these are unsubstantiated rumours . . .'

Bill and the two drivers were also transfixed by the live broadcast, although Bill was the only one in the room struggling to conceal his true emotions. He was distraught that his warning had clearly come too late and wondered if Berrettini and his team would show up before Shomani and his monster of a father disappeared. All he could do was hope.

Yossi warily led the way inside the car park with Berrettini, Vargas and Hembury just a few steps behind. All of them had their weapons drawn, locked and loaded, ready for anything that might come their way. It took less than thirty seconds for the Mossad agent to spot a harmless-looking white door tucked away in the far right-hand corner of the ground floor. It led onto a narrow corridor with a second door at the end. He assumed it belonged to the apartment Bill had referenced in his text. Yossi gestured towards it with his free hand and the group slowly crept in that direction.

Inside, all eyes were glued to the TV screen as speculation grew by the second regarding the fate of the prime minister. None of them had any idea of what was happening just outside the apartment.

Yossi gave a final affirmative nod to the group before carefully reaching for the metal door handle, which he slowly eased downwards. He could sense by the lack of pressure, the door was unlocked – a bonus he hadn't expected. However, he didn't know what was waiting for him on the other side and took one final deep breath before he was good to go.

The door burst open and Yossi flew through it, flanked by Vargas and Hembury, with Berrettini just a couple of steps behind. The two PJB fighters reacted like a pair of rabbits in the headlights, desperately reaching for their weapons, while Franklin did a double take in horror.

Shomani had been standing with his back to the door, so as he spun around to face the intruders, he was a good half a second behind his men, who already had their guns semi-drawn. Yossi's reflexes were razor-sharp, and he fired two headshots within a split second of each other that virtually decapitated the fighters before they could get a round of their own away.

Vargas fired at Shomani, also going for a headshot, but he was on the move and the bullet ripped into the top of the PJB leader's right shoulder, propelling him backwards, where he crashed against the far wall, before slamming to the floor. He roared with pain. The bullet had blown a giant hole through his collarbone, which had shattered into tiny fragments.

It was all over in less than three seconds.

Franklin remained rooted to the spot in horror, alongside

Bill who was splattered with blood spray from the gaping head wound of *Call of Duty* man, whose body had slumped to the floor, immediately in front of him.

Shomani was a natural warrior, and despite the excruciating pain that engulfed the upper part of his torso, he instinctively reached inside his thobe for his weapon. A move spotted by Yossi, who spoke fluent Arabic.

'One more inch and I'll blow your head clean off what's left of your shoulders.'

The terrorist leader knew he was in the presence of an elite marksman and stopped in his tracks, slowly dropping his left arm to the side of his body.

Berrettini stepped further into the room and stared down at Shomani.

'No need for Arabic, Yossi. Unless I'm mistaken, this man is the chief of the PJB's military wing and I believe he speaks perfect English. I'm sure he'll have plenty of time to demonstrate his bilinguistic talents after we hand him over to our friends at Mossad.'

Yossi leaned forward to take a closer look and instantly confirmed Berrettini's identification of the Arab leader, who was sprawled on the floor in front of him.

'Khaled Shomani – if I'd recognised you earlier, the first headshot would have been yours. Hand over your weapon and roll onto your stomach with your hands behind your back.'

While Yossi attached a pair of heavy-duty solid-metal handcuffs, banned by all other police forces around the world, to Shomani's wrists, Vargas and Hembury stared intently at the face of the monster they'd been chasing across the globe for over a decade. Hembury had met him once in person, eleven years earlier in San Francisco, but Vargas had only ever spoken to him on the phone or seen him on a screen.

The TV commentary was still streaming and was loud enough for all of them to hear. Franklin glanced at the screen and then beamed a defiant smile in their direction.

'It seems we succeeded in cutting off the head of the snake – a blow the Jews will never recover from.'

He flicked his eyeline towards Vargas and issued a chilling warning.

'You'll soon come to regret the day you decided to hunt me down.'

Berrettini retaliated with a line he knew would cut Franklin to the quick.

'Bill, step aside and come over here.'

Bill didn't need to be asked twice and stepped away from his father towards the FBI deputy director. Franklin's arrogant smile vanished as the realisation of his son's betrayal hit home. He glared at Bill, a terrifying look of menace etched across his face, before spitting out an accusation drenched in pure venom.

'So, it transpires you really are your mother's son.'

Bill was shaking with fear and didn't reply but Berrettini had heard enough.

'Yossi, let's get these scumbags out of here and hand them over to your boss.'

A few minutes later, the seven men left the apartment together and made their way towards the car park exit. Yossi and Vargas had guns pointing directly at the back of Franklin and Shomani's heads, while Berrettini, Hembury and Bill walked one step behind. As they reached the entrance ramp, Bill spotted the black Mercedes he'd arrived in the night before, parked up about ten yards away.

At the same moment, Yossi tensed up – he'd caught sight of the bodies of two men sprawled on the ground, halfway between himself and the car. Their throats had been slashed and thick trails of blood were leaking tiny rivers onto the concrete floor. Bill almost vomited on the spot as he recognised the lifeless corpses of Wojciech and the driver who'd brought him to Jerusalem from Jordan. Before Yossi could react, a single shot rang out and a 5.56 millimetre round penetrated the right ventricle of Shomani's heart, and the military leader of the Palestinian Justice Brigade was dead before his body hit the ground.

A second later, three Taliban fighters emerged from behind the Mercedes, armed with M16 assault rifles, which were aimed at the remaining six men. Yossi knew his Beretta was no match for the semi-automatic weapons and slowly lowered his gun, a gesture Vargas mimicked. The Afghans, dressed head to toe in black, moved around the front of the car and walked forward in a line, stopping about ten feet in front of Yossi, who was standing slightly forward of his colleagues, next to Franklin.

The Taliban fighter in the centre, who was clearly the leader, still had some discharge emanating from the muzzle of his M16, which he lowered before speaking.

'Hand the American over, and I'll let you live.'

Berrettini knew better than to move, so spoke from where he was standing.

'Who are you?'

The only reply he received from the leader was a raising of his assault rifle, which he aimed directly at the head of the FBI deputy director. Franklin broke the uneasy silence.

'They're Taliban, and you can't hand me over.'

Franklin's plea for help was met with a short burst of gunfire that whistled over their heads.

Yossi's response was to kneel and calmly lay his pistol on the concrete floor.

'We've no choice but to do exactly as they say.'

Franklin's eyes flashed around in his head, as his brain desperately searched for a way out. He knew the fate in store for him in Kabul and there was no way he could endure the extreme levels of torture and prolonged pain awaiting him in the Afghan capital.

Yossi slowly rose to his feet and began walking backwards, leaving Franklin to face his destiny on his own. Vargas and Hembury followed suit, as did Berrettini and Bill, who didn't feel an ounce of remorse for his father's plight.

The Taliban leader signalled to his colleagues to approach Franklin who, bereft of his wealth, power and influence, cut a pitiful, solitary figure. Suddenly, he looked ten years older. He flinched as both his arms were grabbed in a vice-like grip by the Afghan fighters who approached from either side. For a moment, he stayed rooted to the spot, twisting his head around, almost in an *Exorcist*-type motion, to glare back at his other enemies who were watching the event play out in silence.

Franklin's eyes zoomed in on Bill with pinpoint accuracy and his son felt as though they were burning holes directly through his retinas.

'You've betrayed your own bloodline with your actions and your inevitable punishment will be severe – I'll personally ensure it.'

Vargas felt a cold chill run down his spine. The scene he was witnessing between father and son was surreal. Franklin suddenly lost eye contact with Bill as he was jerked forward by his two assailants, who lifted him off the ground and began moving as a threesome towards their leader. He knew it was futile to resist and was already thinking ahead, frantically searching for solutions. Within a matter of seconds, he was bundled into the middle of the back seat of a waiting Ford Explorer, parked up about twenty feet away from the Mercedes.

As the SUV pulled away, its tyres screeching, Vargas swore he heard a harrowing scream mixed into the ear-piercing sound that echoed around the empty, cavernous car park. Moments later, the Ford took a hard right onto the street, fish-tailing as it disappeared into the Jerusalem traffic.

# Chapter Sixty-Two

Jerusalem, Israel

25 September 2023, Yom Kippur
Day of Atonement

Back inside the car park, Yossi was on his cell, calling for backup but, unsurprisingly, every Mossad asset in the capital, was unavailable, with the city in total chaos following the attack on the synagogue. Berrettini resumed control and walked across to Shomani's corpse before turning to the group.

'Guys, these bodies aren't going anywhere. I suggest we decamp back to the hotel until I can reach Bekher.'

\* \* \*

It was four hours later when the Mossad chief finally returned Berrettini's call. The FBI deputy director was in his suite, accompanied by Vargas and Hembury, watching the rolling newsfeed on TV. Bill had checked into a separate room and

Yossi had left the scene after dropping them off at the King David Hotel.

Berrettini switched the call to speaker and placed his cell on the edge of a glass coffee table in the centre of the room. Bekher's voice sounded slightly hoarse and weary, testament to the unrelenting calls the Mossad chief had been on since the bombings.

In a dramatic announcement three hours earlier, Israel had confirmed the assassination of the prime minister. Over fifty world leaders had already condemned the outrageous strike and the US president had issued a statement from hospital, where he was recovering from cuts and bruises, pledging his full support to the Israeli State.

'Mike, I've just had a debrief from Yossi. It sounds as if you guys went through the wringer as well today. It's a miracle you survived. You called this event days ago and I just didn't take it seriously enough. It's incredible to believe Franklin was joined at the hip with Shomani. And a tunnel that took almost two years to build was right under our nose. This is a colossal fail-ure of intelligence and I'm at the heart of it.'

Berrettini glanced across at Vargas and Hembury.

'Doron, we're all on the same page here. It's not your personal screw-up.'

'Are you kidding? I watched as my prime minister was blown into a million pieces. Meanwhile, although the ten attacks we had intel on from Franklin's file were all thwarted one way or another – it turns out the bastard had a few more targets up his sleeve that weren't on that list.'

Vargas jumped in; his voice almost paralysed with concern.

'Buenos Aires?'

'No, Nic. All we know about so far are Jo'burg, Paris and Sydney – over ninety deaths and hundreds injured in three coordinated attacks at prominent city synagogues. Franklin's filthy signature is scrawled all over it. Guys, I've got to go but let's pick this up in the morning, and, Mike, I'm truly sorry.'

As soon as Bekher rang off, Vargas grabbed his cell and called his assistant, Juan Torres, who'd promised to keep a personal vigil over his in-laws, who right now were inside the Templo Libertad in Buenos Aires, along with hundreds of other worshippers. Vargas cursed as the call went straight to voicemail, and after a couple more attempts, he tried his father- and sister-in-law's phones, with the same frustrating result. Then his heart sank into his boots as he recalled the recent visit for his wife's memorial service, when he'd discovered that the historic structure had no phone signal whatsoever.

* * *

Seven and a half thousand miles away, on a different continent, with a six-hour time difference, a blacked-out Cadillac Escalade pulled up about twenty yards away from the entrance of the most famous synagogue in Argentina. Sitting in the front passenger seat was Bruno Guzmán, the self-proclaimed leader of the Victory Nationalist Party. In the back, were three of his most fanatical followers, waiting on his cue to exit. All four of them were wearing black linen two-piece designer suits, with semi-automatic machine guns balanced precariously on their laps.

Guzmán knew the two security officers guarding the entrance were retired Jewish policemen, who were happy to earn a few extra dollars every weekend, donning uniforms and pistols they hadn't fired in years, if ever. Consequently, getting in would be simple, and once inside, they'd have a field day.

Unfortunately for Guzmán, he hadn't factored in an unscheduled intervention from Juan Torres, who'd put a precaution in place. Vargas had pleaded with him to swamp the synagogue with a team of officers, but that request had been turned down by his superiors, due to a lack of solid proof of an imminent attack. Torres wasn't about to let his boss down, however. He'd persuaded one of his best men, Santino Ramos, to take a day's leave, and at that moment, he was standing in front of the synagogue, having replaced one of the two regular guards – his eyes firmly focused on the black SUV.

Guzmán took a final drag on a non-filtered Camel, before flicking the stub into the passenger well of the rental, where he trod it into the thick pile carpet with the sole of his left shoe. He reached inside his jacket pocket, retrieved a fine-knit black balaclava and pulled it tightly over his head. His men followed suit, and then he gave the signal.

They exited the Escalade together and headed straight for the street-level entrance of the synagogue, their weapons on display and aiming forward.

Ramos had watched them all the way and wasted no time in pulling out his Glock 17, just as one of Guzmán's thugs set himself to begin the onslaught. Ramos fired first and two rounds carved open the stomach of the gunman, who never saw them coming. Guzmán and his two other men were quick to react and dived to the ground, before discharging their weapons. A hail of bullets blew away the regular security guard, who was rooted to the spot, paralysed by fear. Ramos refused to be intimidated and held his ground, crouching low in a classic firing pose, and four more carefully aimed rounds took care of Guzmán's other two men. But the fascist leader was no slouch either, and was canny enough to use one of his men's fallen bodies as a shield. He barrel-rolled along the sidewalk, where he tucked in behind it before firing another blast of rounds in Ramos's direction. Only one hit the target but it proved lethal. It penetrated the left atrium of the police officer's heart, and Ramos's body slumped to the ground.

Guzmán leaped up and surveyed the carnage that surrounded him. Five bodies were strewn on the sidewalk, a testament to an unexpected firefight that had gone spectacularly wrong for the neo-Nazi. His mission was already a failure, but there was one last act he could still carry out that might just redeem him in the eyes of Hitler's grandson. It would take less than a minute to achieve, and then he'd get the hell out of there.

The chaos created by the shoot-out had sent screaming pedestrians running for their lives, but inside the heart of the packed synagogue, hundreds of members of the congregation were singing a much-loved communal prayer in unison, unaware of the mayhem unfolding outside.

Guzmán ripped off his balaclava and threw it away, along with his machine gun, which clattered menacingly along the ground. He calmly smoothed his hair and drew a small handgun from the back of his waistband, before carefully walking though the freshly created human cemetery and entering the huge doorway, framed by two heavily panelled wooden doors. Everybody inside the large prayer hall stood facing forwards and no one paid any attention to the well-dressed man who slipped in the back, moved to the end of the aisle on the right-hand side and strolled down it, as if he were returning to his seat.

The number of the seat he was aiming for was engraved on his brain, as was the name of the man he knew would be occupying it. As he approached, he could clearly make out the back of Gabriel Kapel standing upright with a black-and-cream prayer shawl wrapped around his shoulders and a red silk yarmulke held in position on his head by a small grip.

Guzmán was less than five yards behind him when he raised the Glock in his right hand and prepared to blow the head off Vargas's father-in-law. He knew the killing would provide a fatal wound to the chief inspector's heart, which would bring him huge kudos from Franklin, as well as a welcome financial bonus. At that moment, nothing mattered other than pulling the trigger. He'd killed before in cold blood but had never known such a buzz of excitement and anticipation flowing through his veins as he felt right then.

But in an instant, the colour drained from Guzmán's face as Juan Torres, who'd taken Kapel's seat, spun around and fired a point-blank shot that blew a gaping hole directly between his eyes. The look of shock and bewilderment on his face was still present as his body collapsed in a heap on the wooden floor and his expression remained for a few seconds while the synapses in his dead brain continued to fire.

The singing of a familiar Hebrew prayer was instantly drowned out by hysterical screams as panic ensued inside the large hall. Hundreds of worshippers threw their bodies to the floor underneath the wooden pews, while others fled towards the exit. A few minutes later, the Argentine detective called his boss for a debrief, and when Vargas heard the news, he knew the madness that had haunted his life for over a decade was finally over.

*Five Days Later*

The four participants on the zoom call were located in three different countries: Hembury was sitting alongside Berrettini in his FBI office in Washington, Vargas was back in Buenos Aires, also at his work desk, and Bekher, who was at home in his apartment in Tel Aviv, was the last to join.

Vargas smiled warmly at the Israeli spy chief, who'd suffered a huge battering of public abuse for failing to keep his premier safe and was fighting to keep his job.

'Doron, it's good to see you. How are you holding up?'

'To be honest, Nic, it's a shitshow over here. Things are turning pretty ugly – the country is in mourning, while the PJB are revelling in their success. Fortunately, I've managed to keep Franklin's name out of it, so as far as the Israeli people are concerned, their prime minister was assassinated by Shomani and his cohort with nobody else involved. But the events of the last few days have helped me make a decision – a big one. I've lost the confidence of the cabinet and, tomorrow morning, I'm handing in my resignation. I'm going to take a year off and get to know my family again. Life's far too short.'

The other three men nodded as a gesture of their understanding and Hembury began to tear up. He could sense the raw pain and suffering in Bekher's voice and it reminded him of his own plight. Berrettini broke in for the first time.

'Doron, what's your intelligence on Franklin? I assume he's no longer a live threat?'

'Mike, we've no idea how the Taliban got him out of Jerusalem. We found the Ford Explorer abandoned a few miles away from the car park, close to Jaffa Gate, so we assume they switched vehicles and escaped while the city was still in chaos. We believe they took him to Kabul, but we've heard nothing. The fact they risked sending a kidnap team into our capital tells us just how badly they wanted him. Normally, we'd treat such an incursion as an attack against the Israeli state, but, let's face it, none of us is going to grieve for the soul of that evil maniac.'

A brief silence followed as the three other men on the zoom had no appetite to contradict the Mossad chief. They all suspected Franklin was destined for a slow, barbaric death at the hands of the Taliban leadership, who'd spent the previous eighteen months tracking him down. None of them going to mourn the loss of the man who'd tormented their lives for so long and caused so much death and destruction along the way. Finally, after eleven long and torturous years, they could close the book on John Franklin and Adolf Hitler's evil legacy.

# Epilogue

Zürich, Switzerland

*Twelve Months Later*

Goehner and Roths, established in 1865, was one of
Switzerland's oldest and most esteemed banks. It was
based in a majestic Gothic style, red-brick building on
Bahnhofstrasse, an exclusive avenue in Zurich's business quarter. Their motto, which was modestly displayed on a small
brass plaque above the main entrance, promised 'Personal
Service and Discretion'. Everyone in the banking community
knew that, in this instance, discretion was a code word for
collusion.

After the Second World War, prominent Nazis used the
bank's secret facility as a laundering house for stolen funds –
either cash, bonds, gold, or other treasures – in return for
paying exorbitant interest rates that often ran at an eye-water-
ing thirty per cent.

The bank's general manager, Rueben Goehner, was a direct
descendant of one of the founders and his family was amongst

the wealthiest in Zurich. He was a man who liked his considerable wealth to be on display at all times, courtesy of Armani suits, Hawes & Curtis Egyptian cotton shirts and Crockett & Jones Pembroke brogues, which meant that, at any one time, he was clothed in over ten thousand dollars' worth of designer garb. He was just over six foot tall, in his fifties, with a full head of salt-and-pepper hair, immaculately groomed to within an inch of its life. His slightly elongated face was balanced perfectly by a pronounced set of cheekbones and enormous perceptive blue eyes that were slightly intimidating.

Goehner was sitting behind his Parnian desk, which had been constructed from four types of exotic wood, staring across at a potential new client whose personal wealth topped a staggering ninety billion dollars. He'd do whatever it took to ensure the funds, currently held by the bank in the name of the client's recently deceased father, stayed where they were, even if that meant agreeing to less favourable terms. He turned the charm factor up to record-breaking levels in a desperate attempt to maintain the status quo.

'Mr Bush, it's been my establishment's honour to look after your family's assets for almost eighty years. I feel we share a special bond that can never be broken.'

Bill feigned a hint of a smile. He knew full well that the man facing him was happy to look after dirty Nazi funds, as long as he could turn a healthy profit. In truth, the fact he'd been his father's personal banker was a good enough reason in itself to despise him. Sitting next to Bill was his father's former lawyer, another hateful Swiss character, Leon Brummer, whom he also planned to dispense with, once matters were resolved.

Bill was still coming to terms with his new-found wealth and wasn't sure how he planned to handle it. The sums involved were simply overwhelming and the root of the money was pure evil. He was now an orphan, and was about to inherit everything, and although he loathed the two men in the room, for now he needed to play their games.

'Just how rich am I?'

Goehner produced a cartoonish smarmy smile before flicking his eyes to the desktop computer in front of him.

'Impetuous, just like your father. They say the apple doesn't fall far from the tree.'

His comment was met by a stony glare from Bill, so he quickly moved on.

'Well, Mr Bush, you have liquid funds in excess of fifty billion dollars and assets worth at least the same again.'

The Swiss banker was referring to the stolen gold and precious artworks stashed in the bank's secret vaults, which had lain pretty much untouched for over eighty years. Bill showed no reaction whatsoever, so Goehner ploughed on.

'There should have been considerably more, but eighteen months ago your late father withdrew a great amount of cash from the main deposit account – almost twenty-five billion.'

Brummer didn't want to be rendered redundant in front of Bill and followed up with his own assessment.

'Then there's the three private jets, the super yacht and fifteen prime properties, located in cities all over the world. Mr Bush, you are, without doubt, one of the wealthiest men on earth and it will be my honour to—'

Bill cut him dead and rose to his feet.

'I want everything put into my name as soon as possible and

all assets liquidated. I'll be in touch to instruct you on the details of where I want the funds to be sent.'

Goehner was crushed but tried to maintain a smile in the hope his client might change his mind, somewhere down the line. He stood and offered his bony hand, which Bill ignored.

'Thank you, Mr Bush. I look forward to hearing from you soon and do enjoy your new-found wealth.'

Bill had already turned his back on Goehner and was heading for the door and some fresh air. As soon as he exited the building and began walking away, he was hit by a tsunami of high-end fashion outlets. Bahnhofstrasse had the reputation of being the most expensive shopping strip in the world, and every designer name was represented within a mile stretch.

He paused briefly to glance in the window of a Vacheron Constantin store, where watches routinely went for over a million dollars apiece. One caught his eye that was marked up for two million, and he smiled to himself when he realised he could afford to buy it without a second thought. Not that it held the slightest interest for him. Then the insanity of the situation kicked in and he realised he could afford to buy the entire contents of that shop and those of every other store on the street too, without breaking sweat.

He began to hum to himself as he turned away from the window and continued walking down the street, wondering what he'd do with the rest of his life.

# Author's Note

I t was just over four years ago when I began writing *The Counterfeit Candidate* and, to be perfectly honest, at that time I'd no plans whatsoever for a sequel, let alone a trilogy. However, the characters somehow took on a life of their own and here we are, three books later. The first draft of *The Last Reich* was completed in early 2023, nine months before the momentous events of 7 October, which rocked the world to its very core. I guess the adage that truth is stranger than fiction is particularly poignant in this case. *The Last Reich* is of course a work of fiction, as is the Palestinian Justice Brigade, an organisation I created for the purposes of the plot, as Franklin needed a collaborator based in the Middle East.

I hope you enjoyed the story as much as I loved writing it. I tried my hardest to keep you guessing right up until the last page as to how things might play out. Although *The Last Reich* is a standalone novel, it's also the last in a trilogy, so if you want more of the same, try *The Counterfeit Candidate* and *The Führer's Prophecy.* If you've already read all three books, I hope you enjoyed them and were happy with the conclusion. I agonised over it for a while, wondering how to end it, but, finally, giving

Bill the last word somehow seemed right, as he was key in bringing down his monster of a father; a sociopath, driven by hatred and racism – a man as deluded and evil as his paternal grandfather.

I love reading thrillers, and with all my books, I attempt to write the sort of story I'd like to read. My literary heroes are truly great thriller writers such as Ludlum, Baldacci, Brown, Forsyth, Grisham, Hayes and Higgins, who've all heavily influenced my writing style and are masters of delivering page-turning masterpieces.

I've now begun work on my next book, a story that features Vargas and Hembury, coming together once again, in a brand-new adventure. I've included the first few chapters to give you a taste of it. Hopefully, it'll be ready for release in 2025.

I love hearing feedback from readers, so please feel free to message me on my Instagram – @klein443 – or check out my website, brianklein.tv, for news. Thanks again for sticking with me for the first three books and I hope to see you again very soon with the new one.

Brian Klein

# Acknowledgements

Writing a book begins as a solitary process but ends up being a collaborative one and, once again, I feel myself indebted to many people who have helped me along the way. Chief amongst those by far is my wife Charmaine, who has become my editor-in-chief and go-to sounding board and has helped my process improve in so many ways. She comes up with great suggestions for parts of the story and then works through several drafts with me when we hone the manuscript to within an inch of its life. She's brilliant at what she does, and her changes improve my writing no end. I'd also like to thank Victoria Woodside for her painstaking copy-editing, which she undertakes each time with great enthusiasm.

Inspiration for ideas comes from many places and I must thank an old family friend, Bill Breckon, who told me, over a typical Italian lunch, the fascinating true story of the Tempio Maggiore. At the time, my wife and I were staying in Florence, visiting him and his family when he regaled us about the celebrated synagogue and Hitler's failed attempt in 1944 to destroy it. As soon as I heard the incredible tale of its survival, I had to visit the site, and as you know from the story, it ended up playing a major role, as Franklin became obsessed with its history.

I'm thrilled to be starting an exciting journey with a new publisher, Little, Brown, who have taken over all my books, and I must thank my agent, Jon Smith, for his tremendous belief in me and determination to create a relationship with such a wonderful publishing house. I want to end by thanking their Publishing Director, Andreas Campomar, Project Editor, Holly Blood, and the entire Little, Brown team.

NEW IN 2025

Keep reading for a sneak peek at
Brian Klein's next book

# Prologue

Munich, Germany

August 1922

The five-cylinder, liquorice-black motorcycle carved an erratic path through the narrow cobbled streets in downtown Munich, weaving through the early evening traffic as though it was standing still, heading directly for the Hofbräuhaus beer hall on Platzl 9. The young student on board was in a hurry and for most of the journey kept the hand throttle fully depressed, maintaining the machine's top speed of fifty-three miles per hour. Thirty minutes earlier he'd received news from his technical college that he'd successfully graduated, achieving an honours degree in Agriculture, and was eager to celebrate the achievement with his friends.

The infamous drinking establishment was a magnet for right-wing students and members of the National Socialist German Workers' Party, whose members were more commonly known as Nazis. Although he wasn't a member, the twenty-one-year-old student shared many of the controversial views of the party's charismatic leader, Adolf Hitler, especially his anti-Semitism, and was seriously considering joining the fascist organisation.

As soon as he reached his destination he parked up and ran inside, forcing his way through large clusters of drunken revellers who'd overflowed onto the street. He made his way upstairs, navigating the rear, congested staircase, which led to an alcove on the first floor, where he knew a small group of his college friends would already be in place celebrating. He wasn't a great drinker and, four hours later, found himself lying on a filthy, threadbare mattress on the floor of a shabby basement studio flat, wrapped in the arms of a young girl, whose naked limbs entwined him like a ravenous anaconda. As he stared into her liquid blue eyes, he'd no recollection of meeting her and his instincts screamed at him to get the hell out. Those feelings of extreme anxiety melted away as soon as she leaned forward to gently caress him on the lips, before lightly pulling away to whisper in his ear. Her voice was like a purr and the silky tone made his entire body tingle.

'You were a virgin. I can tell. How was it?'

He felt a deep wave of embarrassment engulf his senses and closed his eyes, desperately trying to recall anything from the previous few hours. He glanced around the room looking for clues, but none were forthcoming.

'I don't know. I can't remember. What's your name? How did I get here?'

Her lips parted slightly and her smile was intoxicating.

'My darling, you only had to stumble down a few steps. We're in the bowels of the Hofbräuhaus. I'm a waitress here and this cesspit comes with the job. My name is Franka. What's yours?'

He peered at her through his rimless, pince-nez glasses that, remarkably, were still firmly in their rightful place, which he mused was somewhat of a miracle. Her heart-shaped face, perfectly framed by pin-straight, shoulder-length honey-blond hair, had an air of natural beauty. He knew the entire episode was entirely out of character and cursed his friends who'd persuaded him to switch from beer to schnapps.

He was twenty-one and, however tempting it might have been, he'd no intention of getting involved in a romantic relationship. He was a man with serious political ambitions and had far bigger fish to fry. He managed a fake half-smile, as he replied to her question.

'My name is Heinrich.'

Franka burst into a sudden bout of teasing laughter.

'My god, were you named after a prince?'

His smile morphed into a frown.

'Actually, I was. Prince Heinrich of Bavaria. My father is a schoolteacher and tutored him when he was a boy.'

He spoke so earnestly the young waitress had no doubt he was telling the truth. Forty weeks later to the day, Franka gave birth to a healthy girl, but as she was seventeen and unmarried, she'd little choice but to hand her over to a Protestant orphanage, located on the outskirts of the city. After the night she conceived, and throughout the pregnancy, Franka never heard from Heinrich, although he covertly obtained the details of the institution that had taken over the welfare of the baby. He kept the secret of his daughter's illegitimate birth from his family and close friends but vowed that when he achieved political power and financial wealth, he'd make up for his bad behaviour and his little princess would be the beneficiary of his success and proud to know the identity of her father.

# Chapter One

Buenos Aires, Argentina

October 2024

It was just after three in the morning when the second prisoner broke his vow of silence. The man known as 'Manuel' made the decision to talk after being shown a short video featuring the mutilated body of his brother, who'd embraced torture and certain death rather than give up the information his interrogator required. Manuel knew he'd no stomach to match his sibling's bravery, so compliance was his only option.

The inquisitor glanced up at the CCTV camera mounted on the low ceiling and gave an almost imperceptible nod. In a small open area directly outside the makeshift cell, his employer caught the gesture on a twenty-inch black-and-white monitor positioned on a small metal table. He rose from his chair and moved towards an arch-shaped solid oak door, grabbed the end hub of the giant iron bolt and slid it sideways through its rusty mechanism.

Moments later a short, stocky bull of a man marched into the dimly lit cell and surveyed the scene. He allowed a malevolent smile to break out on his lips as he glared at the pathetic figure slumped in the far corner of the room, his hands tied by black leather restraints to the back of a steel chair cemented to the floor. His head was bowed in a gesture of subservience and the beads of sweat dribbling down his forehead were the product of unbridled fear, rather than pain.

The man who was clearly in charge of the interrogation leaned down over the prone figure and grabbed a fistful of oily hair in his right hand, yanking the prisoner's head upwards until the two men's eyes were barely inches apart. When he spoke, his voice was a sinister whisper. Its chilling guttural quality added a sense of foreboding. Inside the prisoner's scrambled brain, it sounded like the voice of a demon.

'Now, Manuel, I've only two questions for you and I'm sure you know exactly what they are. But just in case you have memory failure, I'll ask you once again. Who did you pass the USB over to and where is it now?'

# Chapter Two

Buenos Aires, Argentina

Twenty-four hours earlier

C hief Inspector Nicolas Vargas of the Buenos Aires
Police Department was enjoying a beer in El Alamo,
the only sports bar in the city centre showing a live US
basketball game his friend, Troy Hembury, was desperate to
watch. The African American, who was Director of Internal
Security for the White House, had arrived earlier that day on
the red-eye from Washington and was a huge fan of the LA
Clippers, who were playing a top-of-the-table grudge match
against the Boston Celtics. Hembury had come to Argentina for
a two-week break and was staying as a house guest of Vargas at
his new apartment in the fashionable neighbourhood of
Recoleta, the bohemian district in the north of the sprawling
city.

The pair were sitting together in a small, circular red-leather
booth waiting for the live transmission to start. They'd been
friends for well over a decade, having met in 2010 at a law

enforcement conference in Vegas, when Hembury was working as a lieutenant in the LAPD, a post he held for over twenty
years before joining the White House staff.

In many ways the men were far closer than brothers, having
forged an unbreakable relationship, working together on
several heart-stopping cases that had generated front-page
news across the world. They'd formed a remarkable alliance
with senior figures inside Mossad and the FBI, helping the
respective intelligence agencies combat two international
terrorist attacks in the Middle East. The last episode had taken
place just over a year ago and this was the first time they'd met
up in person since.

The headline-making history they'd been part of creating
didn't really mean much to either of them, particularly
Hembury. He was living on borrowed time, due to a grade
three tumour, burrowed deep inside his brain. It was currently
being kept at bay by an unlicensed drug that was being clinically trialled – aimed at patients like him, who had an imminent death sentence hanging over their head and nothing to
lose.

Vargas, the city's most celebrated detective, thanks to the
notoriety of some of his previous high-profile cases, was also a
deeply troubled man, but for completely different reasons. He
was a widower of almost fifteen years and had never come to
terms with the tragic loss of his wife. The drug that kept him
alive, however, wasn't synthetic. It was an unrelenting barrage
of work, which filled his every thought and helped preserve his
sanity.

Hembury was sixty-three, exactly ten years older than
Vargas as, remarkably, they shared the same birthday. He was

eighteen months away from retirement and relishing the thought of it. If his body could hang on.

'Less than two years to go, Nic, and if the drugs hold up, then it's just me, my tropical fish and twenty-four hours a day of ESPN sports.'

Vargas's reply was laden with scepticism, as he gestured towards the basketball players warming up on the huge flatscreen hanging above the bar.

'Right, I'll give you three months with your feet up, and as soon as your beloved team start losing, you'll be itching to come back.'

Hembury grinned and was about to reply as two servers laden with trays approached their corner booth, just as the game was about to start. The enormous food platters covered every inch of the round wooden table the men were seated at, with a banquet of ribs, chicken wings, corn, guacamole, pickles and fries, which just about left enough room for their pint glasses. Vargas burst into laughter as his friend dived into the ribs.

'Christ, Troy, we could feed the entire Clippers team with this feast. What happened to your healthy eating regime?'

Hembury demolished the pork meat and wiped the barbeque sauce off his lips with a napkin.

'Don't worry, I'm still on it, but basketball brings out my primitive urges and—'

Hembury never got to finish his sentence, as his eyeline flicked across to the front entrance of the bar, where a young man burst through the door like a whirlwind, then came to a sudden stop as his eyes darted around the restaurant like a pair of frantic pinballs, until they settled on Vargas. After a moment of recognition, he ran towards the detective, whose right hand instinctively dropped to the Glock 17 holstered across his chest.

The stranger was in his late twenties, olive-skinned with jet-black hair, which was badly overgrown and formed a seamless join with his dark beard, which was slightly better groomed. His hazel brown eyes were panicked with fear and his body was vibrating like a cheap washing machine, as he slowly opened the palm of his left hand, revealing a small blue USB drive.

'Chief Inspector, you're the Nazi hunter, right? The policeman who exposed Hitler's grandson?'

Vargas grimaced as the stranger made the questions sound like an accolade. His reply was laced with anger.

'What do you want with me?'

'Take this drive and share it with your colleagues. It has the names – the names of *Die Spinne*—'

Before Vargas could reply, the man grabbed his hand and passed across the USB and turned to leave.

'Who are you?'

The stranger stopped in his tracks and half-turned to face the chief inspector.

'I'm known as Manuel.'

# About the Author

Before becoming a full-time novelist, Brian Klein worked as an award-winning television director for over thirty years. His work still regularly appears on Netflix, Amazon Prime, BBC and Sky. Among his directing credits are twenty-eight seasons of the iconic car show, *Top Gear*, which in its heyday was the most popular factual entertainment TV show in the world, with over three hundred million viewers watching in over one hundred countries.

As a student, Brian studied modern history and politics at Queen Mary College, University of London, majoring on the origins of the Second World War.

*The Last Reich* is his third publication. His previous two are *The Counterfeit Candidate* and *The Führer's Prophecy.*